Isabella Bradford is a pseudonym for Susan Holloway Scott, the award-winning author of more than forty historical novels and historical romances. Her bestselling books have been published in nineteen countries and translated into fourteen languages with more than three million copies in print. Bradford also writes as half of the Two Nerdy History Girls, an entertaining history blog that is also on Twitter and Pinterest. She is a graduate of Brown University, and lives with her family outside of Philadelphia.

Praise for Isabella Bradford:

'Richly researched and beautifully written' Karen Harper, author of *The Last Boleyn*

'Wickedly entertaining' Mary Jo Putney, *New York Times* bestselling author

'A vivid portrait of an intriguing woman with all her flaws and strengths. Rich in period detail, the novel also has all the ingredients necessary for a compelling read: conflict, suspense, intrigue, and the romance between Sarah and John Churchill, one of history's great love stories' Susan Carroll, author of *The Silver Rose*

By Isabella Bradford

The Wylder Sisters Trilogy
When You Wish Upon a Duke
When the Duchess Said Yes
When the Duke Found Love

When the Duchess Said Yes

ISABELLA BRADFORD

ETERNAL
ROMANCE

Published by arrangement with Ballantine Books,
A division of Random House, Inc.

First published in Great Britain in 2012
by ETERNAL ROMANCE
An imprint of HEADLINE PUBLISHING GROUP

1

Cataloguing in Publication Data is available from the British Library

ISBN 978 0 7553 9673 3

Offset in Sabon by Avon DataSet Ltd,
Bidford-on-Avon, Warwickshire

Printed and bound by CPI Group (UK) Ltd, Croydon, CR0 4YY

Headline's policy is to use papers that are natural, renewable and
recyclable products and made from wood grown in sustainable forests.
The logging and manufacturing processes are expected to conform to the
environmental regulations of the country of origin.

HEADLINE PUBLISHING GROUP
An Hachette UK Company
338 Euston Road
London NW1 3BH

www.eternalromancebooks.co.uk
www.headline.co.uk
www.hachette.co.uk

When the Duchess Said Yes

CHAPTER

✿ *1* ✿

London
April 1762

It was duty that had drawn the Duke of Hawkesworth back to England. More specifically, duty, and lawyers, and a woman he'd never met but was bound to marry.

Bored already, Hawke sprawled in his chair in the playhouse box, pretending to watch the abysmal opera before him. He'd been away nearly ten years, long enough that he suspected those in the other first-tier boxes were desperately trying to decide who he must be. It wouldn't be easy. He knew he'd changed, grown from a schoolboy to a man, and he'd grown into both his broad frame and his title. Thanks to a long-ago Mediterranean grandmother, he had dark hair and dark eyes, and his face was so unfashionably tan after the long voyage that those in the other boxes had likely all decided he was swarthy, even foreign.

The thought made him smile. Well, let them peer at him with their opera glasses and whisper behind their fans. They'd all come to recognize him soon enough.

"Those two dancers with the scarlet stockings," whispered the Marquis of Petershaw, an old friend and the first to welcome him back to London. "The ones with the golden hair. A delectable pair, eh? Sisters, I'd wager. Should I send our compliments for a late supper, the way we did in the old days?"

"We were randy schoolboys in those 'old days,' Petershaw, ready to mount anything female that didn't kick us away," Hawke said, bemused. "We weren't exactly discerning."

Petershaw's round face fell. "I judged them a fine pair of doxies."

"They are, they are," Hawke assured him, not wanting to belittle his friend's tastes. But the truth was that Hawke's own tastes had changed with the rest of him, and in comparison to the vibrant, voluptuous women he'd left behind in Naples, English females seemed pale, bland, and thoroughly insipid, just as English food now tasted underseasoned and overcooked. "I'm not in the humor for such entertainment, that is all."

"You, Hawke?" His friend's brows rose with disbelief. "I've never known you to refuse feminine company."

"You forget my reason for returning," Hawke said, as evenly as he could. "I am to be wed, and my days with that manner of strumpet are done."

"Perhaps on your wedding night," Petershaw said, "but not forever. Not you."

Hawke only smiled, letting his friend think what he pleased. Petershaw would anyway, regardless of what Hawke told him.

"No, not you," Petershaw declared with a suggestive chuckle that also managed to be admiring. "Not at all! I'm going to send a note down to the tiring room for those little dancers, and I'll wager you'll change your mind before the evening's done."

He went off in search of a messenger before Hawke could answer. Hawke sighed, sadly wondering if he'd lost his taste for English friends, too. But then Petershaw could afford to be impulsive with dancers, milliner's assistants, and whatever other pretty faces caught his fancy. He was a third son with no need to wed or sire heirs, and he was completely free to scatter his seed wherever he pleased.

But the truth was that Hawke's smile masked a great many misgivings about his own upcoming marriage. He was, of course, obliged to follow through with the betrothal that Father had long ago arranged for him. It wasn't only a matter of honor, of not abandoning some poor lady of rank at the altar. No, Father had mistrusted his only son so thoroughly that he'd bound this marriage and his estate together into a tangled knot of legal complexities and obligation that could never be undone. Father couldn't prohibit him from inheriting the dukedom, but he could—and had—restricted the estate necessary to support the title. In other words, unless Hawke married the lady of Father's choosing before her nineteenth birthday, he would become a duke without a farthing.

Restlessly Hawke tapped his fingers on the polished rail before him. Accepting his fate didn't mean he found it agreeable. Far from it. Ten years had passed since Father died, yet Hawke still resented both him and that infernal will. Still, though his father expected him to marry, at least he didn't expect him to be faithful. Their family had been founded on the legitimized by-blows of a king and his mistress a century before, and every Duke of Hawkesworth since had followed suit and kept at least one mistress. It was a tradition Hawke fully intended to continue. He'd marry this lady, remain honorably faithful to her long enough to produce children, and then, with the title secure, his duty complete, and his family well provided for, he'd depart for Bella Collina, his beloved villa in Naples, never to return.

In theory it was a most excellent plan, one that had

given Hawke much comfort on the long voyage to England. But as he idly glanced around at the well-bred faces in the other boxes, his heart sank. He'd forgotten how unappealing his fellow aristocrats could be, and one lady after another struck him as smugly complacent as they preened in their jewels and costly gowns, their painted faces and towering white wigs no more attractive to him than the two dancers that Petershaw had spotted.

Glumly he wondered what his bride would be like. Wynn, his agent, had written that she was a beauty. But then every bride was considered beautiful, and what, truly, could Wynn have written instead? There was no portrait enclosed, never a favorable sign. Wynn had mentioned that the lady had been raised in the country and wasn't accustomed to society, let alone to sitting for portrait painters, but Hawke had immediately imagined some bland, stolid, milk-fed creature, more like a farmer's daughter than an earl's, with a round face and wispy pale hair.

By unfortunate coincidence, his wandering gaze had settled on exactly that sort of young lady, not two boxes away, who set off her pasty pallor and snub nose with black velvet patches scattered over her cheeks. To Hawke's dismay, she'd noticed him, too. She smiled, flashing teeth marred by too much sugar and tea, and coyly winked at him over the blades of her fan.

He nodded curtly in return, only enough to be polite, then swiftly turned away, back toward the portly singer.

But before his gaze reached the stage, it stopped, stopped as completely and abruptly as a gaze could be stopped. He couldn't look away if his life depended upon it, and in a way, perhaps it did.

She was standing alone at the front of an empty box, leaning forward with her hands on the railing. From her pale pink gown and the strand of pearls around her throat, she appeared to be a lady, but she bore no resemblance to any of the other ladies in the entire house. If she was alone like this, unattended, then she was likely a courtesan, some wealthy gentleman's costly plaything despite her youth.

Not that Hawke cared, and in a way that made her even more fascinating. He'd stolen women away from other gentlemen, and he was quite willing to do it again. She was undeniably pretty, even beautiful, and fresh in a way that wasn't fashionable for London, let alone for whores. Her face was bare of paint and artifice, rosy and glowing by the light from the stage, and her hair was unpowdered as well, so dark that it blended into the shadows around her. She was tall, too, with a slender grace that didn't depend on tight lacing, and the way she bent forward, offering a generous view of her breasts framed by the pink silk, was unconsciously elegant.

That was it, then, the intangible that compelled him to look at her. She was a beauty who didn't seem to care about being one, unashamed of being unaware. It charmed him, he who'd been sure he'd seen and admired every kind of female beauty; no, it captivated him. And the longer he watched her, the more intrigued he became.

In his eagerness, Hawke leaned forward, too, almost as if mirroring her pose. Suddenly she looked from the stage directly toward him, as if she'd felt the power of his interest clear across the playhouse. She looked at him openly, studying him without any coyness or coquettishness, and slowly raised one hand to smooth a loose curl behind her ear. Automatically he smiled, more with pleasure than with any seductive motive, and to his delight, she smiled in return.

He had to learn who she was, no matter the inconvenience this would cause to his wedding plans. His unwanted bride had already waited a good long time for him, and surely she could wait just a little longer. He had to meet this beauty as soon as possible. At once he rose, intending to leave his box and find her, and crashed directly into Petershaw.

"Here, Hawke, no hurry," he said, his broad face beaming as he put his hands on Hawke's shoulders to steady himself. "I've made certain that those two little hussies will be waiting for us after the performance, and then—"

"Damnation, Petershaw, not now." Hawke untangled himself from his friend. "That beauty in pink, there, in the box directly across the way. Do you know who she might be?"

He turned back to point her out to Petershaw.

The box was empty. The girl was gone.

Hawke swore again, and raced through the door of his box into the corridor. She couldn't have gone far. Her box was on the same ring, and if he hurried, he was sure to find her.

But the opera's second act had just concluded, and while applause rippled through the house behind him, the doors to all the other boxes opened and their occupants streamed into the corridor in search of refreshments or one another. At once the narrow passage was filled with people, with the ladies in their wide hooped skirts claiming three times the space. Though Hawke did his best to press through, by the time he'd finally made his way to other side, the young woman in pink was nowhere to be found, and doubtless long, long gone.

"Whose box is this?" Hawke demanded of the attendant standing beside the door.

"The Earl of Farnham, my lord," the man said.

"Your Grace," Hawke corrected impatiently. He didn't know Lord Farnham, but then he didn't know much of anyone in London now. "I'm the Duke of Hawkesworth."

"Forgive me, Your Grace," the man said, mortified, and bowed hastily. "I did not know."

"There was a young woman here this night, dressed all in pink," Hawke said. "Was she a guest of Lord Farnham's? Do you know her name?"

The attendant's brows rose with surprise. "Lord Farnham's not in attendance tonight, Your Grace. Forgive me for speaking plain, but his lordship must be eighty if he's a day, Your Grace, with scant interest in young ladies."

"You saw no young woman in pink?"

"No, Your Grace," the man declared soundly. "None at all."

"What is this all about, Hawke?" Petershaw asked beside him. "Who the devil is this chit in pink that has you in such a steam?"

Hawke sighed with frustration, and a certain amount of confusion as well. He didn't know why finding this girl had become so important to him; he could not put her smile from his thoughts, nor, truly, did he want to.

"I do not know who she is, Petershaw," he said, "beyond her being the most beguiling creature imaginable. It would seem she has vanished clear away."

"Now that's the Hawke I recall, always with his nose to the trail of a vixen." Petershaw grinned slyly. "Where's that dutiful, dull bridegroom now, eh?"

Petershaw had intended it only as a jest, a sly and slightly envious jab at Hawke's reputation with women. But instead it struck Hawke as a sobering reminder, as determined to douse his desire as a bucket of water from an icy river. It should have been, too, especially for a man such as Hawke, who seldom denied himself anything. As delectable as the smiling girl in pink might be, she was not for him. For the foreseeable future, he was doomed to keep to only the most respectable of paths, and grant to his bride exclusive rights to his honor, his title, his fortune, and, most of all, his cock.

A sobering reminder, indeed. A grim, depressing, damnably sobering reminder.

CHAPTER

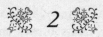 2

Lady Elizabeth Wylder, second daughter of the late and lamented Earl of Hervey, sat squeezed into one corner of her older sister's coach, bound to meet her destiny at the masquerade at Ranelagh Gardens.

Her gown was green silk with scattered spangles on the skirts and bodice that itched terribly beneath her arms. On her hands were silver mesh mitts that also itched, and so many silk flowers had been pinned into her hair that she felt like a barrow at Covent Garden. Sewn to the back of her gown, over her shoulder blades, were two small wired wings, likewise covered with spangles. Because of the wings, she couldn't rest back against the feather-stuffed cushions, but was forced to crouch forward on the very edge of the seat, a posture that made her queasily feel every bump and cobblestone beneath the carriage's iron-bound wheels. The wings and the rest of the costume had been the idea of her older sister, Charlotte, and as she'd stood before her dressing glass, Lizzie—for she had always been called Lizzie, not possessing the innate grandeur to be a true Elizabeth—had judged the entire rig to be unconscionably hideous.

She was supposed to be a charming fairy. Instead she felt a complete fool, and when she thought of how vastly important this evening would be for her, she could only despair.

A despairing, queasy, itchy, hideous, complete fool of a fairy: oh, yes, surely His Grace the Duke of Hawkesworth would be all eagerness to meet *her*.

"I trust that for once Hawke will keep his promise and join us tonight," her brother-in-law, March, was saying. March was Charlotte's husband and the Duke of Marchbourne, who was tall and wonderfully handsome and not afraid to show exactly how much he loved Charlotte. He was dressed as King Arthur, though the extent of his costume seemed to be the brass crown now sitting on his lap, and a cape trimmed with imitation ermine over his regular dark clothes. "It's been one empty excuse after another with him since he returned to London. Surely he must be the most selfish rogue in all creation."

"He'll come tonight," Charlotte said. "Who can resist a masquerade?"

"He'd best not resist this one," March grumbled. "He's been in residence at the Chase for nearly a fortnight by now, and it's past time that he called upon us."

"His Grace will join us tonight," Lizzie said, echoing her sister with resignation. If she'd liked her costume, he wouldn't have appeared, but because she hated what she wore, he was certain to join them. "I am sure of it."

March shook his head, unconvinced. "It's ungallant of him to treat you like this, Lizzie, and I do not like it."

Precariously balanced on the seat as she was, Lizzie smiled her gratitude at March. At least he was being gallant on her behalf, even if so far the Duke of Hawkesworth wasn't. When, on her eighteenth birthday last year, Mama had told her that Father had long ago arranged a marriage for her, too, Lizzie had nearly expired with joy. Six months ago, she had come to London to stay with Charlotte and March and prepare for her wedding. Of course she'd imagined her future husband to be a second March, as eager to fall in love with her as March had been with Charlotte. It was possible, even likely, since the two dukes were distant cousins.

"Be easy, March, be easy," Charlotte said fondly, reaching across to pat her husband's knee. Naturally, she was dressed as Queen Guinevere, in a brilliant blue damask costume. The widespread hoops beneath her skirts weren't exactly medieval, but they were very fashionable for this year in London, and also the reason that Lizzie was so squeezed into her corner.

"Hawke has just spent weeks and weeks at sea on his voyage home," Charlotte continued. "You can't expect the poor man to launch instantly into wooing without a few days' rest."

March frowned, his dark brows drawing together. "It would have been more proper if he had," he said. "Did he live so long among those Neapolitans that he took on their dallying southern ways? It's an insult to the family, and to your sister in particular."

"Lizzie understands the virtue of a little patience, March," Charlotte said with one of her famously beatific smiles. "She's waited nearly a year for Hawke to return. I'm sure she can wait another few days without perishing."

But Lizzie's smile was anxious, not beatific. She couldn't help it. She *had* waited nearly a year for this gentleman, her bridegroom, whom she'd never met, and now, it seemed, the waiting was almost done.

"I won't have to wait even a day longer if he comes tonight," she said, then corrected herself. "*When* he comes tonight."

"As soon as he meets you, Lizzie, he'll see what a prize he's been missing," Charlotte assured her one more time. "And you are a prize."

Lizzie supposed she was a prize, mainly because people had been assuring her that she was one all this last, long year. Being a Wylder meant she was also a lady, and their family was so desirably old and venerable that they'd likely been waiting to brandish their swords against William the Conqueror. She'd a handsome marriage portion, too, all of which was sufficient for her to qualify as a prize.

True, her personal qualities weren't quite so sterling. She had no genteel accomplishments. She couldn't play the pianoforte, or sing, or recite sentimental French poetry. She wasn't exactly plain, but she knew she wasn't as radiant and charming as Charlotte, nor did she possess the golden beauty and sweetness of her younger sister, Diana.

To be sure, there *had* been a small, unfortunate incident when she'd first come to town to stay with Charlotte and March. At a private ball, a so-called gentleman (or, at least, that was how Lizzie had always thought of him; in truth, he'd been a rather indisputable gentleman, a viscount) had attempted more familiarity with her behind a potted orange tree than she'd found pleasing. She'd denounced him, loudly and colorfully, and boxed his ears, too. But despite his having earned this treatment, she was the one who'd earned the unfortunate sobriquet of "Lizzie Wyldest" in the scandal sheets, a distressing term for a future duchess.

But she was clever and amusing, and she could tell jests like a firecracker, even the bawdy ones she'd overheard in the stables. Because she'd been raised near the sea, she could row a boat and trim a sail. On a horse, she could outride every man she'd ever met, and she could outlast them on the dance floor, too, so long as a minuet wasn't called. She liked to laugh, and to make others laugh with her, and she could as much as guarantee that the Duke of Hawkesworth would never be bored in her company.

Which, in her own estimation, really did make her a powerfully fine prize, even for a duke. Was it any wonder that it stung both her heart and her pride that the duke had taken so wicked long in claiming her?

"If I'm such a prize, Charlotte," she said, "then why didn't he come back to London sooner? No one ever speaks of that."

"Yes, we have, Lizzie," Charlotte said patiently, looking down to check the catch on her pearl bracelet. "I've explained to you before that a gentleman like the duke has many affairs to settle and arrange before he can make such a long voyage."

March grunted. "It's time to be honest with her, Charlotte. Tell her the truth. Hawke had an idle, indulgent bachelor's life in a villa overlooking the Bay of Naples that he was loath to leave, complete with a pretty Italian mistress or two as well."

Lizzie gasped, a small gasp for all the shock and disappointment it contained. Her first dream of an adoring bridegroom had become more threadbare and worn with each month that the Duke of Hawkesworth had delayed his return to England, but she'd still cherished it. She'd imagined endless excuses for his delays, from storms at sea to perilous illnesses. But to be left dangling for the sake of an exotic Italian mistress or two, unwillingly left behind in a villa—oh, she'd never imagined anything so *humiliating*. How could she possibly compete with Italian mistresses, especially when she was dressed as an infernal fairy?

"Really, March." Charlotte glared at him, and there was nothing beatific about her expression now. "Lizzie doesn't need to hear such things."

"And I say it's past time that she did," March said. "Far better for her to know the truth now, before she meets him, than to be led forward in blind trust."

"I've no wish to be blind, March," Lizzie said, struggling to make sense of what he'd just told her—and rather ungallantly for March, too. "But—but *two* mistresses? Are you certain of that?"

"Perhaps not at once," he admitted. "But pay heed to what I'm saying, Lizzie. It's not you but the whole notion of marriage that has made Hawke so balky. His delay has had absolutely nothing to do with you or your person, except that you're the lady he must marry."

"Ah," Lizzie said slowly. "I suppose that's a small comfort."

But it wasn't, not at all. She wanted to be a prize, not a punishment, and her dream of a gallant, ardent suitor was now tattered well beyond repair.

Charlotte slipped her arm around Lizzie's shoulders. "What March is trying to say, lamb, is that it's up to you to be charming and clever, and show Hawke that the wedded state truly can be a blissful one. He's only twenty-seven. Nearly all gentlemen have a past of some sort. No lady can reasonably expect otherwise."

Lizzie scowled. "And yet I am expected to be entirely pure and innocent, with no more past than a new-hatched chick in the nest."

March frowned, too, glancing uneasily at Charlotte. "You do not have any, ah, past of your own, do you, Lizzie? Any, ah, indiscretions that I've not been told of?"

"Of course she doesn't, March," Charlotte said impatiently. "You know that. Mama might have been careless with our education, but she made sure that Ransom Manor was as good as a convent for keeping us away from temptation and mischief."

With an indignant harrumph, she turned back to Lizzie. "What you can do is to make Hawke forget his youthful adventures. Once he meets you tonight, he's sure to be enchanted."

Lizzie looked down at her hands in their foolish fairy mitts. "Why must I be the one to do all the charming?

Shouldn't he be trying to please me, too, and make me forget all about his strumpets?"

She didn't miss the pointed glance that Charlotte and March exchanged.

"That is what we hope," Charlotte said with great delicacy. "That once Hawke meets you, that he'll want to do nothing more than please and love you, as you deserve."

"But you don't *know* that he will," Lizzie said, her first disappointment swiftly turning into resentment, and then anger after that. "That's what you truly mean, isn't it? Then I shall spare him the trouble. If he doesn't wish to marry me, then I've no desire to marry him, either, and that's an end to it. We should simply turn about and go home."

Furiously she began to pull off the spangled mitts, until Charlotte laid her hands over Lizzie's to stop her. "What he wants doesn't matter. His duty—"

"A pox on his duty!" cried Lizzie. "I'll go back home to Ransom and marry some—some *fisherman* who'll love me for myself. Why should I agree to being any-one's *duty*, just because he's a duke?"

"Because neither of you has a choice," Charlotte said, her voice suddenly firm. "You know this match can't be broken. It's been arranged for years. And it is a most excellent match, Lizzie. Father chose well for you, as he did for me."

Lizzie made a wordless, outraged moan. "Father didn't know I'd have to compete with harlots!"

"The harlots and their mischief have been left far behind in Italy, where they'll never trouble you," March said, much too heartily for Lizzie's tastes. "Your sister is right. This is an excellent match. You'll become a duch-ess, a peeress, and your children will be descended from kings. You'll be mistress of several houses, and you'll have every jewel and frippery a lady could wish. Most ladies would trade their souls to marry an English duke."

Of course Lizzie knew that every word of what he said was true. The same contracts that Father had signed to provide for her and protect her in such an advantageous way also sealed her doom. She knew she must marry the Duke of Hawkesworth, and it wouldn't matter if he'd kept an entire harem of mistresses. Just as Charlotte said, she knew she had no choice.

But all that sensible knowing had been done by her head. Her heart longed for more from a marriage, much more, and a single, slow tear of angry frustration slipped from her eye and fell onto the green silk of her lap.

"There now, you mustn't cry," Charlotte said, her usual gentleness returning as she drew her handkerchief to wipe the tear from Lizzie's cheek. "No gentleman likes to see a weeping woman. Look, we're here at the gates. Come, lamb, collect yourself to make a proud show, before the footman opens the door."

Lizzie pressed her fingers over her eyes, willing back her tears. It was strange that while her pride had suffered so grievously from Hawkesworth's neglect, she now clung to that same pride for support. She would be strong, and she would not weep. No matter what the duke had done in the past or what future they would be forced to share, for now she was still Lady Elizabeth Wylder—and she was determined to follow her sister's advice and make a proud show for herself.

And if there was ever a place for a proud show, it was Ranelagh Gardens. Lizzie had often visited the gardens with her family, but she'd never attended a masquerade like this one. Even before she stepped from the coach, she was astonished by the number of people gathered before her inside the iron fences. Despite the sizable entrance fee—two shillings and sixpence!—that was charged to keep out those who weren't quality, the crowds were thick, laughing and chatting as they strolled the long walks beneath the trees. In the distance rose the Rotunda like a fancy tea cake, the centerpiece of the gardens; while it was a welcome refuge on cooler evenings, tonight the air was so warm and pleasing that no one went inside. Even the musicians had moved out-of-doors with their instruments, and their music drifted in the breeze in the most charming way imaginable.

Nearly everyone wore something fanciful, whether no more than an extralong plume in the hat or a full diamond-patterned Harlequin costume. Many were masked as well, in half masks of black or white satin, or grotesques of papier-mâché that hid the entire face. Even the gaudiest costume gleamed and shimmered beneath the light of the lanterns that hung in the branches overhead, and now Lizzie realized that her green fairy costume wasn't hideous, as she'd feared, but exactly right.

As she walked beside Charlotte, her skirts fluttered about her legs and the spangles danced like true fairy dust, and the wings that had caused her so much grief in the carriage now trembled delicately on her back. She was glad, doubly glad. Earlier she'd wanted to look fine to win Hawkesworth's favor; she still wished to be pleasing to his eye, of course, but now she also wanted him to realize what he'd missed by lingering so long in Naples.

In the middle of one of the long canals stood a Chinese-style pavilion with a pointed, tiled roof like a pagoda's. The pavilion was open on all sides and had been contrived to look as if it floated on the water. March had reserved half of the pavilion for their exclusive use, ordering a table set with refreshments and armchairs brought for their ease and use until they went inside the Rotunda for dancing. Most important, March had ordered several of his own liveried footmen in addition to the gardens' attendants to stand guard and keep curious others at a distance.

These were the times that made Lizzie realize exactly how very grand the Duke and Duchess of Marchbourne were in comparison to ordinary Englishmen, or even to lesser peers. For all that March was kind and generous to her, to the world, he had royal blood in his veins, which made him the next thing to a prince. March and Charlotte acted as if there were nothing extraordinary about taking tea while strangers stared in awe, but Lizzie found it disconcerting, and felt more like the caged animals in the Tower menagerie than privileged noble folk.

Would it be like this for her, too, once she was married and a duchess in her own right? Throughout her childhood, she and her sisters had done as they'd pleased, and no one had taken any particular notice. At least she'd take Hawkesworth's name as well as his title and become Elizabeth Halsbury, which meant that Lizzie Wyldest would finally be put to rest. But would people bow and curtsey to her as they did to Charlotte, even as they took note of every detail of her dress and jewels and how she styled her hair? Would wagers be made in clubs and taverns on the sex of her first child, too, and breathless reports of her every action be printed in the papers?

"This is most agreeable, March," Charlotte was saying, languidly waving her painted ivory fan before her face as she rested her arm on the latticework railing. "And what a delightful place for Lizzie to have her first conversation with Hawke."

Lizzie was unconvinced. She was anxious enough about meeting him without having to do so before an audience. Nibbling on a biscuit, she perched on her chair with her back straight, both from nervousness and to preserve her wings, and wistfully watched the ordinary folk as they walked by, laughing and flirting and stealing kisses without a care.

"How will we recognize His Grace when he comes?" she asked. Hawkesworth had never bothered to send a portrait of himself to her, not even a miniature—another example of his indifference. In the beginning, Lizzie had imagined him to be every bit as handsome as March, but as the months had dragged by, she'd unconsciously begun altering that image in subtle ways, now picturing him in her mind as shorter, stouter, coarser. "Do you know what his costume will be?"

"Oh, no doubt something florid and Italian," March said. He unhooked his watch from the chain at his waist and set it on the table, opening it so that they all could see the face and the time: an oversized golden reminder keeping the time until Hawkesworth's scheduled appearance. "I expect I'll have no difficulty telling it's him."

"But he's sure to have changed while he's been away."

March smiled. "I'll know him, Lizzie. We were often together as boys, and I doubt even Naples has changed him beyond recognition."

"I cannot wait to make his acquaintance." Charlotte reached out to squeeze Lizzie's hand. "We'll have such a splendid time together tonight, won't we?"

Lizzie attempted a smile, then tried to concentrate on watching the crowds before them, wondering which gentleman might turn out to be her husband. She was appallingly nervous, her palms damp inside her mitts and her shift clinging moistly to her back beneath her stays. Though she tried not to look too often at March's watch on the table, it sat there like a ticking conscience, relentlessly counting away the minutes.

They'd arrived early, because March believed in promptness to a fault. But soon the time appointed for Hawkesworth's arrival came and went. He was a quarter hour late, then a half hour, and still he did not appear. March and Charlotte pretended not to notice, maintaining cheerful, empty conversation as if nothing were amiss. Yet Lizzie knew they were furious with Hawkesworth and pitied her, and she didn't know which was worse.

Finally Charlotte rose. "Come, Lizzie, I am weary of sitting," she said, holding out her hand. "Let's walk about, just the two of us, and leave March here with his wine."

March waved them on, as if this were exactly what he'd planned from the beginning, but Lizzie also saw him glowering at the watch on the table. She could almost—almost—feel sorry for Hawkesworth, having to face a solemn lecture from March on timeliness, breeding, and good manners as soon as he finally arrived.

If he arrived.

And as Lizzie's spirits sank lower, all she could do was to wish the vilest, most humiliating, and most excruciating pox possible on the shameful tardiness of His Grace the Duke of Hawkesworth.

CHAPTER

3

Hawke climbed from the hackney cab, paid the driver, and sauntered toward the gates of Ranelagh Gardens. It wasn't either appropriate or customary for an English duke to travel in the anonymity of a hackney, but Hawke liked the lack of fuss that came with the worn leather seats. His father's lumbering old carriage with the gold-picked wheels and the family coat of arms painted on the door remained in perfect working order in the coach house at Hawkesworth Chase, and his helpful (too help-ful, really) agents here in London had anticipated his return by purchasing a suitable team of matched grays to draw it, plus engaging the stable boys, grooms, driver, and footmen that were a ducal coach's necessities.

But what was the point of wearing a costume to a masquerade only to trumpet his identity with a carriage like that? No, Hawke would rather arrive like this, unknown and unnoticed in a dark blue costume that blended into the night, and pay for his ticket like any other mortal Englishman. The fox-faced girl at the booth winked and smiled invitingly, and told him when she was free for the night. Hawke nodded and winked in return, then moved through the gate.

Very well, then, he wasn't entirely unnoticed, and he smiled as he considered both the ticket girl and then the woman he'd been with when he'd last worn this costume, a lascivious flame-haired courtesan who'd been his companion for Carnival revelry along the canals of Venice. A splendid time, that, and exactly the kind of pleasurable diversion that he must now put behind him. He sighed deeply, almost a groan, and made his way further into the gardens.

He'd postponed this meeting a half dozen times already, and he was determined not to put it off again; otherwise he risked offending his cousin March beyond reconciliation. By temperament, he and March had little in common—March could be as serious and solemn as a preacher, and painfully earnest in the bargain—but they shared a common bloodline. Both their families (and that of two more cousins as well, the Duke of Breconridge and the Duke of Sheffield) had descended from ennobled bastards of a long-ago king and his royal mistresses, a kind of fraternity of dishonor that bound them more tightly than many true brothers.

March's father had also arranged for him to wed one of the Earl of Hervey's daughters, and in typical March fashion, he had obediently done so. March had always done what he was supposed to, while Hawke almost never did. Now March seemed determined to see that Hawke followed the same fate, arranging this introduction with the lady and generally shoving him headfirst toward matrimony. Misery must definitely love company, Hawke thought with gloomy resignation, dragging his feet like a condemned man with each step he took toward the Chinese pavilion.

He could see the pointed tile roof now, and thought he could make out March and the ladies inside, too. He took a deep breath, then another. Damnation, he wasn't ready for this. One more walk around the gardens to settle his nerves—that was what he needed. A few more minutes to prepare himself, and then he'd join them.

Briskly he turned away from the pavilion and down the next path in the opposite direction. He knew perfectly, pitifully well that he was being a wretched coward, but so be it. A few more minutes of his blissful bachelor life was worth it, and then, at last, he'd meet the lady he must marry.

Arm in arm, Lizzie and Charlotte strolled in silence through the crowd, one of the tall footmen in the March-bourne livery close behind them. The last gray of twilight had faded, replaced by stars and a quarter moon in the night sky. Neither sister spoke a word of the Duke of Hawkesworth, but when they came upon a group of Charlotte's friends, Charlotte joined their conversation with eager relief.

Lizzie hung by her sister's side, listening, but with nothing to contribute to the animated talk of husbands and babies. Impatiently she turned back toward the pavilion, wondering if perhaps Hawkesworth was there by now. Its pointed red roof and swinging lanterns showed through the trees, beckoning her to come. It wasn't that far away; surely there'd be no harm in her returning by herself to see if the duke had appeared, then coming back for Charlotte. She looked for their footman, who'd been distracted by a giggling young woman in a black mask and yellow gown cut so low that her breasts threatened to pop free.

Likely the footman wouldn't notice if Lizzie walked back to the pavilion, either, and quickly, before he did, Lizzie plunged resolutely into the crowd, her wings bouncing against her shoulders. Without Charlotte or her footman, Lizzie felt like everyone else who was in costume, and she liked it. The merriment was contagious, and for the first time in this whole wretched day she felt her spirits rise. She couldn't keep from grinning. No one knew she was an earl's daughter, or that she was betrothed to a duke, or that she wasn't simply some lady's maid out for a lark, and it was a vastly fine feeling indeed.

"Hey, ho, my pretty fairy!" called a man in a Roman warrior's helmet, bowing to her over his tin sword. "Come scatter your magic over my way!"

Lizzie laughed and shooed him away. She knew Charlotte—and, far worse, March—would not be happy to see her alone and behaving so freely, but she was willing to risk their displeasure for a few minutes. She was sure she was safe enough as long as she kept to the path among so many others. Besides, she rather liked the idea of surprising Hawkesworth and March, popping up unexpectedly in the pavilion like a true fairy. She chuckled to herself, imagining their faces.

"My lady in pink," said another man beside her. He wore an ink-blue costume edged with silver, cut close to display his height and broad shoulders to best advantage. The upper half of his face was hidden by a black mask, but his smile was both charming and oddly familiar.

"Not your lady, sir," Lizzie said, adding a toss of her flower-laden head for emphasis, "nor am I clad in pink."

She began to hurry past him, but he deftly stepped before her to stop her short.

"Forgive me my boldness, sweeting," he said, "but when last I saw you, you did wear pink."

She glared at him. He spoke like a gentleman, but no man, whether a gentleman or otherwise, had the right to block her way like this.

"A pox on your boldness, sir," she said, more sharply than before. "You're barbarously mistaken. You are a stranger to me, and we've never so much as seen each other before. Now pray let me pass, so that I—"

He pulled off his mask, and she gasped.

"So you do remember me," he said, bemused. "I suppose I should be honored."

She did recall him. She couldn't deny it, for she'd been the one who'd acted boldly. What had it been, a week ago? Ten days? March and Charlotte had taken her with them to the opera. It had been Lizzie's first opera, and she'd been enchanted. But March had insisted they leave their box before the first act was done, to avoid the crush and more easily make their way to visit with friends on the opposite side of the playhouse. Other acquaintances had stopped them first, and while they'd talked, Lizzie had slipped into an empty box nearby to hear the last aria of the act.

But in the middle of that aria, she'd had the oddest sensation, as if someone or something were calling to her. She'd looked up and discovered the handsomest gentleman she'd ever seen watching her as if they'd been the only two in the playhouse. He'd leaned forward, toward her, and into the reflected light from the stage. His features were strong and regular, his brow and hair dark, his eyes—oh, such eyes, even at a distance!—burning with a fiery intensity, and an unabashed interest, too. No man had ever looked at her that way, not once, and she was thankful for the shadows that masked her inevitable blush.

And though she'd known she shouldn't, she'd smiled. She hadn't been able to help herself. She'd smiled, and he'd smiled in return, a slow, easy smile, full of wicked charm that had made her cheeks grow warm. She'd felt like a heroine in a romance with a mysterious secret admirer, and her heart had raced with excitement. Who knew what would have happened had not Charlotte called to her, drawing her away. When she later searched for the gentleman again from her seat, he was gone, his box empty. She'd been disappointed, but relieved, too, and in her mind, that had been that.

Until now, when he stood not a playhouse away but directly before her, still watching, still smiling at her with that same wicked charm.

"I must go," she blurted out. "My—my friends will miss me."

"So will mine," he countered. "I don't care. You shouldn't, either."

She shook her head, trying to shake away his argument. She didn't want to tell him March's name or Charlotte's, either, any more than her own, for fear of scandal.

"But my friends care very much for me, and I for them," she said carefully. "Why should I oblige you instead?"

His smile was warm, and unlike the smiles of most men, it not only reached his eyes but filled them.

"Because you are singularly beautiful," he said. "Because you are as sweet as the first peach, and luscious as the first rose."

"Goodness." Her eyes widened. She'd never heard such deliriously fine rubbish slip from a man's lips, not with such utter conviction, and certainly never offered up to her.

"Yes," he said thoughtfully, as if this were new to him, too, though of course it couldn't be. "Yes, you are. I haven't been able to put you from my thoughts since I saw you at the opera."

She felt her resolve melting and her resistance with it, dissolving right here among these crowds of people. She knew she shouldn't believe so much as a word. And yet, because of the phantom Duke of Hawkesworth, who had found it a bothersome trial even to be in the same country with her, she longed to believe these honey-sweet words from this unbearably handsome gentleman. The duke had had his mistresses; what harm could come of her having these few moments?

"A dance," he said, offering his hand to her. "I've always wished to dance with a fairy. Come, the floor can't be far. I can hear the musicians from here."

"I can't accept," she said, looking down at his proffered hand with far more regret than she should have. "If I were seen dancing with you, I would be ruined."

"Then no one *shall* see us." He didn't wait for her to take his hand, but claimed hers instead. Swiftly he ducked between the trees and hedges, leading her into a small clearing inside the greenery. Although the crowds on the walk could clearly be heard a few feet away, the space was surprisingly private, and designed to be so, too. Lizzie stopped short, frowning at the single white-washed bench, clearly meant for trysting.

"This is madness," she said, pulling her hand free. "I can't stay here with you."

"Hush," he said softly, bowing low before her, all dark-clad elegance. "Do you hear the music? Pray honor me with this dance, my fairy queen."

She shouldn't, she shouldn't, yet there she was, taking his hand. He was taller than she was, so tall that she had to tip her head back a bit to meet his eye, rare for her with anyone. He drew her forward, into the center of the little clearing, and they turned with the music. Of course he danced well, assured in his steps without the fussiness of a dancing master. Likely he did everything well. A gentleman like him would. Moonlight splashed full across his face, and Lizzie sighed.

"Oh, my, look at you," she whispered with a certain despair as he guided her through the steps of the dance. "I know that is monstrously rude of me to say, but—but *look* at you."

He cocked one dark brow. "You say that as if I'm the Tower of London, a site to be recommended to visitors."

"I say that because you are so handsome." Her smile felt as wide as a common fool's, and she couldn't make herself look away from his dark eyes, his black hair, and the clean, sharp line of his jaw. "Perhaps the most handsome man I've ever seen."

He laughed again, a sound she was sure she'd never tire of. "You're only saying that because I said you were beautiful."

"I'm saying it because it's the truth." His shoulder beneath her hand was wide and strong, made for her to lean upon. "I'm not very good at dissembling, you see. I'm much better with the truth."

"A beautiful woman who cannot lie." He placed his hand on the small of her back, finding a place below the wings. "What a rare and wonderful creature."

She frowned, concentrating on keeping her spangled skirts clear of her heels without tripping him, too. "But you, sir, are not being truthful. I am not beautiful, especially not the way you are. I am comely, but not beautiful. Everyone says so."

"Then everyone is wrong, sweeting, and that *is* the truth."

"No." The silk flowers in her hair wafted back and forth on their wire stems as she shook her head. "My cheeks are too round and my hair too dark, and I have a bump in the middle of my nose from falling from an apple tree when I was six. So I will grant you comely, even striking, but not beautiful. No. *You* are beautiful, like the plaster statue of Adonis I saw last week in the museum."

"Not quite." His laugh had dropped to a chuckle, so warm that the sound tickled down Lizzie's spine and back up again. "Adonis. My God. Didn't your mother tell you that a pretty face can hide an ugly soul?"

"Hardly." Her smile turned wry. "She would say a pretty face would be the first one asked to dance at a ball."

"Then that explains why you are here with me now."

He drew her closer, close enough that she felt the plush velvet of his coat against her bare skin. Their dancing slowed to a sway as he leaned closer, his face over hers while the lights in the branches twinkled overhead.

She knew he was going to kiss her. She also knew that if she'd any sense of decency, she'd turn away and deny him. But then she likewise knew herself, and was dreadfully aware that there'd be no denying anyone, however deserved. Instead she raised her mouth a fraction, challenging him.

"You can't explain fairies," she said. "We are beyond reason and capture."

"Not to me," he said. He bent lower, his mouth brushing over hers. "Kiss me, my fairy queen."

Her heart racing with anticipation, she closed her eyes and offered her pursed lips, the way she'd observed other ladies do.

But observation wasn't experience, and at once she could tell she wasn't doing it right. She realized that as soon as his mouth found hers and without a word he demanded that she relax and kiss him in return. She'd no idea a man's mouth could be so firm and so soft at once, or able to coax her lips to part so that their mouths joined, too, all wet heat and sensation. Her knees turned wobbly and she held on to his shoulders so she wouldn't collapse. He pulled her closer, the spangles on her gown catching on the silver braid of his coat. His arm tightened around her waist in a way that only made her want to kiss him more, and when he finally broke away, she felt light-headed, full of wonder, and regretful that it had ended.

"Oh, my." She touched her fingertips to her lips to see if they'd changed, and smiled up at him from the cozy nest in the crook of his arm. "How extraordinary."

"Most extraordinary." He smiled, too, with a very

male pride, as he ran his open hand up and down her back.

She chuckled with happiness. "A first kiss is supposed to be extraordinary."

"Our first, yes," he said, "but I'd wager it won't be our last."

She frowned a bit because he'd misunderstood. This had been her first kiss ever, not just with him, but then his hand slid lower, his fingers spreading over her bottom in a way that also was extraordinary—perhaps a bit too much so.

"My carriage isn't far, nor is my house," he said, his invitation warm against her ear. "We can have the whole night to explore more of your fairy ways together."

He pulled her hips close to his, and shockingly she felt the hard length of his cock in his breeches, heady proof that she'd not been the only one to be moved by their kiss.

But in that instant Lizzie realized the reality of what she'd done, and what he wanted her to do. Swiftly she stepped apart, away from his caress.

"I must go." Her voice sounded odd, breathless and throaty and not her own. "I've been gone too long. My sist—my friends will miss me."

"Not as much as I shall," he said winningly, reaching for her again. "Come, lass. I promise you that was only the beginning."

"I—I can't," she stammered, panicking as she skittered backward. He was every bit as handsome and charming and tempting as ever, but now fear and regret washed over her like an icy bath. What would the Duke of Hawkesworth say if he ever learned that she'd gone into the bushes with a stranger and let him kiss and embrace her? Worse yet, what would March say? Oh, truly she *was* Lizzie Wyldest! No matter how Charlotte pleaded on her behalf, March would order her immediately packed back to Dorset and ignominy, and likely spinsterhood, too.

"I must go at once," she said breathlessly, "before my friends worry and come hunting for me, and—and you do not wish them to find you."

"Let them," he said with a grandly dismissive sweep of his arm. "I'll fight them all for your sake."

She rather believed he would, and part of her was delighted by his bravery, like that of a knight of old. But these weren't olden times and she couldn't let him fall into the hands of March's burly footmen, and in despair she played her final card.

"You can't," she said. "I won't permit it. There'd be no point to fighting, anyway, for I am promised to wed another."

Not trusting herself, she didn't wait to measure his response. She ducked beneath the branches and fled into the crowd, her skirts flying and her wired wings bobbing against her back.

"Lizzie!" Charlotte held her arms out to her, obviously relieved. "Where have you been? We've been hunting all over for you."

Lizzie flung herself into her sister's embrace, hugging her tight. Her heart was still pounding, her thoughts confused by all that had just happened. And what would she do if the gentleman followed her?

"Are you unharmed, Lizzie?" Charlotte asked. "Poor thing, I can feel your heart."

With a shuddering sigh, Lizzie broke away, struggling to compose herself.

"I'm fine, perfectly fine," she said. "I went to the privy, that was all, and then I couldn't find you again."

She hated herself for lying to Charlotte, but the truth was so shamefully grievous that Lizzie could never confess it, not even to her sister.

Charlotte's contrition made it worse. "Oh, please forgive me, Lizzie, forgive me if you can. That was all my fault, for becoming so caught up in the tattle of the day that I forgot you. Here now, sit beside me and calm yourself before we return to the gentlemen. You're very jumbled now, and I want you to be serene when you meet Hawke."

She led Lizzie toward the nearest bench, conveniently emptied for them by a footman who'd shooed away the bench's other, less worthy occupants. Seated at her sister's side, Charlotte smoothed Lizzie's hair, tucking the stray wisps back beneath her flowered wreath.

"You're flushed," Charlotte said with concern. "Are you feverish? Do you feel unwell?"

"I'm well enough." Quickly Lizzie looked down, fearing what her eyes might betray. "But if you please, Charlotte, shouldn't we return to the pavilion?"

Charlotte rose and smiled slyly. "To the pavilion, and to meet your bridegroom, too. I suppose you've every reason to feel feverish, dear Lizzie, haven't you?"

Perhaps she *was* feverish. Certainly all the way back to the pavilion her stomach was twisting in knots as she struggled to balance her conscience against her giddy excitement. She must banish the nameless stranger from her head *now*, and instead anticipate meeting the man who would be her husband. She must put from her mind the only kiss she'd ever had, and concentrate on her dutiful marriage and the honorable kisses that would come from her husband. Duty, honor, respectability appropriate to her rank and position, to her husband and the children they'd have together: that was what mattered, not the folly of a meaningless embrace and a kiss from a man whom—with luck—she'd never see again.

A man whom, if Lizzie was honest, she would never forget.

Yet as soon as she and Charlotte reached the canal,

they could see that March was alone at the table in the pavilion. He wasn't sitting, either, but standing, his expression severe and his hands clasped behind his waist. His watch was no longer open on the table but tucked back in its waistcoat pocket. None of it augured well.

"I have sent for the carriage," March announced even before they'd reached him. "Our evening here is done. Hawke has only now sent word that he regrets that he is unable to attend us this evening. Regrets, my foot. My only regret is that he is such a selfish, ill-mannered rascal."

"Oh, Lizzie, I am sorry," Charlotte said. "The man's behavior is appalling, to show you so little regard."

But though Lizzie nodded solemnly, as she was expected to do, inside she was vastly relieved. She wouldn't have to smile sweetly at one man while another's kiss was still on her lips. Her secret was safe, and she wouldn't be called Lizzie Wyldest again.

And at least for this night, the duke's absence and neglect didn't wound her. How could it? For this night, there was at least one man in London who believed she was as sweet as the first peach, and luscious as the first rose.

CHAPTER

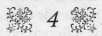

4

Hawke was not by nature a man who found much profit or goodness in the early hours of the day. To his mind, more and more interesting things occurred as the day progressed, with the absolutely most fascinating taking place well after boring, sensible folk had long since retired. Those first hours after the cock's crow were tedious and dull and far too bright, and it was Hawke's habit to pass them with the curtains drawn, snug in his own bed (or someone else's, if a pleasing female opportunity had presented itself).

This was, of course, the expected regime of a gentleman in Naples, where no one of rank or fashion ever ventured out before noon, and Hawke had continued to keep the same hours here in London as well. All of which explained why the ebony panther clock on the drawing room mantelpiece had just begun chiming eleven as Hawke finally appeared to take his breakfast.

Granted, he was only slightly more awake than asleep. His eyes were still heavy-lidded and his jaw unshaven, and despite the pleas for ducal propriety from his manservant, Giacomo, his feet were bare and he wore only his silk banyan wrapped loosely over his nakedness. Yawning, he dropped into a leather-covered armchair near the fire and watched Giacomo pour his coffee:

very black, very thick, very potent, the way the Turks drank it.

"Excellent, Giacomo," he murmured, sipping the coffee. He spoke Italian with Giacomo, with the southern lilt he'd acquired over the years. "You earned your passage for your coffee alone."

"You are kindness itself, sir." Giacomo touched his forehead and bowed so low that his waist-length pigtail with the red ribbon bow flipped forward over his head. Before he'd come into Hawke's service, he had apprenticed as a barber, and he was terribly vain about his own appearance, a true macaroni. But Hawke considered Giacomo's endless primping a fair trade for his skill with a razor and his gift for making Hawke eminently presentable in the shortest of time.

That, and the coffee. He closed his eyes, savoring the heady fragrance. He needed this even more than usual this morning. It wasn't that he was suffering from the aftereffects of a raucous night. Far from it. He'd spent the last two nights and the day in between making his way through every fashionable resort he could imagine—clubs, dining houses, playhouses, gaming dens, pleasure gardens, even the better class of bagnio and brothel—trying to find his fairy queen again. Surely a beauty who had appeared alone at an opera and at Ranelagh had to have a name, and a reputation to go with it. Yet every time he'd described her, he'd met with only blank faces and shrugs, coupled with the occasional pitying shake of the head. He'd begun to feel like one of Fielding's Bow Street runners, except that they were successful and he was not. She'd said her affections were taken, and clearly that lucky gentleman, whoever he was, had her securely squirreled away in keeping in a private house.

He could see her in his thoughts as clearly as if she stood before him still, and the memory of her kiss was just as vivid. She had beguiled him thoroughly, fascinated him as if she'd cast a true fairy spell over him, and then vanished completely into the night.

"The curtains, sir?" Giacomo asked, already poised to pull them open. It was another of the servant's admirable qualities that he never let the morning light intrude unbidden, and with a sigh Hawke nodded and opened his eyes to the scene from his drawing room window.

He was still half surprised to see the regimented English garden of his family's London house instead of the familiar Bay of Naples with Vesuvius wrapped in a haze in the distance. Hawkesworth Chase stood on the grounds of an ancient royal hunting park, one of the many rewards given by the old king to the first Duchess of Hawkesworth for generously sharing her favors. Although the deer, the old lodge, and the chase were long gone and the house had been absorbed by the spread of London in the last hundred or so years, the place still retained its original name. Hawke's father had made some improvements, but it remained a rambling, old-fashioned mansion of brick and stone, with octagonal towers at each corner and a hawk with spread wings carved over the door.

But what made Hawke most uncomfortable about the place wasn't the unstylishness of the façade or the small-paned windows. It was the overwhelming sense that this was still his father's house, not his. His mother had moved to the dowager's house soon after his father's death, and Hawke himself had left for Italy. Almost nothing had changed since he was a boy, with every chair and painting in exactly the spot that his father had decreed. It wasn't exactly that Hawke believed in ghosts, but he swore he could still smell his father's tobacco in the hall and hear his voice in the library, worrying over politics with other members of the House of Lords. To the consternation of the servants, on Hawke's return he had chosen to sleep in his old boyhood bedchamber rather than in the rooms once occupied by his father, rooms reserved for the duke, with those for the duchess close by.

The duchess. Not his mother, but his wife. He tipped his head against the armchair's tall back and muttered a halfhearted oath aimed at nothing in particular. Could anything else spoil his morning more completely?

"Forgive me, sir, a small interruption," Giacomo said beside him, and reluctantly Hawke turned. With Giacomo stood one of the footmen, and both wore the sort of pained expression that servants always adopted when bearing unwelcome news. "You have a visitor, sir. His Grace the Duke of Breconridge."

"Brecon? Here?" Immediately Hawke sat upright. There could be only one reason why his eldest cousin would come to the Chase at this hour. "Tell him I'm not at home, or tell him I'm still abed, or—"

"Too late, dear Hawke," Brecon said, entering the room as if it belonged to him. He handed his hat and his gloves to the footman, sat in the chair opposite Hawke's, and motioned for Giacomo to pour him coffee, too. "You make yourself damned elusive, cousin. Fortunately, my skills as a huntsman are excellent, and you weren't going to escape me any longer."

"Good day to you as well," Hawke grumbled. Richard, Duke of Breconridge, was the eldest of the quartet of cousins descended from the royal bastards of the same king. If March was like a brother to Hawke, then Brecon was like an uncle, a half generation older at forty-two. Brecon had long ago married and produced three stalwart sons, which had given him the confidence to offer advice, friendship, and solicitude to the younger cousins as they'd lurched their own ways toward manhood.

Not that Brecon was a doddering graybeard. He was a worldly, witty widower who knew everyone worth knowing in London. Celebrated both for his embroidered French waistcoats and for his mistresses, he was as adept with his sword as he was with a bon mot, and perfectly capable of making ladies of every age swoon with delight at his gallantry. Secretly Hawke had always wanted to be like Brecon, a much more dashing model of a duke to emulate than his father had been.

But not now, not when Brecon was sitting before him, as elegantly dressed as Hawke was not, and with a steely set to his handsome face that instantly put Hawke on his guard. Clearly Brecon was here to ask difficult questions, the sort of questions to which Hawke had no suitable replies to offer in return.

"A good day to you as well, cousin," Brecon said agreeably. "Or rather, what is left of it. By my recollection, you were born an Englishman, no matter that you've spent the past decade attempting to prove otherwise. Perhaps now that you are once again in London, you might at least attempt to keep London hours."

Hawke set his cup down on the table and folded his arms over his chest. "Is that why you've come, then? To lecture me on the hours I choose to keep?"

Brecon smiled. "Oh, we both know that's not the case," he said easily. "Hawke, you dishonor yourself by ignoring your bride."

Hawke knew this was true, but he hated hearing it from Brecon. He *did* feel dishonorable, which made him speak even more dishonorably.

"Is that why you are here?" he asked. "Did the harridan herself send you?"

As soon as he'd spoken, he wished he hadn't, and seeing Brecon wince at the cruel words only made it worse.

"Unkind, cousin," he said "most unkind. The lady is no harridan, as you will realize at once if ever you deign to call upon her. And no, unlike you, she is too well-bred to involve me in her private sorrows."

Hawke shook his head, as if that were enough to make all of this go away. "If my father hadn't—"

"This is not about your father, Hawke, but you," Brecon said firmly, leaning forward. "This is not about love, or desire, or whatever other nonsense has filled your brain. This is a contract, a legal obligation that you must obey, or be considered a scoundrel—a scoundrel who, as I recall, will also be without a bent shilling to your name if you continue to ignore the lady beyond her next birthday. I would say your father knew you better than any of us realized."

Abruptly Hawke rose, going to stand before the window with his back to Brecon. Every word was bitterly true, especially the part about his father.

"I have every intention of going through with the marriage," he said, his voice hollow and strained. "I would not have made the journey from Naples if I hadn't."

"True enough," Brecon said evenly. "But the delay does not serve you well, nor does the way you have pushed aside the lady bound to be your wife in favor of some insignificant jade you met in Ranelagh."

Hawke turned back sharply. "How could you know of her?"

Brecon swept his hand through the air. "How could I not, given how publicly you have hunted for the whore and scorned the lady?"

"But if you had seen her, Brecon," Hawke protested, once again imagining his fairy in green. "Her beauty, her grace, her—"

"Forget her," Brecon said curtly. "She will ruin you if you don't."

Hawke groaned and thumped his fist against the window in frustration. *Ruin* was a word more usually applied to what an unscrupulous man could do to a woman, yet Brecon was absolutely right: if Hawke persisted in chasing this phantom, he would in fact be ruined, dishonored, and broken in every way that a gentleman could be.

All for the sake of a girl with spangled wings and a merry laugh, a girl as sweet as the first peach and luscious as the first rose.

"We are invited to take tea this afternoon at Marchbourne House," Brecon was saying. "I have taken the liberty of accepting for you, and further, I will be bringing my carriage to gather you at half past two. If the weather holds, I imagine we'll repair to the duchess's garden. Most agreeable."

"Your Grace," called one of the footmen solemnly from the doorway. "Lady Allred."

"Mother?" Hawke turned from the window in disbelief. The morning had descended from bad to much, much worse. He and his mother were not particularly close, though she'd been the first one he'd called on when he arrived in London. He'd been that dutiful. But he'd never expected her in turn to come here, and as far as he knew, this was her first time back since she had remarried and left the dowager's cottage. She'd come with a reason and a purpose, and he could already guess what that must be.

"Yes, yes, Hawkesworth, your mother, as if even you would forget." She sailed across the room toward him in a black gown topped by a yellow silk capelet and an oversized feathered hat on her head. She had always prided herself on presenting a fashionable figure, and though she must be nearly fifty—Hawke wasn't entirely certain—she still did. She wore a great many jewels on her fingers, on her ears, and draped over her person, her habit for both day and night, and as she drew closer and into the sunlight from the window her sparkle increased. She waited for him to bend down low enough so she could kiss his cheek, then stepped back to study him critically.

"Are you ill?" she asked, scowling fiercely at the tuft of black hair on his bare chest where his banyan had fallen open. "They should have told me at the door if you are. Is that why you are still in your undress? Because you are ill?"

"No, Mother, I am not ill," he said wearily. "I am in perfect health."

"Then cover yourself like a Christian," Lady Allred ordered sternly, the plumes on her hat twitching. "How can I address you about poor Lady Elizabeth if you're parading about in your nakedness like some wicked pasha?"

Defensively he pulled his banyan more closely about his body. "There's no need for you to address me like I've been sent down from school."

"That is true," she said. "Sensible talk accomplishes nothing with you. It never has, and it never will. What is required is a good thrashing. Why are you treating your future wife so shamefully, Hawkesworth? My friends speak of nothing else, and what defense can I make for you? You, my only son?"

"We were discussing exactly that when you arrived, Lady Allred," Brecon said, coming to bow with his usual grace. "Good day to you, ma'am. How vastly handsome you look."

Hawke could have sworn his mother blushed beneath her paint.

"Why, thank you, Breconridge," she said. "Forgive me for taking no notice of you. I am simply so distraught over Hawkesworth's behavior that I am not myself."

Brecon bowed his head, his expression both sorrowful and aggrieved.

"It is a deplorable situation, ma'am, to be sure," he said, as if Hawke wasn't there. "Most gentlemen would rejoice at the prospect of marriage to so admirable a lady."

"Exactly so, Breconridge," Lady Allred said. "Such a pretty little thing, too. I must say she is bearing up well, considering. What lady wishes to be scorned, and by such a rogue as my son?"

Hawke sighed with exasperation. He felt like a beleaguered fox at the end of the chase, with the baying hounds nipping close at his exhausted heels.

"I'd dared to hope Hawkesworth would have secured the title with a son or two of his own by now," his mother was saying. "How I should loathe to see the dukedom slip from the family because he was too proud to—"

"It has been resolved, Mother," Hawke said. "Brecon and I are going to Marchbourne House this afternoon to take tea with the ladies. If Lady Elizabeth finds me tolerable, I will wed her before the cream cakes are passed, and present you with your first grandson by supper."

Lady Allred snorted. "Such rubbish!"

"But Hawke and I are attending tea this day with March's good lady and Lady Elizabeth," Brecon said. "That part of it is true."

Hawke took a deep breath. If he'd gone this far, he might as well jump entirely into the well.

"I'm sure Charlotte would welcome you to the party as well, Mother," he said, bowing as Brecon had earlier. "I would be delighted to escort you."

"No, no, that is very kind of you, Hawkesworth, but unnecessary," his mother said, though clearly pleased. "I would not wish to interfere in your personal affairs."

Hawke's brows shot high with cynical amazement. "You, Mother?"

"Yes," she said demurely, retying her hat's silk bow at the nape of her neck as she prepared to leave. "I have never been a meddler, and I won't begin now. Good day to you, Hawkesworth. Pray make yourself agreeable to the lady, and if you can, pray remember to wear stockings and shoes."

Three hours later, Hawke sat facing Brecon in his cousin's carriage. Giacomo had taken considerable care with Hawke's appearance, all the while as he shaved and dressed him fairly purring about how much he was looking forward to serving a duchess as well as a duke. Hawke wished he shared the valet's enthusiasm. After so much attention to the brushing of his coat, the polishing of the silver buttons on his waistcoat, and the precise tying of his neckcloth, he felt more like a well-dressed dish being carried for presentation at the dining table than a jolly bridegroom.

"I'm surprised you didn't put me in manacles to make sure I didn't escape," he said glumly to Brecon.

His cousin smiled. "I considered it," he said. "But Giacomo would have had my head if I'd dared put irons over your shirt cuffs."

"I am in no humor for your witty diversion, Brecon," he said, unhappiness making him curt. "None at all."

"Then I'll beg you to have a thought for the lady," Brecon said. "She is only eighteen, an innocent, with none of your experience or knowledge of the world. Consider how daunting you must be to her, and her distress at this meeting. She will look to you not only for protection but for guidance. Think of all the things you can share with her, and the pleasure that will bring to you both."

"That's easy enough for you to imagine, Brecon," Hawke said grudgingly. "You loved your wife."

"I did love her, more than I'd ever thought possible." Brecon's face softened, the way it always did when he spoke of his late wife, Henriette. She had died of smallpox more than a dozen years before, yet it was clear that

Brecon had never stopped grieving her. "On our wedding day, I'd no such feelings. I'd never been permitted her company unattended. I knew none of her likes or dislikes, nor what pleased her most. All I knew of her was that her smile was shy and that she blushed at anything, and that she was the daughter of the Duke of Culverton. Yet from that unromantic beginning, love grew, just as I hope it shall for you and Lady Elizabeth."

Unconvinced, Hawke stared from the carriage window. His parents had lived in civilized distance from each other, and his father had always discreetly kept a mistress; the last one had even been mentioned in Father's will. That seemed to Hawke to be a much more reasonable arrangement than hoping for Cupid to come along with the union of fortunes, estates, and titles that was to be his marriage. The best he could pray for now was that the well-bred and eminently suitable Lady Elizabeth wasn't so homely that bedding her would be a trial, conducted behind closed bed-curtains with the candles doused.

"Ah, here we are," Brecon said as the carriage rolled through the gates to Marchbourne House. "We're fortunate in the weather. Tea in the garden will be pleasant indeed."

It had been a decade since Hawke had visited Marchbourne House, and he had to admit that it compared more favorably than he would have thought to the grand Italian houses designed by Palladio. If Hawkesworth Chase was a Tudor ramble, then March's house was as elegant and precise as a minuet, with everything done in the best classical manner.

As he and Brecon were ushered through the house and past room after richly furnished and appointed room, all marble and gilt, Hawke began to feel self-consciously protective of the old Chase. It wasn't that there wasn't money to bring it up to snuff—his bankers assured him he'd plenty, or at least he would so long as he married—but Hawke had sadly neglected his London house in favor of his Neapolitan villa.

But March, however, had had no such divided loyalties, and his house was more imposing than many royal palaces Hawke had visited. He'd been told that Lady Elizabeth had been living here as a guest for some time. He hoped she hadn't become too accustomed to such grandeur, or else she was bound to be disappointed in the Chase.

They followed the footman out the back door and into the walled garden at the rear of the house. The garden was a formal arrangement of squared paths framing beds of blooming flowers, scenting the air with their blossoms, and in one corner was a small fountain with a dancing stone faun. In the center of the garden stood a small green-painted summerhouse, raised to catch any breezes that came over the tall brick walls from the park beyond. A table was set for tea with gleaming silver pots and tableware, porcelain cups and saucers, and more flowers in a vase in the center.

All Hawke saw was the young woman sitting on a stool to one side. She was dressed in a dark gown with a white kerchief over her shoulders and a white ruffled cap on her curly, carroty hair, plain country dressing if ever he'd seen it.

But clothes could be changed, he told himself firmly, and fashion could be bought. He'd paid his share of mantua makers' bills, and he knew a clever seamstress could find elegance and style in almost any woman. The girl was bent over some sort of handwork, the cloth bunched in her hand as she purposefully jabbed a needle in and out of the cloth. At least she was industrious and not idle, he thought, desperately striving to put the best face on matters even as his hopes plummeted.

But even at this distance Hawke could see that she

was no beauty, her form round and sturdy, and when she raised her needle to the sun to rethread it, squinting with one eye closed, he saw that her cheeks were badly pockmarked, her lips narrow and pinched, her eyes pale and lashless. There wasn't a scrap of humor or good nature anywhere on her person or face, not one single feature of pleasantness that might make for an agreeable companion.

No wonder they'd brought him to a walled garden, or he would have bolted straightaway.

"Gentlemen!" March had spotted them, and rose to wave, grinning. "At last you are here!"

Still focused on the young woman sewing, Hawke felt as if his feet (or rather his shoes; his mother needn't have worried) had taken root on the path of crushed shell. He simply could not go forward.

"Courage, cousin, courage," Brecon said softly beside him, taking him by the upper arm to nudge him forward. "It's only March."

It was indeed only March, striding toward them. He'd never seen March look so relaxed or so informal, in his waistcoat without a coat, the sleeves of his shirt rolled carelessly to his elbows. He also appeared happier, too, his smile wide and easy. Clearly whatever insult Hawke might have caused at Ranelagh had been forgotten and forgiven.

"I cannot tell you how glad I am to have you here," March said, grasping him fondly by the shoulders. "Here in my home, and here, too, in London. But come, there is someone I wish you to meet."

Hawke's smile grew stiff and forced as they walked to the summerhouse. The young woman put aside her stitchery, bowed her head, and curtseyed deeply. Hawke supposed that was proper. After all, how often would any woman, even one of rank, ever be confronted with three dukes at a time? He swallowed hard. Usually he'd no trouble at all addressing women, but his brain had frozen and every word had fled, leaving him with a fixed, sickly smile pasted on his face.

"My dear angel," March said proudly. "Peg, present the young fellow."

The woman stepped into the summerhouse and returned cradling a small baby in her arms. The child had a round-cheeked face with huge, staring blue eyes, and yet even amidst the yards of trailing linen, he still somehow bore an unmistakable resemblance to March.

"My second son, George," March said, carefully taking the baby from the nurse.

So the stern-faced woman was the infant's nurse, not Lady Elizabeth. Hawke almost laughed aloud from relief, and at his own folly.

"He is named for His Majesty," March was saying, rocking the child gently against his chest with astonishing familiarity. At least it astonished Hawke, who happily had no familiarity with babies in any form. "Always useful to honor the king, isn't it, Georgie?"

He tickled the baby's cheek with the back of his finger, and at once little Georgie smiled, a beautiful, toothless smile, with a string of drool trickling from his chin.

"Aren't you the hearty young gentleman?" March said, clearly besotted. "Aren't you a proper rascal? Three months old, and look at the size of him!"

"A most excellent lad," Brecon agreed. "You and Charlotte have every reason to be proud of that brave little one. Hawke, the next babe will be yours, yes?"

"I should hope not," Hawke said, so quickly that the other two laughed. How could a mere baby make him feel such a fool?

"That's how I felt, too," March said, "until the child was my own. A shame you weren't in time to meet the twins, but since they'd both begun to wail, the ladies took them in with their nurses. I expect Charlotte and

Lizzie to be back any moment. Here, Hawke, why don't you hold Georgie, just to get the proper feel of being a father?"

Before Hawke could protest, March had placed the baby into his arms, a transfer received with such stiff-armed clumsiness on Hawke's part that he marveled that March would trust him with his son. The baby never stopped moving, kicking and wriggling and waving his small impotent fists in Hawke's face while making the most alarming chirps and small cries.

"I do not believe he likes me, March," Hawke said, desperately wishing March would take his offspring back before Hawke caused some hideous harm to it.

"He likes you fine," March assured him. "If only Lizzie could see you now! There is nothing that melts a woman's heart faster than the sight of a large man with a small baby."

"Lizzie?" Hawke repeated, not daring to take his gaze away from Georgie. "Is she another nursemaid?"

Again March and Brecon laughed. "No, no, that's what we call Lady Elizabeth within the family," March said, "and so you shall, too, once she gives you leave."

But Hawke was too occupied with watching the infant, who likewise stared at him, until at last the child decided to concede the contest. Georgie blinked twice and squawked, then spit up a dramatic amount of foul-smelling curdled matter directly onto the front of the coat that Giacomo had so lovingly prepared.

Instantly Peg reappeared. "Pray permit me to take his lordship, Your Grace," she said briskly, carrying the baby away before he launched another assault.

"Well, now, you'll forgive Georgie for that, won't you?" March said apologetically, handing Hawke his own handkerchief for mopping. "At least he gave you a proper salute."

"A salute?" Hawke said, aghast. No mere blotting

with a handkerchief would redeem his coat, and the more he tried, the worse the mess seemed to become, the smell now clinging to his hand as well as his coat. If this was what baby heirs did, then his mother could find her grandchildren beneath a cabbage leaf, for he wished nothing further to do with the creatures. "That is what you call it? A *salute*? Damnation, March, I reek worse than a sailor at the dog end of his leave, and I—"

"Ah, at last," Brecon said pleasantly. "Here are the ladies to join us."

CHAPTER

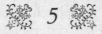 5

"I can't bear to look myself, Charlotte," Lizzie said. "Tell me, tell me quickly! Is he truly there?"

"It would appear that he is," Charlotte said as they walked through the garden together. "Finally! I knew we could trust Brecon to capture him. Come now, Lizzie, you're dawdling. You don't want Hawke to think you're reluctant."

"Why shouldn't I, when he certainly has been?" Lizzie's heart was racing so fast and her stomach was twisting into such knots that she prayed she wouldn't expire here on the garden path beside the roses. "Does my gown look well enough? My hair hasn't come unpinned, has it? Do I—"

"You look lovely," Charlotte assured her for what must have been the thousandth time. "That gown becomes you most wonderfully. Hawke is sure to be enchanted. You're like a fresh blossom in the garden."

In any other circumstance, Lizzie, too, would have been enchanted by her gown: a pale yellow brocaded silk, strewn all over with a pattern of pink and deep red carnations, with double-flounced cuffs at the elbows and a delicate lace scarf tied loosely over her shoulders. Coral beads circled her neck, and pearl drops hung from her ears. Because they were out-of-doors, she wore a wide-brimmed hat of Milano straw with a froth of yellow ribbons on the crown. Charlotte had pinned the hat to tip coquettishly low over Lizzie's face to shield her from the sun, but Lizzie was more thankful that she could hide beneath the curving brim.

"That's curious," Charlotte said. "The gentlemen seem to be fussing about something. Now Hawke has taken off his coat and thrown it off to one side. What *is* happening, I wonder?"

"Perhaps he is mad," Lizzie said glumly, still not daring to look up and judge for herself. "I am doomed to wed a madman."

"Oh, he's not mad," Charlotte said. "But faith, he *is* handsome, and tall, and very well made. Oh, Lizzie, you are most fortunate!"

"He is all those things?" Lizzie asked, her voice squeaking upward. "Truly?"

"He is," Charlotte said, lowering her voice to a whisper as she sank into a curtsey. "And now he has come to greet us. Your Grace, let me welcome you to our home."

At once Lizzie, too, dropped into a deep curtsey, staring down at the crushed white oyster shells of the path. Among three dukes and a duchess, her rank was so inferior that it was likely quite appropriate for her to remain bent over this way for minutes on end. Without lifting her head, she could just see the toes of a gentleman's well-polished shoes with gleaming silver buckles. No, her future husband's shoes, she thought with a small thrill—here, now, finally, before her.

A second pair of men's shoes appeared, shoes that belonged to March, and a shadow that must belong to the third cousin, Brecon.

"Charlotte, my dear, may I present my cousin, Hawke," March said. "Hawke, my wife Charlotte."

"Duchess, I am most honored," he said, and Lizzie saw his shadow as he bowed in reply to her curtsey. Her heart was beating so loudly in her ears that she scarcely heard his words—though she did hear that his voice was deep and manly.

"Good day to you, Duke," Charlotte said, ever correct. "I am most honored to welcome you to our home."

Lizzie knew she was next. There was no escaping now, and she prayed she'd not shame herself by doing or saying something regrettable. She felt her sister's hand rest lightly on her shoulder, a gesture of both comfort and presentation.

"But I know this is the lady you are most eager to meet, Duke," Charlotte continued. "May I present my younger sister Lady Elizabeth Wylder?"

"Lady Elizabeth," he murmured, and she felt his fingers take her hand, strong and sure, to raise her up. She had practiced this with Charlotte. She knew what to do. Slowly she stood, with as much composure as could be managed when her knees felt like jelly. She straightened, made herself smile, and lifted her face to meet his gaze with what she hoped was the grace worthy of a duchess.

Her small shriek of bewilderment was not part of the plan.

He gasped, and barely bit back an oath.

Neither spoke. Neither looked away. Neither moved.

"Well, now," Brecon said with satisfaction. "I've never seen a couple so instantly enchanted with each other that they were literally left without words. I should say we have a match, eh?"

"Indeed we do," declared March, equally pleased. "I told you she was a beauty, Hawke."

"That you did, March," Hawke said slowly. Still he stared at Lizzie, almost as if he feared she might vanish if he looked away. "I doubt there could be another like her anywhere."

Lizzie's face burned, both with embarrassment and with confusion. She understood his double-edged remark, even if no one else did. How could her stranger from the opera and from Ranelagh turn out to be the Duke of Hawkesworth? Was this some sort of hideous jest, a humorless trick on her innocence?

But if it was a trick, then clearly neither Brecon nor March was party to it. They were too busy beaming and doting to have done anything so low. Swiftly Lizzie looked to her sister, hoping to find an explanation there. But Charlotte's face showed only delight as well.

Clearly none of her family knew, and with growing frustration she turned back to the gentleman who still held her hand. Now that his first shock had faded, she read in his face the same confusion as she felt herself, and more than a little anger. Well, let him be angry, she thought. She was angry, too, and with far more reason.

"Have you no reply to His Grace, Lizzie?" her sister prodded gently. "Faith, I've never known you to have not a word to say!"

Lizzie had a great deal to say, so much that she scarcely knew where to begin. But just as she opened her mouth to start, the stranger—or rather, Hawkesworth, her intended husband—spoke first.

"If you please, Duchess," he said, smiling winningly at Charlotte. "I have a request to beg, that I might hear Lady Elizabeth's first words to me alone, so that I shall be able to recall them forever with perfect clarity. It's selfish of me, I know, but—"

"How could that be selfish?" exclaimed Charlotte, pressing her palms together with a rapturous sigh. "It's vastly gallant of you, and I would not dream of denying you. March, you have no objections, do you?"

"So long as you stay within sight in this garden," he said, "you may keep from our hearing as far as you please."

Brecon chuckled. "What manner of mischief could

they possibly contrive, with the three of us to serve as vigilant duennas? Besides, they'll wed soon enough."

"I thank you," Hawkesworth said solemnly. He waited until the three returned to the summerhouse before he turned to Lizzie.

"Shall we walk together, Lady Elizabeth?" he asked with a pleasant smile as he tightened his hold on her hand.

"I should rather walk straight into the river than walk with you," she said with vehemence, not moving from where she stood.

"I can assure you that I share much the same preferences regarding your company, Lady Elizabeth," he said firmly. "But I hold my cousins in the highest regard, and I would not disappoint them for the world. For their sake, you will walk, and you will smile, and you will appear to them as if there is no other place in creation you would rather be."

"Your cousins, but my sister," Lizzie said. Where was the sweet romance she'd dreamed of over all those long months? Where was the courtly lover she'd imagined? She took a deep breath to steady herself, then another. "None of them must ever know that we have met before."

"No," he said curtly. "Why the devil would there be any use in them knowing that?"

"Then walk." She pulled her hand free of his, tucking it into the crook of his arm instead. She smiled up at him, the picture of adoration. "Make a better show of it for them, sir. It shouldn't be difficult, considering your gift for being false."

He lurched forward, dragging her along with him. "Hah, that is rare to hear from your lips," he said. "Who is the duplicitous creature who led me into the bushes at Ranelagh like any other common jade?"

She gasped, outraged. "You would dare call *me* duplicitous? Consider, sir, that you had come to Ranelagh for the express purpose of meeting your intended bride—a meeting that you, sir, had already avoided repeatedly—and yet you were so easily misled to dally with another and abandon your true lady?"

His eyes widened with equal outrage, his hair tossing around his face in the breeze. At Ranelagh she'd thought his eyes were brown, but now, in the sunlight, she could see they'd blue in them, too, an unusual combination that, in other circumstances, she would have found most intriguing.

"You make little sense, Lady Elizabeth," he said. "You would fault me for dallying with you, because it meant that at the same time I was being unfaithful to you?"

She scowled, struggling to make sense of her own tangled argument. It was not easy, and having his thoroughly handsome self so close beside her did not make it any easier to think.

The last time she'd seen him, he'd been dressed like the night, all in dark velvet. Now, with his scarlet silk waistcoat and his linen shirtsleeves billowing about his arms, he seemed more a kind of avenging angel, though she wasn't sure what exactly he'd be here to avenge.

"Where is your coat?" she asked. "Why did you take it off?"

"I had no choice," he said defensively. "March's infernal brat puked down the front of it."

"Little Georgie?" Oh, prize baby, she thought. Clever little fellow for having displayed such judgment! "He did that to you?"

"Yes, he did," he said. "Now answer my question, if you can. Do you believe I've betrayed you with yourself?"

She sighed, because it didn't make any more sense that way than it had before.

"Yes," she said at last. "That is precisely what I meant.

You'd no notion of who I was, so you were being false to me, even as you paid your attentions to me."

"Why would you tempt me into such a trap?" he demanded. "What was your purpose?"

"What purpose could I possibly have?" she asked. "What could I have hoped to achieve by pretending I was other than who I am?"

"You tell me, Lady Elizabeth," he said. "I'm sure you'd planned some deceitful female trickery, some cunning way to dishonor me. Why else were you, a lady, alone and unprotected?"

"Because I didn't believe I'd need any protection," she retorted, "especially not from the man I am supposed to marry."

He made a grumbling noise deep in his chest. "There is no supposing about it. You will marry me, Lady Elizabeth, and by God, I'll marry you. Our meddlesome dead fathers have seen to that, reaching up from the grave to bind us together."

That shocked Lizzie. Her father had died in a riding accident when she was very young, so she'd only the haziest memories of him, but she still respected those memories, and him with them. "Do not speak of my father that way."

"Why not, when I speak only the truth?" he said. "Neither of us would be here now if those selfish old men hadn't made this devil's bargain between them."

Somehow they'd fallen into step together as they'd walked the paths. Lizzie noticed, and purposely broke stride, not wanting to accommodate him in any fashion. Betrothal or no, how could she possibly marry such a man?

"I wish you to the devil, sir," she said bitterly, "and a devil's pox on you, too, to rot your carcass for all eternity."

He looked at her sharply. "Now those are pretty words for a lady."

"Why shouldn't I use them, and worse, toward you, when you've not behaved like a gentleman?" she said. "You tricked me, sir. You must have known who I was."

"How could I have known?" he said, stopping to throw his hands out in exasperation. "It wasn't as if you wore a lettered placard about your neck, proclaiming your identity to the world. 'Lady Elizabeth Wylder, a teasing little baggage.'"

Lizzie gasped again, fairly seething. He'd stopped at the corner of the path, where a large mulberry bush hid them from the sight of the summerhouse. Not that it mattered. She was too furious to restrain herself, even if they'd been standing before every last one of her relatives.

She drew back her arm, and with all her force swung around and struck her palm across his cheek.

"There," she declared. "*That* is what you deserve, sir, that and more!"

She expected him to grab his cheek, swear, stamp off, or do some other typical mannish thing. It would have been gallant of him to have realized his errors and apologize, though she doubted very much he'd do that. He might have been gallant in the moonlight at Ranelagh, but in the light of the sun, he hadn't a shred of gallantry anywhere about his handsome person.

Which, really, explained what he did next.

He grabbed her by the wrist and jerked her close against his chest, circling his arm around her waist to hold her fast. She sputtered with surprise, but before she realized what was happening, he had bent her back over his arm and was kissing her.

She tried to break free, struggling and twisting against him, but succeeded only in knocking her hat off her head. Hawkesworth wasn't about to let her go. This kiss was purposeful and relentless, with none of the sweetness she remembered from the last time. But to her consternation, the more she fought against him, the more arousing the kiss became. It was almost as if he'd magically taken her anger and turned it against her, changing it into something equally fiery but very different. Soon she realized she'd not only stopped fighting but had curled her hands possessively over his shoulders. She liked how he tasted, how he smelled, how he kissed, and how his body felt pressed against hers. She liked all that a great deal.

What she didn't like, however, was *him*, and with that as a reminder, she finally broke free, though she remained rocked back against his arm, her hands resting peacefully upon his red-silk-covered chest.

"Why did you do that?" she demanded, though as demands went, it was quite pathetic, and more a breathy whisper.

He smiled down at her with pure male triumph and happiness, the first real smile she'd seen from him that day.

"I wasn't sure you were the same woman I'd kissed before," he said. "And thank God, you are."

"You're—you're *vile*," she sputtered, shoving hard against his chest. He let her go and didn't try to stop her as she hurried away from him, her heels crunching on the shell path. She had never been this disgusted with herself.

He might even have laughed.

"Why, Lizzie, here you are," Charlotte said as she reached the summerhouse. She sat with a teacup in one hand and surprise on her face—surprise, and questions, too. Self-consciously Lizzie reached up to smooth her hair. She hadn't realized that her elaborately arranged hair was coming unpinned and that a tangled, heavy piece of it was flopping awkwardly over her left shoulder. She shoved it back behind her ear and folded her hands neatly at her waist as if nothing untoward had happened.

"Lady Elizabeth," Hawkesworth called, coming up behind her. "Your hat."

"Thank you," she said with murderous civility. She snatched the hat from his hands and jammed it back atop her head. "Sir."

"How chivalrous of you, Hawke," Brecon said, helping himself to another tea cake. "What delightful lovebirds! Have we determined a date for the wedding, then?"

"Never," Lizzie said, and before anyone could say otherwise, she turned on her heel and fled to the house.

As much as Hawke enjoyed company, there were definitely times when solitude held a special allure.

After yesterday's unfortunate afternoon at Marchbourne House, he wasn't sure he ever wished to venture into company again, leastwise not company that included his cousins or the woman he was ostensibly to wed. After a merciless night of unrest, he gave up on trying to sleep as the sun was rising, and to Giacomo's dismay carried his coffee himself downstairs to the old ballroom.

Since returning to London, he'd turned the ballroom into his makeshift picture gallery. In Italy, art wasn't an ornamental flourish but a part of life, and Hawke had embraced it like one more lover. Even as a boy he'd been fascinated by the murky portraits and landscapes that had hung in their houses, and he'd secretly stare at them for hours; it had been one of the deeper conflicts with his father, who had wanted him to take an interest in something more useful if tedious, like politics.

It wasn't until Hawke had traveled to Italy that he'd

been finally free to indulge himself. He'd collected pictures not like most Englishmen did—for their prestige and monetary value—but simply because he liked them. They amused him, pleased him, and brought him peace. He'd brought a score of his favorites along with him from Bella Collina, the ones he couldn't bear to leave behind, and this morning they were all the company he wanted.

He'd arranged the paintings himself, some on easels and others leaning against the walls of the vast, empty room, not bothering to have them hung for what he expected would be a short stay in London. A ballroom was meant to be lit by candlelight and filled with music and laughter, but he liked it best this way, comfortably silent except for the birdsongs from the garden outside the tall windows and filled with the even, gentle sunlight from the north that was most perfect for viewing pictures.

He set the single chair (for he hadn't seen the reason to have any more in the room) before one of the largest paintings, a landscape of the Bay of Naples at sunset that he'd commissioned from a local painter. It was not so much a great painting as an exact one: the view was precisely the same as the one from Hawke's villa, and with a contented sigh and his cup of coffee in his hands, he prepared to lose himself in the scene's beauty.

But this morning he couldn't. Instead of the peaceful reverie he craved, he looked at the painting and thought only of how Lady Elizabeth compared to the women he'd left behind in Naples. With a frown, he pulled his chair to the next picture, an amusing vignette featuring a traveling theater company rehearsing their next play beside a stream.

Yet all he could think of now was how his own well-ordered life seemed to have deteriorated into a farcical scene from a bad comedy, just like the one shown in the painting. If he'd been a character in such a play, then he would have been delighted to discover that the girl he'd been pursuing was the same lady he was betrothed to, and everyone would have lived happily ever after. But he wasn't in a play, and he didn't trust coincidence like that. It didn't make sense in real life, especially in *his* real life. Having Lady Elizabeth equally unhappy and full of suspicion didn't help matters, either, nor did he enjoy bearing the blame for her distress—blame that March, Brecon, and Charlotte, too, were determined to heap upon him.

No, no, this wasn't right. Grumbling to himself, he moved to the one picture that was sure to make him smile: a nearly life-sized portrait of a reclining Venus, shamelessly nude except for her jewels. The Venus was a masterpiece, painted by Titian, a true master. It had been one of the first paintings he'd bought, and usually the goddess's bounteous attributes could make him forget anything.

But this morning when he looked at her, his thoughts raced back to Lady Elizabeth: astonishingly beautiful, amusing, clever, and, when she was in a good humor, graceful and charming beyond measure. An earl's daughter or not, she had also revealed herself to be a termagant of the first order, with a fiery temper to match.

Of course she wanted nothing to do with him.

And equally of course, he had never been more insanely attracted to a woman in his life.

Almost desperately Hawke tried to focus on the painted Venus, her creamy flesh, her seductive smile. He'd wager fifty guineas that Lady Elizabeth's breasts were every bit that fine, round, and tempting. It was difficult to gauge with modern women, who barricaded their charms so tightly behind whalebone stays and hoops, but he'd bet Lady Elizabeth was—

"Good day, Hawkesworth," his mother said briskly,

entering unannounced, the plumes on her oversized hat all a-flutter. "I told the footman not to bother calling my name. This was my house long enough that I should know my own way to my own son, even if he insists on sitting alone in his undress in the ballroom. Is this another of the Italian customs you have acquired?"

He rose and bowed, taking care to keep his banyan closed. "If you insist on appearing without warning, Mother, then you will find what you find."

"Indeed," she said, coming around the easel to claim his chair. She stopped abruptly before the painted Venus, wrinkling her face with distaste. "I suppose that is Italian as well?"

"It is," he said evenly. Unable to resist, he added, "She's beautiful, isn't she?"

"Shameless harlot," Lady Allred said, her nose high with disdain as she sat, purposefully turning the chair and her back to the painting. She sat with practiced care, arranging her silk skirts to cover her feet. "I trust your wife will put an end to that sort of trumpery. That is, if you can ever make yourself sufficiently agreeable to the poor lady that she'll agree to wed you."

Glumly Hawke stared into his mostly empty coffee cup. He longed for more, but if he summoned Giacomo, then he would have to be hospitable and offer refreshment to his mother as well, and he'd no desire to encourage her to stay any longer than was necessary.

Which, knowing his mother when she'd things to say, could be very long indeed.

"I know you don't wish me to linger, Hawkesworth," she said as if reading his thoughts. "But I heard of yesterday's debacle with the Wylder girl, and I cannot conceive of how you misplayed your hand so badly. What do you propose to do next? How will you redeem yourself?"

Hawke frowned and tapped his fingers against the

side of the cup, wishing his mother didn't insist on treating him as if he were still a twelve-year-old sent down from school for bad behavior.

Little wonder he thought longingly of Bella Collina, so agreeably distant from London.

"I am meeting with my solicitors later today, Mother," he said at last, striving to sound businesslike and in control. "Since this marriage is a contract instead of a love match, it seems better to turn the arrangements over to the fellows who execute such things on a regular basis."

"Oh, Hawkesworth," said his mother, wincing as if she'd just smelled an unpleasant rot. "That is preposterous."

"I've given the situation much thought, Mother," he said. Not that he'd tell her the real reason for turning to the lawyers: that he didn't entirely trust himself to be with Lady Elizabeth again. He needed time away from her to cool his passions, or God only knew what kind of insanity he'd commit with her. "I know what I am doing."

"No, you do not," Lady Allred said. "Love match or arrangement, every marriage is a kind of partnership, and not one made by lawyers, either. For people like us, it is also a way to cement important fortunes and families. You must demonstrate an agreeable face to your bride and a willingness for compromise, and you must show the lady at least a smidgeon of wooing."

"Oh, yes, a smidgeon," Hawke said. "I can't see Father showing you any more than that."

Lady Allred smiled serenely, touching a gloved finger to one of the plumes in her hat.

"You would be surprised what your father showed in the early days of our marriage," she said. "If he hadn't, I doubt that you or your sisters would be here now."

Hawke gulped, not wishing any further information from his parents' bedchamber.

"The wooing part is also being addressed, Mother," he said. "I'm not the complete dolt you think me."

Her gaze narrowed. "I have never once called you a dolt," she said. "You are unbearably selfish, even for a man, but you are not a dolt."

Hawke grumbled, refusing to discuss his doltdom any further. "I have already arranged to send a small token to Lady Elizabeth today, by way of apology and regard."

His mother glanced at him suspiciously. "Not flowers, I hope. You are a duke, you know. More is expected from you than mere ephemeral blossoms."

Flowers were exactly what Hawke had intended, though he could scarcely admit it now. In desperation he glanced around at the paintings lined up on their easels, and seized the smallest one.

"I am sending her this," he said, holding the painting with a flourish for his mother to see, as if he'd planned it all along. "It's a tempera panel, and more than three hundred years old."

The painting was a jewel in its own right, the ancient paint still bright and gleaming as if it were enameled, a prize he'd bought on a trip to Florence. Two lovers in lavish ermine-trimmed clothes from some forgotten royal court sat facing each other beneath an apple tree whose fruit hung like bright red ornaments. Hawke had bought it mainly because he'd liked the two dogs in studded collars that sat beside their owners: a white greyhound beside the woman, and a black one beside the man.

The longer Hawke looked at the painting, the more he realized he didn't really wish to part with it, but now he didn't have a choice. If he didn't trust Lady Elizabeth about her past, then how was he to trust her with his pictures? But perhaps this was what everyone meant about sacrifices made for love: if he offered a gift as significant as his greyhound painting to Lady Elizabeth, then perhaps she'd begin to find him a bit more agreeable, too.

His mother, however, understood none of this, any more than she realized the true value of the painting.

"Very nice," she said, barely glancing at it. "An untraditional gift, but I suppose Lady Elizabeth must learn of your penchant for buying foreign pictures soon enough. You can give it to her yourself this afternoon at Lady Sanborn's house."

So at last his mother had come to her true reason for calling. "Lady Sanborn, Mother?"

"Yes, yes, Lady Sanborn," she said, smoothing her black lace shawl over her shoulders. "Surely you recall her, Hawkesworth. The dowager Countess of Carbery. She has been among my acquaintances forever. More important to you, she is Lady Elizabeth's great-aunt."

Of course she was. When Hawke had first arrived in London, he hadn't been able to find a soul with personal knowledge of Lady Elizabeth. Now there seemed to be a fresh relative on every tree branch.

Carefully he set the little painting back on its easel. "Recall, Mother, that I am to marry Lady Elizabeth, not Lady Carbery."

"Don't be impertinent, Hawkesworth," she said. "You made such a misery of your first meeting that Lady Sanborn and I decided we'd no choice but to involve ourselves. You will begin again, and attend Lady Elizabeth in Lady Carbery's drawing room this afternoon at four."

"A misery," he repeated, marveling at her choice of the word, and how inadvertently—for so it had to be— that was exactly what his meeting with Lady Elizabeth had become. "What if I have other obligations for this evening?"

"Then you must make your apologies," Lady Allred

said, rising to leave. "Pray do not be late. Lady Elizabeth will not wait forever."

He kissed her cheek as she expected, and escorted her to the door. Then he returned to the pictures, especially the one he was giving to Lady Elizabeth. He hoped she appreciated it. He hoped she liked it as much as he did, because, really, he was giving her a small part of himself with this painting. Truly, it was much easier to send flowers to ladies.

He sighed, running his finger lightly around the gilded frame. It was irrational, yes, but he was almost certain she would like it. Treasure it, even. Why else would it be so easy for him to imagine her eyes wide with pleasure when she saw it, her gasp of delight, and, if he was lucky, the deliciously sweet kiss of thanks she'd impulsively grant?

It would not be such a trial to be civil to her. In fact, it would be quite the opposite: a pleasure, a delight, a blissful experience. Seducing a wife couldn't be that different from seducing any other woman, and he'd always enjoyed that. And, as with any other woman, once the delight and the pleasure began to fade, he could turn elsewhere, except that this time he needed to sire a child or two before he left.

He smiled to himself, thinking again of his soon-to-be wife. His *wife*. His mother could babble on all she wished about how Lady Elizabeth wouldn't wait forever. The unholy truth of the matter, though, was that now he was the one who couldn't wait.

CHAPTER
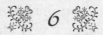
6

Lizzie had done a great deal of thinking in the day and night since she'd run from the garden at Marchbourne House. She'd had plenty of time alone for thinking, too. First she'd shut herself in her bedchamber, too mortified to appear until Charlotte had cajoled her to come down for supper. As soon as that dismal meal was over, she'd swiftly retreated back upstairs, claiming to be too exhausted to stay awake any longer. But instead of sleep, she'd tossed and turned and thrashed about, her thoughts racing feverishly this way and that the entire night long, with absolutely no useful conclusions having come from any of it.

She had defiantly declared that she'd never wed Hawkesworth, but even she knew how empty a threat that was. She'd have to marry him. Neither of them had a choice, exactly as he'd said. At least her father had made sure she'd never be jilted, though that was small comfort indeed.

She desperately wished her mother were here to hug her and tell her everything would work out for the best. She wished her younger sister, Diana, were here, too, to tell her of new kittens in the barn at home, and how hard the wind had blown the night before, and how what might have been the remnants of a genuine sea monster had washed up on the beach in the morning. Even better, she heartily wished herself back home at Ransom Manor, where she wouldn't disappoint anyone.

It wasn't that she didn't find Hawkesworth acceptable. Far from it. In appearance he was all that a bridegroom should be; if anything, her sister hadn't done him full justice when she'd described him as handsome, tall, and well made. Bowing before her in the garden with his dark hair tousled by the breeze, he'd been *dazzling*. And when he'd kissed her—ah, she'd been dazzled by that, too.

But everything in between had been decidedly without dazzle. She'd had months and months to imagine what their first real meeting would be like, and he'd destroyed every one of those dreams in a matter of minutes. He had been neither charming nor romantic. He had been blunt and direct, and he'd insinuated—no, he'd spoken it plainly enough—that she'd somehow tricked him into their meeting at Ranelagh. It made no sense, no sense at all, and she'd hated how he'd mistrusted her so much that he'd actually believed such foolishness. That mistrust had hurt, and had made her say and do things that she wasn't proud of, things that no honorable lady should ever have on her conscience regarding a gentleman.

Especially the gentleman she was to marry.

But no matter how grim her betrothal had seemed in the middle of the night, it had grown markedly worse in the morning. That was when Charlotte had told her that their Aunt Sophronia had decided to take matters into her own overbearing hands and personally oversee the next meeting between Lizzie and Hawkesworth. Aunt Sophronia was the dowager Countess of Carbery, her late father's oldest aunt and a looming presence in society. Because she'd no children of her own, she was perfectly happy to suggest the correct guidance of everyone else's. She was one of the reasons that Mama had retreated as far from London as she had to raise her daughters, and after Lizzie had witnessed how much Aunt Sophronia meddled in Charlotte's life, she understood why.

Now it was Lizzie's turn. First Aunt Sophronia had dictated her dress for the afternoon: a plain blue silk lutestring, with a white linen kerchief tucked securely into the top of her bodice to hide even a hint of décolletage. If that weren't grim enough, her aunt had also insisted that Lizzie pin her hair tightly away from her face, and wear a linen cap over it for good measure.

Pointedly not including Charlotte in her invitation, Aunt Sophronia had then sent her own coach to Marchbourne House to fetch Lizzie, and installed her here, in the reception room of her house, overlooking St. James's Square. The room was large and echoing, with excessive gilding on the walls and furnishings and so many looking glasses that Lizzie kept seeing a hundred versions of herself reflected every way she turned. Likely that, too, was part of Aunt Sophronia's plan for suitable humility, as she explained in a lengthy lecture on what was proper conversation for young ladies in Lizzie's position and what wasn't. Clearly Aunt Sophronia assumed that Lizzie knew none of the former and far too much of the latter—which was rather true, though Lizzie would never admit it—and so the lecture continued on and on while Lizzie struggled not to yawn outright.

Finally Aunt Sophronia finished, or at least paused, and turned to feeding chunks of cake to her three fat white spaniels. While she did, Lizzie was permitted to stand by the tall window, waiting for her first glimpse of Hawkesworth's arrival. At least she hoped he'd arrive and wouldn't return to his old disappearing ways.

But as Lizzie looked out at the square, a carriage drew

up before the house. The footman opened the door, and Hawkesworth stepped out.

"He's here!" she exclaimed excitedly, leaning closer to the glass. "He's here, and—and he's brought someone with him."

As she watched, Hawkesworth handed out a tall, older lady in an extravagant dark gray gown fluttering with a great many ruffles, and even more jewels draped over the ruffles. She did not wait to take his arm, but sailed toward the house and left him to follow.

"He is not a 'he,' Elizabeth," Aunt Sophronia said sternly, popping another morsel of frosted cake into the open mouth of one of the dogs. "He is His Grace to you until you are wed and he raises you to be his equal. And that someone accompanying him is His Grace's mother."

"His mother!" Lizzie looked down with new interest at the woman who would become her mother-in-law. Her own mother was warm and comfortable, always eager to put others at ease. Even from two floors up, Lizzie could tell that Hawkesworth's mother wasn't like that, and she felt a fresh wave of trepidation wash over her.

"Elizabeth, please, come away from the window directly," Aunt Sophronia said, briskly dusting the cake crumbs from her hands. "His Grace must find you waiting for him with genteel attendance in your chair, not peering from the window like an idle parlor maid. Quickly now, sit beside me, and hold that book as if you were reading it. *If* you have ever done such a thing."

Swiftly Lizzie hurried across the room, dropping into the chair beside her aunt. Belatedly she realized she'd sat on the book, and jumped up to rescue it from the chair. She glanced at the title on the spine and laughed.

"Sermons, Aunt?" she said. "I've *never* read a book of *sermons.*"

"I should never have guessed that of you." Her aunt

sighed with exasperation. "Now pray stop laughing. It makes your face red and common. Sit straight, Elizabeth, ankles crossed, and hold the book gracefully, gracefully, with your head raised so your eyes are downcast. Let His Grace discover you engaged in a becoming pursuit."

Obediently Lizzie struggled not to laugh or even smile, smoothing her skirts and crossing her ankles so that just the tiny pointed toes of her shoes peeked out from beneath her petticoats. She drew her shoulders back straight as Aunt Sophronia had insisted, taking care not to lounge against the chair, and relaxed her arm to hold the book open before her. It wasn't easy to keep her chin up and her eyes down; she felt as if she were being aloof and looking down her nose instead of keeping her eyes downcast with perfect noble serenity.

It was, she decided, wicked hard to behave like a duchess, not that a duchess could ever admit that any task was difficult for her to perform.

She could hear voices on the stairs, Hawkesworth and his mother being escorted by a footman. She forced herself to focus on the words before her, which proved impossible, since she was holding the book upside down. Quickly she turned it around just as the drawing room door opened and the footman announced the guests.

She rose, and at once sank down into a curtsey, the book still in her hand, exactly as her aunt had bidden her do. She held the pose, even as the three white dogs yipped and yapped and bounced around her skirts with excitement.

"What a pretty child, Sophronia," said Hawkesworth's mother, raising her voice over the dogs. "Quite charming."

"She is indeed, Mary," said Aunt Sophronia, even as she was swatting at the dogs. "Down, down, I say. Hush, you bad boys!"

Lizzie didn't answer, not sure if being spoken of by Lady Allred was the same as being addressed. She couldn't speak to the dowager duchess until that lady took notice of her, just as she couldn't stand upright until the duke had acknowledged her, too.

She hadn't long to wait. Hawkesworth's hand took hers, exactly as she remembered, and at his touch, excitement rushed through her again, also exactly as she remembered. Finally she looked up, and if her face grew red and common again when their gazes met, well, then, she could not help it. His expression was studiously somber, and she couldn't yet tell if he was unhappy or perhaps even angry with her.

"Good day, Lady Elizabeth," he said. "I trust you are recovered from your, ah, indisposition of yesterday?"

If he wished to dismiss her grabbing her hat from his hands without thanks, shouting in his face that she'd never marry him, and then running off without his leave as an "indisposition," then she was gratefully, instantly happy to agree.

She smiled, which was doubtless common of her, too, but she was too relieved to worry overmuch about it. Even duchesses had to smile sometimes.

"Good day, Your Grace," she said. "I thank you for your concern, but I can assure you I am entirely recovered."

"Entirely?" His mouth and voice held that solemnity, but his eyes sparkled with amusement, a shared secret between them. Perhaps yesterday, when they'd spoken so sharply to each other, had been the anomaly, and the other time at Ranelagh had been the one that mattered. Perhaps her giddy dreams of love and romance weren't to be dashed after all, but only needed this fresh beginning, exactly as Aunt Sophronia had predicted.

"I am absolutely, entirely recovered, sir," she said. Daring greatly, she squeezed his fingers, a tiny, barely discernible squeeze, but enough to make him squeeze hers in return. If she weren't supposed to be so infernally proper and duchesslike, she might even have reached up and kissed him herself.

"I am glad of it," he said softly, and with his gaze not leaving hers, he began to introduce her to his mother.

"Mother, may I present my betrothed, Lady Elizabeth Wylder," he said. "Lady Elizabeth, my mother, Lady Allred."

Hawkesworth might not look his mother's way, but Lizzie knew that she should, and did, and she dropped a second curtsey, full of respect.

"Oh, Hawkesworth, she is lovely," Lady Allred declared, being the kind of lady who declared rather than merely spoke. "How fortunate for you! Look at me, Lady Elizabeth. Hah, as I thought. Your father's face is quite alive in yours, particularly in the eyes. I vow you must hear that often."

"Thank you, my lady," Lizzie said, surprised and pleased. Mama always said that she was the only one of her daughters to resemble Father, and Lizzie believed it the greatest of compliments, even if it meant she wasn't as beautiful as either Charlotte or Diana. "I am most honored, my lady. My mother has told me the same as well."

"Then you must be a comfort to her," Lady Allred said, "because every time she looks at you, she must see her late consort. What book is that you read?"

"A book of my choosing," Aunt Sophronia said quickly, as if fearing what Lizzie herself might answer. "A collection of Reverend Fullingham's sermons for ladies. I thought it wise for her to prepare herself for the sacrament of marriage, and what better way than through the guidance of Reverend Fullingham?"

"An excellent, edifying choice." Lady Allred nodded with approval, and the plumes on her hat nodded as well. "Tell me, Lady Elizabeth. In light of your readings, what is the best quality for a wife to possess?"

"The best, my lady?" Lizzie said, stalling. Having not read a word, right side up or otherwise, of Reverend Fullingham's sage advice, she was hard-pressed to answer. "There are so many, my lady, that it is difficult to choose one."

Lady Allred's eyes narrowed a skeptical fraction. "If there are so many, my dear, then it should be no trial to name one."

"Yes, my lady." Lizzie glanced down at the closed book in her hand, wishing the words inside would suddenly and conveniently appear on the cover. "I should say the best quality is, ah, being dutiful, my lady. Yes. A good wife should be dutiful to her husband in all matters."

Lady Allred smiled, approving again. "Do you hear that, Hawkesworth? Your intended duchess aspires to be dutiful to you in all matters. That is far better than you deserve, you know. Even if she achieves that worthy goal in only half of those matters, you will be a fortunate husband indeed."

Hawkesworth smiled, making a half bow of acknowledgment, and Lizzie was certain she'd seen a slight twitch around his eye to prove that, had the two older ladies not been present, he would have winked as well.

Aunt Sophronia laid her hand on Lady Allred's arm.

"My dear Mary," she said, their friendship sufficiently long and fond that she could be familiar. "Shall we retreat and leave these two to their own private conversation?"

"We shall," Lady Allred said, drawing an elaborate lace fan from her pocket and snapping it open. "Though mind you, Hawkesworth, Lady Sanborn and I shall be out of hearing, but not out of sight. Now come, Sophronia, I wish to see this new trick that you claim your pup can do."

"It is no idle claim, Mary, I assure you," Aunt Sophronia said as they walked away. "My darling Swan will jump higher than any trained beast in the circus, so long as I hold his treat in the air. Isn't that so, my own little fellow? Won't you do that for your mama and her friend?"

"I should rather like to see Swan jump that high myself," Hawkesworth said, watching the older ladies and the dogs retreat to a settee at the far end of the drawing room. "A leaping dog can be wicked amusing."

"My aunt exaggerates, sir," Lizzie said. "Swan is more wicked fat than wicked amusing. Cannot you see how his belly nigh drags on the floor? All he does is eat the cake that my aunt feeds him, and even then it must be frosted, or he'll not touch it."

Hawkesworth laughed, that wonderful warm chuckle that she remembered from Ranelagh. "Truly?"

"Truly, sir," Lizzie said. "I would never lie about such a thing. Would you sit, sir?"

"Ah, so that's part of the script, isn't it?" He bowed and indicated her chair. "Those two may be fussing over the dogs, but all the time they're keeping a weather eye on us. Your chair, Lady Elizabeth."

"Thank you, sir," Lizzie said, sitting with care so that her hoops wouldn't spring up. She'd never worn hoops in the country, and she still found the cane rings unpredictable. Thoughtfully Aunt Sophronia had arranged for them to sit on side chairs, not armchairs, to minimize the risk of hoop mishaps. Now it was her turn to wave a purposely languid hand toward the other chair for him. "If you please, sir."

"And thus we begin again, Lady Elizabeth," he said. "That is their reason for bringing us together, and I suppose it must be ours as well."

"Oh, yes," she said fervently. "Let us forget those other times ever happened."

"Most of them," he agreed, all amiability. "Though there are certain pleasurable parts that I'd hate to let slip from my memory."

She blushed, for there were more than a few things she wouldn't forget, either.

He pulled his chair nearer to hers before he sat, so his long legs were nearly touching her knee.

"To begin, you must call me Hawke," he continued. "All my friends do, and I've no intention of being one of those men who require their wives to remind them of their own rank."

"Thank you, Hawke," she said, strangely shy. She'd kissed him, yes, but somehow calling him by this shortened name seemed so *familiar* and worldly. "I am grateful for that."

"You shouldn't be, since it comes with a condition," he said, leaning closer. "You must permit me to call you Elizabeth."

"Lizzie," she corrected. "That's what my friends and family call me."

He made a face of mock severity. "I do not know if I can do that," he said. "I've never heard of a duchess named Lizzie."

"Then I shall be the first," she said. "Or more likely, I shall be Elizabeth as a duchess, but Lizzie to you."

At once she realized how imperious and forward that sounded.

"That is, you may call me whatever you please," she said quickly. "I did not mean to order you like that, as if you were no better than fat little Swan."

"I will forgive you only if you offer me a bite of cake," he said, managing to keep his voice so perfectly even that she didn't realize at first that he was teasing. "Mind you make the bites precisely square and with icing that you have spread yourself."

She blushed with pleasure. She did not possess an abundant knowledge of gentlemen and their ways, but she did know that they didn't bother to tease unless they were interested.

Of course, having two sisters made her perfectly capable of teasing him in return. Slowly she opened the book of sermons, holding it up as if she were reading aloud to him, her eyes modestly downcast and intent on the page before her.

"When the ladies study us from across the room," she began, "they will see me sharing a favorite edifying passage with you."

"Yes, they will," he said, smiling and nodding at his mother and Lady Sophronia. "But am I correct to suppose that what they will see is not what is happening?"

"Why, yes, you are," Lizzie said. "Because in reality, I am imagining myself standing on my tiptoes, on this chair, with my hand raised high and a small cube of iced cake—*pink* iced cake, with silver French dragées pressed into the icing—held in my fingers, whilst you leap as high as you can into the air and attempt to snatch the cake from me. *That*, Hawke, is what I am imagining, even as I turn this next page of the good Reverend Fullingham's book."

She did turn the page, and finally raised her gaze to meet his.

His well-mannered drawing-room expression was gone, and in its place was the same look she'd seen in his face when he'd asked her to leave Ranelagh with him so they might better explore her fairy ways. Though he smiled still, he looked hungry, in a masculine, wolfish sort of way that had nothing to do with scampering little dogs. It was exciting to realize she could inspire such a look simply by teasing him, but at the same time she felt like an inexperienced swimmer who had drifted well out beyond her depth.

"Truly?" he asked. "Those were your thoughts, Lizzie?"

"Yes," she said, her cheeks warming with excitement.

"What if I told you that I would never be that obedient, or agreeable to tricks?" He leaned a little closer to her. "What if I said that if you kept that sweet little cake too long from my reach, I might tire of the game and simply seize it for my own?"

She had the distinct feeling he was no longer speaking of the cake alone.

"But waiting always makes the treat sweeter," she said. "Didn't you learn that as a boy?"

He slipped his arm over the back of her chair, behind her shoulders. "Recall that I'm a duke, and I don't have to wait for anything that I want."

She raised her brows, incredulous. "Nothing?"

"No," he said, and smiled. "Not even pink frosted cake with silver dragées."

She blushed and quickly looked back down at the book. His arm wasn't touching her, but she was acutely aware of it there. Part of her wished to scuttle away like a nervous little mouse, but the other part of her wanted to lean back against his arm and let it curl around her shoulders.

"Then perhaps you should be the one reading Reverend Fullingham's sermons, not I," she said. Absently she looked down at the page she held open, which seemed to be a sermon about how bearing poverty with humility displayed rare virtue: not exactly applicable to a duke who'd always been granted whatever he wished as one of the wealthiest gentlemen in the country. "There must be plenty here that might be useful to you."

"Oh, I'm sure of it," he said easily. "I'm a duke, not a

paragon. I never claimed otherwise. Unlike you, my ever dutiful Lady Lizzie."

"Ah, you mean what I said to your mother." She closed the book, holding it cradled in her hands. "To be truthful—for I am that, Hawke—I haven't read a single one of the good reverend's admonitions. Not one. Aunt Sophronia thrust the book into my hands before you arrived, for show."

He chuckled at that. The arm on the back of her chair moved lower, and she felt him toying with the wisps of hair that curled on her nape, tendrils that had slipped loose of the neat linen cap. She'd never realized how sensitive the back of her neck could be—at least how sensitive it was to his featherlight touch, barely grazing her skin yet sending tiny ripples of sensation down her spine. She wondered if her aunt and his mother could see what he was doing from across the room. She hoped they couldn't, because she didn't want him to stop.

"I like truth," he said softly, "especially in a lady. Though you've confessed that virtue to me before, at Ranelagh, didn't you? If you have said it twice, I suppose it must be the truth. You are truthful regarding truth."

She smiled wryly, looking back down at the book. "It is, and I am. Which must make me thoroughly dull to a worldly gentleman like you."

"Not at all," he said. "I'd hardly scorn the rarity of an honest lady. But why didn't you confess that to my mother as well? Why did you speak of being dutiful instead?"

She twisted on her chair to face him, letting his hand drop to her shoulder.

"Why?" she repeated, incredulous because to her it seemed so perfectly obvious. "Because you and I are dutiful, Hawke, as dutiful as any two people can be. Why else would we be here together, sitting in this room on these chairs, unless we were aware of our duty not only to our fathers but to each other?"

He turned his head to one side, frowning a bit and making Lizzie wish she were more adept at reading his handsome face.

"I suppose we are dutiful," he said thoughtfully, as if he'd never considered such a notion before. "We are."

"It doesn't displease you, does it?" she asked wistfully, and immediately wished the words unsaid.

But at last he smiled, the smile that lit his entire face. For the first time, she thought she saw not only desire there but respect as well, and even a bit of affection.

"My own Lizzie," he said. "Truly you will make me the most fortunate of men."

"Oh, Hawke." Though she'd take being his own Lizzie over being his duchess any day, she did wish he'd make her some sort of pretty lover's speech, the way the heroes did in novels and plays, instead of falling back on the same words his mother had used. But perhaps pretty speeches would come in time, and she leaned closer, hoping he'd dare to kiss her even with the two older ladies standing guard.

But Hawke turned away before he could take note of her willingness, and instead of kissing her he beckoned to one of the footmen who stood by the door, and then with surprising impatience rose and went to meet the footman halfway. Lizzie's consolation was being able to watch him; this was a view she didn't ordinarily see, and she unabashedly admired him. His coat was pale gray and perfectly tailored to display his height and the breadth of his shoulders; his dark hair was held back with a black silk ribbon.

She was so busy ogling him that she almost regretted it when he returned, carrying a flat linen-wrapped parcel that he'd taken from the footman. Until, that is, he came to stand before her, the package in his hands.

"I know it's common for gentlemen to offer their brides some costly jeweler's bauble," he said, carefully unwrapping the linen. "But I wished to give you something that cannot be bought in London, not for any price, and something that only I could give to you."

He pulled away the last length of linen, and though he still held the object facing away, she could see now that it was some sort of framed looking glass or picture.

"If it's from you, I am sure to like it," she said, her curiosity growing by the second. "Please, Hawke, might I see?"

Looking down at the picture in his hands, he visibly took a deep breath. His uncertainty surprised her, but she found it endearing, too, that he'd worry so over pleasing her with his gift.

"Please," she said softly, more to reassure him than to beg.

"Very well," he said, and handed the picture to her.

She took it and gasped. She'd never seen anything like this painting. An elegant lady and gentleman, married or at least lovers, sat beneath a tree with their dogs. Though the picture was clearly very old—even her uneducated eye could tell that—the colors were as bright as jewels, the gold leaf shining, the detail precise and charming. The painting of the gentleman in his fur-trimmed clothes offering a white primrose to the lady in her ermine-edged robes was the most exquisitely romantic object she'd ever held in her hands. And now, to her wonder, it was hers.

"It's more than three hundred years old, tempera on panel," he said, rapidly explaining and apologizing at the same time. "It may seem peculiar to modern tastes, I know, but it's always been one of my special favorites, which is why I wished you to have it. But if you'd rather I bought you a bracelet or some such, I will understand, and—"

"This is *perfect*," she whispered, unable to look away from the picture in her hands. "Why would I ever long for a bracelet when you've given me a gift like this?"

He dropped back into the chair beside her. "You like it, then?"

"How could I not, Hawke?" she said. "I shall be the first to admit that I know nothing of pictures—our house at Ransom had only a few gloomy ones from the old queen's time that scared me when I was little—but even I can tell that this is special, and right, and—and I cannot believe you would give it to me."

"It's easy enough to learn the history," he said eagerly, studying the picture over her arm. "But not everyone can *see* paintings, with their heart as well as their eyes."

She glanced at him, surprised by what she saw. She hadn't realized how much of his charm was a mask, a guise of pleasantry worn before the world. Yet when he spoke of the painting, the mask had vanished, and his face suddenly became much more alive and almost boyishly enthusiastic.

"Is that how you see?" she asked, her excitement matching his. "With your heart?"

He nodded, raking his hair back from where it had slipped across his forehead. "Most Englishmen can't, you know, being hopeless Philistines. All they can see in art is expense and value and how many guineas were spent to impress the squire in the next county. Italians discover beauty everywhere. To see like that, Lizzie, is a rare gift, a marvel, a—"

"Ah, very good, Hawkesworth," Lady Allred said. "I see you have given Lady Elizabeth your little token."

Lizzie looked up, startled and disappointed. How had her ladyship and her aunt managed to appear so suddenly and so silently, very like thieves in the night, to spoil her conversation with Hawke?

"To be sure, it is a most curious gift to offer one's betrothed, but then my son never will follow the usual custom," Lady Allred continued. "Show the thing to your aunt, Lady Elizabeth, so she might understand."

Reluctantly Lizzie turned the painting, wishing she could keep Hawke's gift entirely to herself. She wasn't precisely sure who Hawke's "hopeless Philistines" might be, but she could guess that Aunt Sophronia would be one.

"Gracious, that is a curiosity," her aunt said, her painted brows arching with bewildered dismay. "I know taste is a variable quality in matters of art, but couldn't Your Grace have found a painter with more ability for so important a gift for my niece?"

Lizzie didn't answer, but at once looked to Hawke, who was already looking at *her*, and making it clear without any bothersome words that he was thinking exactly the same thing as she.

Finally he sighed deeply, a sigh of commiseration that was also meant for Lizzie alone, and reluctantly turned to her aunt.

"Your niece shows a wondrous appreciation for fine painting, Lady Carbery," he said, adding a slight bow to deflect notice from how he'd just insulted Lady Sanborn's own lack of taste. "With your permission, I should like to invite her to call upon me at Hawkesworth Chase, so that I might show her my collection of pictures."

"Certainly not, Hawkesworth," Lady Allred said sharply before Lizzie or her aunt could reply. "It would not be proper. If after you are wed you insist on showing those *pictures* of yours to your wife, then I could not protest, but now—"

"Then I will marry her at once," he said, taking Lizzie's hand. "Will Thursday suit you, Lady Elizabeth?"

"Thursday, Your Grace!" exclaimed Aunt Sophronia with genuine horror. "That is but three days away. No decent wedding can take place with only three days' notice."

"You are being ridiculous, Hawkesworth," said his mother, equally outraged. "Even three months would be a prodigiously short time to arrange a wedding between persons of your rank."

But to Lizzie's infinite joy, Hawke's expression did not change, nor did his resolve falter. After all, he was a duke, and accustomed to getting whatever he pleased.

"Three weeks, then, three weeks from this day," he said evenly. "There, I'm the very spirit of compromise. Is that agreeable to you, Lady Elizabeth?"

What was three weeks when she'd marry him in three minutes if she could?

"Yes, Hawke," she said, her smile wide and her heart full. "Oh, yes."

CHAPTER

 7

"A ruby?" asked Brecon with surprise. "For Lady Elizabeth's wedding ring?"

"Yes, a ruby," Hawke said as Mr. Boyce, the jeweler, carefully placed the ring on the velvet-covered tray before him. "A ruby full of fire, like her."

But Brecon, sitting at the jeweler's table beside him, could only frown. "Diamonds alone, white and pure, would be a more suitable choice," he suggested. "She's your wife, Hawke, not another of your little Neapolitan inamoratas. Surely there must be scores of diamonds in your family waiting for you."

"There are," Hawke said. "As you can well imagine, Mother attempted to force them upon me in the name of tradition. But I'd rather my wife had a new stone, without any family entanglements. She'll be the first to wear it, and she'll make it hers."

Carefully Hawke took the ring between his thumb and forefinger and held it up to the sunlight coming through the shop's window. Countless shades of red danced from the square-cut center stone, flashing this way and that as he turned the ring. The ruby was surrounded by two rows of diamonds, and the stones were set in heavy gold, with a band fashioned like a swirling vine around the finger. He'd had the jeweler make it from his own description to be sure it was unique. It was a substantial ring, a ring meant to catch attention and be noticed, exactly like Lizzie herself.

Brecon sighed, unconvinced. "I trust you are right, Hawke," he said. "But then I've no notion at all of what would please a lady of her tender years."

"Pray hope that I do," Hawke said. Yet just as he'd been sure Lizzie would like the old painting, he was equally certain that she would like this for her wedding ring. He couldn't explain why. Even he would have to admit that he didn't know his bride, and yet he had not a single doubt as he handed the ring back to the jeweler. "All you need do now, Boyce, is add the engraving inside."

The jeweler puckered his mouth with worry. "Forgive me, Your Grace, but is that wise? We have not fitted the ring to the lady's finger, and if an adjustment must be made after the wedding, then the sentiment will be marred."

"Bad luck in that, Hawke, no mistake," warned Brecon. "The ladies will be all aflutter over that. Better to wait and have the sizing made right, with the lady's finger here to measure."

"It's right as it is," Hawke said confidently. "Go ahead, Boyce. Mark our initials on the inside, and have it sent to me tomorrow."

The jeweler bowed and retreated into the next room, leaving Brecon to let out a small *harrumph* of disbelief.

"Aren't you the cocky bastard, Hawke," he said, and only half in jest. "First you choose your bride's wedding ring, then you declare you know the very breadth of the finger it will grace."

"I should know it," Hawke said defensively. "Procuring Lady Elizabeth's ring is the only task I'm permitted in this entire rigmarole of a wedding, and if that is all, then I intend that ring to be as perfect as it can be. What else am I to do? Three weeks, Brecon, only three weeks between the day I agreed with the lady and the day we are to wed, yet I've never had time stretch so interminably long."

Brecon shrugged. "You shall survive," he said. "Three weeks is a veritable wink of an eye compared to the whole span of your wedded life with the lady."

"But that is just it, Brecon," Hawke said, exasperation in his voice. "I had always heard that betrothed men and women were supposed to be together, and yet I have seen Lady Elizabeth but once in the last fortnight, and that was with the harpies hovering."

"By 'harpies' I suppose you mean your esteemed mother and Lady Sanborn," Brecon said wryly. "Really, Hawke. Likening those dear ladies to the foul, vicious creatures that plagued the Greeks is a bit harsh. Did you know that March calls Lady Sanborn 'the dragon,' likely for much the same reason?"

"Most appropriate, too." Restlessly Hawke drummed his fingers on the jeweler's counter. "I cannot fathom how much worse it will be when Lady Elizabeth's mother finally arrives tomorrow."

"Lady Hervey?" asked Brecon with surprise. "Oh, Lady Hervey's no harpy, nor dragon. You'll never have meddling from that quarter. She's a lovely lady, more like another sister than a mother."

"Well, then, the others are bad enough," Hawke grumbled. "They invent a score of empty reasons for me not to see her alone. Even my letters to her have been returned unopened, my very pen and paper having been deemed too 'inflaming' for her so close to the wedding. Inflaming, for God's sake! I should show them true fire, and then they'd have genuine cause for worry."

Brecon smiled. "Clearly they fear you already, cousin, else they'd not take such care guarding their little innocent. But likely they are engaged in their preparations as well. Ladies live for weddings."

"There's less effort to launching a fleet than to make one lady presentable for the altar," Hawke said. "Damnation, Brecon, our fathers arranged this marriage years ago. You'd think these women would have at least begun their infernal preparations, wouldn't you?"

"Not women," Brecon said succinctly. "Ladies. There's a world of difference between the two, especially as far as spending goes."

Hawke nodded glumly. Brecon was right: he'd never conceived of such an absolute orgy of spending as that surrounding his bride. He'd previously considered himself wise in the many ways of feminine spending, but after watching his future wife's family pillage the finest of London's shops and its tradespeople's wares, he realized he'd understood nothing. In these three weeks, an entire wardrobe had been cut, stitched, and fitted for Lizzie. He was told of countless trips to milliners, mantua makers, jewelers, and likely other female shops that he didn't know existed. Vast quantities of linen, china, and plate must all be purchased, as if he'd none in his house already.

"Hymeneal hysteria," Brecon said sagely. "All the ladies wallow in it, from the most ancient dowager to the youngest girl in the nursery. Be grateful your engagement will last for only three weeks, and not two years or so."

Hawke shook his head, still unable to find the reason in this. "But why is it necessary for her to have an entire phalanx of women to guard her from me? Her sister, her aunt, my own confounded mother and sisters, and now her mother and another sister of hers, newly arrived from the country to join in the hennish excess. I vow they seem to multiply by the day."

He had never been more frustrated in his life, nor

could he ignore the irony of his situation. Lady Elizabeth Wylder was unlike any other woman he'd known. Of course, the others in his life had been very much of a piece: obliging, beautiful, and far beneath him in rank, slipping from his bed and his life as easily as they'd slipped into it, leaving happily with a monetary remembrance. They'd expected nothing more, and beyond the obvious, they hadn't offered much, either.

But Lizzie was different. She could tease him, make him laugh, and make him think, too. Even more astonishing, she'd responded to the little Florentine painting with exactly the same fervor that he himself had. He'd seen it in her eyes, the excitement that a picture or statue could make him feel. He'd been amazed, and shocked as well. Before that afternoon in Lady Sanborn's drawing room, he'd simply assumed that women didn't respond to art the same way as men did. Seeing Lizzie's face light up had been a *revelation*.

Her beautiful face, of course, and the beautiful rest of her as well, a rest of her that his imagination had pleasingly undressed over and over from her snug-laced stays and modest gowns. He had only kissed her twice, but those two kisses had haunted him day and night, driving him half mad from wanting her. That amazed him, too. If anyone had asked him on the voyage from Italy how he intended to spend his last nights as a bachelor, he would have jovially predicted that he could be found in the choicest brothel in London and would not budge until his wedding day. Yet he was so fascinated by his future wife that he'd lost all interest in bacchanalian revelry. The devil only knew why or how, let alone how long his interest would last, but for the present, Lizzie had simply ruined him for other women.

In short, she *deserved* that ruby ring.

"You're besotted, cousin," Brecon said, his smile wide as he echoed Hawke's own thoughts. "Ten minutes we have sat here, and I'll wager you thought it ten seconds, so lost were you in dreaming of your bride."

"I'm not some wretched mooncalf, Brecon," said Hawke, his sharpness betraying how close Brecon was to the mark. "And I'm done dreaming."

Brecon laughed indulgently, not at all what Hawke wished to hear in the circumstances. "True enough," he said. "The wedding's almost here, and your wedding night with it."

"That's not what I meant," Hawke said as the jeweler returned with two more boxes. "I've plans. Are these the other pieces, Boyce?"

"Yes, Your Grace, exactly to your specifications." Boyce set the larger box on the table and with a showman's finesse slowly opened the lid. Inside lay an elaborate necklace with gold-set rubies and diamonds to match the ring. The diamonds were arranged to look like ribbon bows, with the large rubies dangling from them like cherries from a tree.

Brecon whistled low with approval. "Did you raid the Tower for the crown jewels, cousin?"

"Almost," said Hawke, holding the necklace up to the light. Even to him, the sum that Boyce had told him when Hawke described what he wanted had been staggering, likely enough to support a small village for a year. But he intended to marry only one wife, and he wanted to do it properly.

"Most excellent, Boyce," he said with satisfaction. "I can already picture this around Her Grace's throat. Is that the bracelet?"

"Yes, Your Grace," the jeweler said, opening the second case. The bracelet inside matched the necklace and the ring, with more diamonds and rubies glittering against the dark velvet. He particularly liked the clasp, made to look as if it were the bow tying the bracelet around the wrist. "Pray, shall I have it sent with the necklace?"

"Thank you, no," Hawke said, taking the necklace from the case. Briefly he held it to the light, as he had the other pieces, and then tucked it into his waistcoat pocket. He rose from the chair, giving his pocket an extra little pat as safekeeping. He *had* made plans, his own special touch to enliven wedding preparations that had been entirely too regimented. He was weary of being kept apart from Lizzie, and believed that seeing her—one way or another—was completely within his rights.

"The previous arrangements will stand, Boyce," he continued. "I thank you for your swift service in this matter. Brecon, I shall see you tomorrow. Good day."

"Hold now, you cannot dismiss me as easily as that," his cousin said, hurrying to follow him from the shop. "What do you intend to do with that bracelet?"

Hawke smiled, though he'd no intention of telling Brecon anything. "I told you," he said. "I've plans."

"I trust you won't do anything foolish, Hawke," Brecon warned earnestly. "You've only a few days until the wedding. Pray don't dishonor your bride with some manner of impulsive foolishness."

"Foolishness, Brecon? You should know me better than that," Hawke said, squaring his hat on his head with purposeful disdain. "I've never willingly done a foolish thing in my life, and I don't intend to do so now."

But impulsiveness: ah, now that was altogether different. . . .

Lizzie stood in the center of Mrs. Cartwright's back room while three journeywomen mantua makers plus Mrs. Cartwright herself fussed about her, smoothing and pinning the silk sleeves of yet another gown in place. In the beginning, Lizzie had found the process exciting.

After a lifetime as the second sister, it was wonderful to finally be the center of everyone's attention, and the clothes that were being made for her were extraordinarily beautiful, fit for the duchess she was to become.

But the novelty of her position had soon worn away and was replaced by the tedium of standing still for what seemed to be hours on end. Unlike gentlemen's clothing, which was made from patterns, ladies' dresses were draped and fashioned directly on the body, and required that lady's body to be present. It didn't help that Aunt Sophronia and Charlotte had attended every fitting, too, making all the choices of fabric and trimmings as they gave the mantua maker excruciatingly specific directions.

Lizzie sighed again. How many extraordinarily beautiful gowns (and stockings and stays and shifts and shoes and night rails and hats and cloaks and all the rest) did a duchess truly require, anyway? And what was the purpose if she couldn't show them off to Hawke?

"Lizzie, please, you must stop wriggling," Charlotte scolded. "These women cannot do their work properly if you won't stand still. I vow you're worse than the twins, and they're only two."

Lizzie sighed dramatically. "I wouldn't wriggle a bit if His Grace were here," she said. "*He* would amuse me."

"His Grace at a fitting?" Aunt Sophronia exclaimed. "Why, what could be more improper?"

"I remember how March came rushing in to interrupt Charlotte's before they were wed," Lizzie said. "I haven't forgotten. The scandal sheets were full of it."

"The scandal sheets are full of a great many sordid things that should not concern you, my dear," Lady Allred said severely. "The less frequently a lady's name appears there, the better."

Glumly Lizzie raised her arm to oblige the seamstress's pins. She'd always loved the story of March being so *impassioned* that he'd ordered Aunt Sophronia out of the fitting room so that he could take liberties with Charlotte. That was how the gossips had described it— "taken liberties"—and because Charlotte had always refused to tell more, Lizzie's imagination had supplied all kinds of thrilling indiscretions. Her own betrothal seemed sadly lacking in this kind of excitement. She knew that Hawke was capable of it—she had only to recall Ranelagh—but she'd been so well and oppressively chaperoned that there'd been no opportunities. She hadn't seen him since he'd declared the date for their wedding, and though she told herself it was all due to Aunt Sophronia and the others ordering him away, she still couldn't quite keep the doubts at bay, and wondered if he'd gone back to his former, neglectful ways. The little painting had been a perfect gift, but couldn't he at least have sent her a love letter to tuck beneath her pillow, or flowers from his garden to prove she remained in his thoughts?

"Thank you, Your Grace, we are finished for the day," Mrs. Cartwright said, curtseying to Charlotte as the highest-ranking lady in the room. "The gowns will be delivered to Marchbourne House tomorrow, exactly as you wished."

Relieved to be at last freed from her role as a flesh-and-blood pincushion, Lizzie let the women dress her in her own clothes once again, while the others spoke of the final details of the new gowns around her, almost as if she weren't there. Becoming a duchess might make her feel like a caterpillar magically transforming into a butterfly, but these three weeks in the cocoon were wicked tedious, and she barely hid another yawn behind her hand.

"I wish you'd take more interest in your wardrobe, Elizabeth," Aunt Sophronia scolded. "You must be guided to develop your taste, so that you will learn to dress according to your rank. You must make His Grace proud, you know. Whatever would he say if he were to see you in the ragamuffin clothes your mother let you wear before you came to town?"

"We weren't ragamuffins," protested Lizzie, ready to defend not only her old clothes but her mother, too. "We were *comfortable*, as children should be, and if His Grace can't understand—"

"Lizzie, please," Charlotte interrupted swiftly, always playing the peacekeeper. "I'm sure you'd like some air after all those fittings. Why don't you wait in the carriage, and we shall join you there as soon as we are done?"

Lizzie sighed, knowing that Charlotte was right. Nothing would be gained by quarreling with Aunt Sophronia, especially over something her aunt would never concede. Her mouth tight, Lizzie instead turned toward the door and her sister's coach waiting outside. One Marchbourne footman hurried forward to open the shop door for her while another let down the carriage's folding steps. At the same time, the tall footman deftly managed to block the pavement and hold back other passersby and curiosity seekers, granting Lizzie a clear path to the carriage.

But not everyone had been pushed away. To one side of the pavement stood a man in a green feathered cap with a hurdy-gurdy hanging from a leather strap around his shoulders. As he turned the instrument's crank, music filled the narrow street, the rolling, buzzing notes bouncing off the glass shop windows and drowning the noise from horses and carts. Best of all was the musician's companion, a grinning capuchin monkey dressed like a tiny gentleman, perfect from his satin breeches to his miniature cocked hat. Unperturbed by the looming footman, the monkey danced a smart little jig to the music, bowing and scraping just like any other courtier.

Fascinated, Lizzie stepped around the footman to better see the monkey, clapping her hands in time to his dance. The monkey skipped away, stretching the long gold chain around his neck taut until he capered beside the tall wheel of a hackney. The song ended and he bowed again, this time pulling his little hat from his head and holding it out toward Lizzie.

"Aren't you a bold little beggar?" she said, laughing as she reached into her pocket for a coin to put in his proffered hat. The monkey deserved it; it had been ages since she'd felt so lighthearted. She joined him with a merry little skip of her own and bent down to his level with the coin in her fingers.

With avaricious haste, the monkey grabbed for the coin, then suddenly froze. He wasn't looking at the coin or even at Lizzie, but behind her, his tiny wrinkled face anxious with fear. He grimaced, baring his teeth, then let loose an ungodly shriek of distress.

Startled, Lizzie frowned and drew back, and began to look over her shoulder to see what had frightened the monkey. But as she turned, a heavy rough cloth smelling of horses and tobacco suddenly swept over her, covering her as completely as a shroud.

She cried out, her words muffled by the blanket that was now being wrapped around her. Strong arms grabbed her around her knees and lifted her from her feet. She punched and kicked as hard as she could, yet still she felt herself being carried, then tossed onto an unyielding bench or seat. She heard men shouting, a door close and latch, horses' hooves, and the scrape of wheels on paving stones. She was in a carriage, then, and as she kicked and clawed against the tightly wrapped blanket and the weight of her kidnapper—obviously large, heavy, and strong—crushing upon her, she felt the lurch of the carriage moving forward, then increasing in speed.

That was enough to make her stop fighting and lie still. Think, she ordered herself sternly even as her heart raced with fear. *Think*. She tried to recall all the novels she'd read where the heroine had been kidnapped like this, but romantic heroines tended to swoon becomingly and wait for the hero to arrive on a snow-white charger to rescue her. That wasn't likely to happen, not on the streets of modern London. Besides, she'd never swooned in her life.

Think, think, *think*.

She hadn't been chosen at random, and she wasn't going to be sold into some distant sultan's harem or even into a Covent Garden brothel. She'd been kidnapped because of who she was, no doubt because she was going to marry a wealthy nobleman and could fetch a handsome ransom. This kind of peril wasn't something she'd ever considered about becoming a duchess, and it didn't seem entirely fair, either, especially since she was still just Lizzie. In fact the more she considered it, the more her fear became mixed with anger. How dare this ogre, whoever he was, believe he could profit by bundling her up like an unwanted litter of kittens? At least if he expected to be rewarded for her safe release, then he wouldn't hurt her.

Which was not to say she'd make the same assurance toward him.

She felt him relax his grip on her, doubtless lulled by her lying so still beneath him. More fool he, she decided fiercely, and before he could realize that she wasn't in the grip of a proper maidenly swoon, she shoved forward and freed herself of the blanket, and of him. In front of her was the window of the hackney—for so it must be, from his plain and grimy condition—and at once she threw herself at it, shoving aside the flapping black curtain so she could shout from the window for help. That would draw attention, even in a crowded London street, and attention would be her salvation.

But before she could, her kidnapper recovered enough to clap his hand over her open mouth.

Lizzie would have none of that, and bit his palm as hard as she could.

The man jerked his hand away and swore vehemently. The oath was in Italian, and though Lizzie didn't understand a word of it, at once she recognized the swearer.

"You!" she cried furiously, twisting around to face Hawke. "How could you do this to me, Hawke? To *me*?"

His expression managed to be both outraged and bewildered as he cradled his bitten hand against his chest. "How the devil could you *bite* me?"

"What else am I to do when you thrust your hand into my mouth?" She shoved herself free of the blanket and clambered onto the seat, keeping as far away from him as was possible in the narrow hackney. "You terrified me, and likely have my poor family worried to death. You even scared that little monkey, and for what? For *what*?"

He was still rubbing his palm. His clothes were anonymously plain and unducal, a dark, threadbare jacket and breeches and a plain white shirt open at the throat. On his feet were well-worn top boots, the sort worn by jockeys, hunters, and other such disreputable sorts. Clearly he'd adopted such a costume to be unnoticed—as if any man as tall and well made as Hawke could go unnoticed anywhere.

"I'd no intention to frighten anyone," he said. "And the monkey was well compensated for his part."

"You mean to say his owner was compensated for *his* part, not the poor little monkey," she retorted. Bracing herself with one arm against the rocking hackney's side, she reached up and rapped against the roof to signal to the driver to stop.

"What the devil are you doing?" Hawke demanded.

"I'm stopping this cab so that the driver might turn about and take me back to Mrs. Cartwright's shop."

"He won't," he said. "At least not unless I'm the one to order it."

Lizzie scowled, ducking her chin low with frustration. As she did, the sad remnants of her hat slid forward over her brow. Today had been the first time she'd worn it, but thanks to that all-enveloping horse blanket, the brim was now bent and broken and the silk satin ribbons sadly crushed beyond redemption. Her frustration growing by the second, she snatched it from her head and threw it on the seat, a dramatic gesture that only managed to pull a large piece of her hair free to flop over her eyes. She shoved that aside, too, muttering the sort of black oath no duchess should even know, let alone allow to pass her lips.

Hawke's dark brows rose, more with amusement than with shock, which irritated her all the more. He held his hand out to her—not, she noted, the hand she'd bitten earlier.

"Come, Lizzie, be honest," he said cordially. "You can't really prefer a mantua maker to me, can you?"

He smiled warmly, wickedly, coaxing her toward forgiveness with his charm. Standing and swaying with the hackney's motion, she gazed down at him, at the white smile in his sun-browned face, at the dimples, and lower, to the tantalizing glimpse of bare skin revealed by the open collar of his shirt. She'd never seen a gentleman's bare throat before, or the dark curls on a gentlemanly chest, and it was all . . . distracting. How was it possible that even when he was dressed like a threadbare Quaker he remained the handsomest man she'd ever met?

No, the handsomest man who'd just carried her off from her family like some impetuous Gypsy king, and she wanted none of it, or him, either. Resolutely she turned back to the hackney's window and shoved aside the curtain.

"Help me, good people, I beg you! Help me at once!" she shouted to the startled passersby on the pavement as the hackney continued to clatter briskly down the street. "I've been taken prisoner by a—*ooof*!"

This time Hawke didn't try to silence her with his hand. Instead he grabbed her about the waist and tossed her on her back on the hackney's seat, pinning her there with his knees on either side of her legs and her wrists held fast in his hands. Because of the hackney's small size, it wasn't gracefully done, and their arms and legs were tangled together with awkward intimacy.

"What are you *doing*?" she sputtered. She couldn't push away with her hands trapped, and she couldn't kick with him holding her skirts tight around her legs. He was not only a great deal larger than her but a great deal stronger, too, and the harder she struggled, the more she was forced to admit it.

"I should ask the same of you, Lady Elizabeth." He wasn't even breathing hard as he leaned over her, which infuriated her all the more. "Do you wish to see me dragged before a magistrate instead of the bishop?"

"Before a magistrate is where you belong, sir, on account of how you're treating me," she declared. "Not that they'd do anything so grievous to a peer."

"You say that," he said, "as if you wish to see if it is true or not."

With his face so close over hers, she'd no choice but to look at him, squarely and without flinching. For the sake of his disguise, he hadn't been shaved this day, and a fine black prickle of new beard peppered his jaw. If he'd wanted to look like a perfect rogue and rascal, then he'd succeeded admirably, what with the stubble and his tousled hair and that open-necked shirt.

And he really must be very strong, to hold her as effortlessly as he was.

He might not be breathing hard from exertion, but blast him, *she* was.

"We're not married yet, you know." She'd mislaid her lace kerchief, and her breasts now felt both shamefully bare and shamelessly quivering above the stiffened bones of her stays. Beneath her hip, she could also feel the crumpled straw of her hat, the pins poking into her like more little jabs of humiliation. "I'm not your wife yet. I could still bear witness against you in a court of law."

"For what purpose?" he said. "So that you might wizen and waste as a spinster while I am sent to seven years' bondage in some forsaken tobacco colony?"

She didn't want that, not one bit, especially not when explained in that fashion, but she was still too angry with him to admit it.

"You would deserve it," she said, as tartly as she could under the circumstances, and under him. "You have behaved like—like a *cur*!"

"A cur," he said, and for the first time she heard an answering anger in his voice, too. "Damnation, Lizzie, don't you know why I contrived this whole ridiculous business? Haven't you guessed?"

"I have not, sir," she said. "How could I? You have as good as abandoned me this past fortnight, until this—"

"Lizzie, each day I have tried to call on you," he interrupted, "and each day I have been denied."

Abruptly Lizzie went still. "Denied? I never denied you, not once."

"Perhaps you didn't," he said, "but your family and their servants did. I wrote to you, and my letters were returned unopened, with the advice that you were too distracted to receive them. I couldn't find even one of

March's house servants willing to be bought to carry a message to you."

"You did that?" She stared up at him, perplexed and frowning, and thinking of how both her aunt and sister had assured her that it was for the best that she not see Hawke again until the wedding. They hadn't out-and-out lied and told her he'd shown no interest in her, but they hadn't exactly confessed everything, either. She'd been all too willing to believe that he was being neglectful. She'd never imagined that her family could be to blame, even if now it all made sense.

"I did do that," he said. "At least I tried to."

"Now you've done this," she said. "Abducting me, I mean."

He smiled crookedly. "I could not conceive of a better way to see you alone. I thought you'd be amused. I'd no notion you'd be frightened."

"Or angry." She could say that because she'd realized she wasn't either angry or frightened any longer. She wasn't exactly sure when both had faded away, but they had, which made her present ungainly position with him atop her entirely unnecessary. She wasn't going to fight him, or try to jump from the cab. She didn't need restraining at all. So why, then, was neither of them making an effort to rise? "What you did made me monstrously angry, Hawke."

"Or angry, then," he said. "I didn't intend to do that, either. But I'd every intention of doing this."

He lowered himself to kiss her, and to make it easier for them both she raised her lips to meet his. She liked kissing him this way, lying on her back with her hands still held over her head, almost as if she couldn't help herself. Maybe she couldn't. She kissed him eagerly, with all the longing and uncertainty of this last fortnight coalescing into a feverish edge that she hadn't expected.

Kissing him made her happy, and she couldn't keep back a low chuckle, just from sheer delight.

He felt it, too. She could see it in his eyes when he finally broke away: desire, yes, but surprise that bordered on wonder.

"Are you going to take me to Gretna Green?" she asked in a breathless whisper. "So we can be married there by the blacksmith?"

"Gretna?" he said, that wonder changing to abject horror. "I wouldn't wish dreary Scotland on a dog."

"Or a cur?" she asked, faintly disappointed. She couldn't imagine traveling all the way to Scotland in a hackney, but the *idea* of eloping had been exciting.

"Especially not on a cur." He kissed her again, an excellent way to put Gretna Green from her head. He was kissing her still when they both realized that the hackney had stopped, and likely had been stopped for a while. The cab swayed as the driver climbed down, just warning enough for Lizzie to wriggle free and sit upright. Her hair was a tangled mess, her kerchief was gone, and her skirts were crushed and rumpled, and when the driver unlatched the door, she was sure her cheeks were red with shame, too.

"Where are we, Hawke?" she asked warily. She could see a brick wall overgrown with greenery, and a blue-painted arched door. "What place is this?"

"The place where we're meant to be." He climbed down and turned to offer his hand to her. "Come with me, sweeting, and I'll show you."

CHAPTER

8

When Hawke had first conceived of this little adventure to carry off Lizzie, he'd been carousing very late with friends at his club, and perhaps had had too much inspirational brandy. As a consequence, he had planned parts of it very well, and other parts not at all. He hadn't thought of it exactly as an abduction, since he meant to return her after a few hours. An abduction did sound far more exciting than a borrowing, however, and arranging the hackney, the hurdy-gurdy player and his monkey, and his own costume, all with the goal of Lizzie's astonishment, had entertained him and reminded him, too, of certain midnight larks he'd survived in Italy.

Rattling away through London in a hackney in the middle of the day, however, wasn't exactly the same as pretending to be a masked *bandito* from the mountains, racing into town to steal a perfectly willing young harlot from some brothel or another. He hadn't expected to frighten Lizzie (though in hindsight he contritely understood why she must have been terrified), and he hadn't expected her to be so angry with him that she'd bite his hand, either. He thought she'd find it all to be just a grand, romantic gesture, the way he'd meant it to be.

But then Lizzie wasn't a wine-sodden strumpet from

Naples. She was an English lady, soon to be his wife and his duchess and, with luck and application, the mother of his children, too. All of which made what had happened next completely inexplicable.

He'd kissed her. He'd meant to do that. What he hadn't planned was how she'd kissed him back. With her arms still over her head, she'd *undulated* beneath him, arching as luxuriantly as a cat. The fiery temper that she'd launched at him before had somehow magically transformed into passion. She'd been simmering when she'd kissed him, opening her mouth with greedy anticipation for more, even chuckling deep in her throat with pleasure as they'd kissed.

How a virgin lady—and he'd never doubted that she was both—could be so innocently, so wickedly seductive, was beyond his reason. It made no sense. The only thing he knew for certain was that she had made him half mad with lust and as hard as a ramrod in his breeches, and if their journey had been five minutes longer, he would have taken her then and there, on the seat of a hackney cab.

How the devil had she done that to him, anyway?

He smiled at Lizzie now as he handed her down, thankful that she couldn't read his thoughts as he struggled to regain his composure so that he could continue the rest of this afternoon. At least he could see that she wasn't in a much better state than he: her cheeks were charmingly flushed and her mouth swollen from kissing him. Her clothes were wrinkled and mussed, and her hair was tumbled down around her shoulders, with loose pins sticking out every which way. If ever there was a portrait of a lady in beautiful, lustful disarray, here it was.

"My hat," she said suddenly, clasping the top of her head where it should have been. "I can't go without a hat."

She climbed back into the cab long enough to return with a doleful expression and the crumpled remains of her hat in her hands. Already handsomely paid, the driver closed the door, climbed back on the box, and drove off, leaving them alone together beside the wall.

"Look what you did, Hawke," Lizzie said sadly, more to the broken straw and crushed satin than to him. "Even to be decent, I can't wear it now, not like this. It's quite ruined."

"Then don't," he said. He took the hat from her, and before she could stop him, he sailed it over the wall and into the bushes and trees on the other side. "I'll buy you a hundred more when we're wed."

She made a small shrieking wail of grief for the sake of the lost hat.

"I can't go about London with my head bare," she protested, spreading her fingers over her head as a make-shift covering.

"Why not?" he said, unable to keep from reaching out and curling a lock of her long, lustrous hair around his finger. He hadn't realized how long it was until now, falling nearly to her waist and thick with rippling waves. "You have beautiful hair. If it were up to me, you'd always wear it loose, and never let a pin near your head again."

"Wear my hair loose!" Her eyes widened, scandalized, but she didn't pull away the lock that he held. "Faith, no lady would ever dare show herself like that."

He pressed the lock to his lips, then let it spring free to fall against her breast, a situation he rather envied.

"You will be a duchess, Lizzie." His gaze still lingered on the dark curl against the swell of her breast. "*My* duchess. You can set the fashions as you please, and not be bound to follow any others."

"It's not a question of following a fashion," she said. "No respectable woman steps out-of-doors with her head uncovered and her hair loose. It's shameless and slatternly."

She shook her hair back over her shoulders and, with her fingers as combs, briskly began to section it for braiding.

"Don't," he said softly. "Leave it down for me."

She blushed again, but froze with her arms raised and her hands behind her head.

"It *is* shameless, Hawke," she protested weakly. "You shouldn't see me with it down until we are wed."

"We shouldn't have kissed like that until we are wed, either, but we did." He smiled slyly, coaxing her. "Besides, no one will see you here."

She dropped her hands, silently agreeing to his wish, and looked about her. "You still have not told me where you have brought us."

They stood in a narrow alley between two high walls of weathered old Flemish-bond brickwork, with no clues beyond the tall, overhanging trees as to what might lie on either side. Of course he knew exactly where he and Lizzie were standing, because everything within sight and a good deal beyond belonged to him—not that he'd wanted to tell her so just yet. He'd lost face in the hackney, and he meant to regain it.

"I vow you'll find no fault with our destination," he said. "Beyond that door, you'll find a veritable garden of delights."

Skeptical, she went to the blue-painted door and tried the latch.

"It's locked," she said, pressing her shoulder against the door to be sure. "Unless you have the key, Your Grace."

He grinned and drew the old-fashioned iron key from his pocket with a flourish.

"I do in fact possess such an article," he said, dangling the key before her, "for a price."

She looked at the key, then back to him.

"As a duchess, I believe I must be above price," she said, "just as I must be above fashion. A duchess should be more resourceful than to pay out whatever any blaggard demands."

Not waiting for him to answer—or to ask his price for the key—she turned to face the wall. She bent down and pulled the back of her skirts forward between her legs, tucking the hems into the waist strings of her petticoats. She'd created a pair of voluminous, makeshift breeches, the sides billowing out over her hips and backside and her slender legs sticking out from the bottoms in yellow clocked stockings.

It was all he could do to keep from laughing out loud.

"For a lady with concerns for her propriety, Lady Elizabeth," he called, "that's the silliest rig I've ever seen. The key will only cost you a kiss."

"Keep your key, sirrah," she said over her shoulder. "I wager I'll be in that garden soon enough without it."

She reached up to one of the protruding bricks, then set her feet on another as if the bricks were small, shallow steps. That was how she used them, too, clambering nimbly up the wall with a *shush* of her petticoat-breeches. The wall was at least twelve feet high and meant to keep out intruders, but she scaled it with a rope dancer's ease. At the top she slung one leg over the wall as if she were riding a horse, then perched there, displaying a fine length of her leg in her yellow stockings and red garters, her feet in heeled, flowered shoes with glittering buckles.

"La, look at you down there," she said with triumph, shaking her hair back over her shoulders. "Have your feet grown roots to that spot, sir?"

He shielded his eyes with his hand to stare up at her. She was something rare to see, like some sort of beautiful pagan pirate-queen. "Where did you learn to climb walls like that?"

She grinned. "I told you before. I'm a lady of many qualities and accomplishments."

"Pray can you warn me of others," he said, "so that I may be prepared."

"Oh, there are too many to enumerate," she said grandly, swinging her legs. "It will be much more entertaining for you to discover them yourself, one at a time."

"I can only imagine." What he was imagining in particular after seeing her sitting astride that wall made him think of how fine she'd look astride *him*.

"Most likely you can't," she said cheerfully, turning to look on the garden side of the wall. "Just as you can't enter this garden before I will."

Without further warning she disappeared, dropping down the far side of the wall. Quickly Hawke thrust the key into the lock.

Of course it stuck and did not turn.

"Lizzie?" he shouted. "Lizzie, open the door from your side."

He heard her laughing. "What manner of jest is that, Hawke?"

"It's not a jest. It's the truth," he said crossly, wanting very much to be on the other side with her. It was his garden, not hers, and she'd no right to keep him out. "The lock is old and stuck, and will not open from this side."

"Then perhaps you should follow my lead and breach the wall like a man," she called, laughing still. "Boarders away!"

No man likes to be laughed at by a woman, and as a duke, Hawke liked it even less than his ordinary brother would. He ripped off his coat and dropped it, then felt for a foothold on the old bricks. His feet were much larger than Lizzie's and the bricks were less accommodating, but he persisted, pulling himself up to the top of the wall.

"You did it, Hawke!" exclaimed Lizzie. She was standing in the shadows of a large tree, watching him. She'd untucked her petticoats from their makeshift breeches, and she appeared to be hopping up and down with excitement. "Oh, you did it!"

But the way she said it made it clear that she hadn't expected him to do anything of the sort, which in turn only made Hawke crosser still. Wives were supposed to believe in their husbands, even when they pursued foolishness such as climbing brick walls.

"Never doubt me, Lizzie," he said, more gruffly than he'd intended, as he swung down from the wall. "Not in this or anything else."

She heard that sternness as a warning, or perhaps a dare. Before he'd dropped from the wall to the grass, she'd taken off with a wild small whoop, bunching her skirts in her hands to free her legs in those yellow stocking and running as fast as she could.

Hawke followed. If he'd been asked earlier, he would have sworn that English ladies did not possess the ability to run. At least he'd never witnessed one moving through a garden at any pace beyond stately, or, if tested, a serene amble, without revealing the existence of limbs inside her petticoats.

But Lizzie ran. There was no other way to describe it. She ran, and ran fast, darting through his beautifully maintained formal gardens like a wild deer through the forest. She ran beneath stone arches, past beds of flowers, around a fountain, and through the allée of poplar trees. Doves fluttered up as she passed, disturbed from their nestings. Still Hawke followed, racing after her and determined to catch her, too. Just as she'd not behaved the way he'd imagined in the hackney, she wasn't following his plan now, either, denying him that pretty dream of them walking genteelly through the gardens while he pointed out this flower or that fruit.

It irritated him, this headstrong demonstration of unexpected athleticism. She'd no right to behave like this. It annoyed him. And, if he was honest, it excited him no end, and inspired him to run faster still.

He was closing the distance between them, and now he could hear her breathing hard, panting with exertion as she pushed onward. Her legs might be swift, but she did wear stays, and surely that cage of whalebone must be restricting her breath. Still she pressed on, her long hair streaming behind her.

But he'd another advantage, too. He'd spent his boyhood roaming this garden. He knew every tree and path, and she didn't. When he saw her head for an arbor—a small marble folly built like a Roman temple, now overhung with grape vines—he knew he'd won. The end of the arbor was blocked with an ancient marble sarcophagus that his grandfather had brought (without its long-forgotten occupant) from Rome, and beyond that was a sharp drop to a false waterfall.

As Hawke watched, she reached the sarcophagus and leaned over it, realizing too late that there was no way to cross it. Swiftly she turned, looking for another outlet. Then, at last, she looked at Hawke. Her breasts were rising and falling rapidly above her bodice, her cheeks flushed and her lips parted. Wearier than she wished to admit, she leaned against the sarcophagus, tossed back her hair, and slowly, slowly smiled at him.

"I won," she said breathlessly. "I outran you."

"The hell you did," he said, coming to stand before her. "Don't ever run from me again."

"No," she said, slipping her arms around his shoulders. "No."

For a fraction of a second he wondered whether she meant no, she wouldn't agree, or no, she'd never run from him. But then all logical thoughts fled from his brain, leaving nothing but the blood-thumping perfection of her kissing him.

Of course he kissed her in return. She parted her lips at once for him to deepen the kiss, and at once it seemed they were back where they'd left off in the hackney. She was a-simmer again (and so was he, really), this time not from anger but from the running, warm and willing, only this was better, much better, because they weren't wrestling in a tiny space.

Here he could run his hands down her sides, following the narrowing of her waist to the swell of her hips beneath her silk skirts and below the stiffened tabs of her stays, then up again to her breasts. How fortunate that she'd mislaid her kerchief, and there was nothing to keep him from her warm, satiny flesh, thrust up high by her stays for him. He touched her, lightly stroking the top of her breast. She arched against him, pressing herself against his fingers, and it was easy enough to lift her breast free of her stays. He filled his hand with her, relishing the incredible softness, and gently flicked his thumb over her nipple. At once it stiffened, and she made that same delighted, surprised chuckle of eagerness.

That was all the encouragement—or was it permission?—that he needed. He grabbed her by the waist and lifted her onto the edge of the sarcophagus, her feet dangling and her legs apart. He kissed her again with growing intensity, and leaned between her legs into the mass of her petticoats. His cock was thick and ready in his breeches, pressing hard against his fall. If he pushed aside her skirts, there'd be nothing else to stop him. He could take her now, here. She'd be his wife soon enough. What would a few days either way matter, when—

"*Hawke!*" Abruptly she froze in his arms, her eyes wide and full of panic. "Oh, no, oh, my, look, *look*!"

He'd no wish to look at anything other than her loveliness, but reluctantly he followed her gaze and turned.

Hell. How had he become so intent on her that he had forgotten the rest of his plans? There on the other side of the arbor was the refreshment he'd ordered, precisely arranged beside the goldfish pond: a table with a drifting white cloth, crystal decanters with wine and two goblets, a silver plate of sweet biscuits, a porcelain bowl overflowing with roses, a pair of cushioned chairs. If that were all, then there'd have been nothing to disturb her.

But because he was a duke and she was going to be a duchess, there were also three footmen in white-powdered wigs and his gold-laced livery, standing at attention as they waited to serve, and a French violin player, also waiting with his instrument in hand. Four men who, though they were pretending otherwise, had just been granted a most excellent view of the next Duchess of Hawkesworth's legs, and worse, her right tit.

Hell, hell, *hell.*

Lizzie was already wriggling herself free of him, and he obliged by stepping back and blocking the servants' view while she put herself back to rights. He'd lived his entire life in the view of servants and didn't give their presence any thought. But he gathered that Lizzie's upbringing had been different, without much of a staff, and he could understand her discomfiture. Ladies could turn shy over the strangest things.

"I'm sorry," he said gruffly, and he was, too, though not quite for the things that he needed to apologize to her for. "Everything will be all right. They won't repeat what they've seen."

"The devil they won't!" She glared at him as she tucked her breast back into her bodice, clearly furious and embarrassed at the same time. Now that he'd seen how her anger could lead so conveniently to arousal, he was doubly sorry that their little game here was done. "I dare you to show me a single servant in any house, in any country, who wouldn't tattle what he'd just seen. And a fiddler!"

"He's a violinist, not a fiddler," Hawke said, not helping but not knowing what else to say under the circumstances. "A Frenchman."

"A *Frenchman*!" She made a low shriek of frustration. "How wondrous fine, Hawke. Now my good name will be tattered not only in London but in Paris, too."

"No, it won't, Lizzie," he said, trying to placate her. "And what does it matter now, anyway? Once you're my wife, nothing's scandalous between us."

She made a low, grumbling sound to show she didn't agree. She was bending over to retie her garters, and he saw nearly as much of her breasts as when he'd pulled her bodice down.

"Who are those men, anyway?" she said as she stood upright, settling her stays around her waist. "Do you know them? Whose servants, to be in this park?"

"It's not a park," Hawke said. "These are my gardens. My house is there. You can just see the chimneys through the trees. Hawkesworth Chase."

"This is all yours?"

"Mine," he said, nodding. "I've another house, too, Halsbury Abbey in Somerset, along with one more in Scotland somewhere that I've never visited. But they'll all be yours as well as mine. Ours."

"Ours," she repeated softly. "Then those footmen will be mine as well. Oh, Hawke, I'll have no respect at all from the staff after this!"

She buried her face in her hands, and he put his arms around her, drawing her close.

"They'll respect you, Lizzie, I'm sure of it," he said. It was odd to comfort her like this, and he felt awkward doing it, patting her shoulders. His experiences with women seldom involved comforting, but he supposed it must be expected with a wife. "Now come with me, and act as if there's nothing amiss. If you can do that, then they will, too."

She heaved a shuddering sigh, then lifted her head from his shoulder.

"You are perfectly, perfectly right, Hawke," she said, visibly laboring to compose herself. "So long as I act like their duchess and their mistress, then they've no choice but to treat me as such."

"True enough," he said heartily, relieved.

"It is true," she said, raising her chin with resolve. "Life is much like a game of cards. Bluffing *is* everything, isn't it?"

He smiled, and tried not to think of how many other ways she fell back on bluffing. "There are cherry tarts on that table."

She gasped, her attempts at a peeress's composure gone as her face lit with girlish delight. "Cherry tarts! Do you know, Hawke, that those are my very favorite thing in all the world?"

"I do know," he said as he offered her his arm. "I made inquiries."

He had, too, sending a maid from his kitchen to the cook at Marchbourne House to discover Lady Elizabeth's fancy.

"You did?" she asked, her eyes melting appreciatively when she looked at him. "For me?"

"All of this is for you, my own Lizzie," he said gallantly. Most women would have squealed with delight over the prospect of owning this garden and house, but Lizzie seemed to care more for the tarts. It was oddly endearing, and he liked her all the more for it. But then he was on familiar ground here, giving women gifts they desired after he'd kissed them. "Every last bit of it."

His confidence continued as he led Lizzie to the table

and seated her himself. Likely the footmen (being men) did wish to ogle her further, but instead they served with their usual decorum, and that, too, put her at her ease. The French violinist played the romantic Albinoni adagios that Hawke had chosen, which also made Lizzie sigh with enjoyment. She sipped her sherry and tossed crumbs to the goldfish, and the way she savored the cherry tarts, licking the sugary syrup from her fingers, could only make Hawke smile.

"One more, my dear," he said, motioning to one of the footmen. "Because they are your favorites."

"You spoil me, Hawke," she said cheerfully as the footman set a fresh porcelain plate with another tart before her. "I vow I'll—faith, Hawke, what is this? Oh, my. Oh, *my*!"

Carefully she uncurled the ruby and diamond bracelet from around the base of the tart where Hawke had placed it. She held it up, the stones glittering in the late afternoon sun, and stared at him incredulously.

"For me?" she whispered. "You would give such a thing to me?"

He laughed, his happiness a match for hers. "I told you everything here was for you," he said. "Here, let me help you with the clasp."

She held her wrist out to him. "How vastly, vastly beautiful," she murmured, still in awe. "It's not real, is it?"

He laughed again. "The Duchess of Hawkesworth will never wear paste stones," he said. "Rubies and diamonds are what you deserve."

She stared down at the bracelet, overwhelmed. Then she left her chair and came to perch on his lap, looping her arms around his shoulders.

"Rubies and diamonds and cherries," she said shyly. "Cherries! However can I thank you, Hawke?"

She kissed him again, clearly no longer caring who

watched. He was glad of that, and he threaded his fingers through her hair, cradling her face before him as he kissed her, and—

"Forgive me, Your Grace."

Hawke could not believe he'd heard so intemperate an interruption; he ignored it and continued to kiss Lizzie. But when the interruption was followed by an impressive throat-clearing, he knew he'd no choice but to look up. Giacomo was standing before him, holding a silver salver that carried a single letter.

"Giacomo, you fiendish rascal," he said, falling into the Italian the two always used together. "I trust that this is a message from His Majesty himself, to disturb me at this time?"

Giacomo bowed, the sort of graceful, noncommittal bow at which he excelled, and presented the salver to Hawke.

"I regret, sir, that this is not from His Majesty," he replied, also in Italian. "But it is from His Grace the Duke of Breconridge, whose servant impressed upon me the need for great urgency."

It didn't take a genius to guess what and why Brecon would have sent him word, and with a muttered oath Hawke took the letter and cracked the seal.

"What is it, Hawke?" Lizzie asked with concern. "What is wrong?"

"We are, by my cousin's reckoning," he said, and handed her the note, written in Brecon's impeccable hand:

> *Marchbourne House*
> *Four of the clock*

My dear Hawkesworth:
I regret to bear the most Unfortunate News that
Lady Elizabeth Wylder has been borne away by some
Criminal of the lowest order, & at present remains
Missing & torn from her Family. The Hearts of those
who Love her Most are distraught, & I urge You to

*come directly to us here to decide what Course must
next be taken for the Lady's safe deliverance. Not a
minute is to be lost.*

*N.B. However, as I do grievously suspect that this
is No News to you, & that the Lady is in your Safekeeping, I beg that you return her At Once, to end
the Suffering of her Family, & before the Magistrates
are consulted & admitted to our Confidences.*

Yr. s'v't.,
B.

She read it once, then slipped from his lap to read it
again with more care. Hawke sighed and reached for his
glass for more sherry.

"I wanted to show you my pictures next," he said ruefully. "They would have amused you, I think. But now—
now I suppose I must return you, as Brecon says."

"We must go at once, Hawke." She refolded the page
and handed it back to him. "If you please, have your
people prepare your carriage."

"I shall see that it is done, my lady," Giacomo said
in English, bowing, and leaving to obey—obeying her,
really, as if she were already his mistress.

"I told you that you'd have no trouble with the servants," Hawke said, emptying the glass. "But then,
Giacomo has always had a weakness for the fair sex."

But Lizzie wasn't laughing. Her expression was solemn, far more solemn than he'd expected, and she stood
with her hands clasped tightly before her waist. In gaudy
contrast to that somber pose, the rubies and diamonds
at her wrist sparkled in the late afternoon sun, a reminder of what they'd shared earlier.

"I have made my family suffer, worrying over me, and
for no reason," she said softly. "I should have sent word
that I was unharmed, and with you."

"You were gone for only a few hours," he protested.

"And I was the one who carried you off, as a lark. It wasn't your idea. Surely they'll forgive you for that."

She shook her head, looking down. "Likely they will. They only wish the best for me, you know. But how can I forgive myself?"

He frowned, at a loss for what to say. He could not fathom why she should worry so much over her family's reaction. It was her life, not theirs. He'd turned his back on his own family for a good ten years with no harm to any of them. What difference could a few hours make to hers?

Yet clearly to her it did. He watched her braid her hair, scraping it back from her face into a sensible plait that doubtless she'd coil into an even more sensible bun.

What had become of the carefree girl he'd chased through the garden at a breakneck pace? Where was the merry, willing nymph he'd kissed in the arbor? What had her family done to her to make her feel so damned guilty over a few hours of pleasure with him? Damnation, he was the one who was going to marry her. Didn't his wishes count for anything? He sighed and rose.

"Come," he said, reaching for Lizzie's hand. "By the time we reach the stable yard, the carriage will be ready."

She offered a tremulous smile of gratitude and squeezed his fingers, for which he in turn was grateful as well.

But the ride to Marchbourne House in the coming dusk was made in silence, and in silence he handed her down from the carriage when they arrived. He saw eager shadows silhouetted by candlelight at the drawing room windows, doubtless her family of keepers eager to swallow her back into their lair. His footman trotted before them, and one of March's was already waiting to open the door.

Yet at the last possible moment, Lizzie stopped and turned toward him.

"I wish to thank you for this afternoon, Hawke," she

said, her words tumbling out in a rush. "For the cherry tarts, and the French fiddler, and the bracelet and—and everything else. I will never forget it, not so long as I live, and I cannot wait until we are wed."

He hadn't expected that, nor the odd little tug in his chest that her words seemed to cause.

"I cannot wait, either," he said, raising her hand to his lips. "Not at all."

"Lizzie!" Charlotte hurried down the steps, her skirts flying, and flung her arms around her sister. "Oh, my dear little sister, you cannot know how happy I am to see you safe!"

Over Lizzie's shoulder Charlotte stared at Hawke, her gaze flinty and full of reproach. Then she swept her sister toward the light and into the house, and away from him.

He stood there, unsure what to do next. He could have climbed back into his carriage and left, ridden away as if he'd planned to do so from the beginning. He was hardly dressed for the customary splendor of Marchbourne House, still in his common dark linen breeches and shirt, and those none too fresh, either. Like a rascal meant for the gallows at Tyburn, he thought, imagining already what they'd say when they saw him. Joining that anxious company inside would earn him nothing but scolding and faultfinding for what he'd done, and he'd a distinct feeling that his explanation— that he'd only wished to be alone with Lizzie—would likely fall on the deafest of ears. Lady Sophronia and his mother would come after him like the harpies they were, while Brecon and March would be harsher and again call him a scoundrel, a rogue, and much more besides.

He could ride away now and spare himself. But the painful truth was that he wished to stay in Lizzie's company, if only for as long as they'd let him. He didn't care what they said of him. All he wanted was to have her to himself, which in a few days he would.

The Marchbourne footmen were still holding the door, expecting him to enter. At least the servants welcomed him, he thought dryly. So would Lizzie, and she was the only one of the lot who really mattered.

He squared his shoulders and followed her.

CHAPTER

9

"How cross is Aunt Sophronia with me?" Lizzie asked her sister, clutching at her arm. "You must tell me before we go inside. And Lady Allred? I'll wager she's absolutely furious."

But Charlotte shook her head. "The older ladies aren't angry at all, leastways not with you," she said. "They blame everything on Hawke. March and Brecon, too. I do believe they were ready to come after you themselves with pitchforks and muskets if he hadn't brought you back soon."

"It's not Hawke's fault," Lizzie said. "That is, not entirely. He did carry me off from the mantua-maker's shop in the hackney, and he did refuse to take me back when I demanded that he do so. But after that, once we arrived at Hawkesworth Chase and he explained everything to me, I didn't protest at all. He's a very fine gentleman, Charlotte, and very amusing. I was indeed rather willing."

Charlotte rolled her eyes. "You look more willing than those tawdry creatures we see trailing after the men in Covent Garden. I can't begin to think what manner of explanation he could offer that would reduce you to— to this."

"Hawke can be very persuasive," Lizzie insisted. She

wasn't entirely sure herself how he'd changed her mind so completely. She'd begun by being furious with him, and then they'd kissed, and she'd climbed the wall and run away from him to prove she could, and after that, everything had been most splendid between them.

"He's persuaded you right into the scandal sheets again," Charlotte said. "I know there's only a few days until the wedding, Lizzie, but even you might have kept your virtue intact until then."

"I did, Charlotte, I swear by all that's holy!"

"The sorry state of your clothes tells another tale, Lizzie," Charlotte said skeptically. "That is, the clothes you're still wearing. What's become of your hat and your cap, and your kerchief as well? If I could, I'd take you upstairs directly for repairs before you join the company, just to salvage what we can, but Mama insists on seeing you at once."

"Mama's here now?" Lizzie exclaimed. "And Diana?"

She hadn't seen her mother or her younger sister for many months, not since they had returned to Ransom Manor after Twelfth Night, and in that time Lizzie had missed them both sorely. "They weren't supposed to arrive until tomorrow!"

"For once the roads from Dorset were dry, and their journey was easier than expected," Charlotte was saying, but Lizzie had already rushed ahead, into the drawing room where everyone was gathered.

Like the rest of Marchbourne House, the drawing room was very large and grand, with marble columns trimmed with gold, blue silk brocade on the walls, and gold-framed looking glasses that ran clear to the ceiling. Even now it easily contained the large crowd of people gathered in it, including Aunt Sophronia, Lady Allred, and a tall, severe gentleman in a medal-covered uniform who must be her second husband, General Lord Allred. Also present were Brecon and two of his sons; March and Charlotte and their twins, plus the nursemaids to keep them in line; March's secretary and Brecon's man of business; and several assorted clergymen, determined to offer comfort, who had accompanied someone or another. It was indeed a crowd, but for Lizzie, the only faces she saw belonged to her mother and sister, sitting to one side.

They were lovely faces, too, with Mama's golden-haired beauty duplicated in sixteen-year-old Diana. In Diana's lap was curled her treasured cat, Fig, sensibly and soundly asleep. Both women still wore their traveling clothes, with the dust of the road on their skirts, and in addition Mama's face bore the obvious strain of her middle daughter's disappearance and deliverance. That alone was enough to sharpen the edge on Lizzie's guilt as she fell into her mother's arms.

"I'm sorry, Mama, so sorry," she said contritely, holding her mother tight. "I can only beg your forgiveness for the trouble I have caused this day."

"Dear Lizzie, what a curious sort of greeting is that!" Mama exclaimed. "Here now, let me have a proper look at you before you begin wailing over sorrow and forgiveness."

Dutifully Lizzie stepped back, bowing her head modestly and clasping her hands at her waist as a lady should, or at least as Aunt Sophronia had been trying to teach her. Mama, however, wasn't fooled.

"I must say you're looking a bit bedraggled for a bride," she said, her blue eyes shrewdly observing Lizzie's rumpled skirts, haphazardly dressed hair, and missing hat and kerchief. "Even for you, Lizzie."

"Yes, Mama," she said, wincing even at that gentle criticism. "But when I left this house, I promise I was most properly dressed. Charlotte has seen to that. Even when I left the mantua maker's shop, I was turned out well enough. But that was before I, ah, met Hawke."

"She didn't 'meet' His Grace, Celia," Aunt Sophronia declared indignantly, unable to keep quiet any longer. "Not unless being bundled up in a horse blanket from the street and thrown into a common hackney cab before a score of horrified witnesses is how a gentleman chooses to meet a lady in this present, wicked age. It was entirely disgraceful."

"Hawke did it because you wouldn't permit him to call on me, Aunt," Lizzie protested. "He said he tried and tried but was always turned away. He vows that this was the only way he could contrive to be with me, and how could I object to that? Isn't that so, Hawke?"

She turned around, expecting him to be there. She'd assumed that he'd followed her and Charlotte into the house, and for one long, hideous moment she feared he hadn't, but had abandoned her to face her displeased family alone.

Then suddenly he *was* in the doorway of the drawing room, and she couldn't help but grin and hold out her hands to him. Still in his shirtsleeves—for his coat must have gone the same way as her kerchief and hat, and he'd never had a neckcloth that she could recall—and with a decided devil-may-care look to him, he looked the perfect romantic hero, making every other gentleman in the room seem stuffy and overdone by comparison. It was the perfect hero's entrance, too, with him striding confidently across the room to join her. Before everyone he took her hand and lifted it to his lips, his dark eyes fairly *smoldering* with desire and regard for her. If Lizzie were prone to swooning, she would definitely have done so then. Surely she must be the most fortunate lady in London, to have such a bridegroom!

Others, however, did not agree.

"Have you no shame, Hawkesworth, no decency?" said Lady Allred, her quivering indignation a match for Aunt Sophronia's. "I cannot believe a son of mine would behave in such a ridiculously selfish fashion. Where is your honor, sir? Where is your *sense*? What on earth is the reason for the Duke of Hawkesworth to play at being a highwayman, Dick Turpin himself, a robber bridegroom seizing his bride from the city streets?"

"I must agree with the ladies, Hawke," Brecon said, more sharply than Lizzie had ever heard him speak. "You have paid absolutely no heed to my cautions or my advice for decorum. Your behavior toward this lady has been reprehensible."

"But not to me!" Lizzie cried, ready to defend Hawke. He'd already claimed possession of her hand, but she went further and slipped her arm around his waist to prove how closely she considered them bound. "To be sure, I appreciate your concern for my welfare, and I regret any suffering caused by my—my disappearance. But I do not find any fault with this gentleman, who acted from only the most noble of intentions toward me."

Someone—she suspected March—made a derisive snort, which she ignored. Instead she brought Hawke to stand before her mother and sister, proud of him even if he was dressed like the highwayman his mother had called him.

"Hawke, I should like to present to you my mother, Lady Celia Wylder, dowager Countess of Hervey, and my sister, Lady Diana Wylder," she said. "Mama, my betrothed, His Grace the Duke of Hawkesworth."

At once Mama and Diana (with the limply sleeping Fig draped over one arm) rose from their chairs to curtsey to Hawke. Given his rank, this was entirely proper, of course, but it did feel odd to Lizzie, and she was relieved when Hawke quickly stepped forward to take Mama's hand to raise her up.

"It is I who is honored, Lady Wylder," he said, flashing the full force of his smiling charm toward them.

"For you to grant me Lady Elizabeth's hand brings me unspeakable joy."

"You are most generous, Your Grace." Mama smiled and nodded gracefully as she returned to her chair. Though she was nearly forty, she could still muster a considerable share of charm herself. "My Lizzie is a true jewel, and every day I pray for her happiness."

Hawke beamed, interpreting this as a compliment, but Lizzie realized that her mother wasn't exactly welcoming Hawke into the family. Praying for Lizzie's happiness more likely meant that Mama was praying for Lizzie to be happy with another gentleman. Obviously she had been influenced by what she must have heard before she and Hawke had appeared, and now it was going to be a sizable task to convince her to change her mind.

But Lizzie did have one excellent card to play in her favor, at least to begin.

"Hawke believes me to be a jewel, too, Mama," she said, "which is why he gave me this bracelet this afternoon as a token of his regard."

She held out her wrist, the heavy stones sliding forward over the back of her hand. What better way to declare honorable intentions than a gift of rubies and diamonds? There was no mistaking the gasps and oohs and ahhs from around the room: at least Hawke had done something to gather their approval.

"Goodness, sir," Mama murmured, considering the bracelet. "That is a most generous gift."

"Please, call me Hawke," he said. "I'd be most honored if you did."

"Very well, Hawke," Mama said, her smile warming. "You are most kind to me, and to my daughter."

Progress, thought Lizzie with relief. Progress.

"Might I call you Hawke, too, Your Grace?" asked

Diana. "When you marry Lizzie, then you shall be my brother, the same as March."

She smiled winningly, and Lizzie smiled, too, again with relief. At least Diana liked him, and Diana was notoriously picky about whom she liked, especially gentlemen.

"Of course you may call me Hawke," he said heartily. "I cannot think of anything more agreeable than to acquire a new sister along with a wife."

"Thank you, Hawke," she said, bobbing another quick curtsey. She glanced slyly at Lizzie as she settled Fig against her shoulder, and at once Lizzie's relief vanished. "We've nicknames in our family, too. Has Lizzie told you that when she first came to London, the scandal sheets called her Lady Lizzie Wyldest?"

"Diana, don't," Lizzie said sharply. *"Don't."*

"Yes, Diana," Mama said, her voice full of warning. "I doubt that Hawke has any interest in you trotting out ancient, tattling history concerning your sister."

"But I do," he said easily. "I wish to learn everything there is to know about my own dear Lizzie. Tell me, Diana, if you please. Why was she called Lady Wyldest?"

Diana smiled, delighting in the attention.

"It *is* an amusing story, Hawke," she began in a confidential tone, stroking the cat on her shoulder. "When Lizzie first came to town, Lord Nightingale conceived a mad passion for her, even though everyone knew she was betrothed to you. She made the mistake of agreeing to dance with his lordship one night, and he danced her into the library, meaning to *seduce* her right there."

"Diana, please," Mama said again. "That is enough."

But Diana was too far into her tale to stop now. "But when his lordship pressed his suit," she said, her voice rising with excitement, "Lizzie took hold of the nearest volume, a book about African wild beasts, and used it to thrash him, all the while swearing like blazes. She even chased his lordship back into the ballroom, so that all the company could watch her swinging at him with the book. *That* was why the papers called her Lady Wyld-est, on account of the thrashing and because of the African wild beasts."

Lizzie's face burned with mortification. It was not that Diana's telling was untrue—if anything, it was much milder than the actual events—or that she regretted treating Lord Nightingale as she had, for she didn't, his lordship's presumption having entirely deserved the African beasts. What she feared was Hawke's reaction. What gentleman wishes to hear his betrothed described in such a lurid fashion?

"That is all?" Hawke said. "Because she hit Nightin-gale with a book?"

"She *smote* him about the neck and shoulders, and denounced him," Diana said with relish. "Even the musicians stopped playing to watch."

"Oh, well," he said easily. "Nightingale should have known better. Here I'm bound to marry your sister this week, and yet this afternoon she still made me climb over a twelve-foot brick wall and chase her all through the garden before she'd let me kiss her."

Abruptly Mama rose. "Hawke, I trust you will excuse me. I am most weary from our journey, and fear I must retire before I fall asleep here on the carpet."

"Of course, ma'am, of course," Hawke said. "I look forward to seeing you again under less taxing circum-stances."

She nodded in acknowledgment. "Lizzie, you will ac-company me. Now."

Lizzie gulped, for Mama was never stern like this. She nodded and turned back to Hawke.

"Good day to you, dearest sir," she said softly, shy before such a crowd. "I thank you for—for everything."

"I'll call here for you tomorrow," he said, not shy at all. "I'll take you riding in the park, and then we can—"

"I'm afraid my daughter will be too occupied tomorrow to see you, Hawke," Mama said. "The last of the wedding preparations, you know."

"You may see her again Saturday morning before the bishop, Hawkesworth," Lady Allred intoned with all the authority of the bishop herself. "In the chapel at St. Barnabas, and not before."

Hawke sighed, a sigh that managed to be heartfelt, resigned, and full of melancholy regret as well.

"It seems we have no choice, sweeting," he said to Lizzie. "We must wait until Saturday."

Then he deftly tipped her into the crook of his arm and kissed her, long and well and without a care for those who were watching.

And Lizzie—Lizzie kissed him back. If she was going to scandalize her family, why, then, she was determined to enjoy herself in the process.

"Until Saturday, when I shall become your wife forever," she said breathlessly when they were done. "Until Saturday!"

She would have lingered longer still if she dared, but Mama had been so appalled by the kiss that she was already halfway from the room. With one final glance of regret for Hawke, she hurried after Mama.

Charlotte had give Mama a pleasing suite of rooms overlooking the gardens, with everything done in sunny shades of yellow and pale green. Servants had already unpacked Mama's trunks, and there were flowers in the vases and a fire set and burning cheerfully in the grate. But Lizzie knew there was bound to be little cheer in this conversation, and she stood expectantly—or at least in expectant dread—as Mama's maid helped her remove her hat and traveling Brunswick, and change into a simple dressing gown until it was time to make ready for dinner.

At last the maid left them, and they were alone. Mama sat in one of the armchairs before the fire, motioning for Lizzie to take the other as she poured fresh tea.

"Your sister does know how to make me happy," Mama said, handing Lizzie a steaming cup. "Fresh flowers, clean linens, and a pot of India tea are all I require to be completely content."

Lizzie stared down into the cup, breathing deep of the tea's fragrance. It was Mama's favorite tea, and she'd always associate it with her. But only Charlotte would be thoughtful enough to remember the blend and have it waiting for her, and while Lizzie resolved to do the same in the future, she also understood what was truly being said.

Charlotte (and March) made her happy.

Lizzie (and Hawke) did not.

"I am sorry that you do not care for Hawke, Mama," Lizzie said into the tea, unable to keep her wounded feelings to herself any longer. "I am sorry he isn't March and that I'm not Charlotte. I am sorry indeed."

"There you are again, Lizzie," Mama said with a sigh, "apologizing when no apology is required. I have never once wished you were Charlotte, and it is complete foolishness of you to believe otherwise. And I have never said that I didn't care for Hawke. On the contrary, I find him charming, handsome, and attentive, and everything that a lady could wish in a gentleman."

Lizzie smiled, sinking back into the armchair. "Oh, I am so vastly glad!"

"Permit me to finish, Lizzie," Mama said, setting the pot beside her. "I said he is all a lady could wish in a gentleman, meaning a gentleman who will dance with her, and amuse her, and bring her posies and sweets at a ball. But as for being the sort of gentleman that you should marry, the duke strikes me as a complete and unmitigated disaster."

Lizzie gasped with disappointment, pressing her hand over her mouth to keep from bursting into tears. Silently Mama drew a fresh handkerchief from her pocket and handed it to Lizzie.

"I'm sure you think I'm judging him too harshly," Mama went on, undeterred by Lizzie's tears. "But pray consider what we know of His Grace. He has lived his entire adult life in shameless self-indulgence, wallowing in the dissipation of a foreign excess. He has avoided his responsibilities as a peer, preferring to leave his obligations to his properties and tenants in the hands of agents. Unlike his father, who was respected both at court and in Parliament, Hawke has only once taken his seat in the House of Lords, for the form of it, and given only a single speech."

"But he has no interest in politics," Lizzie said tearfully, snuffling through the handkerchief. "He prefers art and painting and—and beauty."

Mama sighed and sipped her tea. "Art and beauty are well enough in their place, Lizzie, but they will do precious little for you. Consider how the duke neglected his obligation to you until the last possible moment, and finally appeared only because he was compelled by the strictures of his father's will."

"I know that, Mama, I know it all," Lizzie said with a little hiccuping sob. "But once he met me, he has become most attentive and—and ardent."

"That is exactly my greatest concern, Lizzie," Mama said, leaning forward for emphasis. "I saw it at once. He is infatuated with you, and is wooing you with the ardor that a man displays for a new mistress, for the novelty of love. But what will happen once the pursuit is done and he has possessed you, and that novelty is gone?"

"Mama, if you could only see him as I do—"

"Lizzie, you scarcely know the Duke!" Mama exclaimed. "How many times have you been in his company? Two, three, four? What can you know of any person in that span? What will you do if, in time, he fails to show you the respect and regard that a good husband demonstrates toward his wife, and his children if you are blessed?"

These were sobering thoughts indeed: dreadful, serious, sobering thoughts. Lizzie swallowed hard. "But I—I cannot break with Hawke. Because Father arranged it, I must marry him."

"You understand the dilemma, then." Mama tried to smile, and failed, and did not try again. "What worries me the most is that you and Hawke are so much alike. I saw it at once when you first stood together before me, and then when he kissed you just now—my, I didn't know where to look, for modesty's sake. I can imagine well enough what occurred this afternoon in that garden bower of his."

"Next to nothing, Mama, I assure you," Lizzie said quickly. But just as she knew no one believed her when she swore that Hawke had not ravished her, she knew, too, that if only the footmen and violinist hadn't been there—or if she hadn't seen them—she most certainly and most happily would have permitted Hawke the final favor. "I swear by all that's holy that I am still a virgin."

"Oh yes, and I am not so vastly old that I need believe you." Mama dropped a spoonful of sugar into her tea, stirring it thoughtfully. "You're both so full of passion, with so little regard for anything but the present day. Of course your love will burn bright in the beginning. How could it not?"

The more Lizzie considered this, the more she wondered at how perfectly Mama had described what she'd discovered with Hawke. They *were* exactly alike, which explained how what began as a quarrel could magically shift to a fiery kiss. She had of course heard the old adage about how those of opposite temperaments were attracted to each other, but why couldn't two of a similar nature love equally well?

"If we are alike, then why can't we keep our love burning together?" she asked. "Why must it die?"

"Because wedded life does not permit it, not even for a duke and duchess," Mama said firmly. "There will be heartache as well as joy, and grief to balance the rapturous bliss. A mistress can insulate a gentleman and keep trouble away from their little nest for a week, a month, a year. For that matter—and though I do pray it not be so!—you could be the one who strays, lured by some handsome lieutenant you've met by chance."

"Mama!" Lizzie said, genuinely shocked. "I would never do such a thing!"

Mama smiled in spite of herself at Lizzie's reaction. "No one can tell the future, Lizzie, nor what strange fates are planned for us," she said. "But an honorable wife has the responsibilities of a household and children that a mistress will never have, and she needs her husband's support, just as he needs hers to manage his own affairs. Such things will keep a marriage strong long after an empty *affaire de coeur* has run its shallow course."

Another hot tear of confused misery slipped from Lizzie's eye, down her cheek, and fiercely she blotted it away. Marriage, as Mama was portraying it, sounded grim indeed, a dreary, dull existence bound by duty alone. No wonder Hawke would not be content with such a fate. Neither would she.

"If all of what you say is true, Mama," she said, "then I would do better to throw myself from London Bridge and spare both Hawke and me the curse of this sorrowful, burdensome marriage."

"Hush, hush, none of that," Mama scolded. "And

that, too, is exactly what I mean about your passions running wild. Listen to you! You sound as if you were some hysterical, invented creature on the common stage, rather than a resourceful young lady of intelligence and breeding."

"But what else am I to *do*?"

"You will be strong," Mama said. "For Hawke, and for your children, but most of all for yourself. It will go against your nature, I know, and it will not be easy, but you can do it. You must be strong, and purposeful, and keep your husband content within your marriage even as you steer the course that you shall take together."

Lizzie stared at her mother, incredulous. Hawke was nearly ten years her senior and a sophisticated man of the world, while she had scarcely escaped from girl-hood, and a country girlhood at that. How was she supposed to achieve so much? Mama might well have told her to sprout wings and fly like an eagle to the moon and back.

And Mama—Mama laughed.

"My sweet little goose, do not gape at me that way!" she said. "I would not tell you to do this if I didn't believe you capable of it. Mind you, Hawke must share the challenge. You must work together. But if you can, if you will, then I know you will be happy all your years together."

She set down her tea and opened her arms wide to Lizzie. At once Lizzie went to her, curling close as if she were still a little girl in need of cosseting over a skinned knee rather than an almost-duchess with her wedding day before her.

"Oh, Mama," she whispered, her eyes squeezed tight. "I do not know if I can do all that."

"You can, you and Hawke together," Mama said, her arms warm about Lizzie's back. "So long as you never lose your love for each other, I am sure of it."

Lizzie didn't answer, striving to store up the comfort of this moment for all the times she'd need it in the future. She would, too; she'd no doubt of it. To become a strong wife, a devoted lover, a mother to an heir (with luck) and other children besides, a conscientious duchess who would guide her duke down only the most righteous of paths—oh, it seemed far too much for her to even consider, let alone resolve to do.

But in two more days she would marry the Duke of Hawkesworth, and at last—at last!—her new life would begin.

Saturday dawned as perfect as only an early summer day in England could be. The skies over London were the brightest of blues, without so much as a scrap of cloud or trace of coal smoke to mar it. The sun offered the exactly perfect degree of warmth, neither unpleasantly hot nor shiveringly chill. The breeze was only of the most gentle variety, seeming to carry the sweetest fragrances of grass and flowers directly from the country. A light dew had fallen in the night at an hour to be of no inconvenience to anyone, but had remained to add the slightest glisten and polish to every blade of grass in the parks and on every brick in every wall. It was, in short, a perfect day, the perfect day for a wedding.

Though Charlotte had longed for Lizzie to be wed from Marchbourne House, Lady Allred had insisted the ceremony be held in the same church where Hawkesworths beyond counting had been wed. St. Barnabas-of-the-Fields had no more relation to open fields than Hawkesworth Chase had to hunting, but together the parish and the old house had somehow miraculously survived. The original church had perished in the Great Fire, but with substantial aid from the Hawkesworth family, a newer, grander one had swiftly been put up in its place, designed by the esteemed Sir Christopher Wren himself. It was not perhaps as entirely fashionable as it once had been (churches and their parishes being no more immune to fashion than other, less spiritual organizations), but it would still make a splendid setting for the wedding.

It was to be a small, family affair, or at least as small an affair as a wedding could be with the bishop of London presiding and the Duke of Hawkesworth as the groom. From fear of gawkers and scriveners from the papers, the guests were limited to the immediate family, and the chapel had been sealed off to all others for the past two days. Still, well-wishers and those who were simply curious had begun to stake out spots in the streets around St. Barnabas the night before, and the guards His Grace had hired to keep the peace were already busy. Everyone wished to catch a glimpse of the bride, to see her beauty, her gown, and her jewels.

At this hour, the bride was standing before her looking glass with her arms outstretched as a pair of feverish seamstresses tacked her flounced lace cuffs inside her sleeves. It was the last step to be done. Lizzie's hair had long ago been dressed into a tall, curling mass atop her head, and the dark weaves sprinkled with sparkling brilliants and pearls. Her veil had been pinned to the crown, drifting like a lace cloud behind her. Her shoes were white silk, with high curving heels and diamond buckles. Her gown was silk damask, a rich, creamy white that made her pale skin glow, and edged with gathered poufs of more lace and silk roses; at least the gown was to be worn once again, when she was presented at court.

The only color in her dress came from the ruby and diamond bracelet on her wrist. Over the past three days, the bracelet's fame had grown like a mushroom in the rain and had become the most tangible (and most valuable) part of the glorious tale of the robber bridegroom, stealing his beauteous lady away from her family.

But for now the bride stood as dutifully still as the two seamstresses demanded, with a large linen napkin tied around over her gown to protect it while her sister Diana carefully fed her slices of oranges and the other women of her family fluttered around her.

"I vow, Lizzie," said Mama, "if you get so much as one drop of juice on that gown, then I shall expire. I am serious, you know. Why must you eat an orange now, when you are dressed?"

"Because I am hungry, Mama," Lizzie said, as if this were the only explanation in the world. "I'd no interest in the eggs or sausages or toasted muffins that Charlotte tried to stuff down my throat earlier, but an orange is exactly what I desired."

"You wouldn't eat earlier because you feared they couldn't lace your stays tight enough to fit your gown," Charlotte said shrewdly. "Now you're likely famished, aren't you?"

"Not at all," Lizzie declared. "I am exactly as a bride should be."

Which was to say that she felt both elated and terrified, eager and reluctant, boldly confident and shy. She hadn't been as worried about her stays not lacing to fit her gown as that, when the laces were tightened, all the butterflies in her belly might have suddenly flown upward and she would have been shamefully ill. Most of all, she longed for the ceremony to be over and for she and Hawke to finally be alone together. With Hawke as her bridegroom, she was positive that her wedding night would be by far the best part of their entire wedding day.

"Look, Lizzie, another gift for you," Diana said as a footman appeared with a silk-wrapped box. "I wonder what this will be."

"That's no ordinary gift," Charlotte said, who had seen the livery on the footman who delivered it. "It's from Hawke. You must open it now, Lizzie, open it at once! You know it's bound to be something most extraordinary."

Pulling aside her makeshift bib, Lizzie hurried to take the box. Inside the white silk was another box, wide, flat, hinged, and covered in dark blue leather with gold embossing, the kind of box that could only contain jewels.

"That box is from Boyce's," Aunt Sophronia said with approval. "I'll grant you the Duke does have exquisite taste."

"Not to mention an exquisite purse to match," Mama said. "To be sure, everything from Mr. Boyce's shop is very beautiful, but also very dear."

"Pearls," said Aunt Sophronia sagely. "That is the only gift proper for a bride from her groom on her wedding day. I'll wager it's a triple strand of flawless pearls."

Lizzie's fingers trembled with excitement as she unhooked the box and slowly opened the lid.

It wasn't a simple strand of pearls.

It was a necklace, yes, but an extravagant necklace of rubies and diamonds to match the bracelet. Large, round rubies hung from intricately looped bows of diamonds set in gold, and even to Lizzie's inexperienced eye, the size of the stones and the quality of the workmanship *were* extraordinary, exactly as Charlotte had predicted.

"Cherries," Lizzie said with delight as she held the necklace up to the window to catch the sunlight. "Hawke remembered that I like cherry tarts above all things, and that's what this is supposed to be. Cherries."

"Cherries!" Aunt Sophronia sputtered with outrage. "Those are not cherries, my dear, but rubies so fine Her Majesty herself will covet them. I cannot conceive what His Grace must have paid for that necklace, but there is no question of a lady of your age wearing such a piece, especially not for her wedding."

Lizzie stared, speechless with disappointment. She understood exactly why Hawke had chosen this necklace for her, and she didn't give a fig as to whether it was suitable or not. She was eighteen, and if she was old enough to be a duchess, she was old enough to wear a necklace given to her by a duke.

Yet if Aunt Sophronia insisted, she'd have no choice.

"What vulgar demon possessed His Grace to send such an inappropriate bridal gift?" Aunt Sophronia was saying, growing more strident with every syllable. "Wrongful it is, indeed, and—"

"It doesn't matter, Sophronia," Mama said, coming to stand behind Lizzie. "His Grace has given the necklace to his bride, and if she wishes to wear it, then she shall."

Aunt Sophronia drew back with shock. No one in the family dared question her authority in what was correct and proper for all situations.

"Lizzie has the dark beauty to wear rubies well," Mama continued, taking the necklace from Lizzie and fastening it around her throat for her. "If they have special meaning between her and the Duke, then all the more reason for her to wear them now."

She gave the clasp a little extra pat. The stones were heavy and cool on Lizzie's skin, and she touched them herself, settling the unfamiliar weight of the ruby drops against her collarbone. She stepped back before the glass, sighing with happiness at what she saw. She wasn't sure how Hawke could have known, but the necklace was quite, quite perfect.

Mama's face showed in the reflection beside her, her own smile so bittersweet that tears stung Lizzie's eyes. At once Lizzie turned and hugged her mother, too overwhelmed for words.

"There, Lizzie, there, no weeping," Mama said, though

she, too, was smiling through her tears. "We want no red noses today to shame the Wylders."

"The carriages are here, Lizzie!" exclaimed Diana from the window. "It's time. It's time!"

It *was* time, and with one last touch to the rubies for luck, Lizzie stepped forward to her wedding.

CHAPTER
10

Six weeks ago, Hawke would have given half his fortune not to be here, in this place. Now he couldn't think of anywhere he'd rather be, because the prize he'd receive was Lizzie.

He stood beneath the trumpeting marble angels that crowned the chapel, and tried to focus on the words the bishop was saying. They were important words, after all, words that were changing his life forever, words that deserved his full and thoughtful attention.

Yet his entire supply of thoughtful attention was being completely diverted to the slender white fingers he held in his hand, and the fingers' owner, who knelt beside him, so close that her skirts brushed against his leg and over his shoes. Those fingers were damp with nervousness, or perhaps anticipation. He liked to think it was anticipation, the same anticipation that he was feeling himself.

He wondered if she was smiling still, if her eyes were as bright and eager as when she'd first seen him waiting for her at the end of the aisle. He'd done his best to dress to be worthy of her—he'd worn the somber dark gray suit of Brecon's recommendation, but Hawke had chosen a waistcoat embroidered with a flamboyant silver and gold leopard pattern because he'd known it would make Lizzie laugh—but all of that was nothing compared to how she had appeared to him.

He'd been blinded, dazzled, thunderstruck. What man wouldn't have been? She'd looked like an angel with the sun streaming behind her, a flesh-and-blood angel and not the stone ones over his head, so beautiful that it had almost hurt to look at her. Then she'd smiled, and she became again his Lizzie, and all he'd been able to do was grin like an idiot since then.

As Brecon had explained it, Hawk had to at least pretend to be listening to the bishop. He screwed up his face to look solemn and grave, then counted to five before he stole another peek at her.

She was staring straight ahead, her eyes wide and her mouth very tight. He'd never seen her—his brave, bold, wall-climbing Lizzie—look so thoroughly intimidated, and he gave her hand a little squeeze of reassurance, a little reminder to trust him. Swiftly she glanced up at him and smiled, a smile that dimmed the jewels he'd given her, and without a thought he raised her hand to his lips to kiss just the tips.

He heard Brecon clear his throat behind him, an ominous warning if ever there was one, and reluctantly Hawke forced himself back to staring at the front of the bishop's vestments.

Blast, how much longer must they kneel here? He'd lost all track of the time and the service. He had already slipped the ruby and diamond ring onto Lizzie's finger, they'd pledged their vows, knelt, and the bishop had said the part about no one putting them asunder. How many more prayers and psalms and admonitions remained to be said before she was well and truly his?

Suddenly the bishop's words seemed as clear as day, as if his sonorous voice was speaking to Hawke alone:

Almighty God, who at the beginning did create our first parents, Adam and Eve, and did sanctify and join them together in marriage; pour upon you the riches of His grace, sanctify and bless you, that ye may please him both in body and soul, and live together in holy love unto your lives' end.

Now *that* was solemn, and daunting, too, especially the part about living together in holy love unto their lives' end. It made him . . . uneasy, especially since he'd just vowed something quite similar to that here beneath the stone angels of St. Barnabas. He intended to love Lizzie quite thoroughly tonight—she was his wife and his duchess, after all, and this was to be their wedding night—and he doubted he'd tire of her anytime soon. He liked her too much for that. In fact, he liked her very much, far more than he'd expected from a match arranged by his father, and was perhaps even halfway to being in love with her.

He knew what that meant, too. If there was one thing Italy could teach a young Englishman, it was how to fall in love, and Hawke had been routinely falling in love for many years now.

But in Italy he'd also learned the other side of the coin, and he understood how it was just as easy to fall out of love as it was into it. Attraction lessened, passion grew cold, charm was replaced by indifference, and the thing was done. It was, to him, as natural a progress as the seasons, and about as permanent, too. In a year or two or perhaps three, what he felt for Lizzie would fade from love to friendship and regard, as was proper for the mother of his children. Such an arrangement had worked out well enough for his own parents, hadn't it? Bella Collina was waiting for him. He'd never expected fidelity that lasted a lifetime, nor was he sure it was even in his blood. How could it be otherwise, when his own dukedom was founded on a long-ago philandering king taking a courtier's wife as his mistress?

Not that any such unromantic thoughts belonged here today, not with Lizzie at his side. He turned to find her smiling up at him, grinning, really, so widely that she might even be trying not to laugh.

"It is customary at this time to rise, Your Grace," the bishop said in a generous whisper. "Afterward, if it pleases you, you may offer your new wife an affectionate salute."

Mortified, Hawke wondered exactly how long he'd been kneeling there, his thoughts a thousand miles away. He scrambled to his feet, then helped Lizzie rise from her cushion, too, struggling to keep from tangling his feet in the billowing sea of her skirts and hoops. She *was* laughing now, that same delicious, droll chuckle that she often made while he kissed her. He'd take that as an unabashed invitation to kiss her again, here, now, and at once he bent down toward her.

But even before he'd leaned down to her, she'd stood up on her toes to take his face in her hands and reached up to kiss him first. It was a true kiss, too, not some polite small peck. Her lips moved eagerly and her mouth opened, coaxing his to do the same. Brazen little baggage, he thought with delight, and swiftly showed her how a husband should properly kiss his wife. He threaded his fingers into her elaborately dressed hair and deepened the kiss further. The bishop had told him to salute her, and before them all, he gave Lizzie a full twenty-one guns.

But apparently by that the bishop had intended only a tiny popgun of a salute, a decorous peck. In addition to Brecon's throat-clearing, Hawke realized the bishop had added his own, too, a sonorous rumbling that even he couldn't ignore. Reluctantly he broke away, smiling down at Lizzie. Her lips were rosy and wet, and as she looked up at him from beneath her lashes, she nibbled her plump lower lip between her front teeth. She reached up to smooth a lock of hair that he'd mussed out of place, the new ruby wedding ring sparkling on her finger. He suspected they were supposed to now turn and walk back to their families for well-wishing and congratulations, but instead he lingered, unable to look away from her just yet. He wanted to remember her like this, her joy making her beauty all the more exquisite.

Then, with another little chuckle, she grabbed her skirts in her hands and ran down the aisle, her high heels clicking on the stone floor and her lace veil drifting out behind her.

He'd no choice but to follow, running past their appalled families.

Even with a brisk start, she was slowed by her shoes and her skirts, and he caught her easily in the entry. She was too breathless for chuckling now, and with his hands around her waist, he pushed her back against a wide stone column.

"What the devil has possessed you?" he demanded.

"You must not swear," she whispered, her voice ragged from running and excitement. "We're in church."

"Answer me," he said gruffly, watching how the rubies were rising and falling on her chest.

"What has possessed me?" She laughed softly, tipping her head back. "You, Hawke. Only you."

He couldn't help kissing her again, and at once she curled her arms around the back of his neck, arching up against him. He half thought of something clever about how he hadn't possessed her yet, that that would come later, but kissing her seemed more important than cleverness, and he concentrated on that instead.

"Hawke," said Brecon sharply, suddenly beside them. "Duchess. May I be the first to congratulate you on your marriage?"

Swiftly Hawke unwrapped himself from Lizzie, though

he held tightly to her hand just to be sure she wouldn't bolt again. One look at Brecon's face as he shook his hand told Hawke exactly how bad his behavior—no, theirs, for Lizzie's behavior had been no better—had been. St. Barnabas was a church and marriage was a sacrament, not a frolic, and though only family were supposed to be present, he'd wager a hundred guineas that the papers would be filled with the first scandal of the newly wed Duke and Duchess of Hawkesworth. On most days, Hawke cared very little about what was whispered or written about himself, but somehow it seemed to be courting bad luck to begin their marriage on such a note.

He stole another glance at Lizzie, who appeared likewise struck with guilty contrition. Her conspirator's grin had been replaced by a much more proper half smile as she curtseyed and accepted Brecon's good wishes. Only a single unpinned curl, trailing awkwardly behind her ear, betrayed her earlier mischief.

And yet, if Hawke had it to do again, beginning with her smiling up at him that way before the bishop, he wouldn't have changed a thing.

"Your Grace," murmured Lady Hervey with her head bowed, curtseying before her daughter for the first time. An hour ago they had been merely mother and daughter. Now Lizzie was a duchess, while her mother remained only a countess, far below her in rank. "May I offer my heartfelt wishes for your happiness to you and His Grace."

"Oh, Mama, please," Lizzie said with a little catch to her voice as she sank down to embrace her mother. "You needn't do this, not with me."

Slowly her mother rose. "Thank you, ma'am," she said, a crackle of admonition in her voice, "but pray recall your new station, and attend to His Grace's wishes before mine."

Lizzie drew back, obviously startled by her mother's response. "Mama, I am sorry if I—"

"If you please, ma'am," her mother interrupted, more sternly this time. "If His Grace is content with you and your decorum, then so must I be."

Hawke's estimation of Lady Hervey rose. When first they'd met several days ago, he'd dismissed Lizzie's mother as a handsome but insubstantial woman, blue eyes and golden hair and not much more. Now he could see that she'd a strength of will he hadn't expected, and further, that she was determined to make Lizzie act as she should for her new role.

Strange how he hadn't considered that himself. As her husband, he could by rights expect—even demand—things of Lizzie that he couldn't have if she'd been only his mistress, but he'd only gone so far as to think of Lizzie as a woman he desired. Obedience, deference, devotion: he hadn't thought of any of that at all.

Who would have dreamed being married would be so complicated?

Nor was Lizzie finding it any less difficult, either.

"You would know if Hawke is content with me, Mama?" she asked, glancing uncertainly from her mother to him and back again. "So soon?"

"Pray recall our conversations, ma'am, and you'll understand," her mother said with weighty significance before she turned to curtsey swiftly before Hawke.

"Your Grace," she said softly, her hands pressed together in supplication, "I pray that you will honor us with your presence and Her Grace's for a small celebration at Marchbourne House."

Hawke frowned, even more confused. Both Lizzie and her mother were waiting in breathless expectation, and so, too, was her younger sister, Diana, standing to one side between March and Charlotte. Even Brecon for once was silent.

Did they really believe he'd deprive Lizzie of that celebration with her family? What manner of ogre did they judge him to be, anyway?

He smiled as warmly as he could, determined to prove them wrong.

"Of course we shall come," he said, linking his fingers into Lizzie's. "My wife and I shall be most honored."

At once they seemed to relax, smiling and laughing and chatting and kissing Lizzie and shaking his hand. The harpies (meaning her Aunt Sophronia and his mother) and the general had finally joined them as well, and just like that, their little gathering had become a proper, respectable wedding party, with everything exactly as a wedding should be.

He shook the bishop's hand, and they stepped into the vestry to sign the registry, Lizzie's signature small and neat, his bold and slashing. There was more congratulating and cheek-kissing as Lizzie took the posy of flowers from Diana, and then, at last, he could lead Lizzie through the chapel door and to the porch, where his carriage was waiting.

Hawke had been anticipating this moment not only because he'd finally be alone with her, but also because he wanted to see her reaction to the carriage itself. He'd ordered his father's staid old carriage bedecked for a bride, with white flowers tied along the windows and ribbon streamers floating from the top. Even the horses wore white ribbon rosettes on their harnesses, and the coachman and footmen all sported more flowers pinned to their breasts and in their hats.

Her reaction was worth it, too.

"Oh, my, Hawke, look what you've done!" she exclaimed, adding a little hop of delight. "I shall be as proud as a princess, riding in that!"

"You're the Duchess of Hawkesworth," he said as he

led her down the chapel steps. "That's better than any princess."

She laughed. "Is it?"

"It is," he assured her, "because you're wed not to any mere prince, but to me."

That made her laugh again, the sunshine warm on her face, and she was laughing still when he handed her into the carriage, her veil and skirts fluttering around her in the breeze. He liked how she laughed, even though there wasn't anything particularly amusing, and he flattered himself that mostly it came from her being so happy to be married to him that it rose up into her wonderful, merry laughter, like the bubbles in champagne.

She tried to make room for him on the seat beside her, but her hoops and petticoats seemed to nigh fill the carriage with white silk and lace, and he settled across from her instead. It was likely just as well. This way he could admire her delicious splendor, and keep himself more properly in check while doing so, too. Their drive to Marchbourne House was not long, and he'd resolved to deliver her there in the same state in which she'd left St. Barnabas.

More or less, anyway. And once they left March's house for good, all bets would be off.

She was still fussing with her skirts when the driver cracked the reins and the carriage rolled into the street. As it did, a hearty cheer rose from the crowd on the pavement, and quickly Lizzie looked from the window.

"Goodness! Who are all those people?" she asked, her eyes widening with wonder.

"Well-wishers and curiosity seekers," he said. "Wave if you like, though you needn't if you don't wish to."

"Of course I shall wave," she said, waving her hand so enthusiastically that she was immediately rewarded with a fresh round of cheers. "If they've been waiting to see me, it would be rude not to."

The notion of a duchess worrying about offending a street full of gawkers made him smile.

"Everyone loves a bride," he said, "but everyone loves a duchess bride even more. You're a rare creature, you know."

She looked away from the window to make a face at him, clearly believing he was only teasing.

"I'm not jesting, Lizzie," he said, bemused. "Hasn't the harpy explained the facts to you?"

"The harpy?" Lizzie repeated. "By which I suppose you mean Aunt Sophronia?"

"I suppose I do," he said, not nearly as teasing as she assumed. "She *is* a harpy, but she likely understands the peerage better than I do myself. Dukes themselves are rare enough. There can't be more than twenty-five or thirty dukedoms left in the kingdom. Of those dukes, at least half are still at school, or confirmed bachelors, or widowed, or in their dotage, which leaves perhaps a dozen with a duchess, and of that noble handful of ladies, I'd wager not one can come close to your beauty."

"One can," she answered immediately. "My sister Charlotte's much prettier than I."

Now he was the one who made a face. "Charlotte? Your sister, and March's wife? You're much mistaken, sweetheart. She can't hold the proverbial candle to you, especially not today."

"You're very kind to say that, Hawke." She smiled, but it was the sort of female smile that was one part indulgence for male idiocy and another part plain unvarnished disbelief, with a dash of melancholy tossed in.

"I didn't say it to be kind," he said. "I said it because it's true."

"But you *are* kind," she insisted, neatly skirting the original question. "You don't want to believe it, because apparently it's not ducal and lordly to be kind, but you are. Otherwise you wouldn't have agreed when Mama asked you to come back to Marchbourne House."

"I would have been barbarous cruel not to," he said. "I do not wish to create havoc within your family as soon as I've married into it. You wish to bid your mother and sisters a proper farewell, and March and Brecon wish to try to make me drunk. Who am I to deny them those simple pleasures?"

"March did," she said promptly, answering his rhetorical question in seriousness. "He refused to go to the wedding supper that Aunt Sophronia had arranged, and instead insisted on carrying off Charlotte directly after the wedding, like Hades with Persephone."

That made him raise his brows. He didn't know which seemed more improbable: March driven to ill manners by desire, or Lizzie quoting ancient mythology.

"Do you intend to carry that analogy further," he said, "and liken Marchbourne House to the blackest bowels of hell?"

"I never meant that!" She scowled charmingly. "What I do mean is that March was so—so *ardent* for my sister that he couldn't wait, and instead swept her away. Charlotte said that he almost didn't wait until her bedchamber, but began to make love to her in the carriage."

"How horrifying," Hawke said dryly, trying hard not to laugh at this astounding sisterly revelation. His dry, dutiful cousin, unable to keep his breeches buttoned! "How mortifying for his eldest son if he had been begotten on a carriage seat."

She grinned. "You were perfectly, perfectly willing to attempt the same with me on a *sarcophagus*. That's far worse."

"Why, that sarcophagus is older than England," he retorted, "and it would have made a splendid foundation for siring an heir. Though it would seem that you, dear Lizzie, preferred St. Barnabas."

"Oh, Hawke!" she exclaimed, blushing nearly as red as the rubies around her neck. "Oh, oh, I do not know *what* made me behave so!"

"I thought you laid the blame upon me," he said, folding his arms across his chest and striving to look stern and undeserving of blame.

"I did, because it's vastly true," she said, pressing her palms to her cheeks in mortification. "I do not know what it is about you, but whenever I am in your company and you smile and look at me and make me laugh, I feel dreadfully *wanton*, and I forget who and where I am and behave quite irresponsibly, and—and—oh, Hawke, you are doing it to me *even now*!"

He laughed, realizing that he couldn't recall a time in his life when he'd been happier.

"There is one sure way to address that trouble," he said. " 'Tis true, we haven't much time left, but we still could follow Cousin March's lead and—"

She slid her hands over her eyes, hiding them.

"Do not speak it, Hawke, not even in jest!" she wailed. "Because I would almost wish that we would, that you would *ravish* me now, here, with those people in the street waving and not knowing, and—and that is exactly what Mama was warning me of today! How can I be a strong and honorable duchess to you if my passions run wild like that?"

He was torn between two desires: to laugh, and to toss up her petticoats and fall upon her like a ravening beast. Neither was appropriate, and both would be disastrous in their own way.

Instead he took the safest course, though one that was disturbing in its own way. "Is *that* what your mother was saying to you? That you must put aside your passions for my sake?"

"Yes," she confessed, distraught. "No. That is, I must

put aside my own foolish passions before I might become the duchess that—"

"Hush," he said softly. "No more, mind?"

She was perilously close to tears—he heard it in the tremble of her voice—and he didn't want the day spoiled like that. He reached across to her, gently taking her hands from her face and kissing each palm in turn. Then he kissed her, sweetly, fervently, devotedly, to make her forget her mother's foolishness.

"You are perfect as you are, Lizzie," he said between kisses and against her cheek and forehead and chin, wherever the words and kisses happened to fall. "Perfect as my wife, perfect as my duchess. And when we are in my house, in my bed, I shall show you exactly how perfectly your passions please me."

She sighed, a deep, shuddering sigh, and rested against his shoulder.

"My own dear Hawke," she murmured. "I shall hold you to that."

He grunted, holding her a little more tightly. "So shall I."

His knee was between her legs, his thigh acutely aware of hers against his, albeit through layers of silk. Her breasts were pressed against his chest, the jewels of the necklace jabbing into his shoulder blade. He'd tolerate the jewels for the sake of her breasts, and try to forget the throbbing demand of his own sadly neglected cock.

Damnation, why did he have to be so blasted noble?

"We've stopped," she said, sniffing as she sat back against the seat and away from him. "We're here."

He was grateful she'd noticed. From the babies onward, her family was standing on the steps of the house, waiting to welcome them, and he needed a moment or two to compose himself and his breeches before he stepped out. As it was, he took his time helping her from the carriage, gallantly handing her the forgotten posy and making sure her hand was tucked securely into the crook of his arm.

She noticed. "I won't run again," she said. "I only did it before to torment you."

"You achieved magnificent success," he said, giving her hand a final pat. "However, you've promised before, to no avail. I'll not take another chance of you escaping now."

"Escaping?" she scoffed. "I'm not escaping, nor do I wish to."

"I'm glad of it," he said, and smiled warmly. "If you please, my Duchess. The others are waiting."

"That's the first time you've called me that," she said. "I like it, Duke."

Her cheeks pinked again, this time with pleasure. He'd always been fond of women who blushed, and he was powerfully glad he'd married one.

"And I like you, Duchess," he said, beginning to move her forward. "A good thing, too."

"Hawke?"

He sighed. At this rate, it would take them at least an hour to reach the steps, another two or three to go inside, and by the time they eventually reached their own house and bed, they'd both be too exhausted to make any inventive, romantic use of it.

"Hawke," she said, undeterred. "You *are* kind."

"Indeed," he said, not stopping or even slowing. "And you, Lizzie, are beautiful."

"Oh, Duke," she said, chuckling.

He was glad, very glad, that the chuckle had returned. March's dogs—an assortment of rambunctious spaniels— had been loosed from the house and bounded past the family and servants, delighted to be free. While footmen and children ran about after them, two of the dogs came racing up to him and Lizzie. While most ladies would have screamed and tried to protect their gowns, Lizzie handed Hawke her flowers and crouched down on the paving stones in her rubies and diamonds and Venetian lace to pet heads and ruffle ears. When a dog sat on her white silk petticoat, she only looked up at Hawke and laughed.

"We needn't remain here long," she said. "You gentlemen have your toasts, I shall change my clothes, and then we'll leave."

"We can stay as long with your family as you need to," he said gallantly, forcing himself to ignore the splendid view of her mostly bare breasts available to him and the dogs. "As long as you wish."

"What I wish, Hawke," she said firmly, "is to be alone with you, and make you keep your promise about my passions."

The nearest dog swiped its tongue across her cheek, and she didn't even flinch. She grinned.

And in that moment, Hawke realized that he'd done the unthinkable for any Duke of Hawkesworth.

He'd fallen in love with his wife.

CHAPTER

11

Lizzie stood before the long looking glass in her sister's bedchamber, studying her reflection. To her disappointment, she didn't appear any different at all, even though she'd been married and a duchess for nearly four hours now. Perhaps it wasn't standing before the bishop that would make the change, but lying with Hawke. Perhaps then she'd look more like a duchess, a peeress, a *wife*. She gave a little shake to her shoulders, a mixture of excitement and anticipation, and a bit of fear, too. She thought she knew what to expect, and yet . . . she didn't.

"I hope Hawke likes this gown," she said to Charlotte as her maid gave her skirts one final tweak. She'd shifted from the elaborate silk damask wedding gown into another, simple and elegant, of pale blue lutestring, and the ruby and diamond necklace and the bracelet had been carefully packed away in their cases, ready to be taken with the rest of her belongings to Hawkesworth Chase. "I hope he won't think it's too plain."

"Your gown?" Charlotte smiled knowingly. "Lizzie, Hawke won't give a fig for what you're wearing now. All that concerns him at present is what you won't be wearing, and the sooner the better, too. That's how men think."

"I suppose you are right," Lizzie said. Hawke had already displayed surprising skill at removing her clothing. She doubted that would change now that they were wed. "Men do have different notions about fashions."

Suddenly one particular notion of Hawke's came to mind. She couldn't walk to their carriage in her shift, which would likely please him most, but she could oblige him in another way. She reached up and began to jerk the pins from her hair, running her fingers through the waves to free them.

"What are you doing?" Charlotte asked, shocked. "Stop, Lizzie, stop. There's no time to redress your hair, not unless you wish to keep Hawke waiting even longer."

"I don't intend to redress it," she said, shaking her hair free and over her shoulders. She seized a brush from the dressing table, and to the horror of Charlotte's maid, vigorously began to brush her hair herself. "Hawke has asked me to wear my hair down, and for him, I will."

"But you can't, Lizzie," Charlotte protested. "You're a married woman, a lady, and now you're a duchess. When he takes you to his house, he'll present you to his servants for the first time. Do you wish their first glimpse of their new mistress to be with your hair trailing down as if you don't know better?"

Lizzie remembered the footmen from the garden who had already seen her in a far more compromising situation than simply with unbound hair. "I can always twist it into a knot if I must."

"But what about now?" Charlotte asked. "You can't go downstairs with your hair hanging down like that. It's not proper. It's not decent."

"Hawke says that as Duchess of Hawkesworth, I don't have to follow the fashions," Lizzie said finally. "I can make them instead. How pleased he'll be to see it down!"

"But shouldn't you wait until you are alone with him, Lizzie?" Charlotte pleaded. "A special pleasure for your husband's eyes alone?"

Lizzie shook her head, relishing the sensation of her hair loose. Her hair was long, nearly to her waist, and rippled over her shoulders like a gleaming cloak. She liked how daring it made her feel, and she also liked being spared the unbalanced weight of having her hair pinned high. She gave her head one final shake and handed the brush to the maid.

"I'm ready now," she said, turning away from the glass. "I've kept the duke waiting long enough. Shall we go downstairs?"

"In a moment." Charlotte dismissed the maid, waiting until the door had closed behind her. "I know that Mama and Aunt Sophronia have both spoken to you of your, ah, wifely duties."

" 'Wifely duties'!" Lizzie repeated with a shudder. "Oh, Charlotte, did they deliver the same sermon to you?"

That conversation in Aunt Sophronia's drawing room had been one of the most embarrassing in her life. Because she and her sisters had been raised in the country and surrounded by animals, they'd few questions about the origins of babies. Any further details that pertained to people had been supplied by the helpful maidservants hired from the local village, girls who'd whisper frankly, even boastfully, of what they'd done with the young fishermen and sailors they intended to marry.

Yet those same acts sounded entirely different as described by her mother and aunt. They had stressed the need for respect and dignity between husband and wife, and how, while love could make anything bearable, a titled wife must never forget that her primary purpose in the marriage was to produce an heir.

This had been most uncomfortable for Lizzie to hear

from her mother, who, of course, had failed at that very task. Mama had held her own circumstance up as an example, wistfully explaining how, because of three daughters and no sons, Lord Hervey's title and estates had escaped the family entirely. The stakes rose immeasurably with a dukedom, and now that Charlotte had so swiftly and ably produced two sons, Lizzie must surely follow. Yet as difficult as this had been to hear, worse still had been Aunt Sophronia's instructions for the best methods for achieving male offspring.

"Could there be anything less romantic than Aunt Sophronia's advice?" Charlotte said sympathetically. "To hear her explain things, it's a wonder any wedded couple continues together."

Lizzie wrinkled her nose with distaste. "All I could think of was the village bull brought to cover the poor cows every autumn."

"Well, yes," Charlotte said, blushing. She flicked open her fan, fluttering it furiously before her face. "But for lack of any other words, I listened too closely to what Aunt Sophronia said, and in the beginning March and I suffered greatly for it. I would not have you make the same mistakes, Lizzie."

"That won't happen with Hawke," Lizzie said quickly, now blushing, too. She didn't want to hear any of Charlotte's bedchamber confessions about her and March, and she certainly wasn't about to volunteer any about Hawke. "He wouldn't pay any heed to Aunt Sophronia, not when he calls her a harpy."

Lizzie hoped the mention of harpies would be enough to distract Charlotte from her present uncomfortable topic.

Alas, it wasn't. "For all that they are cousins, Hawke seems to be a much different gentleman from March in matters of, ah, worldly experience," she said earnestly.

"Perhaps then my cautions are unnecessary. Perhaps you and he have already—"

"I must go, Charlotte," Lizzie said abruptly, turning away. "I've kept Hawke waiting long enough."

But Charlotte caught her lightly by the arm before she could escape.

"Love him, little sister," she said softly. "Love him, and let him love you. That's all I shall say. You needn't please anyone else but each other. Remember that, and you will be happy."

Sudden tears clouded Lizzie's eyes, and she hugged Charlotte close. She knew she'd follow Charlotte's advice and love Hawke, because she was nearly in love with him already. But she couldn't begin to guess if he held the same feelings for her, or if he ever would. All at once she felt woefully inexperienced, as if she were blindfolded and plunging into a deep pool of uncertainty without the swimming strokes to save herself, and she clung more tightly to Charlotte. Married to cousins, they would likely never be far apart physically, but Lizzie sensed that things could not be quite the same between them again. Lizzie's closest allegiances must now be to her husband and her new family, not her old one, a somber, sober realization for any bride.

"No red noses," Lizzie said, finally stepping back with a monumental sniff. "That was what Mama told me this morning. Red noses do not become the Wylder women."

Charlotte laughed, or at least tried to.

"No truer words were ever spoken," she said, looping her arm through Lizzie's. "Now come, I must give you over to your husband the duke. Your *husband*, Lizzie! La, how we often feared I'd never say those words!"

Everything happened very fast after that. They returned to the drawing room, where the others were still gathered, with every face turning their way when they returned, and a smattering of applause in Lizzie's honor as well. But there was no applause from the older ladies, who made it clear that they thought Lizzie should not have come down with her hair loose.

"Elizabeth, please," Aunt Sophronia said, so irritated that she forgot to address her as the new duchess she was. "Pray return upstairs until you are properly prepared for company."

"I know your new lady maid's already on her way to Hawkesworth Chase, Lizzie," March said, more conciliatory, "but surely Charlotte's could help you with your hair."

"My wife's hair requires no help, March," Hawke said, coming forward to take Lizzie's hands. "It is absolutely beautiful as it is, and absolutely as I like it best."

He smiled and kissed her. "You can't know how pleased I am," he whispered to her. "My own beautiful Lizzie! You remembered, and you did this for me."

Lizzie grinned. "Of course I remembered," she whispered back. "Though I do believe Aunt Sophronia would have my head if she could."

"The harpy will never hold sway over you again," he said, and winked slyly. "You're my wife now, and you needn't heed anyone else."

He turned toward the rest of the room, smiling with a grand wave of his hand.

"Dear friends and family," he announced. "My wife and I thank you all for your kindness and hospitality. Now we must leave you and begin our life together. *Auguri e addio*—good wishes and farewell!"

With his hand firmly clasped in Lizzie's, he led her from the room and into the hall, striding so briskly toward the door that she had to skip along to keep pace.

"That is all?" she said breathlessly. "The sum of your farewell? Hawke, I did not say good-bye to my mother, or my sisters, or—"

"You've had all afternoon to bid them good-bye," he

said without stopping, hurrying her down the steps and to the waiting carriage. "No, you've had your entire *life*. Now you're my wife. You don't belong to them any longer. You're mine, not theirs."

He handed her up the carriage's folding steps, and at the top she turned and looked past him back at her sister's house. There was a light breeze, the kind that often rises at the end of the day, making the white ribbons tied to the carriage ripple and dance, and her hair stream over her face. Dusk was just beginning to fall, and the lanterns on either side of the portico had been lit for the night. But the footmen had closed the door after her and Hawke, and though the first candles flickered within the windows, this time she saw no figures at the windows, and not one of her sisters or mother standing behind the curtains to wave a final time to her.

It wasn't that they didn't love her any longer, but that they understood that her life had changed. She had a world of new responsibilities, a household and staff to manage, a station to maintain for her husband as well as herself, children to bear and nurture. Most of all, after a life of not answering to much of anyone, she now, by the laws of church, kingdom, and custom, must oblige and obey every wish of the gentleman standing before her. She'd had months to accept the idea of her marriage and weeks to accustom herself to Hawke, but the reality of it all was suddenly hitting her very hard.

"Lizzie," he said. "What is wrong?"

She looked down at him, standing there below her. In the fading light, his handsome face was sharply angular, his eyes and hair as dark as the coming night. He looked older, harder, faintly dangerous, and much less patient.

"What is wrong?" he asked again.

"I don't know you," she said bluntly. "Not at all."

He sighed. "I don't know you, either, sweeting. But

after tonight I expect we'll both know each other a good deal better."

If that was supposed to comfort her, it didn't. She climbed into the carriage, settling in the far corner.

"I'm sorry, Hawke," she said, feeling oddly helpless. "I'm sorry."

"You've not one thing to be sorry for." He climbed in beside her, not pressing too close, but not keeping apart, either. The footman closed and latched the door, and immediately the carriage began to draw away from the house.

"I don't know what the devil the harpies told you your wedding night with me will be like," he continued, "but it's wrong, every word of it."

"They didn't tell me any words, wrong or right," she said, more wistfully than she wished. The carriage pulled through the open gate, and she resisted turning back for a last glimpse of the house. "They think you've already— already—"

"Ravished you?" he said dryly. "Well, we both know I haven't. Not yet."

She looked down at her hand in her lap and at the heavy new ring, the ruby gathering what little light remained in the carriage like a red flame of its own. There was no earthly reason for her to feel like this, or a way to explain her sudden apprehension, either. It wasn't as if Hawke were some dreadful monster of a husband, or old or infirm or even poxy. Far from it. Earlier this same day she'd been so overwhelmed with desire that she'd behaved quite shamelessly with him in the church. Truly, she couldn't have imagined a more agreeable gentleman to wed. And hadn't every other woman in her family not only survived but prospered in arranged marriages?

"I am your wife, Hawke," she said, still looking down at her wedding ring. "I will be brave, and I won't fear the challenges before me."

"Bravery!" he exclaimed. "My God, Lizzie, I trust that you won't need a huge supply of that to face lying with me."

"I don't know if I will or not," she said. "I've never had to lie with you before."

"My dear, darling duchess," he said, slipping his arm across the back of the carriage seat, and incidentally across her shoulders as well. "I know I'm now your husband, and that I have all manner of medieval rights over your person as well as your fortune. But I will give you my word as a gentleman that I'll never hurt you, or force you, or expect you to do anything against your will. Does that give you the courage you seem to require?"

"Thank you," she said softly, leaning back against his arm. "I couldn't wish for more from a husband."

"Hush now, hush," he said, lightly crossing her lips with his finger. "We'll have no more of that 'husband' talk between us, not just yet. Think of me first as the man who would please you."

She frowned, uncertain. "But you please me already as my husband."

"That's a start, I suppose," he said, sliding closer to her, close enough that she could smell the faint spiciness of his shaving soap. "But I don't mean pleasing as agreeable. A well-buttered slice of toast is pleasing."

"I have never thought of you as a slice of toast, Hawke." The carriage seemed much more intimate and cozy in the dusk. The only light came as they passed the occasional lantern on the street, the brightness slashing briefly across his face. "Not once."

"How gratifying." His voice was low and confidential, as if he were telling her the most delicious secret in the world. Which, indeed, he might be. "When I please you, sweeting, I'll pleasure you, too, as a lover should, and as you deserve."

"As a lover?" she repeated, a little mystified, her own voice dropping to a whisper. She'd always thought a lover was very different from a husband. A lover was wicked and illicit, while a husband was, well, a husband. How the two could be combined was a puzzle that perplexed her, and worried her, too, as not being entirely respectable.

But then he was kissing her, and she realized how relieved she was that he was, finally, doing that. She forgot about respectability and pleasures and other uxorial puzzles, and instead slipped her arms around his shoulders and kissed him more.

In fact, she simply stopped thinking at all, giving herself over to her senses rather than her brain: the teasing feel of his tongue against hers, the taste of his mouth, still ripe with the champagne and brandy—a great deal of brandy, if March and Brecon had had their way—with which he'd drunk to their happiness, the slight bristle of his long-ago-shaven upper lip against hers.

He drew her closer so that she settled more comfortably into his arm and shoulder, as if she'd always belonged there, and her earlier anxieties began to fade. He deepened the kiss, making her blood quicken and warm. If this was pleasing, or pleasuring, or whatever he chose to call it, then she *was* pleased, supremely so. When he slipped his hand beneath her kerchief and into her bodice, she arched to meet him, shamelessly pressing her breast against his hand. Her nipple was already hard, eager for more of his touch, and his small male grunt of appreciation when he discovered it made her laugh softly.

Oh, yes, she was pleased.

"That's my Lizzie," he said, gently tugging and rubbing her breast with delicious results. "My own wicked lass."

She was just beginning to tell him that he was far more

wicked than she would ever be when the carriage suddenly stopped. She frowned, turning to look from the window. They couldn't possibly be at Hawkesworth Chase, not yet.

"Why have we stopped?" she asked, sitting upright and pulling her bodice back over her breast. One thing she'd learned with Hawke was to be prepared for overeager footmen to throw open carriage doors. She ducked to peek from the window, searching for a landmark. "Where are we, Hawke?"

"The place where we're meant to be," he said, and smiled knowingly.

"I have heard that before," she said, giving his arm a small shove as the footman came to open the door. "Tell me honestly, Hawke. Where are we?"

"The Whitehall Steps," he said, as if there could be no other reply. "It's such a fair night, I thought we'd make the rest of our journey by water."

He climbed down and offered her his hand to follow. He wasn't jesting: the carriage was standing before the Whitehall Steps, one of the steep stone stairways that led to the edge of the Thames. Lizzie had never gone on the river, as much as she'd longed to. Charlotte didn't trust the low, narrow wherries for hire that served as waterbound hackneys or the watermen that rowed them, and insisted they always travel by carriage instead.

"Are we going by wherry, Hawke?" Lizzie asked excitedly, trying to see past the steps' stone walls to the landing. "I've always wanted to, you know, but Charlotte said they're not proper for ladies."

"They're not," Hawke said. "Which is why I've arranged something more suitable for you."

With a footman holding a lantern to light their way, Hawke led Lizzie down the steps, keeping her hand tucked into the crook of his arm. She was expecting that he'd hired a more substantial waterman's boat, making sure they'd be the only passengers for the night, but what she saw when they turned the corner made her halt and gasp with amazement.

On the water at the bottom of the steps waited a lavish pleasure barge, lit with hanging lanterns that showed off its gilded, carved woodwork and red-and-black-painted sides. Eight oarsmen and a coxswain dressed in matching white jumpers, black hats, and red scarves around their throats sat ready on their benches aft. To the fore was a small canopied area, hung with striped curtains and furnished with wide cushioned benches and a small table for dining. A servant in gaudy livery that matched the oarsmen's waited beside a large hamper of food and wines. The prow sloped up into a bare-breasted mermaid, much like the figurehead on a grander ship, with another broad bench piled with cushions and coverlets directly behind her. Pennants fluttered from the flagstaffs, and more bridal-white ribbon rosettes, similar to the ones decorating the carriage, had been added to the canopy and to the gilded mermaid herself. The barge was so elegant, so fanciful, so utterly unexpected, that for a long moment Lizzie could do nothing but stare.

"Might I assume that I have surprised you?" Hawke said, enjoying her reaction.

"Of course you have," she exclaimed, "which you know perfectly, perfectly well. Where did you find such a vessel?"

"I have loan of it from a friend with tastes as florid as mine," he said. "It's not quite the Venetian gondola I would have preferred, but it will do well enough to convey us to the Chase. We have our own river stairs, you know, left from the old king's convenience."

"Truly?" She skipped down the last steps with excitement, not waiting for him to follow. "La, Hawke, it looks more fit for royalty than for me."

"But you are my goddess, Lizzie," he said grandly, "which makes you superior to mere royalty. Here, let me help you aboard."

She took his hand because he offered it, not because she needed his support, and deftly scrambled aboard the barge. As she did, the oarsmen tipped their oars straight upward in salute, sending a shower of droplets that caught the lanterns' light like falling diamonds. She laughed with delight and applauded as they pushed off from the shore. With her skirts dancing around her legs, she made her way up to the prow, her arms held out for balance on the moving boat, but still walking with ease.

"Come now, Lizzie, there must be no secrets between us," Hawke said as he joined her. He'd left his hat with the servant, and the breeze from the water had already begun to toss his dark hair around his face. "I was told you were an earl's daughter, but I vow there must be some of Sailor Jack's blood in you somewhere as well."

Laughing, she leaned against the curved back of the mermaid, bracing herself against the boat's movement. Her unbound hair streamed around her, tangling in the breeze, and the delicate silk of her skirts fluttered restlessly around her ankles.

"I don't know if I've any of Sailor Jack's blood," she said, "but our house in Dorset is near the sea, and as a girl I was on the beach and in the waves most days, no matter the weather. I could go aft and row one of those oars quite handsomely myself, you know."

"No!" he said, pretending to be shocked. "A lady with an oar in her hand?"

"I vow I could, Hawke," she declared eagerly, sounding as though she wished he would test her. "Mama swears I'm half fish, and she may be right. Next time we'll take a two-seat wherry onto the river, and I'll show you how well I can handle a boat."

"A two-seat wherry!" he marveled. "I am in complete and utter awe, Duchess. How was I to know you were such a wonder?"

Yet there was something in the way he said it, some faint little twitch to his lips, that betrayed the truth.

"Because I *told* you before, didn't I?" she said, striving to sound as indignant as he had pretended to be shocked. "You needn't be in awe of any sort, considering I told you before how much I loved the water."

"You did?" he said, smiling and forgetting to be shocked.

"I did," she said, likewise putting aside her show of indignation. "I told you all about it, and that is why you've hired this barge for me tonight, isn't it?"

"Or it could be simply because this is a much more pleasant way to travel from March's house to mine," he said, teasing still. He slipped his hand beneath the curtain of her hair to rest his palm lightly on the small of her back, a small, protective gesture that somehow seemed far more intimate than if he'd embraced her out-right. "You must agree with that."

"Oh, I do," Lizzie said. "There's much less dust as well."

That made him laugh, and Lizzie grinned, too. This was a more pleasant way to travel than through the city streets, true, but it was also vastly more romantic. The water around them was dark, reflecting both the moon and the stars and their own lanterns as they glided over its shimmering surface. Having so large a crew of oars-men meant that their passage was effortlessly smooth, and given the hour, there were few other vessels to crowd their way. The daytime boats filled with wares to be sold or men on their business had been replaced by wherries filled with men and women traveling for pleasure, from one amusement to another. There were a few other barges on the water, too, and though none was so grand as theirs, some of these had musicians aboard, and the sounds of strings and flutes along with merry-making and laughter drifted over the water to them.

"Everything looks different from the river," she said. "But there's the block of Westminster Abbey, and over there's the rounded dome of St. Paul's."

"Do you see those four spindly towers?" Hawke said, pointing over her shoulder. The servant had brought them wine, and Hawke handed her one of the cut-crystal tumblers. "That's the old queen's footstool."

"The what?" she asked, sipping the sweet canary as she looked to where he was pointing. Drinking wine with him in the prow of a pleasure barge by moonlight made her feel wonderfully worldly, like a true London lady.

"Queen Anne's footstool," he said. "St. John's Smith Square. The story's that when the royal architect asked Her Majesty what she fancied in a new church, she kicked over her footstool so that the legs stuck upward, and said 'Like that.' Which is why it has the four towers, one for each leg of the footstool."

She laughed, watching him over the rim of her glass. "I should not believe you."

He shrugged. "Believe me or not, I vow it's the truth. Now there, right before us, is the new Westminster Bridge. They were still building it when I first left for Italy, and now no one can recall when it wasn't here. Are you ready to shoot the arches?"

"You mean we'll go beneath them?" she asked with surprise. She'd assumed they'd turn about, not go through the bridge's stone arches. "Can we do that?"

"If we wish to reach the water gate to my house, we must," he said. "The current runs brisk and eddies a bit, that is all."

He set down his glass and shrugged off his coat.

"Here," he said, settling it around her shoulders. "There's likely to be spray, and I want you to be warm."

She clutched the two sides of his coat together to keep it from sliding away. It was heavy on her shoulders, still warm from his body and smelling of him, too. She liked how the weight of it made her feel snug and looked after, as if he were shielding her himself.

"Won't you be cold?" she asked, being solicitous in return. He didn't look particularly cold, standing there with the full sleeves of his shirt billowing around his arms, the white linen luminous in the moonlight. His waistcoat was tailored to perfection, fitting close to display the breadth of his chest and the narrowness of his waist, and everything covered in that exotic leopard pattern, the silver and gold threads winking. She'd never seen a gentleman's waistcoat quite like it. He looked outright piratical, with his dark hair wild and half untied from its queue. "Though I suppose you've that leopard waistcoat to keep you warm."

He smiled. Faith, he was so beautiful, his jaw and cheekbones hard and strong by the swinging lantern's light, his mouth full and sensual in a way that made her long to kiss him.

"You like the waistcoat, then," he said. "You won't find another like it in London. I chose it today particularly for you."

"I do," she said, and she did. It was very much like him, as elegant yet as dangerous as a leopard himself, and it pleased her to think that that was how he wished to show himself to her.

"It horrified Brecon," he said, "making it an utter success, as clothing goes."

"A duke can set the fashions," she said, paraphrasing his own words back to him, "and not be bound to follow any others."

"Then we'll be wild creatures together, sweeting, and the respectable world be damned," he said, his smile wicked. "Here now, take care, under we go!"

He'd warned her, but she still wasn't prepared for the swiftness of the current beneath the bridge. The barge jumped forward and the deck beneath her feet lurched, making her grab at Hawke's arm for support. Glistening with damp, the large square stones of the arch flew by overhead, and spray rained all around them, kicked up by the rapids. Her own startled cry echoed back to her, hollow and unearthly, and then, like that, they were on the other side.

"Oh, Hawke," she said breathless with exhilaration. She swiped the spray from her face, chuckling with delight. "That was wonderful, and mysterious, and *perfect*!"

"I knew you would like it," he said, slipping his hands inside the coat to find her. "You're every bit as wild as I, aren't you?"

Instinctively she'd widened her stance to brace herself against the rocking deck, and now Hawke took advantage of her posture to lean between her splayed legs. He pressed her back against the wooden mermaid, crushing her skirts and making her acutely aware of his size and strength—and aware, too, of how at least part of him wasn't cold in the least. He pressed hard against that place between her legs that seemed to tremble and swell in sympathy even through their clothes, and as he rocked against her, she fell into rhythm with him and the rush of the water and the rise and fall of the oars.

She forgot to be offended, as an English peeress must surely be. Instead her excitement only grew, as if his cock and the dark river and the flying spray were all part of a different, separate world from the London she'd always known. In this one evening, he'd made her forget all the careful training she'd had from Aunt Sophronia and Charlotte. He'd freed the untamed, impetuous girl she was supposed to have left behind in Dorset, the girl who ran barefoot across the sand with her skirts held high around her knees and didn't care who saw her.

"I *am* wild, Hawke," she whispered, surprising herself with her ferocity. "Because of you, because of this night, and I—I thank you for everything. Not just the pleasure barge, but remembering about how I liked the water and—and—"

"I remember everything about you, Lizzie," he said, his voice becoming so low it was almost a growl. His hands were gliding up and down her sides over her breasts, never stopping. "Just as you remembered to wear your hair down for me."

Her heart was racing now, knowing he was about to kiss her. "Charlotte said I shouldn't have left it down until we were alone, that it should have been a sight reserved for you as my husband."

"But I see no other when you are with me," he said. "You blind me to everyone and everything, Lizzie. You are my world, my own."

He kissed her then with hungry possession, and she kissed him in return, every bit as greedy for his taste. He broke away to kiss her throat, small, nipping kisses that made her gasp and shiver even as his stubbled cheek and damp hair brushed against her skin. She didn't really know what it was she desired so intensely, yet still she clung to his shoulders as she arched and rolled against him with abandon.

When he pulled down the front of her bodice, baring her breasts, she again felt nothing but the inevitability of it. Her nipples tightened at once in the cool air, only to be warmed as his tongue laved over them, sucking and biting gently at the tender flesh until she whimpered with longing. She tried to flip her hair from her face and breasts, clinging to her skin in sodden tendrils, and randomly she thought of how she must look the figurehead's twin, a mermaid of flesh and blood to mirror the one of gilded wood. Truly she was a mermaid bewitched by her lover's touch, and she'd no wish to be released from his spell.

"Hawkesworth!" The man's voice was well-bred, raucous, thick with expensive liquor as it echoed across the water. "Hellfire, Hawke, is that you with some damned randy wench?"

And just like that, the spell was broken.

CHAPTER

❧ *12* ❧

Hawke jerked upright, shielding Lizzie. He knew that voice, drunk or sober: Sir Richard Avant, baronet. While they'd ostensibly been at school, he and Avant had shared enough misdeeds and mischief to entertain a whole regiment, and he'd never forget that braying voice.

But not here, not now. And definitely not directed at Lizzie.

He could just make out the wherry with a gentleman beside the waterman, straining to keep pace with them. The barge was already leaving the other vessel behind, the distance between them growing with every second. As it was, he could scarcely see their shadow any longer. He could have ignored Avant entirely and pretended he hadn't heard him. Likely Avant was so drunk that he'd forget he'd seen Hawke, let alone Lizzie.

And yet because it was Lizzie—and because Hawke had been drinking, too, as well as having been unceremoniously interrupted from the most enjoyable seduction of his life—he could not keep quiet.

"Shut your mouth, Avant, you drunken whoreson," he roared across the water. "The lady's not one of your posed wenches, but my goddess, mind? My goddess!"

Avant did not reply, at least not that Hawke could hear. But from another boat came a loud huzzah of approval, and someone else applauded. Satisfied, even vindicated, he turned back to Lizzie.

She wasn't leaning against the mermaid any longer, and after a split second's concern, he found her, huddled on the deck. With his coat draped over her shoulders like a tent, she sat with her arms wrapped around her bent knees and her skirts pulled tightly over them, her face hidden by the damp tangle of her hair. She had also pulled her bodice back in place, which, though regrettable, was probably for the best.

At once remorse swept through him, and he quickly crouched down before her.

"Lizzie," he said softly, smoothing her hair from her forehead. "Are you well?"

Swiftly she looked up. "Of course I am well. I only wished to not be in your way, that was all. Do you know that man?"

"I regret to admit that I do," he said contritely. "Or I did."

"That low, despicable rogue," she said with a fury he hadn't expected. "That vile, disgusting *worm*! He is no gentleman, that is certain."

"No," Hawke agreed, resolving never to give her any reason to call him names. "He's only a baronet. He'd no right to address me so familiarly, not without my leave."

"But what he said of *me*, Hawke!" she said. "I will never forgive him. That is, I will never meet him to be able to forgive him. Is he gone now? Did he flee like the liverish coward he must be?"

"Gone," Hawke said. "Lizzie, I'm sorry that—"

"No!" she said fiercely, throwing her arms around his shoulders. "You have nothing to apologize for, Hawke, nothing! You told him exactly what needed to be said, the filthy rascal, and—and—no one has ever, ever defended me like that!"

She kissed him again, most enthusiastically, leaving

him no choice but to kiss her in return. He'd never been a hero to a woman like this before. He didn't think he'd done anything particularly heroic, considering that no dragons had been slain or maidens rescued. All he'd done was shout insults across the water. But he discovered he liked it—being heroic in Lizzie's eyes, that is, not hurling insults—and he liked even more how it seemed to fan her passions all over again. In fact, from the way she was kissing him, he was guessing she wouldn't mind if he shifted her onto one of the benches and took her here, now, in the barge and under the moonlight, her spread thighs pale against those plump red cushions and—

Damnation, what was he thinking? Here he'd planned this as a romantic little cruise on the Thames to put her at ease, and yet once again his careful planning had been torn to shreds and tossed aside by Lizzie and his own raging cock, surely the most willful pairing in creation.

How the devil was he supposed to woo her like a lady, the way he'd promised, when there was nothing ladylike about her response? How could he possibly conduct a measured, refined seduction when she insisted on plunging on ahead and being so charmingly, wickedly irresistible?

It was just as well they were nearly to the house.

The old brick-and-stone water gate at the end of the garden loomed before them, with servants with lanterns waiting with boat hooks to help draw the barge alongside the landing. He sensed that Lizzie was ready to leap ashore ahead of him—he'd only to recall how she'd raced down the aisle earlier today—and he kept a firm grip on her arm. The last thing he wished was to have to chase her through the garden in the dark.

But to his surprise, she paused on the landing to gaze up at the mossy coat of arms carved into the keystone of the water gate's arch.

"Those are the Hawkesworth arms, aren't they?" she asked. "And now they're mine as much as yours?"

"They are," he said, though somehow he'd nearly forgotten that she was his wife and the Duchess of Hawkesworth. "Or they will be in the morning."

"In the morning," she repeated, glancing slyly up at him. "Faith, I'd never thought we'd have to wait until then."

That was all the encouragement he needed. Swiftly he hurried her through the garden, a footman with a lantern trotting before them. In his haste, he didn't bother with going around to the grand door at the front of the house, but chose the library door instead because it was closer. He shooed away the footman with the lantern because he wanted to kiss Lizzie again without her becoming self-conscious about an audience.

But of course there were no candles lit in the library, not at this hour, making him feel like a thief in his own house. He stumbled over a table in the darkened library and swore, and Lizzie laughed, which made her easy to find in the dark, and easier still to kiss again. His only thought now was to get her to his bed—his soft, comfortable, familiar bed, where he was equally at home in the dark or not—but when she climbed the stairs ahead of him, he'd such a splendid hint of the shape of her bottom through her skirts that he had to stop on the landing to kiss her again, and fondle that bottom as well.

"My bedchamber," he said in between the kisses. "It's closer."

"I'll have to send for my maid to help me undress," she said breathlessly as he half carried her up the last few steps and down the hall. "I can't—"

"I'll undress you," he said, and shoved open the last door, the door to his bedchamber.

His bedchamber.

Lizzie had never seen a gentleman's bedchamber before. Having a childhood with neither a father nor brothers as examples, she had vaguely imagined a gentleman's rooms as some kind of male lair, full of dark, forbidden male secrets and mysteries. Instead Hawke's bedchamber looked much like any other in a large house, though it was literally very dark and old-fashioned, with heavy paneling, carved to resemble draped cloth, that was nearly black. The bed seemed enormous, with carved posts as thick as tree trunks and an overhanging canopy, and when she thought of how soon she'd be lying in it with him, she flushed and looked swiftly away. There were more pictures than in ordinary rooms, not only hanging on the walls but also propped along the mantelpiece and on top of tables; knowing Hawke, that was entirely to be expected.

What she hadn't expected, though, was to find his Italian manservant, Giacomo, standing patiently beside the fireplace. He looked as if he'd been there all day, waiting. Perhaps he had.

"Your Grace," he murmured, bowing as soon as they entered. "Your Grace. *Le mie congratulazioni più rispettoso.*"

It took Lizzie a moment to realize that Giacomo wasn't simply being redundant and that the second "Your Grace" had been for her. The rest she couldn't begin to decipher.

"What did he say, Hawke?" she whispered, hanging behind him. She'd encountered Giacomo only once before, but that time as well she'd been bedraggled. Charlotte's warning about making a good impression as a mistress to her new staff was ringing soundly in her conscience, and when she glimpsed her reflection in the looking glass over the mantelpiece—her unbound hair matted and tangled, her kerchief missing, her once lovely blue silk gown now ruined from the river spray and the dirt from the garden—she realized how completely she'd failed.

"He wished us most respectful congratulations, that is all," Hawke said. "Thank you, Giacomo, but I've no need of you tonight. You may go."

Giacomo nodded, but added an eloquent gesture of dismay. "Shall I send for the maid of Her Grace, sir?"

"No," Hawke said. "Liz—ah, Her Grace wants nothing more, nor do I, except for you to leave us. Now."

Giacomo bowed again and backed from the room, closing the door with practiced silence.

Lizzie groaned. "Oh, Hawke, I've made such a wretched, horrid beginning with your servants! What Giacomo must think of me—"

"He shouldn't be thinking of you at all," Hawke said, unbuttoning the long row of buttons on his waistcoat. He was undressing as casually as if they'd been wed for years, not hours, tossing the embroidered waistcoat carelessly across a nearby table as he sat in a high-backed armchair to unbuckle his shoes. "Though because Giacomo is a man and an Italian man at that, he is likely beguiled by you already. As am I."

"But you are my husband," Lizzie protested.

"And your lover," he said. "Mind, I must be that first."

"My lover, then," she said. "Either way, I should hope you *are* besotted with me."

He'd pulled off his stockings and dropped them to the carpet, and now had turned to unbuckling his breeches at the knee. She couldn't recall seeing a gentleman's bare feet and calves before, large and bony and muscular and . . . hairy. She hadn't known that gentlemen had hair on their legs, and it was oddly embarrassing and intimate and arousing at the same time.

Faith, if she felt like this about his *feet*, what would

happen when he uncovered other, less ordinary parts of his person?

"I told you I was," he said, pulling his neckcloth free of his shirt. "You're remarkably easy to become beguiled by. Or is that with? No matter. Can you truly not undress yourself?"

She blushed. "Of course I can."

Quickly she began pulling out the pins that held the front of her gown to her stomacher. He was watching her, watching her closely. She knew it without looking back, and that knowledge made her fingers unsteady. From long habit without her own lady's maid, she carefully stuck the pins back into the edge of the gown, ready for the next wearing. At once she realized what a frugal, housewifely thing this was to do, with none of the seductive carelessness of a duchess.

She didn't dare look his way, afraid she'd see disappointment on his face.

But what could she do? All the confidence she'd felt on the river, when she'd pretended to be a mermaid, had vanished. She'd no idea of how to undress herself seductively for her husband, and so with a racing heart she simply did it as she always had, shrugging her arms free of the gown, unpinning her stomacher, then untying her petticoats and her hoops. She let it all drop to the floor in a puddle of cloth and cane around her feet, then stepped clear. She bent as gracefully as she could, meaning to gather everything up to later take to her own rooms.

"Stop," he said, his voice gruff. "Leave it."

Startled, she looked up. He was leaning forward in the chair as he watched her. He'd a half smile on his face, and his eyes were heavy-lidded, so intent on her body that she blushed again. She hadn't much left to cover her: her stays, covered in apple-green silk brocade, her Holland linen shift, white stockings, garters, and shoes.

"Your legs are even more handsome than I remember from when you climbed that infernal wall," he said, his gaze not leaving them. "What color are your garters?"

"Blue," she said softly. "Blue silk, embroidered with forget-me-nots."

"Forget-me-nots," he repeated. "As if I'd ever forget anything about you, sweeting. Raise your shift and show them to me."

It seemed an odd request. But then she remembered how she'd felt when he'd first pulled off his stockings; perhaps it would be the same for him to see her garters. She took the hem of her shift and lifted it slowly up above her knees so that he could see not only her garters but the pale skin of her thighs above them.

He didn't blink, but he swallowed, swallowed hard: a sure sign that she'd had a powerful effect upon him. So she'd guessed right. He was intrigued, even fascinated, and she felt her earlier confidence returning.

"I should take off my shoes," she said, almost apologetically. "I fear they're ruined."

"I'll buy you more," he said. "As many as you like."

"Thank you," she said, lowering her voice as if that were a confidence. "You are most . . . most generous."

She perched on the edge of his armchair's footstool, before him but just beyond his reach, crossing one leg at the knee to reach the buckle on her shoe. She took much longer than was really necessary, letting him see her garters again and a good deal more besides as she let each shoe drop to the floor with the same nonchalance that he'd shown with his own clothes.

This time while he watched her, he suddenly rubbed his fingers along the inside of his shirt's collar, as if it had grown too tight. She smiled, thinking that perhaps this business of undressing for one's husband was much easier than she'd imagined.

Much easier, and much, much more enjoyable. She

felt warm all over from his watching alone, almost as much as if he were caressing her.

"Now your stays," he said, his voice rumbling low. "Take them off."

She rose from the footstool, reaching around to the back of her stays. This wasn't going to be as easy, or as graceful, either. Her stays laced down the back and had been pulled tight and knotted by Charlotte's maid this morning. The stays were new, the most stylish pair she'd ever owned, and heavily boned in the French fashion to make the best of her figure. But because they were new, they were also still stiff and even more unyielding, and the more she fumbled with the back laces through her tangled hair, the more flushed and flustered she became.

"I told you I'd help you," he said, standing.

"You needn't." She scuttled backward. "I almost have the knot."

"No, you don't." Impatiently he yanked his shirt free from his breeches and pulled it over his head, dropping it to the floor.

She gasped, stunned by the sight of him. His chest and shoulders were broader and more muscular than she'd realized, narrowing to lean hips. She should have known he'd be this strong, considering how easily he carried her about, but still it surprised her, and made her heart beat faster, too. How could it not? More dark hair whorled over the broad planes of his chest, narrowing to a trail that disappeared into his low-slung breeches. Preserve her, his *breeches*: they were all that covered him now, and there was no mistaking the degree of his arousal—an arousal that she had inspired. Behind that neatly buttoned fall, the shape of his hard cock was undeniable.

And suddenly this flirtatious game of theirs seemed a great deal more urgent.

"I'll have this undone in a moment," he said, coming

to stand behind her. He flipped her hair forward, out of his way, and bent over the knot. He was as good as his word: almost at once the knot gave way and the tension released on her stays.

"How did you do that?" she asked breathlessly. "I thought only lady's maids and stay makers knew the secret of that knot."

"And me," he said, snapping the lace through the eyelets. "You'd be astonished by the secrets I know."

She wouldn't, not at all, and as the silver aglet popped through the last eyelet, the weight of the now-free stays made them slip forward. She caught them, holding them close to her breasts, and as she did, she felt his lips brush over the nape of her neck. She caught her breath and tipped her head back, never knowing that could be such a wonderfully sensitive spot.

"I have wanted you since I first saw you," he whispered, each word hot on her already feverish skin as he slipped his hands inside the now-loose stays to find her breasts, now covered only with the thinnest of linen. He filled his hands with the tender flesh, gently tugging and drawing on her nipples with his thumbs. "At the playhouse, across from me."

"You—you didn't even know who I was," she stammered, amazed she could speak. Her legs swayed weakly beneath her, letting him support her, and that place between her legs felt full and wet, yearning for him.

"That didn't matter," he said, his voice no more than a growl as his hands on her breasts became more insistent, more demanding. "I wanted you then, and damnation, I want you now."

"I want you, too, Hawke," she whispered, shocking herself with her own boldness. She dropped the stays and instinctively pushed back against him, pressing her bottom against his cock, still barely covered by his breeches. "I want you, and—and—everything else."

He grunted and turned her around toward him, every muscle on his face taut.

"You can't do that to me, sweeting," he said, "else I'll be finished before we start."

She wasn't sure what that meant, but she figured kissing him—which was what she'd rather do than talk anyway—would be as good a reply as any. She looped her arms around his shoulders and arched up toward him, offering her lips to him, the same as they'd often done before.

But this time he wanted more than her lips. He slipped lower and tucked his arm beneath her knees, effortlessly gathering her up and carrying her across the room to the bed. With his free hand he tore back the coverlet and dropped her crossways on the bed with her legs dangling over the edge. She started to pull herself backward over the featherbed, but before she could, he'd shoved her shift up to her waist. He hooked her knees over his crooked arms, drawing her back to the edge as he knelt beside the bed.

"What are you doing?" she asked frantically—no, begged, for she truly had no explanation. No one, not even Charlotte, had mentioned this possibility. She propped herself on her elbows to look at him, crouching there wickedly between her spread thighs. She felt exposed and ashamed, fearing that he'd see how wet and swollen she must be. "Hawke, please, don't—"

"Hush," he said softly, his dark hair tousled and his dark eyes glinting like the devil himself. "You must trust me, my Lizzie. You nearly unmanned me, so it seems only fair that I do the same to you."

Before she could answer, he'd lowered his head between her legs, and to her shock he began *kissing* her there. She cried out and again tried to pull away, but he held her fast. He was lapping and licking and teasing her, and to her even greater wonder, she began to like it.

Truly, she must have the soul of a slattern to enjoy such a practice, and yet the more she wriggled, the more delicious it felt, until she realized that she wasn't fighting him so much as moving with him, digging her heels into the bed and arching her hips to meet him.

She clutched at the sheets, twisting them into knots, and made small cries of delight as the pleasurable tension grew within her. When he slipped a finger inside her, she scarcely noticed, and when he added another, gently stretching and stroking her from within, she truly thought it possible to expire with pleasure. One final swipe of his tongue, and she felt as if she'd burst, waves and waves of delight racking her body as she cried his name.

"You liked that," he said, rising over her as she lay spent and panting on the bed.

"I did, my love," she murmured, reaching up to touch his cheek. "How can I thank you?"

"You can't, not yet." He kissed her quickly, leaving the taste of her own honey-sweet juices on her lips. If she felt limp and sated, her bones turned to jelly, then his face was tense with concentration. "We've scarce begun to please ourselves."

Languid, she watched him stand and tear away at the buttons on his breeches, shoving them quickly down his hips. She'd only the briefest glimpse of the cock she'd been teasing all evening—larger, longer, harder than she'd imagined, rising proudly from its nest of black curls. Then suddenly he was between her legs again, nudging her open, pressing into her, pushing that hard length of himself into her passage. His thrusts were quick and forceful, and the gasps she made now weren't of pleasure. Finally he was buried in her as far as he could go, and he lay still, resting his head on her shoulder. She felt crushed and pressed down and full, too full, and all that lovely languid feeling had vanished.

But she was now his wife in every way. They'd—what was the word that Aunt Sophronia had always used?—they'd *consummated* their marriage. She only wished now that this were as pleasing as the first part had been.

He raised his head from her shoulder and kissed her lightly, brushing his lips over hers.

"My own dear Lizzie," he said in a rough whisper. "I am sorry for that. But you only give up your maidenhead once, and I swear to you it will only improve."

She did not believe him, and so she said nothing. Tentatively she rested her hands on his back, and shifted her legs to try to find a more comfortable way to bear his weight.

He groaned, breathing hard, as if he, too, were feeling the same discomfort. "Damnation, but you're tight, even after you spent," he said, his teeth gritted. "No doubt that you were a virgin."

"Blast you, Hawke," she shot back bitterly. "There should never have been any doubt."

"Forgive me." He sucked in his breath, collecting himself. He raised himself up a bit, drawing out a fraction to move back in, then changed the angle a bit, and slid into her again.

She gasped again, with surprise. Who would have guessed her body could accept him like this? She shifted her legs and tipped her hips, taking him deeper. It was as if he were caressing her from within, as if she'd turned outside in, or—or—blast, she couldn't think.

He moved with grace and power and confidence, finding the rhythm that suited them both. Instinctively she raised her knees, then curled her legs around his waist. Oh, yes, it was better, much better, and she moved with him, meeting his thrusts to find her own pleasure. It was there again, the same pleasure he'd given her before, only now it was stronger, more intense. But what made it infinitely better was that she shared it with Hawke, the two of them racing for release together.

"I cannot hold it back, Hawke!" she cried as her body twisted beneath his. "Please, please, oh, do not stop!"

"Let it go, Lizzie," he urged hoarsely, driving hard. "Come with me, sweet."

She couldn't have stopped even if she'd wished it.

Her release burst within her and kept coming in waves, stunning her with the rippling, shimmering, exquisite pleasure that made her cry out and cling to him as she rode it out. He followed soon after, roaring with an animal intensity that thrilled her as he filled her with his seed.

She was hot, sticky, and sweaty, her heart pounding faster than if she'd run across the county, and she was so exhausted she thought she'd never be able to move again, half trapped beneath him as he gasped for breath.

This was what Charlotte had tried to explain to her, but how could mere shallow words describe this? It was the most perfect, uncontrolled madness, and she loved it.

Because she loved him.

She knew that now, without doubt. She loved her husband, and her heart fairly overflowed with it, so much that she felt tears of foolish joy sting her eyes. But did she dare tell him? She knew from novels that men could be skittish about such declarations and were leery of love in general. Was it proper to make such a confession at such a moment?

With a weary groan he rolled onto his back, throwing his arms over his head. She quickly joined him, leaning across his chest. She had a vague recollection of Aunt Sophronia warning her to remain on her back so as to preserve her precious drop of what might be the next duke, but she didn't care. With her splendidly virile new husband, she was certain there'd be more, much more.

She glanced down his length, wryly noting how his cock now seemed as sleepy as the rest of him. He lay now with his eyes closed, his long, dark lashes fluttering over his broad cheekbones, his lips parted as his breathing gradually slowed. Unable to resist, she lightly traced the bow of his lips with her fingertip.

His eyes flew open. "You little minx," he said, his smile slow and lazy beneath her touch. "Come here."

He began to circle one arm around her to draw her close, but she shook him off. She sat up and pulled the tangled, crumpled shift over her head and tossed it aside. "It was strangling me," she explained, sitting back on her heels with her breasts bare for him.

"I approve, you brazen creature," he said, his voice reduced to a well-satisfied drawl. "But leave the stockings and the garters. They amuse me."

She grinned, shoving back her hair and making her breasts bob. She didn't care how brazen this made her; she liked having him look at her the way he was now, his admiration and approval and desire, too, all plain across his face. When he looked at her like this, she forgot she'd ever been the overlooked middle sister. She forgot everything, really, except for him.

Now when he held his arm up for her to join him, she went to him immediately, curling neatly at his side as if she was always meant to be there.

"I'm happy," she whispered, the simplest of truths, and the purest.

"So am I," he agreed. "I told you we'd suit as lovers. Who would have guessed my dry old father would find a lady who suited me so?"

"Yes," she said softly, longing to confess the rest. "Yes."

"Yes, yes, hah." He pulled her up to kiss her. "I'll go farther than that. I love you, sweeting."

She couldn't keep back the tears now. "Oh, Hawke, I love you, too. Oh, could I ever be any happier?"

He grinned down at her, purposefully running his hand down the sweeping curve of her waist to her hip. "I'll do my best to try, ma'am. If I love you and you love me, I'd say we've made a most excellent start."

Speechless with joy, all Lizzie could do was kiss him in return. He was absolutely right. They'd made a most excellent, splendid, rapturous start, indeed.

CHAPTER

❀ *13* ❀

In Hawke's estimation, the night could not have gone any better. Now that it was over, he realized how much he'd been dreading it, and with plenty of good reason, too. He'd never been with a virgin before, but he had heard enough tales of hideous wedding nights to make any man quake and any cock wilt, tales that included sobbing, screaming, fainting, general hysteria, and torrential amounts of blood. He had steeled himself for the very worst.

Instead, he'd been blessed with pure heaven. He'd already been intensely attracted to Lizzie, but now, after last night, he was absolutely enchanted. She'd shown no virginal reluctance or squeamishness, and her maidenhead seemed to have vanished without much suffering or blood.

She'd been eager, adventuresome, and responsive, with a body that was an absolute delight, pale and plump where it should be, yet lithe and acrobatic in the most pleasing ways possible. She'd balked at nothing he'd suggested, and embraced every new possibility with enthusiasm. Only her wide-eyed surprise had betrayed her innocence, and that very inexperience had made him love her all the more for it.

He did love her, too. He wasn't ashamed to admit it,

and for as long as that love lasted, he intended to enjoy every moment of it. The way he understood their marriage, the only real obligation they had before him was to conceive an heir with her, and he couldn't imagine how pleasurable the next weeks would be for him. Surely he had to be the most fortunate gentleman in Britain.

He smiled down at her, curled on the bed beside him. He could look at her all the day long, she was that achingly lovely. She lay with her hair tossed back on the pillow, tucked on her side and still fast asleep. He wasn't surprised; by his reckoning, she'd spent at least four times in the course of the night. That also likely accounted for the blissful half smile on her face as she slept. He only hoped she was dreaming of him.

He slid from the bed, taking care not to disturb her, and glanced at the clock on the mantel. It was nearly ten, early for him to rise if this had been an ordinary morning. He opened the curtains and then the diamond-paned window, letting the fresh air and sunshine stream in. He gave no thought that he was standing before the open window without a stitch on his body. He did this every day, too, one of his long-standing bachelor habits, and besides, the garden and everything else outside the window belonged to him. Who would stop him?

He stretched and returned to the bed, smiling down at Lizzie. She'd rolled away from the sun, burying her face beneath the pillow.

He kissed her shoulder, nuzzling that pleasing hollow between her throat and her collarbone. All he received in return was a noncommittal grunt.

"Good morning, dearest," he said softly. "You may waken or not, but I'm giving you fair warning that our breakfast, and Giacomo, will soon appear."

She rolled over on her back, squinting at the sun, and at him.

"Look at you, Hawke," she said, her voice thick with sleep. "You're naked as Adam in the garden."

"So are you," he said, drawing the sheet over her. "Or rather, as Eve. And I'd rather not share the view with my manservant."

As if on cue, the bedchamber door flew open, and Giacomo appeared, bearing an enormous silver tray with a sizable coffeepot and a plate of sweet buns. Behind him came Lizzie's new lady's maid, Margaret. Giacomo was well accustomed to seeing his master naked, but Margaret was another story, and Hawke grabbed a corner of the sheet from the bed and pulled it around his waist. Lizzie yelped and pulled the rest of her sheet up to her chin.

"Good day to you, Giacomo," Hawke said heartily, as if heartiness could compensate for nakedness. "And Margaret, isn't it?"

"Aye, Your Grace," said the maid, curtseying. She appeared to be the servant version of the harpies, older and stern-faced, though at present that stern face was as red as a beet.

"Good day, Margaret," Lizzie said from behind him, obviously trying hard to sound like a duchess and not like some bold little hussy who'd spent the night rogering him. "Have you ordered my things in my rooms?"

"I have, Your Grace," Margaret said. "I trust my arrangements will be to your satisfaction, ma'am. I have taken the liberty of bringing your dressing gown. I have also arranged for a bathing tub to be brought to your dressing room, ma'am, and whenever it pleases you I will have hot water brought up from the kitchens."

"A hot bath!" Lizzie exclaimed, clearly delighted by the prospect of such luxury. "May I go, Hawke, just for a bit? Please?"

"You needn't ask my leave, Lizzie," he said, smiling. He'd regret parting from her for even a moment, but he could understand that she might wish to wash after last night. "You have the freedom of this house. You can do whatever you please."

"But I'm your wife and your duchess," she said, "and if you wish me to remain, I will."

She was smiling, so he guessed she was teasing, but he wasn't entirely certain. It startled him, hearing her refer to herself like that. He didn't yet think of her as his wife, or rather, he wasn't thinking of himself as *having* a wife. She was simply Lizzie, now his Lizzie.

"Likely Giacomo wishes to make me presentable, too," he said, rubbing his hand over his bristling jaw. "Go—wash and dress. I only ask that you don't dress too thoroughly, mind?"

She laughed, and kissed first his cheek, then his lips. "I'll mind," she promised. "So long as you do the same."

Margaret deftly held up the dressing gown so that Lizzie made the transition from the bed without displaying too much of herself. Still, Hawke had a last, tantalizing glimpse, enough to make certain he wouldn't linger over his coffee. She still wore her stockings, the heels splattered lightly with mud, but she'd lost one of the garters during the night. At the doorway, she paused, slipped her dressing gown down to one side, and blew him a kiss over her bare shoulder, which he returned with a wink for good measure. He was smiling still as he took his coffee from Giacomo, and wondered idly how many such details Margaret and Giacomo would share about Lizzie with the other servants belowstairs.

No, not Lizzie: the new mistress of the house, Her Grace the fourth Duchess of Hawkesworth.

His wife.

"This is your bedchamber, ma'am," Margaret said, opening the door and stepping aside for Lizzie to enter first. "Your dressing room is to the right, and beyond that is your private parlor."

Lizzie caught her breath, her eyes wide. This bed-chamber was at least double the size of Hawke's, and where his had been dark in the style of the last century, hers was bright and airy and modern, with cheery pale yellow walls and white plaster moldings. The furnishing were white and gold, with silver silk brocade for the chairs and the bed hangings. The bed itself was magnificent, with gilded carved posts like twisting vines and an oversized canopy with a swagged cornice, crowned on the corners with clusters of white ostrich plumes. Blue-and-white Chinese vases held flowers from the garden, and their fragrance sweetly filled the room.

The only part of the room that was truly hers was the little painting that Hawke had given her, now proudly set on the mantelpiece.

"How beautiful!" Lizzie exclaimed, awed that such a room now belonged to her. "It's not at all like the rest of the house, at least the parts I've seen."

"It's to the dowager duchess's taste, ma'am," Margaret said. "That's Lady Allred, His Grace's mother. If you please, ma'am, if you'll sit here, I can begin to brush out your hair while the water's brought up."

Already a parade of sturdy-armed footmen had begun arriving, each carrying a pair of tin pails of steaming water to Lizzie's dressing room and the waiting tub.

Obediently Lizzie sat on the bench before the looking glass, wincing as Margaret began to draw the brush briskly through the snarled and matted tangles of her hair.

She knew perfectly well who the daunting Lady Allred was. She was grateful to have Margaret here as a friendly face, and to offer such helpful information about her new household, too. Charlotte, who'd chosen Margaret for Lizzie from her own staff, had been very definite about making sure Lizzie had an ally in her lady's maid. She'd also insisted that Lizzie's maid be an older, experienced lady, and plain enough not to catch Hawke's eye. Lizzie had laughed at that, but Charlotte, not trusting Hawke, had been adamant, and there was little doubt that Margaret's severe features and angular form would never tempt Hawke.

"Your Grace will be changing these quarters to suit your own taste now," Margaret continued. "His Grace will likely expect you to."

"Not at first, I won't," Lizzie said, trying to look about without moving her head and suffering more hair pulling. "It's beautiful as it is. But why is the duchess's bedchamber so much larger that Hawke's—that is, His Grace's?"

"That's because His Grace chooses to keep his old rooms, ma'am, from when he was a boy," Margaret said promptly. "He's never shifted to the duke's rooms, no matter that his father died ten years ago."

That piqued Lizzie's curiosity. Most gentlemen who'd inherited a dukedom would be eager to claim every right and scrap of power that came with it.

But then, as she was learning, Hawke wasn't exactly an ordinary gentleman, either.

"I wonder why he hasn't," she mused. "It's not that the other bedchamber is ordinary, but one would think he'd wish the grander one."

"How should I know His Grace's most privy thoughts, ma'am?" Margaret said. "Some say he cares more for that foreign house of his than for any that are on good English soil, ma'am, and others whisper that he wants no part of his father, not even to sleep in his bed. But better you should ask such a question of His Grace yourself, if you wish more than servants' tattle. Pray excuse me, ma'am, while I go make certain those rascals have prepared your bath proper."

Left alone to her thoughts, Lizzie looked at the new ruby and diamond ring on her finger, turning her hand back and forth to make the stones twinkle in the sunlight. As costly a bauble as the ring might be, its true value should lie in the union it symbolized. After last night, she'd little doubt that Hawke loved her as much as she did him, and she smiled to herself, remembering all the wicked, wonderful things he had taught her.

Yet as splendid as last night had been, Lizzie caught herself also remembering her mother's words to her, her fears that she and Hawke were too full of passion for their marriage to last. They troubled Lizzie, those words. How could what she'd felt with Hawke die away? That *was* love, wasn't it? How could anything that brilliant and full of life—just like the ruby on her finger—not last?

"If you please, ma'am, the bath is of a pleasing warmth," Margaret said, and dutifully Lizzie followed her into the dressing room. A large wooden tub, lined with linen cloth, sat in the center of the room. Crushed lavender blossoms had been stirred into the water, making the steam as fragrant as the water. This was indeed luxury; Lizzie could count on one hand the times she'd had a bath like this, and never to herself, but shared with her sisters. With a contented sigh, she lowered herself into the water, drawing her knees high so the water came clear to her chin.

"I'll wager that's a comfort, isn't it, ma'am?" Margaret said, smiling at Lizzie's obvious pleasure as she began to wash her hair. "Nothing soothes away soreness like warm water, and that's the truth."

Lizzie closed her eyes, relishing the warmth. She hadn't realized she was sore until Margaret had mentioned it, but then Hawke had discovered places in her body that she hadn't known existed. If she wasn't careful now, she'd relax so thoroughly she'd fall asleep.

"Here, ma'am, your chocolate," Margaret said, handing Lizzie a tiny porcelain cup. Lizzie breathed deeply: chocolate and cream and cinnamon, exactly as she liked it made.

"Ah, Margaret," she said, sinking back to her chin in the water. "How you pamper me!"

"A new bride deserves to be pampered, ma'am," she said, drying her hands on her apron. "Those were His Grace's orders as well, that you be given whatever pleases you."

Lizzie smiled as she sipped the chocolate, thinking how vastly fortunate she was to have such a thoughtful, generous, kind husband in Hawke, and how sadly Mama had misjudged him.

"Which gown do you wish me to prepare, ma'am?" Margaret said, opening one of several wardrobes in the dressing room. "If you are beginning your calls today, ma'am, might I suggest the pink striped silk? Or perhaps, ma'am, you'd rather the red riding habit with the black feathered hat? That is suitable for calls in town, ma'am, even if you travel by carriage."

Lizzie flushed. She knew that, as the new Duchess of Hawkesworth, she was expected to call upon every other duchess residing in town, and a large number of other well-placed peeresses as well. It was part of her responsibility as a noble bride, a way of introducing herself to society, and society would expect her to do it. Charlotte had assiduously finished all her wedding calls within the first fortnight of her marriage, and March had even dutifully accompanied her on most of them.

But Lizzie wasn't her sister, and Hawke most definitely was not March.

"Thank you, Margaret," she said. "But I do not believe His Grace has any plans for us to begin making calls just yet."

Margaret's carefully impassive face was more expressive than a torrent of disapproving words.

"Very well, ma'am," she said, each word crisp. "What shall I lay out for you instead?"

"Nothing that cannot be removed in an instant, Margaret," Hawke said, strolling into the dressing room. "I do not wish Her Grace to be burdened in any way sartorial today."

He was certainly setting an unencumbered example. He wore a long striped silk banyan, floating open and loose over his bare chest, red leather Turkish slippers, and a pair of dark, loose trousers. He looked as dazzling and exotic as any pasha. He came to Lizzie in the tub, bending over to kiss her, his freshly shaven jaw smelling faintly of soap.

"Good morning again, my dearest naiad," he said. "I trust you are refreshed and restored."

"Good morning to you again, too," she said softly. Even after last night, she felt oddly shy to be sitting before him in the bath like this, her breasts bobbing in the lavender-scented water while he watched with obvious approval. It was all so *intimate*, which, with Hawke, was going to be how her life would now be. "Margaret was just asking me how to dress for the morning. Have we plans?"

"Only that I intend to lavish you with love and amusements," he said. Without looking away from her, he motioned to Margaret, who immediately brought him both a chair so that he could sit beside the tub and his own cup of chocolate, the dainty porcelain looking too small in his hands. "What other plans must I have?"

Lizzie considered mentioning the wedding calls, simply to measure Hawke's thoughts on them, but he'd already moved on to his own plans for the day.

"I believe we'll view pictures today," he said, frowning at the cocoa. "Only a few, I promise. I don't want to overwhelm you with my tastes."

"Where?" she said eagerly. "To the public gallery at the Foundling Hospital?"

"Nothing so grand, I fear," he said ruefully. "You'll have to make do with the makeshift gallery I've arranged in the ballroom."

"So they are your paintings?" she asked, rising from the tub as Margaret surrounded her in an oversized linen cloth and began to pat her dry.

"Like Venus from the waves," he murmured, his cocoa forgotten and his gaze rapt on her body.

She blushed at his attention, though she enjoyed it, too. "Faith, first I'm a naiad, and now Venus on the waves. What will you have me be next, Hawke? A dolphin?"

"My own Lizzie will do, I think." He rose and took her into his arms, damp and swaddled as she was, and kissed her until she pushed him away, laughing.

"Let me dress, if you please," she said as Margaret patiently began combing her wet hair. "Tell me of your pictures instead."

He pretended to be wounded, holding his arms out forlornly at his sides as if to show how empty they were without her to hold. "You must wait until we're standing before them."

"Very well, then," she said, disappearing headfirst into the fresh shift that Margaret held for her. "Tell me the story behind that scar on your chest."

"That?" He glanced down at his bare chest, as if seeing it for the first time. It was a most exemplary male chest, broad and lean and muscled in all the right places, and looking particularly handsome framed by his open banyan.

But last night Lizzie had also noticed the dramatic old scar that slashed across it, barely visible beneath the curling dark hair, though she'd been too occupied at the time to ask its history.

"That scar," he said at last, "is ancient and dishonorable, received in a duel with an outraged husband. It was in every way my own fault, and I learned my lesson."

"Goodness," Lizzie said, not expecting quite so lurid an explanation. "So that is how you learned to keep away from married ladies?"

"Oh, no," he said, nonchalant. "I learned to be a better swordsman."

She gasped with bewilderment and a bit of wounded indignation, too. Did all noble husbands speak as freely as that to their wives? She wasn't nearly as worldly as Hawke, and she'd no notion of how she should respond to such a comment. That is, until she noticed how hard he was trying to keep from laughing. She shoved her arms into the flowered chintz dressing gown that Margaret was offering, drawing the ribbons tight around her waist. Then she reached into the tub and scooped up a handful of water, flicking it at him.

"Not so harsh, madam, not so severe!" he said, laughing as he backed out of range. "Truly, if I swore away from married ladies, I'd have to keep away from my own darling wife."

Her eyes narrowed, she took her time slipping her bare feet into blue heeled mules before she finally let him kiss her again, all of which was much more agreeable than making wedding calls to ancient friends of Aunt Sophronia.

She was thankful she had Hawke to lead her through the house, for she was sure she'd lose her way on her own. The servants wouldn't have been much help, either, for every maid and footman she saw in the distance vanished almost as swiftly as a mirage, doubtless at Hawke's orders. Clearly he wished to show her his home himself, leading her through it like a magical maze. Unlike most grand houses that she'd visited, the Chase wasn't regular and predictable, but rambling this way and that, with mysterious additions that resulted in halls that ended abruptly and doors with nothing behind them.

To Lizzie's surprise, Hawke displayed these deficiencies with the same fondness as he showed her the house's most admirable qualities: the checkerboard marble floor in the towering Great Hall, the terra-cotta cherubs around the fireplace in the drawing room and the collection of antelope horns on the library wall, the elaborate tracery of the plasterwork ceilings, and the transom-and-mullion windows that divided the light into scores of diamond-shaped patches. Hawkesworths had lived in the house for over two hundred years, and each generation had added their own little touches of style and taste.

Unlike the austere classical perfection of the much newer Marchbourne House, the Chase had an undeniable personality all its own, and in an odd way it reminded Lizzie of Hawke himself: exotic, charming, and not what was expected.

Now he stopped before a small bronze satyr, complete with goatish hindquarters and stubby little horns, that stood on a pedestal in a shell-shaped alcove all his own.

"My grandfather bought this rascal in Rome," he said, resting his hand on the statue's curly head. "When I was a boy, it was absolutely my favorite thing in the entire house. Somehow or another, I convinced myself that rubbing his pointed ears would bring me good luck, particularly at school. Look, you can see for yourself how shiny the ears still are."

She did look, and couldn't resist rubbing the ears herself, which made them both laugh.

"You love this house, don't you?" she said, intrigued.

"I can tell by the way you've tried to show me nearly every single thing in it."

He frowned, turning unexpectedly wary. "I did not intend to bore you, Lizzie."

"You didn't, not at all!" she exclaimed. "I love you, and I love this house, just as it is, because I love you, too."

His wariness remained. "You're in a lovesome humor this day, aren't you?"

"I am," she said with conviction. "I rather thought you were, too."

He smiled, albeit reluctantly. "I am, because of you."

"And a good thing, too," she said, rubbing the satyr's ears again. "I pray that one day you'll be teaching our firstborn this trick, and in time the second- and third-born, too, so that this rascal's ears will be burnished like pure gold."

Finally he laughed and slipped his arm around her waist to lead her further through the house. Yet he said nothing about those children that she hoped were in their shared future, which made her uneasy. Considering that children were the main reason their marriage had been arranged, she thought he'd have wished to imagine them along with her.

But perhaps it wasn't so much the notion of their specific children as children in general that unsettled Hawke. Many gentlemen were like that, wanting nothing to do with their own young offspring until they were of an age to make bows and curtseys and polite conversation. Likely that was all. Resolving not to borrow trouble, Lizzie slipped her arm inside his banyan, taking pleasure in the lean, sleek muscles of his back as they walked together. What could be better than to be with him like this, speaking of personal matters in such familiar, beguiling undress?

"Here we are at last, sweeting." Hawke didn't wait

for a footman, but pushed one side of the double doors open for her himself. "My ballroom picture gallery."

Once again Lizzie was surprised. The ballroom itself was what she expected, ballrooms being much the same in all London town houses: a large, cavernous room with chandeliers, a flat, patterned carpet covering the entire floor, and large cast-iron stoves at either end for warmth in winter. She'd also expected to see the walls covered with pictures clear to the ceiling, the way they were in other London galleries that she'd visited.

But instead the framed pictures, large and small, sat unceremoniously on the floor, leaning against the walls or against chairs, with a few propped on easels. The tall windows along one wall were open to the garden, and before a cushioned settee sat a small table with a white cloth. Doubtless again by Hawke's orders, there were a decanter of Madeira and glasses waiting for them, plus a plate of biscuits and a silver bowl of blood oranges.

"*Benvenuto,*" he said happily, holding out his arms to encompass all the pictures as he backed into the room before her. "Welcome to my most cherished possessions."

She glanced around the room in growing awe. There must be at least twoscore paintings, more than most people ever saw, let alone owned. "Why aren't they properly hung on the walls, Hawke? Aren't you afraid they'll be damaged?"

"They won't be damaged," he said. "No one's permitted in here except Giacomo. And now you."

She shook her head, not understanding. "But why not hang them?"

"Why?" He shrugged carelessly, pouring wine into the glasses. "I suppose because I prefer them this way while I'm here. These are my favorites, my fellow rootless vagabonds."

"Vagabonds? You speak of them as if they'd feet instead of frames."

He grinned. "Would that they did," he said, handing a glass to her. "But I expect someday they'll return home to Bella Collina, just as I will."

"Bella Collina?" she said uncertainly. She didn't like this conversation. He was an Englishman and a Londoner, and Hawkesworth Chase was his home, wasn't it?

" 'Beautiful Hill,' " he translated for her, choosing an orange for himself from the bowl. "It's my villa, my home in Naples, overlooking the bay. Here, since I've dawdled so long this morning, I'll show you only a few pictures now, so I don't overwhelm you."

"But I want to see them all," she begged. If she'd been braver, she would have asked him to explain more of this villa in Naples and why he regarded it as his home exclusively and not theirs, the way he'd described the Chase and his other two houses. She longed to ask him what he meant about returning to Italy and how soon he planned to leave. She was his wife; she'd a right to know. But she was also afraid of what he might tell her, and though she hated herself for being so cowardly, she could not do it. "Show them all to me, Hawke, if you please."

"In time, in time." He smiled happily and slowly slipped a segment of the bloodred orange into her mouth, the sweet juice slipping over her lips. "We're in no hurry, are we?"

He kept his word, picking only a handful of paintings to show her. He'd carefully put two chairs before each one, and she sat close to him while she listened and sipped her wine, her head pillowed against his shoulder and her hand resting familiarly on his thigh.

All of the pictures were, of course, surpassingly extraordinary, and even she could tell they were of a quality far beyond the paintings that ordinarily hung in English noble houses, whether a landscape of ancient ruins, a whimsy of two monkeys beside a huge bowl of fruit, or a scene of some long-forgotten regal procession.

Yet as much as Lizzie enjoyed the pictures, what she liked even better was listening to Hawke's voice as he described each one, explaining the history and the artist's life as well as how he himself had come to buy it, and what made the painting special enough to him that he'd brought it all the way back to London. She loved the excitement in his voice, and she loved even more the obvious pleasure he found in sharing something that was so important to him with her.

"Thank you, Hawke," she said softly when it seemed as if he was done. She leaned up and kissed him. "I hope you'll show me more."

"With pleasure," he said, and went to refill their glasses. She rose, too, following him, only to come to a sudden stop before one painting in particular.

"Goodness," she murmured, blushing furiously. The painting showed a reclining woman without a scrap of clothing beyond her jewels. It was obvious, even to Lizzie, from the setting and from the woman's lack of modesty that she was a courtesan, the sort of low, disreputable woman that Lizzie had been raised to pretend didn't exist. Yet here this naked, scandalous woman was staring shamelessly from the canvas at the viewer—who was, in this case, Lizzie herself.

"What have you found?" Hawke asked, sauntering back to her. When he realized where Lizzie had stopped, and which painting had caught her attention, he grinned. "Ah, my *bella donna*. My mother ordered me never to let you see this painting, you know."

Lizzie swallowed, miserably unsure of whether she should agree with Lady Allred or not. "She is—she's very lovely."

"She should be," Hawke said, gazing down at the painting. "She's Venus, goddess of love and beauty. Does she embarrass you, as she does my mother? Should I banish her to some inner closet for the sake of English propriety?"

"Did you know her in Italy?" she blurted out, before she'd time to regret the question. "The woman who posed for the picture, I mean. Was she one of your mistresses?"

"My mistresses?" He laughed, incredulous. "I'd wondered if the harpies had filled your head with tales of my sinful past. But no, this lady was not one of them. The woman who posed for this artist has likely been dead at least two hundred years."

"Oh," she said, all she could muster. She knew she couldn't be glad for anyone's death, and she wasn't, but she was relieved. Yes. She was *relieved*.

"As for those other women in Naples," he continued, "the ones the harpies could not resist describing to you—they were at best passing amusements, Lizzie. They meant nothing to me, nor I to them."

"No?" she asked, her voice more tremulous than she wished it to be.

"No," he said firmly. "I told you. When we wearied of each other, they were gone. You're different. You are my wife and my duchess, and that will never change, not as long as I live."

He raised her hand to his lips, turning it to kiss the palm. She'd always loved that, the brush of his lips, the way he'd nip lightly with his teeth, and now she knew where it would lead. It was enough to make her body warm with longing for him, the telltale heaviness in her belly and breasts.

She was wrong to question him, to hunt for flaws that weren't there. She couldn't expect him to forget entirely about his life in Naples, any more than she could forget hers in Dorset. He loved her and desired her. What more could she wish?

She chuckled low, her happiness bubbling within her.

"Tell me, Hawke," she said, her voice husky and low. "Would you like me to have my portrait painted in such a way?"

She noticed how he looked at her, from her slippers upward, and not at the painting.

"I should like it very much," he said, "but I would have to kill the painter afterward."

She laughed, and he drew her closer, reeling her into his arms.

"But you could still show me what kind of Venus you'd make," he said, close to her ear. "Pose for me alone. Here, on this settee."

She smiled, intrigued, and already toying with the sash on her dressing gown. "What would you do if I agreed?"

"Why, what every gentleman must do in the company of Venus," he said, his breath warm on the side of her throat. "I'd worship her, exactly as she deserves."

"Then show me," she said, sliding free of the gown and the shift with it. "Show me."

And there in the sunlit ballroom, before a crowd of painted witnesses, he did exactly that.

CHAPTER

14

When Hawke looked back, he realized that it was on the tenth day that the first tiny crack had showed in his marriage to Lizzie. Nor was he surprised that the crack was put there by the harpies, her female relations and his own mother. If there was anyone born to sour milk, kick a priceless porcelain, or end his own idyllic honeymoon, it was without doubt those damnable harpies.

The day had begun delightfully enough. After a pleasing dalliance and a late rising, Hawke had taken Lizzie into the garden for a surprise. At one end of the garden was a long canal that had at one time connected to the Thames. Long sealed off from the river, it had been neglected, but Hawke had had the gardeners clear it of duckweed and muck. He'd added a small rowboat, and this morning he'd put Lizzie to the test, daring her to make good her claim that she could row as well as most sailors.

In their short time together, he'd learned this was exactly the sort of challenge she loved most. At once she'd hopped into the boat, set the oars in their locks, and put her back to the task. With a whoop of triumph, she'd launched, picking up speed so quickly that she almost crashed into the wall at the end of the canal. She'd deftly maneuvered her turn in the narrow space, then invited

Hawke aboard. He'd scarcely sat on the bench when she was off with the same ease and confidence as before, as if his added weight were nothing.

"Why aren't you surprised?" she said as she pulled on the oars. She wore a pink dressing gown and a wide straw hat against the sun, and her face was freckled with tiny specks of sunlight that still managed to slip through the braided straw. "I know you arranged this just because you didn't believe me."

"But I did believe you, sweeting," he said, enjoying himself thoroughly. He, too, sported a straw hat like any other country squire, his shirtsleeves rolled high and his breeches worn and comfortable. "I wished you not to fail but to display your prowess for my admiration."

"Are you admiring me, then?" she asked, ducking her head as they passed beneath the trailing willows.

"Of course I am admiring you," he said, lolling comfortably in the boat. "How could I not? What a pleasing way this is to travel, and how fortunate I am to possess such a talented wife. Perhaps we should take this boat out upon the river, so you might demonstrate your abilities to all the world."

She laughed merrily. "See the Duke of Hawkesworth's exceptional wife, plying the oars as handsomely as a Billingsgate fishwife! Only a shilling, gov'nor, only a shilling to see a peeress toil like a commoner!"

"There is nothing common about you, Lizzie," he said. "Not one thing."

That was not idle flattery. He meant it, just as he meant it when he told her she was the most perfect companion on earth for him. No other lover in his experience could come close to her, which was, he was certain, an exceptional accomplishment for any wife. She was clever and cheerful and she could make him laugh in any number of ways. She was as lovely as the moon in the sky and as adventuresome as Aphrodite herself in his bed. He loved her more than he'd ever loved anyone else, and that both staggered and delighted him, all at once.

This was, of course, not to say that there might be some other lady out there who might be even more agreeable to his tastes, but for now his Lizzie was beyond compare and reproach. He could only pray she felt the same for him, and he was as grateful for his good fortune as any man could be.

The only thing lacking would, with luck, come in time, and that was a child. No matter how hard Hawke tried not to think of it, especially while they were in bed together, he could never entirely put that phantom infant heir from his mind. Producing a son was the entire reason for Lizzie and him being together, and their union would be judged an abject failure if no child appeared. No, *he* would be judged a failure, a useless, unmanly duke who couldn't ensure his own lineage.

Worst of all, without a child, he would never be free to return to Italy.

"You look quite pensive, Hawke," Lizzie said. "How can your thoughts be so dark on such a sunny day? Or perhaps it is the charging motion of our mighty vessel that has made you seasick?"

"I'm enjoying myself far too much to be seasick," he said swiftly, for under no circumstances would he confess his true thoughts. "Were you still musing over rowing me clear to Richmond?"

"Oh, no," she said. "Rather I was thinking how pleasant it would be to have you row me, so that I, too, might grow lazy and drowsy in the sun."

"But I never declared that *I* could row a boat," he drawled, sounding exactly as lazy and drowsy as she had accused him of being. He leaned back further, tucking his hands behind his head. "That was your doing, dearest, not mine."

She stopped her oars and frowned. "You would not do this for me, as I would do for you?"

"You offered, sweeting," he said. "I did not."

The truth was that he was not particularly adept at a mariner's skills, and being male, he'd no wish to display his ineptitude before her. Thus he intended his observation as wry teasing, a jest.

Alas, she did not interpret it that way.

"Then perhaps you will *offer* to row yourself the rest of the way, and straight to the devil, too," she said, spinning the oars in their locks as she shoved them toward him. Before he could stop her, she bunched up her skirts and nimbly hopped to the bank, making him and the boat glide out to the middle of the canal.

"Lizzie, wait, forgive me," he called, but she'd already disappeared into the garden toward the house.

With a muttered oath, he tried to use one of the oars to push the drifting boat back to shore. Instead the oar slipped from his hand and into the water beyond his reach. Swearing again, he grabbed the second oar. He'd more success with this one, pushing the boat to the shore. But as he stood to climb out, the boat rocked and pitched him forward. One foot landed on the grass, while the other went into the water along with his hat. He stumbled forward onto the grass, pulling his foot free of the muck with a sucking sound, and tried to follow her. Water and mud squelched inside his shoe with each step, and his well-soaked stocking drooped around his calf. By the time he reached the house, his oaths had progressed to a colorful blend of English, Italian, and French and were fiery enough to scald the very leaves from the nearby trees.

"Lizzie!" he roared as he came close to the garden door. "Damnation, Lizzie, where the devil are you?"

"I'm here, you great swearing oaf," she said mildly. She was sitting cross-legged on the stone balustrade beside the door, her knees tucked inside her skirts and her hat next to her, in delectable disarray. "Where else would I have gone?"

Her anger seemed to have vanished, which only made his irritation grow, along with the blister from the wet shoe and stocking.

"You were not with me, madam," he said crossly. "That was all I knew with surety."

"Oh, yes, surety." She frowned, looking down at his legs. "Goodness, Hawke. Look at you. What has happened? Did you tumble into the canal?"

"Yes," he said. "It was your fault."

"*My* fault?" she repeated in disbelief, slipping down from the balustrade. She shook her skirts out over her bare legs, and bare feet, too, for somewhere between here and the canal she seemed to have shed her mules. "How can I be blamed for you falling into the water?"

"Because you rocked the boat," he explained, finding it increasingly difficult to remain angry with her when she confronted him with her bare, grass-stained toes. "Because you left the oars in an awkward position, and they fell out of the locks. Because—damnation, Lizzie, because it was."

He should have guessed what was coming from the wicked gleam in her eyes. "Because I was being vastly generous, and you were selfish."

He tipped his head to one side, intending to appear conciliatory without having to outright apologize. "Lizzie, please. Please."

"Because I was right," she continued, backing away from him and into the house. "And you, Hawke, were *wrong*."

He lunged for her, and with a yelp she darted away, running through the house. He followed, of course, though she'd the undeniable advantage over him slogging away in the wet shoe. As he passed through the library and into the main hall, he resolved that the one thing he'd wish otherwise about her was that she was too fast for him to catch.

But as he came around the staircase, he stopped dead. Instead of the pleasing prospect of trapping Lizzie somewhere in the house and kissing her until she accepted his apology, he saw Lizzie standing stock-still before him, her skirts bunched in her hands above her bare legs and a horrified look on her face.

Because standing with her with a hapless footman were the harpies: Lady Sanborn, Lady Hervey, and the most harpy-ish of them all, his own mother. They looked at him, decided he was unworthy of their collective regard, and turned back to Lizzie.

"My dear," his mother said, frosty as usual, "surely there is some more agreeable place for us to converse than this hall."

"Of course, Lady Allred," Lizzie said quickly, motioning to one side. "The drawing room. This way, if you please."

Anxiously smoothing her palms over her skirts, she turned to the footman. "Please bring us tea in the drawing room," she said. "And some biscuits, or whatever else Cook thinks is proper."

The footman bowed and left, and as he did, Lady Hervey placed her hand gently on her daughter's arm.

"Oh, Lizzie," she said unhappily. "So what I've heard must be true. You haven't any notion at all what that footman's name might be, do you?"

Lizzie flushed with misery, her hands clasped at her waist.

"I—I disremember it at present, Mama," she said, a wretched dissembling that fooled no one. "There are so many to learn."

Hawke hadn't seen Lizzie clasp her hands like that since their wedding day, and at once he came to her rescue.

"Good day to you, Lady Hervey," he said, coming to stand at Lizzie's side. He bowed, and if the leg he extended as part of that elegant bow was covered by a sagging stocking, splattered with mud, well then, so be it. "Good day, Lady Carbery. Mother, good day to you, too."

"All the 'good days' in Christendom are not going to sweeten my humor, Hawke," his mother said severely. "Besides, we have come here to see the duchess, not you."

"You cannot banish me from my own house, Mother." He smiled and slipped his arm around Lizzie's waist. "I doubt that anything you wish to say to her is unfit to be said to me as well."

Lady Sanborn sighed dramatically, tapping the ferrule of her parasol with growing impatience on the tiled floor "You might as well let His Grace remain, Lady Allred. We all agree that he is as much a part of the problem as Her Grace."

"If you please," Lizzie said, raising her chin more bravely. "To the drawing room, *if* you please."

Somehow Hawke helped herd the ladies into the drawing room, making sure they were all suitably seated.

Seated, but hardly calmed.

"It is concern that has brought us here, ma'am," his mother began. "Grave concern for you and the duke."

"Here in our house, you may call her Lizzie, Mother, nor would it harm you to refer to me as your son, rather than 'the duke,'" Hawke said, not exactly calm himself, either. "We're all of us family now, whether you wish it or not."

His mother swiveled to face him. "That is exactly the problem, Hawke. You continue to think of her as 'Lizzie'—such an intolerably common name!—rather than as Her Grace the Duchess of Hawkesworth."

Lady Hervey made a small, half-smothered cry of protest. "But she has always been Lizzie, ever since she was small. I see no harm—"

"Elizabeth is the name of our most illustrious queen," Lady Allred said with authority. "Lizzie is the name of a costard-monger in the street, or worse."

"It's also the name of my wife, Mother," Hawke said, "and I'll call her whatever pleases her."

Beside him Lizzie shook her head. Her first surprise at the older ladies' arrival had passed, and now she sat very straight and with her jaw set, determined and ready to stand for herself.

"Elizabeth is my given name," she said, "but I have always been called Lizzie by those who care for me most, and I see no reason for them to change."

Hawke smiled and silently marked a victory for Lizzie. Several footmen and maids appeared with tea and enough sugary accoutrements to supply a phalanx of females, enough to momentarily distract the ladies.

But only for a moment.

"The real concern, Lizzie, is the talk," her mother said anxiously. "You've quite disappeared from sight, and people are beginning to make all sorts of dreadful speculations about you and His Grace."

"They may speculate all they wish, Mama," Lizzie said. "If we had gone on a wedding trip and left the town entirely, then they would have speculated, too. The truth is that we are newly wed and wish to spend time alone, in our own company, to accustom ourselves to married life."

Lady Allred gave a small, derisive sniff, sweeping her glance over them both. "Apparently accustoming yourselves to behaving like heathenish Gypsies as well."

"Forgive me, Lady Allred, but we were pleasing each other, as a husband and wife should." Pointedly Lizzie rested her hand on Hawke's knee, a scandalous gesture even between wife and husband. "If we had been expecting your call, I assure you that you would not have discovered us in this manner."

Proudly Hawke covered her hand with his own. How splendidly she was now defending herself against the harpies!

"'We' are not important, Duchess," said her great-aunt, Lady Carbery. "It is the rest of the world that must see and know you as the Duchess of Hawkesworth, not only for the sake of His Grace but for that of your children as well."

"Ah, our children," Hawke said, unable to resist. "You should be pleased, Mother, by how assiduously Lizzie and I have been applying ourselves to our marital obligations. I vow we've been like veritable rabbits in the spring. I know how much you long for an heir, and I've been doing my concerted best to provide you with one as quickly as possible."

His mother glared at him, not amused, and without answering looked back to Lizzie. "You must make your place known in society, Duchess. If you do not make yourself accepted, then your children never shall be, either."

"That's rubbish," Hawke said, more bored by this argument than angry. "I'm an English duke with the blood of a king. No one ignores me. I ignore them."

His mother muttered wordlessly, and if she swore, she would have sworn then. "I vow, Hawke, there are times that I cannot believe you are your father's son. He understood the responsibilities of his rank and position, and appreciated the good fortune that came with it. If he could hear you now—"

"Then it's an excellent thing he cannot," Hawke interrupted, for this was an ancient tirade indeed from his mother. "I am far different from Father, and as unlikely to change as he was himself."

His mother's mouth was so tightly compressed that

her lips had nearly disappeared, made extinct by whatever force she was using to bite back her words. A good thing it was, too, for nothing she said would change him, or bring back his father, either, in this old and bitter argument between them.

But his mother wasn't the only one who'd fallen suddenly, awkwardly silent. Both Lady Hervey and Lady Sanborn stared studiously down at their teacups, as if the secret to a more genial conversation lay inside.

Hawke sighed and looked to Lizzie beside him, expecting her to offer reassurance and support. But the expression on her face was more doubtful than supportive, more uncertain than reassuring. He'd never seen that particular look from her before, and it unsettled him. She was also blushing, not prettily, but miserably; perhaps that little jest likening their lovemaking to amorous rabbits had been inopportune. He hadn't realized how important her trust had become to him in the short time they'd been wed—until now, when it seemed so suddenly, sadly missing.

It pained him to see the obvious effort it took her to smile at the others.

"Does anyone wish more tea?" she asked, too brightly. "Or whatever else you please. I can send—"

"Thank you, no, Duchess," his mother said. She set her cup down on the table beside her and rose, and the others quickly followed. "I only pray that you consider well what we have said, and take heed before it is too late. Good day to you."

The farewells were swiftly said and curtseys made, with only Lady Hervey lingering to take Lizzie's hand in her own. She didn't seem to care that she stood in Hawke's hearing, too, or perhaps she intended to.

"Tell me, dear, please do," she said, searching Lizzie's face. "Are you happy? Is that the true reason you and the duke have kept yourselves away from the world? That you cannot bear to share your joy?"

Hawke looked past them, pretending not to be listening.

But Lizzie didn't care if he heard or not.

"Oh, yes, Mama, yes!" she said in a happy rush that could not be feigned. "I cannot tell you how happy I—we—are to be wed!"

"That is all I wished to hear," Lady Hervey said, her eyes glistening with unshed tears.

She kissed Lizzie and patted her cheek, then turned to Hawke.

"You're taking excellent care with my daughter, Duke," she said, her smile warm in a way that his own mother's never was. "I trust she is treating you with the same tenderness and regard?"

"Mama!" Lizzie exclaimed, her cheeks crimson, but Hawke only laughed and looped his arms around her.

"I could not ask for more, Lady Hervey," he said. "Nothing at all."

He showed Lizzie that, too, hurrying her upstairs and scattering clothes along the way even before his mother's carriage had left their drive. It was a fine way to spend the rest of the afternoon, made even more enjoyable by having sent the harpies on their way. If Lady Hervey had asked him if he was happy, too, his reply might have been even more exuberant than Lizzie's.

It was that boundless happiness that made him do something he very rarely did. Afterward, when he and Lizzie lay sprawled and drowsy in his bed, he apologized.

"I'm sorry about the boat," he said softly. "I intended it to please you, to remind you of boats you must have had at Ransom. I thought you'd like it. I never intended for things to become all twisted around as they did, and I'm sorry. I'm sorry."

She rolled over, resting her hands on his chest. "You remembered that I'd told you about how I could row. That was the best part. You listened to what I said, and you remembered. And it is a very nice boat."

"Well, then, there you are," he said, an empty bit of verbiage, but the best he could muster when he was feeling so contented. "The canal's likely not much of a challenge, but I can have the boat brought down to the river if you wish."

"No," she said quickly. "No. I saw how the real watermen maneuvered their craft, and there are far too many currents and eddies for me to master."

"Then we can have it brought with us to the country," he said. "There's a sizable pond, almost a lake, near one of the follies at the Hall."

"Now, that would be much better," she said. "I like to row, but I've no desire to drown. Faith, can you picture what the news sheets would say of that? 'Rowing Duchess Lost in the Thames.'"

She laughed, but he couldn't, not at a jest that featured her death. To lose her in any way—no, there was nothing amusing about that. He drew her a little closer, hoping she understood.

She sighed happily, so happily that he'd never have suspected what came next.

"When your mother was here," she said softly, "why were you so sharp toward her?"

He tensed. He couldn't help it. "I wasn't aware that I was particularly sharp toward her."

"You were," she said, "and you know it, too, else you wouldn't be denying it now. You never speak of your father. What about him was so dreadful?"

"Nothing," he said. "Not in the dazzled eyes of the world, anyway, nor in my mother's, either. If you'd like a complete catalogue of his inestimable virtues, you shall have to ask her."

She rested her chin on her hands and looked directly into his eyes so that he couldn't hide. She was good at that; it was a pity she was female, else she'd make an excellent judge on the bench.

"Her catalogue, however inestimable, does not interest me nearly as much as yours," she said, smoothing her hair behind one ear. "Which is why I've asked you."

"Very well, then," he said, adding an exasperated sigh that even he could tell was overdone. "My father was a paragon in every way. He was a confidant to the king, a leader in the House of Lords, a benefactor to whoever needed his aid. Although I was his only son, I am not like him in any way, as my charming mother has repeatedly and endlessly explained in the event I did not realize the fact for myself."

"Ah," she said, gently noncommittal. "Ah."

"What the devil do you mean by that?" he demanded. He wanted her to say more. No, he *needed* her to say more, a realization that appalled him.

"I mean that expectations to be like another are a loathsome burden," she said, clearly choosing her words with care. "For as long as I can recall, my sister Charlotte has been held before me as a worthy model to emulate. I love Charlotte most dearly, but I do not wish to be her. I would suppose that it would be the same with your father."

"I have never once wanted to be my father," he said, thinking of how his father's tedious life had been centered on Parliament and good works, and of how his own, infinitely more pleasant, lay in Naples. "Not once."

"Why should you, when you are such a fine gentleman in your own right?" she said, leaning forward to kiss him lightly. "My dearest, dearest Hawke! Your mother should appreciate you for what you are, not wish you to be what you are not. But just as you have resolved not to change, I think it unlikely that she'll change, either."

"She will not," he said, never more definite about anything in his life. "Not at all."

"But you see, there is the conundrum," she said, smiling wryly. "Your mother wishes you to be your father, when in truth you are much more like her than you will ever be like him."

He scowled, not sure he liked this particular conclusion. He and his mother had been at odds his entire life; he'd often wondered how she'd managed to tolerate him for the nine months necessary to give him birth. How could he possibly resemble the queen of all harpies? Yet the more he considered what Lizzie said, the more he realized how much sense she made.

"The only difference," she continued, "is that you are younger, and therefore still capable of change. That is, if you wish to."

"I am a duke," he said, unable to resist one last bit of stubbornness. "I do not have to change for anyone."

"You were a mere earl before you became a duke," she argued lightly. "You were an earl longer than you've been a duke. Earls can change much more easily than dukes. *If* you wish to."

He sighed again. "How do you wish me to change?"

"*I* don't wish you to change at all," she said succinctly. "That is how I shall be stubborn, for I've no intention of being one of those wives who attempt to make over their husbands. If *you* wish to do things differently in your life, then you will. If you don't, then you won't. I'll be quite content either way."

"Praise be for small miracles," he said with a grunt. "You exhaust me, Duchess."

She smiled, a smile that was dangerously close to being a leer as she trailed her fingers down his chest and over his belly.

"Fah," she said. "I can think of a much more interesting way to exhaust you, Duke."

He caught her hand and raised it to his lips, kissing it lightly.

"In a moment, sweeting," he said. "I have a confession to make first. About the boat."

"Goodness," she said with interest, smoothing her hair back behind her ears, the better to listen. "An apology, a revelation, and a confession! Surely you must have been transformed by your voyage aboard the Boat of Truth."

"Oh, to the devil with your Boat of Truth," he scoffed, unable not to laugh. "I am attempting to speak in complete seriousness. The reason I didn't offer to row you up and down that infernal canal was that I can't. I don't know how. I'm a complete ignoramus when it comes to seafaring."

"Rowing is hardly seafaring," she said earnestly. "I could teach you."

"I think not," he said. "One oarsman—or oarswoman—beneath this roof is enough."

"Oarswoman? Truly?" She narrowed her eyes with disapproval, and he laughed again. She'd never believe he hadn't meant it that way, not that it particularly mattered.

"Isn't that what you are?" he teased. "An oarswoman?"

"*Oarswoman* sounds terribly disreputable, Hawke," she said, swatting him to make her point. "But I do appreciate you not taking the oars and pretending you could do it if you can't. Perhaps that's not being very ducal of you, admitting that you're not able to do everything."

"I am not so vastly stubborn after all, am I?"

"No, you're not," she agreed. "Not vastly. But I am

still grateful you didn't overturn us both, simply for the sake of your pride."

He kissed her then, to show that he was grateful, too, though for a great deal more than not toppling from a boat into the canal.

A great deal more, indeed.

CHAPTER

15

The next morning Lizzie woke early, long before the sun had risen. She lay curled beside Hawke, listening to the steady rhythm of his breathing while he slept and watching the sky gray through the bed curtains. It was the earliest she'd awakened since they'd married, and the first time that she'd heard the birds first begin to chirp and chatter in the garden with the coming dawn.

But the early hour gave her time and peace to think. She had spoken plainly to Hawke after yesterday's visit from Lady Allred, Aunt Sophronia, and her own mother, but in truth she wasn't without fault herself, not by half. While Hawke might have been irritated by his imperious mother, Lady Allred's words had found their mark in Lizzie's conscience. Granted, she and Hawke had only been married a fortnight, but still, in that time she'd done not one single thing that had been worthy of her new station.

Hawke had sworn that he'd broken with his former mistresses when he'd left Italy, and Lizzie believed him. But even as an unworldly bride, she'd slowly come to realize that he'd simply replaced his old mistresses with her, expecting her to be endlessly willing to dally with him whenever he wished it—or, to be sure, whenever she wished it as well. As pleasurable as it was to loll about in her dressing gown and frolic away the day with Hawke (and he had made it so very pleasurable!), the time had likely come when she should be demonstrating at least a smidgeon more interest in the management of Hawkesworth Chase. Even her mother, as gentle and kind as could be, had made that clear when she'd noted that Lizzie still did not know her own footman's name. Aunt Sophronia and Charlotte had worked hard at training her for her new responsibilities, and she'd been terribly ashamed by how obvious it was that she'd completely ignored them.

She sighed and rolled onto her back, resting her hands low over her belly. She wondered if that much-desired heir was already a tiny sprout within her. She wished Hawke hadn't been quite so vulgar yesterday before the older ladies, likening the two of them to rabbits, but it was true. If she wasn't with child, it was certainly not from lack of trying. Wylder women were in general rapid breeders; both her sister and her mother had proudly confided to her that they'd conceived during the first month of their marriages. She felt no different than she usually did, but then, she'd no notion of how different she was supposed to feel.

But whether she was carrying a tiny future duke within her or not, she was determined to begin acting more like a duchess herself. Taking care not to wake Hawke, she slipped from the bed, found her dressing gown, and made her way down the hall to her own rooms. She rang for Margaret, who arrived sheepish and sleepy.

"Pray forgive me, ma'am," she said, her face still puffy and her hair drawn back beneath her cap with obvious haste. "I did not know you planned to rise at this hour, else I would have been waiting."

"Neither did I," Lizzie said cheerfully, "so no harm has been done."

She *was* feeling cheerful, pushing through the new gowns in her wardrobe in search of one that would suit her purpose this morning.

"Might I help you, ma'am?" Margaret said, hovering behind her and clearly horrified by the sight of her mistress choosing her own clothes. "If you please, I might suggest—"

"This will do," Lizzie said, triumphantly pulling out a dark silk gown, blue stripes against a darker blue. "Tell me, Margaret: what is the housekeeper's name?"

"Mrs. Perkins, ma'am," Margaret said, taking the gown from Lizzie.

"And the butler?"

"That would be Mr. Betts, ma'am," Margaret said, already unfastening Lizzie's dressing gown to help her dress.

"Mrs. Perkins and Mr. Betts," Lizzie repeated, determined to remember the names. "Please send word that I wish to meet with them and the rest of the staff in the front hall in half an hour."

Even stern-faced Margaret could not keep from smiling. "Very well, ma'am."

In exactly half an hour, Lizzie walked down the long flight of steps to the hall. A long line of servants stood before her, all neatly dressed and gazing straight ahead. At their head stood the butler, Mr. Betts, a formidable Scotsman with bristling brows and a bulbous nose, and beside him was Mrs. Perkins, no less daunting in a ruffled white cap, the heavy ring of keys that was the badge of her position hanging proudly at her waist. Standing slightly to one side, to show they reported to the master and mistress directly, were Giacomo and Margaret.

There was no need for Lizzie to introduce herself. They all were well aware who she was, which was both unnerving and reassuring at the same time. Even though she knew exactly how this first meeting should go—it should be as regimented as a minuet—her heart still thumped beneath her stays, and she couldn't help but think of how much younger she was than nearly every one of the servants she was to oversee.

"Good day, Mr. Betts," she said, greeting him first as the most senior of the staff. "Good day, Mrs. Perkins."

They bowed and curtseyed, exactly as they should, and then began the ritual of presenting the rest of the staff to Lizzie. More bowing, more curtseying, more awestruck murmurs of "Your Grace," with Lizzie smiling and nodding to each well-scrubbed face that passed before her.

She knew she wouldn't remember all their names now, which was why she intended to ask Mr. Betts for a list to study later, when she was alone. But this would be a good beginning, and when she reached the end of the line, she returned to the front and Mr. Betts, Mrs. Perkins, and the cook, a ginger-haired woman named Mrs. McFarlane. These three were the most important people in the household, and if she wished to have a successful reign as mistress, she knew she had to show them that she not only supported their work but realized that there might be room for improvement.

"Mr. Betts," she began, earning yet another bow. "I appreciate the care you have given to this noble house, and the respect you have shown the family's traditions. But from time to time, I believe it a useful task to review the various tradesmen with whom the household does business, lest they, too, become traditions. Would you please prepare a list for me of all such tradesmen, so that you and I might consider it together?"

Faith, she could have been Aunt Sophronia herself, giving that little speech, but she saw the surprise in the butler's face, followed by a new respect as he bowed again.

With a rising confidence, Lizzie turned next to the

housekeeper. "Mrs. Perkins, I am most impressed with the general tidiness of the house, especially considering how often His Grace has been away. But I wish that more care be taken with the opening and closing of the window blinds and curtains throughout the day, particularly in those rooms that face the southern sun. His Grace is especially devoted to his paintings, and I wish them preserved against the damage of the sun."

That advice had come by way of Charlotte, and Lizzie sent her unspoken thanks as the housekeeper agreed and obviously approved. One more, Lizzie thought, and moved on to the cook. Everyone had warned her that cooks could be temperamental and impassioned, with pride that was easily ruffled—leading to disastrous results at the table.

"Mrs. McFarlane," she began. "I understand that His Grace has left most meals to your choosing."

The cook's mouth worked uneasily. "Not quite, Your Grace," she said. "That is, when His Grace returned from the Continent, he sent down a brief list of courses that he approved, ma'am, with orders for me to prepare them as I saw fit. Mostly dishes that His Grace had preferred as a young gentleman, ma'am."

Lizzie nodded, trying to look sympathetic. At least now she'd an explanation for why she and Hawke had been dining on meat pies and sweet puddings fit for schoolboy tastes.

"While those dishes have been most agreeable, Mrs. McFarlane," she said carefully, "I could see how a cook of your talents, in this house, might long to prepare more, ah, adventuresome fare."

At once the woman's eyes brightened. "I would indeed, ma'am," she said. "If it pleases you, ma'am, I could prepare a menu of new dishes for your consideration."

"I would like that very much, Mrs. McFarlane,"

Lizzie said, relieved. "Considering how much time His Grace has spent abroad, a few dishes in the French manner might be—"

"Where the devil is everyone?" roared Hawke from upstairs. "Giacomo, you dog! Why is it I ring and ring and no one moves their lazy ass to come?"

Immediately Giacomo looked to Lizzie, silently pleading. He couldn't go tend to Hawke without her leave; he couldn't even ask permission.

"You may go, Giacomo," she said quickly, and with a hasty bow he raced around her and up the stairs.

But too late.

"Lizzie!" Hawke bellowed. "Lizzie? Where in blazes is my wife?"

He appeared at the top of the stairs, wearing his gold-striped banyan and obviously nothing more besides. His hair was wild and uncombed and his jaw unshaven, and he glared with fierce incomprehension at Lizzie and the line of now terrified servants.

"Lizzie," he said, scowling down at her. "What the devil are you doing here?"

She smiled warmly up at him, recognizing his fierceness as the usual result of still being half asleep.

"I am addressing the staff, Hawke," she said. "I wish to make your household more orderly for your sake."

"Why?" he asked, still scowling.

"Because you are far too busy with your own affairs to be troubled by household matters," she explained, "while I, as mistress of this house, should be tending to them."

He tipped his head to one side, regarding her with sideways skepticism. "Is this my mother's doing?"

"Not at all," she said firmly. "It is my own."

He grunted, shoving his hair back. "Will you be at it much longer?"

"I believe I'm almost finished." She turned to Mr.

Betts, Mrs. Perkins, and Mrs. McFarlane. "Have you any further questions of me?"

"No, ma'am," Mr. Betts said solemnly. "However, I am certain I speak for all of us in saying how happy I am to welcome Your Grace to Hawkesworth Chase."

"Why, thank you, Mr. Betts," Lizzie said, so genuinely touched that she pressed her palms to her cheeks with surprise, and to keep from crying. "Thank you all."

"Lizzie," Hawke said, "whenever you are done, I wish you to dress for riding in Rotten Row."

"Riding?" Lizzie repeated, her voice rising higher with eager delight. She had enjoyed this time alone with Hawke, enjoyed it beyond measure, but she'd likewise enjoy the chance to go elsewhere with him. And if they were heading to Hyde Park, she might be able to persuade him to call at Marchbourne House on the way, so she might see Charlotte and the children. "In Rotten Row?"

Hawk made a noncommittal grunt. "That's what I said, isn't it?"

Barely recalling her duchess self, Lizzie glanced back to the servants, still waiting upon her wishes.

"Thank you all," she said quickly. "Now—now you may go."

As they scattered, Lizzie ran up the stairs to join Hawke on the landing. He was still scowling, and she wished he'd tell her how well she'd done addressing the servants, but most likely he'd do that later, when they were alone. Besides, she was too excited to let it bother her now.

"You do mean riding horses, Hawke," she said, "and not in some stuffy carriage, don't you?"

"If you wish," he said. "I trust you ride as well as you row?"

"Better," she declared. "You will marvel at my new scarlet habit, Hawke, and the most dashing black hat with a great curling black plume. Let me call Margaret to put out my—"

He caught her arm. "Not yet," he said. "No one dares show their face in the park until noon. Since we're up at cock's crow, we've hours before we need dress."

"Hours?" she said, smiling slyly. She slipped her hand inside his banyan to find his warm skin and lean, muscled torso beneath the silk, like unwrapping a splendid present. "However shall we pass that time, I wonder?"

Being married to Hawke, she didn't wonder at all. But though they retreated back to his bedchamber exactly as she'd expected, and though her sober blue gown was soon left in a rumpled heap on the floor along with his banyan, there was something oddly off about their lovemaking. His early morning grumpiness persisted, and though he pleased her in bed and she him, she couldn't help but sense a disgruntled undercurrent simmering away beneath everything he did or said. She tried her best to coax him from it, yet still he persisted in being sour-tempered, and for the first time since they'd been wed, she was almost relieved to be able to leave him to Giacomo's ministrations and retreat to her own rooms to be dressed by Margaret.

For her own part, she was in an excellent humor. Her first address to his servants—no, *her* servants now, too—had gone much better than she'd expected, and she was both proud of herself and relieved to have survived it. She could scarcely wait to ride with Hawke in so public a place as Hyde Park, and she hoped there would be plenty of her friends and acquaintances there as well so she could display her handsome new husband. Besides, who could be out of sorts when dressed in a brilliant red habit with polished brass buttons?

Lizzie smiled at her reflection in the glass as Margaret carefully thrust extra-long pins into her plumed black hat and through her hair to make sure it stayed in place while riding. She adored this hat—shining black silk with a narrow brim to the front over her eyes like a jockey's cap, and an extravagant curling black ostrich plume on the side of the crown—and she'd be loath to have it bounce from her head to the dirt.

"There you are, ma'am," Margaret said, giving the hat one final pat. "You'll do His Grace more than proud in the park."

"I hope so." Lizzie sighed. "At present His Grace is behaving like a sullen small boy determined to pout, and it is not pleasing."

Margaret shook her head in sympathy. "Men are men, ma'am."

"That's vastly wise of you, Margaret," Lizzie said. "Men *are* men, and more fools are we women for tolerating it. I must hope that Giacomo will have said the magic Italian words to him to make him more cheerful."

But one look at Hawke as she met him showed that not even Giacomo's magic had worked. It was doubly hard for Lizzie to bear because she'd never before seen him dressed for riding, and the effect was undeniably breathtaking. At least it claimed *her* breath, seeing him in close-fitting white buckskin breeches, top boots, a pale gray coat, a darker gray waistcoat with gleaming silver buttons, and a black cocked hat. She doubted any male could wear a pair of buckskins with more elegance, nor would the customary colors of a country gentleman's attire suit anyone better than Hawke.

If only he'd smile . . .

"I like you in red," he said, his gaze sweeping so frankly over her that she blushed to match the wool of her habit. "I've never fathomed why a woman dressed as a soldier in regimentals is so beguiling."

"Because it's not really a uniform," she said, glad he'd taken notice. "Only the color and the facings and the buttons are the same, really. Besides, a soldier doesn't wear stays or petticoats."

"Yes, and they don't have breasts, either," he said. "Every man in the park will be looking at you."

"I only care for one," she said as winningly as she could, yet still he didn't smile.

"I regret that you've pinned up your hair," he said. "This is the first day since we've been wed that it's not unbound."

"I can't leave it down, Hawke, not for riding," she protested. "It would fly all around and smother me, not to mention terrify the horses."

He grunted, that dreadful, noncommittal grunt of his that could still speak volumes without a single word. "As you wish. The carriage is waiting."

Because their house was so far from Hyde Park, they rode in the carriage to the park's stables, where Hawke's grooms would have their mounts saddled and ready. It was not that long a drive across the town, and on every other drive that Lizzie could recall with Hawke, he'd made sure the time passed with pleasurable swiftness.

But today he simply sat across from Lizzie like a beautiful, virile lump, so deep in whatever was plaguing him that he'd only answer her queries with a yes or no. They weren't taxing queries, either—most regarded the weather—so by the time they finally reached the stables, she felt as if she'd been trapped on a voyage from one side of the world to the other.

At least he'd more to say about her horse, a neat small bay with a black mane and tail.

"She's a fine little mare," he said, stroking the horse's nose as the groom held her at the block for Lizzie to mount. "They told me she'd only been ridden by ladies and gently at that, but she's young enough that she'll have sufficient spirit for you."

"She's quite beautiful," Lizzie said, hooking her knee

around the sidesaddle's horn and arranging her skirts over her legs. She could tell already that the mare was a much better horse than she'd ever had as a girl; Mama had only bought ponies and horses of advanced age, preferring to trust the horses rather than her daughters to keep to a respectable gait. "I'm sure we'll get along admirably. Do you know her name?"

"Her name?" He came around to the side, waving away another groom and checking her saddle himself. "She's yours now. Call her whatever you wish."

"Mine?" She grinned. "Oh, Hawke, thank you so much!"

She leaned down, intending to kiss him, but before she could, he'd moved away. It might have been simply that he'd already begun to turn toward his own horse, but Lizzie doubted it, and her joy in the new horse vanished. She'd had enough of this, she decided, watching him climb easily into his own saddle, take the reins of his large chestnut gelding, and urge him on, his thighs tensing in those white buckskins.

No, she ordered herself sternly, she would not be distracted. Buckskin breeches were no compensation for churlish behavior. As soon as they'd left the stable yard and were on the path with no other riders within hearing, she nudged her mare close beside him.

"I cannot begin to fathom what has made you so irksome this morning, Hawke," she began, "or why you are insisting upon carrying that irk here to Hyde Park, where it will plague and ruin this day—"

"*Irk* is not a proper word, Duchess," he interrupted, looking straight ahead and pointedly not at her. "At least not as you are employing it."

"It is so!" she said indignantly. "It's an entirely proper word, and entirely appropriate to your behavior at this very moment. Irk, sir, as in you are being a most grievous, huge *irk* in the bottom. What is wrong with you, Hawke? What has put you in such a black humor?"

He whipped his head around to her. "Perhaps you would do better to look to yourself for the answer to that question."

"Look to *myself*?" she asked, her voice squeaking with such incredulity that the mare's ears swiveled about in protest.

"What else am I to say, Duchess, when I am forced to begin my day in utter confusion," he said warmly, "waking to find my wife is gone from my bed?"

"You were asleep, Hawke," she said fiercely. "Deeply asleep. *Snoring* asleep. You had no notion whether I was beside you or not."

"All the more reason that you should be there," he said firmly. "I trusted that you would be. I believed it so, even as I slept."

"And that is what has you in such distemper?" she asked. "Because I chose to rise before—"

"Stop," he said sharply. "That's Lord and Lady Merton directly before us, and I'll not have it said that we are quarreling."

"Whatever became of not caring what others thought?" Lizzie said, showing she didn't by not bothering to lower her voice. "What of setting our own fashions, and doing what we pleased, and—"

"Hush," he ordered, even as he was forcing himself to smile at the earl and countess riding toward them.

If they'd all been in their carriages, riding through the park on the South Carriage Drive, then everyone would have nodded and tipped their hat and passed on by.

But here on Rotten Row, with everyone on horseback, a simple salute could often lead to a conversation that could not be rebuffed without appearing surpassingly rude, and so it was now with Lady Merton. As soon as

Hawke murmured some sort of polite greeting toward her, she seized upon it, and the rest became unavoidable.

"Good day, Your Graces," she said, her voice ringing over the sandy track. "Might I offer our warmest congratulations on your recent marriage?"

Lady Merton's name was on that list of ladies who were supposed to be receiving wedding calls, calls that Lizzie had not so much as thought of making. Not only was Lady Merton a close friend of both Lady Allred and Aunt Sophronia, but she was also considered an important hostess whose assemblies and parties were much anticipated. Lord Merton was an active member of the House of Lords, with fingers in many political pies at the palace, even if his success was whispered to be as much because of his wife's social skills as his own merits.

They were, in short, people best not offended even by dukes and duchesses, and when Hawke failed to reply to Lady Merton's greeting, Lizzie swiftly did.

"Thank you, Lady Merton," she said, smiling as she reined in her mare. "It is a lovely day, is it not?"

"Indeed, Duchess," Lady Merton said, already shifting her gaze toward Hawke. She had once been considered a great beauty, and though age had diminished her allure, she clearly still expected gentlemen to pay attention to her. "Your Grace, your fair wife is a prize—a prize! Why have you not brought her to see me?"

"We have not called on anyone as yet, Lady Merton," Lizzie said quickly, before Hawke could reply, fearing another version of the amorous rabbits. "We've been, ah, enjoying each other's company."

"You've every reason to lock yourself away with such a bride, Duke," Lord Merton drawled. He smiled a bit too warmly as he appraised Lizzie, his eyes wolfishly keen in his full, florid face. "Doing your duty by her in those honeymoon nights, are you?"

"I assure you, Lord Merton," Hawke said, drawling in return, "that duty was never so pleasurable."

The two men laughed broadly, and Lizzie flushed, while Hawke's smile was so knowing and male that she could have gone after him with her riding crop.

Fortunately, Lady Merton chose to ignore them. "Now that you've emerged to rejoin the world, Duchess, I do hope we can lure you and the duke to us. We have a small group of friends who join us regularly on certain evenings. I hope we might be so honored as to include you among our party next Thursday?"

"Oh, yes!" Lizzie said eagerly. She had read of Lady Merton's gatherings in the scandal sheets, and she'd never dreamed she'd be considered either sufficiently interesting or fashionable to be included. "We would be pleased."

"I am glad of it," Lord Merton said. "It will be a fine way to welcome the duke back among us here in London." Addressing Hawke, he added, "Since you are newly returned from Naples, I would ask your advice on several small affairs relating to King Ferdinand and his views."

"I fear I must disappoint you, Lord Merton," Hawke said, a wariness to his voice that was unmistakable to Lizzie. "I was an infrequent visitor to the Neapolitan court and know next to nothing of Ferdinand's views."

But Lord Merton only smiled. "You are too modest, Duke, too modest by half. You are your father's son, and never was there a more sage gentlemen where foreign policies were concerned."

"I cannot deny that I am my father's son, Lord Merton," Hawke said, the edge to his voice a little sharper, "but I assure you that I inherited none of his political sagacity."

Lord Merton chuckled, his chin quivering over the top of his neckcloth. "That I doubt, Duke. I am certain your nothingness will be worth more than a score of the dim-witted dispatches from our addlepated ambassador."

"No more of your politics, my lord," said Lady Merton, teasing and scolding combined. "We mustn't keep these newlyweds from each other a moment longer. Your Graces, good day. Until Thursday."

Lizzie nodded, as did Hawke, and together they rode away from the earl and his wife. As Hawke had predicted, every gentleman they passed looked at her, just as every lady ogled Hawke. Somehow everyone seemed to know who they were, greeting them with a murmured "Your Graces," polite if curious. But there were no further halts for conversations, nor did Hawke choose to break his silence, either—a silence that Lizzie sensed was the quiet before the storm. She was right.

"Why the devil did you agree to go to their house?" Hawke asked at last. It wasn't the furious demand that she'd been expecting, but more of a resigned query. "Why?"

"Because we should," she said calmly, or at least as calmly as she could, fearing worse to come. "Because neither of us has made any wedding calls, and if Lady Merton was willing to overlook that slight and invite us anyway, then I thought it best that we accept."

"Refusing to obey foolish, outmoded custom as dictated by the harpies is not a slight," he said. Usually when Hawke mentioned the harpies, it was a jest, or at least a wry commentary, but not this time. "I've no desire to make wedding calls, and I don't want to attend Lady Merton's gathering, either."

"We needn't stay long," Lizzie said, surprised by his vehemence. "You enjoy company. I've seen you. I've heard that Lady Merton invites artists and writers, too. You'll likely find all manner of people to amuse you."

"What I'll find are all manner of men who wish to inveigle me into politics," he said, his words marked with unexpected despair. "What could I possibly tell Merton of the Neapolitan court?"

She turned to look at him with concern, the plume on her hat blowing across her face. "You don't have to speak to Lord Merton if you don't wish it, Hawke," she said, brushing aside the feathers. "Likely the rooms will be so crowded you won't even see him."

"He will find me," Hawke said, "just as he found me here today. I give you leave to attend by yourself if you wish."

"Don't be foolish," she said, stunned he'd even suggest such an option. "I belong with you. If you don't go, then I won't, either. I'll send an excuse for us."

"You can't," he said wearily. "We must go. Merton was one of my father's closest friends. Now that you have accepted, no excuse would be considered acceptable."

"I'm sorry, Hawke," Lizzie said softly, sadly. "I'd no notion that accepting would distress you so."

"You've no need to apologize, sweeting," he said. They'd reached the end of the row, and he urged his horse to turn about. "I've no right to keep you locked away. We shall attend. Lady Merton and the harpies will be pleased. And if there's anyone who should be sorry, it's I, not you."

She neatly wheeled her mare about after him, following his lead, if not his logic. "That makes no sense, Hawke," she said. "If I needn't apologize, then you couldn't have a reason for doing so, either."

"But I do." His smile was quick and without humor, as if telling a jest that he knew wasn't funny. "I'm sorry I'm not my father."

CHAPTER 16

Hawke stood on the top of the front steps of the Chase, the afternoon sun warm on his face. He knew he shouldn't be here—as a rule, dukes were not supposed to stand bareheaded on their front steps like shopkeepers—but today was an exception. Lizzie was going to call on her sisters and mother at Marchbourne House. She would be gone only a few hours at most, and she would be back at the Chase in time to sup with Hawke this evening. It was an ordinary though pleasant event in a London lady's life.

Except that it wasn't, not for Hawke. It was the first time since he'd married Lizzie that she'd gone anywhere without him. He hadn't objected, of course; he didn't intend to be one of those overbearing boors of a husband.

Since that disastrous ride in the park last week, he'd done his best to be agreeable and obliging, playing the part of a devoted, ardent lover. He'd taken Lizzie to the opera and the playhouse, to stroll in Green Park and toss bread crumbs to the ducks, to the fairground to marvel at the rope dancers and eat strawberries and cream, and to Spring Garden to the museum of curiosities.

He hadn't mentioned his father again. Hesitantly she

had tried to introduce the subject once or twice, but as gently as possible he'd refused to answer. He had long ago closed the door on his father, and there was nothing to be gained by opening it once again, not even for Lizzie—especially not for Lizzie—to peer inside.

All he wished was for her to be happy. Visiting her sister this afternoon had even been his idea, not hers, a way for them both to forget that tonight was Lady Merton's gathering. Hawke had walked down the stairs with Lizzie, praised her gown one more time, smiled at her excitement, and helped her into the carriage himself, saving that privilege for himself instead of a footman. Now he stood here on the step, his hand raised in farewell as the carriage rolled away from the door and down the drive and away.

Away. How could it be possible to miss her already?

He squared his shoulders and walked past the footmen and back into the house, and he didn't stop until he reached the ballroom and his pictures. Since his marriage, he had been neglectful of these old friends, and he almost felt like a stranger now among them. To be sure, he'd enjoyed sharing his favorites with Lizzie, but somehow it hadn't been the same. Now, alone, he was determined to rediscover the old magic that the paintings had held for him, and he quickly made his way to the far corner. If any picture could still be respite for him, it would be this one, and with a happy sigh he set his chair before the oversized landscape.

This was one of the few paintings that he'd commissioned, and the artist had captured a scene that had always been most dear to him: a sweeping view of Naples, as seen from his balcony at Bella Collina. Everything was there exactly as he remembered, from the tiny fishing boats in the harbor to the hazy mists around the broken top of Mt. Vesuvius in the distance. The details were so complete that he could almost feel the gentleness of the breezes from the water, smell the flowers that grew wild on the rocky cliffs beneath the villa, and hear the warbling singing of his cook from the open kitchen windows below. There had been a succession of women there, too, of course, willing, plump-cheeked women, but the villa itself had always been his real mistress.

He had always been happy with this painting before him, because he'd always been happiest in Naples. Was it any wonder that as soon as he'd left, he'd dreamed of the day he'd return? He'd already secured his inheritance by marrying the lady of his father's choice. All that was left was to sire an heir, and then he'd promised himself he'd set sail again for Naples and never look back at England.

He smiled now, determined to lose himself in the countless small recollections of the villa that had meant contentment to him. Bella Collina, his beautiful hill, the one place on earth where he'd been able to put aside the expectations of his father and of London, the one place he'd been able to be the man he wished himself to be. The villa was his escape, his sanctuary, his personal heaven in this life.

So why, then, on this afternoon, were his thoughts unable to focus on the joys of Bella Collina? Why did he keep looking from the painting out the window to the garden, his thoughts wandering again and again to Lizzie: Lizzie laughing as she ran barefoot with her skirts flying, Lizzie at the oars of the little boat, Lizzie climbing up the wall, Lizzie chuckling and sighing with wanton delight as he made love to her on the grass?

He groaned, rubbing his palms across his face as if that would be enough to settle his thoughts. He loved Lizzie. He'd known that almost from the first time he'd seen her. He loved her more than most men ever loved their wives, and certainly loved her more than he'd ever loved any other woman—a staggering realization. But did he love her so much that he'd forget his life at Bella Collina to live here with Lizzie in London? Could his flesh-and-blood wife truly rival his stone-and-mortar mistress?

It was clear to him that Lizzie was perfectly content, even eager, to follow the life and duties that the harpies and the rest of society had laid out for her and, in time, their children, too. While she might have been his own Lizzie Wyldest in those first blissful weeks together, he'd be a fool if he believed she'd forever throw over the traces of her breeding for his sake. Becoming his duchess would be only the beginning for her, not the end. She'd heed the harpies' advice, just as she'd once again begun pinning up her hair, and no matter how in love he was, he'd no intention of being hauled along into docile obedience with her.

He was his own man, a duke, and not even marriage could change that. Over and over he repeated it to himself, as if repetition were enough to make it so.

So why, then, could he not imagine living without Lizzie?

"Your Grace?"

Swiftly Hawke sat upright, pretending he'd been doing anything but wallowing in his own despair—not that Giacomo would ever be so ill-mannered as to notice.

"What is it, Giacomo?" he asked. "Why do you disturb me now, you impudent rascal?"

As usual, Giacomo took no offense, but merely bowed. "As you requested, sir, Monsieur Theobault has arrived. He waits in the hall."

"Where, like all Frenchmen, he is doubtless ogling every one of my parlor maids," Hawke said dryly, or at least as dryly as he could given the gloominess of his thoughts. Monsieur Theobault came to him highly recommended. "Fetch my small sword, Giacomo, and have Theobault meet me in the sunken garden."

Art might have failed him today, but surely violent exercise would not, and with a sigh Hawke left behind his paintings and headed for a lengthy, exhausting session with the French swordsman.

Lizzie ran up the stairs as soon as she returned home, certain she'd find Hawke at his desk in his study. He'd told her he'd intended to spend the afternoon reviewing accounts and correspondence, matters he'd ignored since they'd wed. Men could lose themselves in business affairs, she guessed. She couldn't: though they'd been apart only three hours, she'd missed Hawke almost as much as if the time apart had been three months. It wasn't that she'd not enjoyed herself at Marchbourne House—she'd loved seeing her mother and sisters again, enjoyed laughing and gossiping and playing with Charlotte's children—but being there had only made her realize how much she longed to be back here with Hawke.

It wasn't just love that had pulled her back. There was concern mixed in, too, an uneasy concern that she couldn't quite explain. Ever since the ride in Hyde Park, Hawke had not been the same.

Oh, outwardly he was unchanged, as generous and attentive as ever, but something intangible was different. It was almost as if he'd become *reserved*, holding back from her in a way the Hawke she'd wed never would.

Lizzie suspected that at the heart of it was what he'd said about not being like his father. She wasn't certain, because he refused to speak of it, but she knew him well enough by now to realize that he wouldn't deny it so vehemently if in fact it weren't true. Tonight they were to go to Lord and Lady Merton's house, and it was that invitation that had begun his unhappiness. Lizzie wasn't sure what might happen, or even if, at the last moment, he'd decide they wouldn't attend after all. Whatever he chose to do, she wished to share it with him, which had been much of her reason for hurrying back home.

But to her surprise Hawke's study was empty, with no sign of him having done any work, and she ran through his rooms until she found Giacomo.

"Where is His Grace?" she asked breathlessly. "I thought he'd be here, but he's not."

"His Grace is in the sunken garden, Your Grace," Giacomo said, bowing grandly as he always did. "He is entertaining Monsieur Theobault, ma'am."

"Monsieur Theobault?" The name meant nothing to her. "Who is that?"

"A master in swordsmanship, ma'am," Giacomo said.

Immediately Lizzie thought of the long scar across Hawke's chest, and how he claimed he'd received it fighting an outraged husband.

"What need does he have for swordsmanship?" she asked, more confused than suspicious. "Surely he has no need to defend himself in that fashion here in London."

"No, ma'am," Giacomo said. "It is my understanding that His Grace wishes the challenge of the exercise alone, with no further purpose."

"Then he will not mind if I watch him," Lizzie said, turning to leave. While she and her sisters had engaged in a greater number of mannish activities than most girls, even their mother had drawn the line at sword fighting, and she was curious to see it done.

"Forgive me, ma'am, if you please," Giacomo said, actually daring to step forward. "If you would watch His Grace, ma'am, pray take care not to alarm him. A startlement when armed, a surprise—ah, I would not wish it!"

He threw his hands skyward, too horrified (and melodramatic) to explain further.

"I understand, Giacomo," she said, though she

couldn't tell if his concern was more for her or for Hawke. "It's never a wise idea to surprise anyone who has a sharp blade in his hand. I will take care."

She did, too, slipping out a side door to make as little noise as possible, and taking off her shoes and stockings as well. By now she knew her way around the Chase's gardens, and it was easy enough to find the sunken garden. Despite the name, it never had truly sunk, but simply sat three steps lower than the walk around it. It wasn't much of a garden, either, but more of a large, square area paved with flat stones, used by an earlier Hawkesworth for outdoor banquets when such events were in fashion.

But as Lizzie drew closer, she realized that the garden was being used for a much different activity now. Not wishing to be a distraction, she stayed behind the thick hedge that surrounded the garden, watching through the leaves and branches.

The only time she'd seen gentlemen fighting with swords had been on the stage, with actors who artfully swung tin blades at each other. This wasn't like that, not at all.

Hawke and the Frenchman stood several paces apart, slowly circling the outside of the paving stones. The swords in their hands were not pretend but wickedly real, the blades gleaming dully in the fading light. This was an exercise, not a true duel, but the possibility of injury was undeniable, and the master's young assistant standing to one side oversaw not only water and wine for refreshment but a small surgeon's kit, open and ready on the ground at his feet.

Both men were dressed almost identically, in white shirts, dark breeches, and polished boots, the simplicity of their attire accentuating the drama of their movements. Theobault was shorter than Hawke, powerful and stocky as a bull, with black leather gloves and a leather strip wrapped tightly around his queue in a military fashion. Clearly they had been here a long time: their shirts hung damp and heavy with perspiration and their breeches clung to the muscles in their thighs and buttocks. Both were breathing hard, their lips parted, their hair damp, and their chests rising and falling from exertion.

This was a side to Hawke Lizzie hadn't known existed. Every muscle in his body was taut as he watched the other man with fierce concentration. He swung the sword gently in his hand, almost as if the blade had a life of its own, while he watched for his opponent to move.

Abruptly Hawke lunged forward, his blade catching the other man's with a sharp, metallic clash that made Lizzie jump. The men came close together to engage, then retreated, and engaged again, their swords crashing and scraping together with the violence of each parry and thrust. Just as suddenly—at least to Lizzie's untutored eyes—both once again retreated to the outside of their invisible circle. Breathing hard, they let their arms drop for a moment of rest before they once again began their attacks.

Safely behind the hedge, Lizzie watched, her hands clenched tightly with excitement and her breath coming in quick little gasps. She'd never seen such studied, mannered aggression, such barely controlled male power, especially not from Hawke. It was astonishing, alarming, and infinitely more arousing than she'd ever thought possible. No wonder ladies weren't usually privy to such exhibitions.

"Once more, Monsieur?" Hawke asked, and Theobault bowed his acquiescence. Again they took their places and positions, making ready. This time the Frenchman moved first, lunging forward. Deftly Hawke parried his attack, twisting sideways with animal grace. He turned, charged, and with the tip of his blade caught the guard of the other man's sword. Before Theobault realized what had happened, Hawke snapped the Frenchman's sword from his fingers and flipped it spinning up into the air, where Hawke caught the hilt with his free hand.

But instead of being angry at being caught out like this, Theobault only laughed and applauded.

"Bravo, sir, bravo," he said, bowing extravagantly. "You've learned the lesson so well that you outdo my own humble skills."

Hawke grinned, handing both swords to the assistant. "Rather, I learned your own trick sufficiently well that you could permit me to win without dishonor."

Theobault bowed again and cocked one brow, as much as admitting that Hawke was right. Again they laughed together, with Hawke clapping the Frenchman on the shoulder for good measure, and when the assistant brought them glasses of wine, each attempted to be the first to raise his glass to the other.

It was, decided Lizzie from her hiding place, one of the most bewilderingly male sights she'd ever seen: how one moment the two could have fought with such murderous intent, and then the next acted as if the other were his dearest companion.

But the surprises weren't quite done. As she watched, Hawke emptied his glass, gave one final thump to Theobault's shoulder, and then headed directly toward where Lizzie was hiding.

She gulped and began to scuttle away, not wanting him to catch her, but apparently it was too late for that.

"Lizzie, my love," he said, coming around the hedge to block her way with the same swiftness he'd just demonstrated with his sword. "Did you enjoy that?"

"How did you know I was there?" she said defensively.

He smiled wickedly. "I saw you through the hedge as

soon as you came. The sunlight caught you. Now tell me: did you like seeing your husband perform so admirably?"

"It frightened me," she admitted. "I kept thinking of what would happen if you slipped, or were caught off guard, or—"

"That wouldn't happen," he said, blithely dismissing her worries. He caught her arm and drew her close. "Theobault is good, but I am better. Come, kiss me."

She fluttered her hands a bit against his chest, weakly protesting such a bold command, but because she did wish to kiss him as much as he did her, she soon was doing exactly that, even if he was sticky with sweat and smelled worse than a stable. Or perhaps she kissed him because he was like that, reminding her of his animal grace as he'd lunged with the sword; she wasn't going to stop to philosophize over her reasons.

But Hawke would, and did.

"So you did like it," he said, his voice a low growl. "I can tell. All women are bloodthirsty at heart. There's nothing that warms your fair hearts like witnessing men fighting."

"That's rubbish," she said, even though it was completely true, as she relished the delicious way he was kissing the side of her throat. Still, she felt she should defend womankind in general from his male assumptions. "Completely. Though perhaps it excites men to believe it so."

"Rubbish yourself," he said, sliding his hand down to caress her bottom through her petticoats. "I say it warms your heart, your blood, and other parts of you, too."

She shoved him away, laughing, and glanced back over her shoulder to see if the Frenchman and his assistant were gone.

"You're in a rare humor now, aren't you?" she said.

"No more swordplay for you, Duke, if this is what results."

"You know what results," he teased, taking her arm to reel her back. "I've a much more interesting sword that's ready for play, Duchess, if you should care to see it."

She smiled her invitation. This was the way he'd been when they'd first wed, and she much preferred it to the more careful, distant Hawke she'd had this last week. If crashing about with swords had brought back her bridegroom, then she'd hire Monsieur Theobault herself.

"Then best bring that sword of yours into the house," she said, looking pointedly down at the front of his breeches. "I don't wish to be eaten by the bugs out here. We've at least an hour before we must dress."

But once they were in the house, he surprised her again by taking her not upstairs to his bedchamber, as she'd expected, but to another room, opening an old-fashioned parlor so seldom used that Lizzie hadn't yet wandered into it.

"Why are we here?" she asked, hopefully expecting some intriguing new diversion possible only in this room.

"I wish to show you another picture." He began to pull open the heavy brocade draperies himself, letting the late afternoon sun spill into the room. "Three pictures, actually."

"Pictures?" Lizzie said, disappointed. She liked looking at pictures, liked it very much when Hawke was the one explaining them, but she'd thought he'd other things in mind. These weren't even the usual bright-colored Italian paintings that he usually favored, but instead the kind of dark, life-sized portraits of old ancestors that hung in most grand English houses. "Pictures."

"Pictures, sweeting, and people." He returned, standing behind her with his arms around her waist to hold her close. "Do you know who that old rogue is there, over the fireplace?"

Dutifully Lizzie looked up, leaning her head back against Hawke's convenient shoulder.

"Of course I know," she said, "because there's another portrait of him in Charlotte's house, and besides, you have the same rascally dark eyes. That's the lusty old king who's your great-great-something-grandfather, the one who gave your family the dukedom."

"Indeed he is," Hawke said, leaning closer, until she could feel the warmth of his words against the side of her neck. "A most charming rogue, they say."

"Like you," Lizzie said, tipping her head so that he had to kiss her.

Which he did, albeit more briefly than she wished.

"Do not distract me," he said, pretending to scold. "Though likely His Majesty would approve. Do you know the lady beside him?"

To the king's right was a portrait of a richly dressed lady who was covered with jewels. Despite wearing the stiff, heavy clothes of another century, she was still undeniably beautiful, with curling chestnut hair and an opulent figure. But what caught Lizzie's eye was less obvious: the sly humor in her smile, the shamelessness in how she gazed from her gilded frame, one brow elegantly cocked. Lizzie had seen the same expression before, a bit bolder, a bit more daring, but nearly the twin in confidence and attitude. She should recognize it, because now, three generations later, it belonged wholly to her husband.

"The first duchess," Lizzie whispered, almost in awe. "That's who she is, isn't she?"

"Who else could she be?" Hawke said, his admiration unmistakable. "Catherine Wellwood Halsbury, first Duchess of Hawkesworth. The finest harlot in a court filled with them. They say the king was hers from the first day she arrived at Whitehall Palace."

Lizzie looked from the rakish, swarthy king back to the voluptuous first duchess. They seemed eminently suited to each other, and she understood why they'd been such notorious lovers. As an afterthought, she finally looked to the last of the three portraits: a sour gentleman with a wispy ginger mustache over downturned, disapproving lips. He seemed to have no place with the other two.

"And that sorry fellow is the Earl of Southwell," Hawke said, idly running his hands up and down her sides. "They say old Roger's spirit was as mean as his face. I've never thought he deserved Catherine, husband or not."

Lizzie stared up at his painted face, trying to find a bit of sympathy for a man who'd been so publicly cuckolded. Yet Hawke was right: he did look too mean-spirited for the glorious Catherine.

"How could he be an earl if she was a duchess?" she asked. "That makes no sense."

"But it does," Hawke said, his caresses becoming more purposeful as he drew her back more tightly against his body. "The king made her a duchess after the birth of their first son, the one who's my ancestor. Practical creature, she signed the royal patent and became a duchess, and claimed all the power and riches she could get. Roger, however, would have none of it, and in disgust left for Paris, where in time he died a stubborn earl. I've always been grateful that sorry worm's no blood kin of mine."

"Not at all," she whispered, pressing her bottom against the fall of his breeches to feel the hardness of his cock. "I understand why she must have loved the king more."

"What choice did she have?" Hawke said, kissing the

place beneath her ear that always made her shiver. "Every woman would believe herself in love if her king desired her."

"*I* wouldn't," she said, turning to face him and loop her arms around his shoulders. "I already love my duke. Besides, our king is newly wed, and besotted with his own wife."

He kissed her lightly, feathering more kisses over cheeks and brows. "That's hardly the point, is it?"

She frowned and pulled back a fraction in his embrace. "Then what is the point, Hawke?" she asked breathlessly. "Why tell me of your faithless grandmother now?"

He slipped his fingers into her hair, holding her face before his. "Because when I was fighting Theobault, all I could think of was you, and how I would never let you slip from me, the way Catherine's husband did."

"But I would never leave you for anyone else, Hawke," she protested. "I love you, and you are my husband, and I—I am not faithless, like that first duchess."

He shook his head, barely listening to her. The earlier fierce aggression that she'd seen when he'd a sword in his hand still lingered in his face, but now it was tempered by a desperation that she'd never expected, and which wrenched at her own heart.

"I would not let any other man have you, Lizzie," he insisted. "I want you to know that. For your sake, I would challenge His Majesty himself if I had to."

"But I already know that of you, Hawke," she said gently. "You are that honorable, that loyal, to me, and I never would doubt you."

"That doesn't matter," he said gruffly. "What does is you, Lizzie. Only you. I would rather die on another man's sword than surrender you. I do not believe I could live the rest of my life without you."

"Oh, Hawke," she murmured, reaching up to kiss

him. She wished he wouldn't speak with such violent finality of swords and death together with devotion, but such things must have been in his thoughts after this afternoon. Besides, even the mildest of gentlemen could fall into unexpected, raging jealousies; hadn't March himself once fought a duel to defend Charlotte's honor? "Such brave words for you to say!"

"They're true words, sweeting," he said, tightening his arm around her waist as if fearing he'd lose her even now. "Every one."

"My darling husband," she said, kissing him again. "That is what it is to love and be loved, or very nearly. Come upstairs with me now, and together we'll discover the rest."

CHAPTER

17

They were late arriving at the Lady Merton's little gathering, so late that it would have been disgraceful in anyone of a lesser rank.

Hawke didn't care. The later they arrived meant the less time they had to be in actual attendance, which also meant the fewer of his father's friends he'd have to tolerate.

He'd other reasons not to care about being late, too. He'd spent much of the afternoon matching blades with one of the best professional swordsmen in London, and he'd acquitted himself reasonably well. Better yet, Lizzie had hidden herself to watch him, and he'd had the double pleasure not just of performing well but of doing so before his awestruck wife.

Lizzie hadn't exactly understood what he'd been trying to tell her before the old portraits of his louche ancestors, but then, he wasn't exactly sure what had happened there, either. His original intention for showing her the paintings had been to tell her that he intended to always defend her honor the way that sour old Roger hadn't. He'd never meant to question her fidelity, or even hint that she resembled avaricious, sinful Catherine. Somehow, however, with Lizzie wriggling so wickedly against him, he'd lost his train of thought and the purpose of his conversation, too.

Not that it had mattered, for they'd both benefited well enough when they'd retired to his bed. He doubted the old king and his mistress could have been any more spectacular in the royal bed than he and Lizzie, amusing each other until it was well past nightfall. Giacomo (and likely Margaret) had his work cut out to make Hawke presentable for evening, but Hawke had been much too content to take notice of the muttered jibes in Italian that had accompanied his dressing.

The pleasurable satisfaction lingered still, with Lizzie insisting on sitting beside him in the carriage, where they could continue to kiss and dally, no matter the mussing that might occur to her gown: a rare and excellent quality in a lady. They'd time for dallying, too, since they were so late that their arriving carriage was stuck behind a line of others whose owners were already leaving.

Finally they stopped before Lord Merton's door, and Hawke stepped out first to hand Lizzie down. Her gown was a froth of ruffled white muslin, covered with swirling embroidered flowers and vines in silver threads that twinkled by the light of the house's flambeaux. She'd chosen to wear the rubies and diamonds he'd given her, too, all of them, the bracelet and necklace as well as her wedding ring, a fiery show that would likely make every lady in the house sick with envy. What every man would notice, however—after Lizzie's obvious beauty— was the warm glow to her cheeks and the softness to her eyes, the undeniable look of a woman who'd been recently pleasured.

Except that of all those gentlemen, he'd be the only one who knew how she felt and tasted and made little chuckling cries of joy when she came, because he was the one who'd done the pleasuring, and the only one she loved.

"What are you thinking?" she asked as they walked up the steps.

He smiled. "I was thinking how I'll have the most beautiful lady in the house on my arm," he said, his words close enough to the truth, "and how that makes me the most fortunate of men."

"Oh, Hawke, you say such pretty nonsense," she said, her smile small and tight as she clung to his hand. "Faith, I am so wicked anxious!"

"What reason could you have to be anxious?" he asked, genuinely mystified. How could a lady who fearlessly clambered up walls and rode with aplomb be nervous about a drawing room filled with stuffy folk? "You're likely much more familiar with these affairs than I am, considering how you trailed after March and your sister."

"I never was taken to any house like Lady Merton's," she said. "I was considered too young. Likely they'll all still believe me too young, though because I'm your wife now, no one will be able to say anything."

"You're fine exactly as you are, sweeting," he said, kissing her cheek. He'd forgotten she was only eighteen. Compared to graybeards such as Merton, she would be a babe in the cradle. She left him briefly, disappearing for a few moments to wherever it was that ladies went to shed their cloaks and pelisses and dust fresh powder on their hair and noses, and returned to take his arm.

"I am ready, Hawke," she said, her jaw set and determined. Yet when she tucked her hand into the crook of his arm, he felt how she trembled, her uneasiness all too real. "I only pray I won't say something unwise to shame you before so many important gentlemen."

"I told you, Lizzie, you'll do extraordinarily well," he said, reassuring her again. He knew that likely all those important gentlemen would be so busy ogling her that they wouldn't hear one word, wise or unwise, that she spoke, but he saw no reason to tell her that. "Pray recall that you are my wife, and that to be wed to me demonstrates untold bravery."

Finally she laughed: not her usual boisterous laugh, but enough that he knew she'd do perfectly well. They entered the large parlor, and the footman announced them. It was, he realized, the first time they'd been paired that way in public, the Duke and Duchess of Hawkesworth, and he liked the way it sounded. He liked it very much.

They walked slowly through the crowded room, nodding and making small greetings. He had lived abroad for so long that most of the faces were as new to him as they must be to Lizzie, or so changed that they might as well be new. Yet because of who they were, and newlyweds at that, every person they passed smiled warmly, as genial as if they really were all the dearest of friends, or more accurately, the dearest of his father's friends. Calming Lizzie's worries about this evening had put his own to rest, too. If the evening proved no more challenging than this, then they'd be fortunate indeed.

"Duchess, Duke, please, please forgive me!" Lady Merton sank in a curtsey before them, the diamonds in her white-powdered hair winking by the candlelight. "I should have been waiting to greet you, but I was called away to an unavoidable emergency among the servants. How very honored we are to have you both here with us this night."

"We are the ones who are honored by your invitation, Lady Merton," Lizzie said, in the perfect murmuring voice that a duchess should employ. Clearly she'd drawn on some inner resource of self-possession to overcome her fears, composing herself to stand straight and serene. This must be the work of the harpies, he thought, all their careful training to prepare her for this moment. She'd always been beautiful; now she was almost regal as well, with all traces of his Lizzie with the grass-stained toes and tangled hair gone. "Your home is most lovely."

Hawke could only stare, stunned by her transformation. He remembered how once she'd told him how she'd always been overlooked in her family, the middle sister no one noticed. She wouldn't be overlooked now, nor likely ever again, and it wasn't because of all those diamonds and rubies, either. She was Elizabeth Wylder Halsbury, Duchess of Hawkesworth, and even in this group of high-ranking ladies she'd stand out. She'd be fine, more than fine.

Which was just as well, because clearly Lady Merton intended to make up for her earlier neglect and claim Lizzie as her prize.

"If you please, Duchess, I hope to prise you away from His Grace so that I might present several other ladies to you," she said, holding her gloved hand out to Lizzie. "Everyone wishes to offer their best wishes to you on your recent marriage. Besides, I know how the gentlemen do wish to speak of affairs away from our tender ears. Isn't that so, Duke?"

But before Hawke could answer, Lord Merton appeared, bearing down upon him beneath his tall white wig like a ship-of-the-line under full sail. The earl made a leering, muttered greeting to Lizzie—or rather to Lizzie's breasts—then turned the full force of his attention toward Hawke.

"I was beginning to think you'd found other amusements than us for this evening, Duke," he said, his smile more scolding than welcoming. "Though with a bride such as yours, all is forgiven. Here are two other gentlemen I wish you to meet. Lord Cousins, Lord Bonny."

Hawke bowed politely, swallowing back his rising discomfort. Both gentlemen were cut from the same glittering cloth as Lord Merton: gentlemen of his father's generation whose lives were concentrated on the House of Lords and the court, men with shrewd eyes, cold hearts, and ruthless ambition for power.

"We are heartily glad to have you back among us, sir," said Lord Bonny, his hands resting over a floridly embroidered waistcoat that stretched tight over his abundant belly. "England needs young gentlemen with your experience to help lead her forward."

"That is generous of you, Lord Bonny," Hawke said, thinking how his past in Naples, devoted as it had been to art and to pleasing himself, had very little in it that would benefit England. "But I doubt I've the kind of experience that you require."

"Nonsense, sir," said Lord Cousins, his face reminding Hawke of a half-melted candle. "You are being too modest. You are newly returned from Naples. You will have fresh advice for us on the new king there, and his leanings. Ah, what a tragedy for England that he wed into the Hapsburgs and the Bourbons!"

"The Neapolitan queen appears a fair little lady," Hawke said carefully, the best information he could muster. "I have seen her at balls, and she danced quite prettily. She's already given the king a pair of sons and a daughter, too."

All three men laughed indulgently at that, in a way that irritated Hawke.

"Ah, the bridegroom speaks!" Lord Merton said. "Of course fecundity is on your mind, Duke, and who would dare fault you for it? But we would know of Her Majesty's other, more useful qualities."

"Is it true she is conniving and clever?" Lord Cousins asked eagerly. "Does in fact she make the king her pawn? Does she incline the country toward the wishes of the Austrians and her mother, and thereby to France rather than England?"

Hawke cleared his throat, his irritation growing. "I

fear I was never such a fixture at Ferdinand's court that I would be privy to such information."

"It is wise to be careful, Duke, especially in a place with so many ears," Lord Merton said, nodding sagely. "I like reticence in a man. A most necessary quality for profitable relationships."

"Your father, rest his soul, possessed both wisdom and reticence," Lord Bonny intoned as if speaking from a pulpit. "How fortunate we are to have his son with us now! What we shall all be able to achieve together, what we shall accomplish!"

Hawke clasped his hands behind his back, the only way he could contrive to keep them from making fists of frustration at his sides. He felt as if he were a schoolboy again, trapped and cornered once more by his father's expectations.

He glanced past Lord Bonny's frizzy wig, searching for Lizzie. She stood in the center of a ring of ladies, clearly the center of attention, just as he was here. The only difference was that she was elegant and composed, a perfect duchess, while he was shambling and incoherent. He desperately longed to be there beside her, with her, though it was patently clear that she'd no need of him at all.

He forced himself to collect his thoughts and return to the conversation he'd no wish to pursue.

"You may see many likenesses between my father and me, my lords," he said, displeasure in his voice no matter how he tried to contain it, "but I fear you would discover in time that there are far more dissimilarities than otherwise, especially regarding political affairs."

"Oh, that would come swiftly enough, Duke," Lord Merton said with a dismissive sweep of his thick-fingered hand. "As soon as you take your seat in the Lords—"

"I have taken my seat, my lords, years ago," Hawke

said, "and then I likewise left it, with little intention of returning to it."

All three lords stared at him, aghast. Now that he'd begun, Hawke plunged ahead, unable to stop.

"Regrettably for your plans, I do not share my father's interests, nor likely ever shall," he continued, each word clipped. "I wish nothing to do with the House of Lords or any other 'profitable relationships' here in London."

"Your frankness amazes me, Duke," rumbled Lord Merton, attempting to placate. "Surely in time—"

"There will be no time, Lord Merton," Hawke said curtly. "In fact, I do not plan to remain long in London, but to return to Naples."

"A wedding trip, eh?" Lord Bonny asked slyly. "What could be more romantic than the southern climes with your lovely duchess?"

"Her Grace will not be joining me, but remaining here in London with her family," Hawke said, more sharply than he'd intended. "My villa in Naples is my permanent residence."

My villa in Naples is my permanent residence. That had always been his private plan, a reassuring notion that he'd clung to ever since he'd realized the restriction of his father's damnable will. He would obey his father's wishes, and his reward for doing so would be Villa Collina and his old life. It had always made comforting sense, knowing that he'd a way to outfox his father one final time.

But a private notion and a bold declaration were entirely different things, and even without seeing the shocked faces of the other men he realized at once just how harsh his words must have sounded. How could he be married less than a month, yet already planning a way to part from a seemingly perfect wife?

Doubtless these worldly gentlemen were imagining every kind of explanation behind his words: that the young duchess had some terrible malady or impairment, or that the duke had no interest in women in general, or perhaps that he'd another, illicit family waiting in Italy. None of their imagined explanations would be right, of course. But what could he possibly say that would be any more logical, or without the unsavory hint of betrayal or abandonment? They wouldn't understand; they couldn't.

And if he was honest, he wasn't sure he understood himself any longer, either. He felt a sudden wave of nausea, the kind that followed an unexpected blow to the stomach.

"Pray excuse me, my lords," he muttered. Not waiting for their permission, he turned and plunged into the crowd.

He meant to join Lizzie. He needed to, after what he'd just said.

He only got halfway.

"So you are here, cousin," Brecon said, his smile warm as he caught Hawke by the arm. "Merton told me you were expected—boasted of it, to be true—but I'd begun to doubt his word."

"Good day, Brecon." Hawke took a deep breath, not wanting to appear anything but composed before his older cousin. Brecon was as perfectly at ease as he always was, his clothes impeccably stylish without being overdone or French, his manner relaxed and gentlemanly. But with one look at Hawke, Brecon's perfect smile vanished, and he took Hawke firmly by the shoulders, as if he feared he'd need support.

"What is wrong, Hawke?" he asked quietly. "You're white as your shirt. Are you ill? Should I call for your carriage to take you home?"

Hawke shook his head, reaching to take a glass of wine from a passing servant's tray.

"I'm well enough, I promise you," he said, drinking

deeply. "An unpleasant conversation with company I did not desire. A passing lapse, that is all."

It was clear that Brecon didn't believe him, but that he also knew better than to push Hawke. Instead he simply nodded, accepting Hawke's explanation.

"I am glad to see you among society," he said evenly. "You and your lovely lady. Marriage agrees with you, yes?"

"Yes," Hawke said, searching again for Lizzie. She was sitting now, apparently held so rapt by some delicious tattle that she wasn't moving, her eyes wide and her lips barely parted. It was a very unguarded, very Lizzie expression, and he felt a fresh surge of love for her.

"I can see that it does," Brecon said, following his glance. "You smile when you look at your wife."

Abashed, Hawke shrugged. "I've always had a weakness for beauty."

Now Brecon smiled, too. "Don't pretend it's not more than that. You love the lady."

"I do," Hawke said softly, unable to keep from looking once again at Lizzie. "I do. How could any man not love her?"

"Not any man," Brecon said. "You're her husband, and that's the only one who should."

They laughed together, a comfortable shared laughter between cousins who happened to be friends.

"That's better," Brecon said, clapping him on the shoulder. "And you no longer resemble a corpse. Truly Lizzie must be a goddess, able to raise the dead! Come, I wish to pay my respects to her."

Together they made their way through the crowd. Lizzie spied them when they were still several paces away, her face lighting in a way that was endlessly gratifying to Hawke. He didn't need Brecon to tell him he loved her. The proof was before his eyes, grinning up at him.

"Oh, Hawke, I'm so vastly glad you're here!" she exclaimed, seizing him in a quick, impulsive hug and adding a kiss for good measure. She wasn't being a grand duchess now; she was simply being Lizzie, the way he much preferred. "And Brecon! How good it is to see you, too."

She kissed him, too, a good cousinly kiss, then to Hawke's surprise pulled forward a small, plainly dressed man with a terrified expression on his olive-skinned face. Hawke supposed he'd every right to be terrified, seeing as Lady Merton had been directing a loud, one-sided conversation at him.

"This is someone you must meet, Hawke," she said, beaming as she gave the little man a reassuring pat on his sleeve, "not only because he is a genius as an artist, and I know you like artists, but also because you are likely the only person in this room who can speak with him properly. Hawke, Signor Antonio Petrocelli. Signore, my husband, the Duke of Hawkesworth."

Silently the man bowed low before Hawke—too low, really, for Hawke's comfort. Signor Petrocelli didn't need to grovel as if he were some heathen pasha. Yet Hawke could sympathize with his plight. He knew firsthand what it was like to be in a foreign place without the faintest idea of what was being said, and he, too, had had people like Lady Merton shout at him, only in German or French or Arabic, in the misbegotten belief that any language was made more comprehensible by volume. Besides, Lizzie was right: he did like artists. He reached down and took the man's hand, intending to shake it.

"Good day to you, signore," Hawke said in Italian. "I welcome you to London, and I look forward to seeing your work."

Petrocelli gasped, his eyes filling with tears. He bent and kissed the back of Hawke's hand—a gesture of respect common in Italy, but uncomfortably out of place in Mayfair—and answered in such a torrent of grateful Italian that Hawke could barely make it out himself.

"Merciful heavens," Lady Merton said, taken aback. "Whatever did you say to him, Duke?"

"Only that I wished to see his work," Hawke said, "and that I welcomed him to London."

"He's just arrived last week from Rome, a fearfully long voyage," Lizzie explained. "Poor man, he must be overwhelmed by such a journey and by London, too!"

She fetched a sheet of paper from a nearby table and handed it to him. "Look at this, Hawke. I know I don't see or admire art as well as you do, but doesn't that look exactly like me?"

The drawing had been quickly done in black pencil, likely for the artist's own pleasure rather than for presentation to a potential patron. Certainly the way Petrocelli was standing now, waiting for Hawke's reaction with his palms pressed together before his mouth in agonizing, silent supplication, proved that. Petrocelli must have been drawing Lizzie when Hawke had seen her across the room, when she'd been listening with her eyes wide, for that was exactly how he'd captured her. A few sure lines, an artful smudge or two for shading, and there was Lizzie, with the haste of the sketch reflecting her own vibrancy.

He was impressed, and he felt the first, familiar rush of excitement when he'd discovered an artist new to him. He'd wish to see finished paintings, of course, but if this sketch was any indication of the man's gifts, then Hawke would happily commission him to paint Lizzie, and perhaps himself as well.

"This is very fine, signore," he said in Italian to the

artist. "Very fine indeed. With whom did you study in Rome?"

"Pompeo Girolamo Batoni, Your Grace," Petrocelli answered, rolling the name off his tongue with considerable pride. "I was honored to be part of his studio in the Via Bocca di Leone, and assisted in his drawing academy."

"I can see Batoni's influence in the purity of your line," Hawke said. The man should be proud of a connection to Batoni, in Hawke's estimation the only modern Italian painter worth a damn. "I should like to see more of your work, if possible. Did you paint fashionable portraits in Rome?"

Petrocelli nodded, again close to tears. "I did, Your Grace, I did," he said. "With great success I painted many English gentlemen who had come to visit Rome."

"Yet you came here?" Hawke asked. Just as he'd earlier felt so ill at ease among the politicians, he was now enjoying himself tremendously. Speaking Italian, discussing art and painters: what could be better?

"I was invited by Master Sir Lucas Rowell, Your Grace, to your magnificent city," Petrocelli answered in Italian. "Sir Lucas wishes me to inspire your English painters to greatness."

"Sir Lucas Rowell," Lizzie said eagerly, beckoning to a man of middling age and height whose face was dominated by a turnip-shaped nose. "Now, that much of your conversation I could understand! Here is that very gentleman, Hawke, waiting to make your acquaintance as well. He is a most esteemed painter, perhaps the most esteemed in London, and he's painted Charlotte and March and, oh, everyone else. Hawke, Sir Lucas Rowell. Sir Lucas, my husband the Duke of Hawkesworth."

Hawke's smile grew more reserved. He didn't know which of the portraits at Marchbourne House could be blamed on Sir Lucas, but he did know that most of those he'd seen appeared to be dreary daubs, with flattery in place of talent.

"Your Grace," Sir Lucas said, his voice lushly obsequious from long years catering to noble patrons. "Your servant, sir. I am most honored to make your acquaintance at last. There are so few Englishmen in the highest ranks who take a true interest in the fine arts."

Lizzie nodded eagerly, fluttering her lace fan before her with excitement. "I've told them all about you, Hawke, how much you love your paintings, and what a wondrous collection you have."

"Pray tell me, sir," Sir Lucas asked, lowering his voice in awe. "Is it true that you possess a Titian Venus, and that she is here in London with you?"

Swiftly Hawke glanced at Lizzie. It was clear as day that she'd told these others of his treasures propped on the floor of his ballroom. She smiled in return and came to slip her hand fondly into his, unaware that she might have erred in sharing this particular information with others. Aside from his private attachment to the pictures, he was well aware of their rarity and monetary value, and wished she hadn't described them so thoroughly in public, just as he wouldn't wish her telling strangers of how much income his properties brought him each year.

But Lizzie, his Lizzie, was far too ingenuous to think that way.

"I knew you dreaded coming here tonight," she said softly, so only he could hear, "and feared there'd only be stuffy older gentlemen who'd try to speak to you of Parliament. But I found the artists for you, didn't I? I found you the guests who knew who Titian was, didn't I?"

He smiled and lightly squeezed her fingers to show he appreciated what she'd done. Later, when they were alone, he could explain why it wasn't wise, no matter her intentions.

"Yes, Sir Lucas," he said. "I do in fact have a Venus by Titian, the prize of my little collection. After my wife, she is the beauty of our house."

"Oh, Hawke," Lizzie said, blushing before the others. "Not now."

But Hawke wished it *was* now. No matter whether artists were present or not, when she looked at him that way, he longed for the evening to be done so that he might take her home, where they'd be alone.

"I congratulate you on your good fortune in both areas, Your Grace," Sir Lucas said. "You are a lucky man."

"Indeed you are, Duke," Lady Merton said briskly. "Which is why I hope that we can prevail upon you to share your good fortune with others."

"Yes, yes, Hawke, you must listen to this," Lizzie said. "I'm certain you'll agree that it's wonderfully important."

If he'd heard only the others, he would have refused even before they'd asked, but because it was Lizzie asking, he listened.

Sir Lucas cleared his throat portentously. "I'm sure Your Grace is aware of the sad state of painting in Britain, and specifically in London," he began. "For a land that is so blessed in other ways, we are without any galleries for inspiration, any museums, even any academies for instruction and furtherment. How can our own native painters prosper in such a parched wilderness?"

"Sir Lucas is opening an academy of art," Lizzie said, helpfully slicing through his rhetoric. "He needs patrons."

"Patrons with an understanding of pictures, and an appreciation of the suffering of the soul that a true artist must endure," Lady Merton said solemnly. "Recognizing so noble a cause, Lord Merton and I were among the first patrons of the new academy. Of course His Majesty was first, as is proper."

"We should become patrons, too, Hawke," Lizzie said earnestly. "You'd like it."

"Of course," Hawke said, happy to oblige her in so small a way. Though Lizzie might not realize it, such appeals for support were common, and he subscribed to all manner of charities and noble causes. It was part of being a duke. He'd speak to Wynn in the morning about this one, and have their names added to the list with a suitable contribution to match. "We shall be honored to be included, Sir Lucas."

"I am the one who is honored, Your Grace," said Sir Lucas, bowing with a sweeping arm more fit for an actor than for an artist. "I dare to hope that one day I might show my students the matchless beauty of your Titian Venus so that they may drink in her loveliness."

Hawke made some sort of vague reply, neither listening nor caring. Like so many such noble projects of admirable intentions, this one probably would never come to fruition, and besides, he was more concerned with encouraging Lizzie to bid farewell to the company than with hearing more of Sir Lucas's bombast.

Yet when they were at last back in their carriage and she was nestled comfortably beside him, Hawke had no choice but to return to Sir Lucas, Signor Petrocelli, and his own precious pictures.

"I understand that you meant it for the best, sweeting," he began, "but I'd prefer if you didn't cry out to the world that I have a Titian and a Tintoretto sitting in my ballroom."

She twisted around to face him, her head leaving his shoulder: not a good sign. "But Sir Lucas and the signore are artists themselves, Hawke. I thought you would enjoy speaking to them about paintings, the way you do with me."

"I did, and I thank you for it," he said quickly. "At least I enjoyed speaking with Petrocelli. Rowell is a self-important bag of wind."

But she was shaking her head, her jewels clinking softly with the motion.

"You're always saying how in Italy, art is a part of life," she insisted. "I thought you'd be happy to share your pictures, and by doing so perhaps make London a little bit more like Italy. Sir Lucas and Signor Petrocelli would *understand* the magic, just as you do."

Hawke sighed, wishing this were going better. "Lizzie, you and I look at my pictures and see their magic. Others will look at them and see only their great monetary value. They're priceless."

"That makes no sense, Hawke, even from you." The passing light from lanterns outside fell across her face, showing her unhappiness. "How can your pictures be of great monetary value and yet priceless?"

"Because if they were lost or fell into the wrong hands, they would be gone forever from my life," he said finally. "I can explain it no better than that. They cannot be replaced, not for all the money in the world."

"Like you," she said wistfully.

"Like me?" he asked, not following.

"Like you, Hawke," she said again. "You could never be replaced in my life or my heart, not by any other man, ever, ever."

He hadn't expected that, not at all. He could just make her out in the shadowy corner of the carriage, hugging her arms to herself. She was watching him, her eyes filled with an impossible sadness, as if they'd somehow already been parted.

"Come here, love," he said gruffly, reaching out to pull her close. "You know you could never be replaced in my heart, either."

Yet even to his own ears, it all sounded hollow and

false, words spoken more because they were expected, not felt.

"You know I love you," he said, trying again. "You must know that, Lizzie."

She sighed and curled against him, letting him hold her close.

"I know you love me," she whispered against his waistcoat. "I know you do."

But the sorrow in her voice betrayed her doubt, and when he began to think of all he'd said that night, he could not blame her. Damnation, he could not.

CHAPTER 18

Lizzie sat on the edge of the chair, sipping her chocolate and pretending that everything was as it should be. Outwardly it was. She was dressed in her favorite striped silk dressing gown, taking breakfast with her husband. Earlier, he had made extravagant love to her, so long and well that it had been nearly eleven by the time they'd risen, and this breakfast should more rightly have been called dinner. The day was warm and sunny and full of languid promise; the windows were open to the garden, and she could smell the heady late-summer scent of the ripening plums and peaches on the trees nearby.

But things weren't right. While they'd still been abed, Hawke had announced that he wished to take breakfast in the ballroom with his pictures, a tacit reminder of all he'd said last night in the carriage. It hadn't exactly been a quarrel, but it hadn't been pleasant, either. What she'd been left with was the distinct impression that somehow his pictures were worth more to him than she herself was. She'd been shocked, but most of all she'd been hurt, wounded more grievously than he'd ever know.

Ladies of her rank often discovered to their sorrow and chagrin that they shared their husbands' affections with a mistress. But how was she to fight back if his other love wasn't flesh and blood but old pieces of stretched canvas covered with oil and pigments, items that represented a time in his life that she'd no part of? She'd thought the pictures were something they'd shared. She'd never dreamed they were her rivals.

Now he sat in silence beside her, his coffee in his hand, studying the one picture that made her most uncomfortable. It wasn't the Venus that Lady Allred had wished to banish. It was the scene from his window of his villa in Naples. On the first day he'd brought her here to the Chase, when she'd climbed over the wall to make him run after her in the garden, he'd proudly explained to her how this house, a country house in Somerset, and another in Scotland would all belong to her, too, once they were wed. *Ours:* that was what he'd told her.

But he hadn't included Bella Collina among those houses, not once. The villa was unquestionably his alone, and never more so than now. He sat sipping his coffee and studying the painting propped before him with his back to the open window, pointedly preferring the painted Italian scenery to the real English one behind him.

He was so lost in the picture that there was no conversing with him, which made the task before her infinitely more difficult. Last night while they were riding home she'd meant to tell him what she'd done earlier, to confess her impulsive act. But once he'd told her how badly she'd erred by telling Sir Lucas and Signor Petrocelli about his pictures, there was no possibility of a confession. In most circumstances, she considered herself to be brave, at least braver than most other women. But she'd been a wretched, hopeless coward over this, and each silent moment that passed was only making it worse.

With no stomach for her chocolate, she poked her finger at the foam on the top, chasing the iridescent bubbles around the edge of the cup. It was almost noon now. Perhaps they wouldn't come. Perhaps they'd interpreted her invitation as only an idle pleasantry, not to be acted upon. Perhaps—

The knock at the door echoed so loudly in the room that Lizzie jumped, spilling her chocolate on her gown. She leaped to her feet and grabbed a napkin, furiously blotting at her skirts as Hawke called for the footman to enter.

But it wasn't a footman. It was Mr. Betts, the butler, signifying something or someone important.

"The Countess of Merton and Sir Lucas Rowell are here to see you, Your Grace," Mr. Betts said as he stood before Hawke. "Lady Merton says they have come at Her Grace's invitation."

"Impertinent woman," Hawke said, scowling. "Doubtless the countess suspects me of not keeping my word and comes to dun me in person for her scheme, with her pet painters in tow. Tell her we are not at home, Betts, and that she is mistaken. Can you imagine that, Lizzie? For her to say that you—"

"I did, Hawke," Lizzie said miserably, crumpling the chocolate-stained napkin in her hand. "Last night I invited them to come view your pictures . . . it was before you—you informed me that it displeased you so."

Hawke set his cup down on the table so sharply that the porcelain rang in muted protest. "You did what?"

"I invited them here." Lizzie raised her chin, determined not to cower. She was still his wife, still his duchess, and still at heart Lizzie Wylder. "I invited them here because I believed it would give you pleasure, Hawke. Most people enjoy sharing the things that make them happy."

His expression didn't change. "You presumed a great deal, Lizzie."

"Yes, Hawke, I did presume," she said as firmly as she could. "I presumed that you would wish to do good with your life and to share the blessings that have been yours from birth. I presumed that since you did not wish to follow your father into Parliament, that you would instead wish to be yourself and help in the founding of this academy for the arts. I presumed that you might actually wish to improve your own country and its people, rather than mooning away after your—your *infernal* Italy."

At last Hawke rose, looming over her. His lips were pressed tightly together with displeasure, his dark brows drawn low over his eyes. Most telling of all was the vein to one side of his forehead, throbbing in a telltale way that she'd learned never meant good.

"Are you quite done, Lizzie?" he demanded. "Is that all you have to say in judging me?"

She drew her shoulders back and raised her head with defiance, not letting him have even half an inch's height in advantage over her.

"I am done, thank you." She turned to Mr. Betts. "Please show Lady Merton and Sir Lucas in."

Betts bowed and withdrew, and Lizzie turned back to Hawke, folding her arms over her chest, the trailing sleeves of her dressing gown like wings.

"You may leave now if you wish it, Hawke," she said. "You needn't stay on account of my obligation to Lady Merton. But as long as I am your wife and your duchess, then this house and its contents are mine as well. I won't explain the pictures as well as you would, but I've heeded your lessons well enough to make an acceptable presentation to my guests."

"Have you?" he asked, incredulous. He seized her by the hand and pulled her down to the far end of the row of paintings. He pointed to a painting of a sweet-faced saint, her eyes turned to the heavens in prayer. "Tell me. Who painted that?"

"Andrea del Castagno," she answered promptly. "It is *St. Catherine, on the Wheel of Her Martyrdom.*"

He grunted and pulled her to stand before another painting, a Madonna and child. "What of this one? Who's the painter?"

"Giovanni Bellini. *Our Lady of the Doves.*"

He grunted again and pointed to another, a long panel showing a procession of noblemen. "What of that? Who's the painter?"

"That's a trick," she said at once. "It's *The Duke of Urbino Returning After the Hunt*, with his castle there in the background, but the painter's name is lost, and his work now anonymous. You told me that yourself."

"Hah," he said, pouncing on her answer with competitive triumph. "You are wrong. The painter's name may be unknown, but he is called the Master of the Greyhounds, on account of how he put those dogs in every painting."

"You never told me that, Hawke!" Lizzie cried with frustration, jerking her hand free of his. "How could I know if you kept that from me?"

He didn't answer her question. "I see I must stay," he said instead, "to spare us both the ignominy of you offering misinformation to our company."

"A pox on you, Hawke, for not playing fair!" she exclaimed furiously. "And a pox on your greyhound master, too, and a—"

"The Countess of Merton," Mr. Betts announced. "Sir Lucas Rowell."

At once Hawke sauntered over to greet them, his smile wide and welcoming, as if this were entirely his idea. He left Lizzie no choice but to swallow her anger and follow him in her chocolate-stained dressing gown, even as his back offered a wide and inviting target.

"Lady Merton, I am honored," he said. "Rowell,

good day. I hope you will find some measure of delight in my little collection."

For the next hour he played the ideal host, putting aside all the animosity that he'd shown earlier. Each picture had an anecdote of its own, an explanation that Hawke told with his inimitable style, making the visitors by turns laugh and then nearly weep.

Following and listening, Lizzie found her anger gradually falling away. Though he'd never admit it, he was doing *exactly* as she'd hoped he would, sharing the pleasure of his collection with others. It seemed possible that he might actually have listened to her words, and possible, too, that he could take an interest in the new academy. If he could become part of that here in London, then perhaps even Naples might lose its hold on him. Yes, she'd presumed in inviting Lady Merton here, but if the result was as wonderful as she dared to hope, then all of her presumption would be entirely justified.

"Your Grace, I am for once truly speechless," Sir Lucas said when they were done. "Such beauty! Such passion! I can only beg the privilege of bringing my apprentices here so that they, too, might see such rare works of genius."

Hawke only smiled benignly, neither agreeing nor refusing.

"I will be eager to see how the paintings are finally arranged and hung, Your Grace," Sir Lucas continued. "That will surely be the mark of a true connoisseur such as yourself."

"I rather like how they are arranged at present," Hawke said. "I see no reason for a permanent hanging when the paintings won't remain in London."

Lizzie frowned. What could he mean by that, anyway? Did he intend to have the pictures removed to the country, to Halsbury Abbey?

"So you do intend to return to Naples, Your Grace?"

asked Sir Lucas sadly. "Ah, and here I had hoped you would play a larger role in our little venture."

"In time, yes," Hawke said, as if this were the most natural reply in the world. "I have, of course, kept my villa there against my return."

Lizzie listened, stunned. What was Hawke saying, prattling on about returning to his villa like this? What *was* this nonsense?

"Oh, Duke, how it pains me to hear it!" Lady Merton said. "When my husband told me last night that you intended to return so soon to Naples, I could scarce believe it. Though I assure you we will look after your dear bride here in London after you depart."

Lady Merton was smiling indulgently, but Lizzie pushed past her to grab Hawke by the arm to make him meet her eye.

"What is this nonsense, Hawke?" she demanded, her heart beating painfully in her chest. "Answer me, if you please. Why haven't you told me you're planning to return to Naples? Why haven't you told me?"

His hospitable smile remained, but his face flushed.

"Later, sweeting, when we are alone," he said, his voice full of warning. "Not before our guests, if you please."

"Why shouldn't I speak before them," Lizzie demanded, "when it would seem they know far more of this matter than I?"

"Duke, I thank you for your kind tour of your pictures," the countess said, belatedly realizing how she'd misspoken. "Come, Sir Lucas, we've taken more than our share of Their Graces' time. Good day to you, Duchess. You have been most kind."

They hurriedly retreated, scarcely waiting for the footman to usher them away.

"Are you happy now, Lizzie?" Hawke said sharply before the door had even closed after them. "Is that what you wished? To behave like such a shrew that everyone in London will speak of nothing else?"

"All I care of is what you speak to me, Hawke," she said, desperation driving her as she clung to his arm, "and it had best be the truth. What did you tell Lord Merton? What did you say to him?"

"Enough of this, Lizzie," he ordered, trying to pull free. "You are raving like a madwoman, without any sense or reason."

"If I am mad, it is because you have driven me so!" she cried furiously. "Why won't you answer me?"

"Why should I, when you are behaving like this?"

"Because I am your *wife*." She was weeping now, hot, bitter tears of anger and loss, tears she didn't try to hide. "Because I love you, and I thought you loved me."

"Damnation, Lizzie," he said. "I do love you."

"Then why won't you answer me?" she cried, and in her frustration she flew at him, drumming her fists against his chest. "Why would you leave me if you loved me?"

She saw in his eyes the instant his temper broke, his anger spilling over to match her own. He grabbed her by her wrists and shoved her back against the wall, trapping her there with his body.

"Listen to me, Lizzie," he said, breathing hard, "and mark every word that I say. I love you more than I've ever loved any woman, and no one, not even you, has any right to say otherwise."

"Then what devil possesses you to—"

"*You* are my devil, Lizzie," he said, kissing her hard before she could answer, his mouth grinding down on hers and his body shoving her back against the wall. Yet it was a kiss of possession, not the love he claimed, and Lizzie knew the difference, twisting her mouth away from his.

"Love!" she cried bitterly, struggling to break free of

him. "Do not speak to me of love, Hawke, not when you treat me like this!"

"Then there is your answer, your proof," he said, setting her free so abruptly that she staggered to one side. "Love doesn't last."

She gasped and went still, shocked. "*My* love will!"

He shook his head, his chest rising and falling with emotion.

"No, it won't," he said with maddening finality. "It won't, any more than mine will for you. In six months' time, a year, perhaps two, it will be done between us, the way it happens for every man and woman."

"It didn't with my parents, and it won't with us," she said, desperation making her frantic as the tears streamed down her cheeks. "Not with me, not with you! We are *married*, Hawke, pledged to each other so long as we live!"

"You're so young, Lizzie," he said. "When you're older and have seen more of the world, you'll understand the truth of what I'm saying. If your father had lived longer, I'm sure he and your mother would have come to a similar agreement, much as mine did."

"An agreement?" she cried. "How could the end of our marriage be no more than an *agreement*?"

His smile was more a grimace. "You know why we wed, Lizzie: for the sake of children and our families. We've obeyed, and when children come, then our obligations to each other will be done."

"But what of having our love grow with our children, of sharing our lives?" she asked, her voice breaking along with her dreams. "How could you turn away from that?"

His expression was fixed, looking past her. "I'm sure you'll find other, ah, interests to fill your life, just as I will."

Though she didn't need to, she still turned to follow

his gaze. Behind her sat the painting of the view from Bella Collina.

"Naples," she whispered miserably, so overwhelmed by the truth that she sank to her knees. "So they were right and I was wrong. Oh, Hawke, how could you? How *could* you?"

He said nothing, nor did she truly expect him to, not after everything else he'd said before. Yet when she heard the door open and then close softly, she knew she'd more answer than she'd wanted. With a broken cry, she bent forward beneath the weight of her sorrow and wept.

She sobbed and sobbed until, at last, her tears were spent. With a shuddering sigh, she slowly rose to her feet, wiping her swollen eyes with her sleeve. She went to the table that held their half-eaten breakfast, the rolls now hard and dry and his coffee and her chocolate cold and unappetizing.

She opened the top of the silver coffeepot to look inside. As she'd hoped, it was nearly full, the coffee thick and black the way Hawke preferred it, and thicker still for being cold. She lifted the heavy pot carefully, not wishing to squander a drop as she carried it across the room to the picture of the view from Bella Collina. With the same thoroughness with which she'd water a potted flower, she poured the cold, black coffee over the entire surface of the painting.

Upstairs in her rooms, Lizzie could tell from Margaret's anxious expression that word of what had happened had already spread through the household. Of course it would: the first quarrel between the duke and the duchess was sure to be news. Doubtless now everyone in the servants' hall was waiting breathlessly for news of a passionate reconciliation, with wagers already being made on the exact time.

She almost felt sorry to have to spoil the anticipation by leaving.

"I shall dress for traveling, Margaret," she said as evenly as she could. "The quilted Brunswick, if you please."

"Yes, Your Grace," Margaret said, clearly so ready to burst with questions that, against all her training, one slipped out. "Will you be joining His Grace in the park?"

"In the park?" Lizzie repeated. "Did Giacomo say that was where he'd gone?"

"Yes, ma'am," Margaret said. "He dressed for riding, took his favorite horse, and said not to expect him for dinner, nor supper."

From that description, he could be anywhere in town, and she fought back the automatic pang of wifely concern on his behalf. He was a grown man. He could find his dinner and supper well enough without her.

"I should also like you to pack a small trunk for me, Margaret," she said with fresh resolution. "Clothes necessary for a sojourn in the country. Pack for yourself as well. You will be accompanying me. I should like to leave within the hour."

"Yes, ma'am," Margaret said. "May I ask how long we'll be away?"

"A fortnight, to begin," Lizzie said. Hawke would expect her to flee to her sister or mother, but as Duchess of Hawkesworth, she intended to show more independence. "Have the stable ready the traveling coach, and a rider sent ahead to inform the housekeeper at Halsbury Abbey to prepare for my arrival. Hurry now, I haven't time to waste."

She hadn't, either. She wasn't sure exactly how long it would take Hawke to come back to his senses, but she'd no intention of being here to witness it. He wasn't the only one who could run away from responsibility.

Resolutely she began to decide what things she needed

to take with her. The old saying was that absence made the heart grow fonder. She could only pray that it was true.

Determined to prove his point, Hawke did not return home for five days. He had intended to teach Lizzie A Lesson, the way that men were always supposed to, and he had planned to spend at least a week carousing in expensive brothels to prove that he intended to do whatever made him happy, no matter if he was married or not.

But it had taken less than an hour in the first expensive brothel for him to realize that independence wasn't necessarily as excellent as he'd imagined, at least not in London. The brandy he was served was abysmal, and the company around him—callow boys down from university, old bachelors, and other straying husbands like himself—was not much better. Even worse were the women sent to tempt him, women whom he'd recalled as being wondrously tempting, but who now seemed weary and unenticing compared to Lizzie.

To Madame Mosley's disgust and contempt, he had soon departed, and instead spent the night and the next four besides sleeping staidly at his club. Among his old friends, he knew that this probably raised more eyebrows than if he'd stayed with the whores, but so be it.

Five nights away from home was the recommended time for A Lesson. To Hawke's surprise, however, it also proved the correct time for a bit of self-reflection.

He was shocked by how much he missed his wife. Not a minute of the day seemed to pass in which he didn't wonder what she was doing, think of what her reaction would be to something, or imagine her charming, chuckling laughter. The five nights in that Spartan bed at the club were even worse, because his thoughts of Lizzie had taken a decidedly more lustful turn, so much so that real sleep became impossible. What man desired his wife like this, anyway?

He had always believed that love did not last. He knew it from his own experience, and he'd only to look at the marriages of his parents and his acquaintances to see equal proof that wedded love—especially when the marriage was arranged—had as little chance of lasting as a guttering candle's flame.

He'd been determined to be as civilized about it as his parents had been. Once the thing was done, he would retreat to Bella Collina, and Lizzie could do whatever she pleased here in England. He'd make sure she and the children had a sizable income for expenses, and so long as she was relatively discreet in her activities, she'd be free to do as she pleased. What more could she wish? How could any husband be more understanding, more obliging, than that?

Yet when at last he climbed the steps to the Chase's front door, it took all his willpower not to take those steps two at a time. Mr. Betts himself opened the door to him, greeting him with his usual impeccable demeanor.

"Where is Her Grace?" Hawke asked, already striding toward the staircase. "In her rooms?"

"No, Your Grace," Betts answered. "Her Grace is not at home."

"Ah," Hawke said, hoping he kept the surprise from showing on his face. All the time he'd been away, he'd imagined her pining for him, alone in her bedchamber.

"Here you are at last, Hawke." His cousin Brecon stood in the door that Betts had not yet closed.

"His Grace the Duke of Breconridge," Betts announced.

"Thank you, Betts, I can see him well enough," Hawke said crossly. In ordinary circumstances he would have welcomed Brecon, but now his smiling cousin was bound to ask too many questions Hawke would rather not have to answer. "Good day, Brecon. You have caught me on my way to my bed. A damnable headache."

"That's what comes of late hours at Madame Mosley's house, you know," Brecon said, handing his hat to Betts. "The brandy she serves would give a dog the headache."

"I wasn't there last night," Hawke said. "Which you most likely know already."

Brecon's shrug was wonderfully noncommittal. "If you are too ill to see me, then I'll console myself with the company of your far more agreeable wife. Betts, please send word to Her Grace that I am here to attend her."

"Lizzie's not at home," Hawke said curtly. "You can't see her, any more than I can."

"How disappointing," Brecon said. "Where is she, pray? I have just come from Marchbourne House, and March and Charlotte haven't seen or heard from her in days, either. They're rather concerned, you know."

"They haven't?" Hawke said, instantly anxious. "Betts, where *is* Her Grace?"

"She took the traveling coach to Halsbury Abbey on Monday, sir," Betts said. "Beyond that I cannot say."

Hawke swore. "Did she leave me a letter or message?"

Betts managed to look properly gloomy. "No, sir. There has been no further word from Her Grace."

"But what in blazes would she be doing at Halsbury?" Hawke exclaimed. It made no sense. Lizzie had never been to Halsbury Abbey. All she'd known of it had been what he had told her in passing. He hadn't been there himself since he'd returned to England, and God only knew what state the place was in. "I must go bring her back to London directly. Betts, have the stable bring round a fresh horse. I'll leave as soon as it can be arranged."

"Not before we have a small conversation, cousin."

Deftly Brecon stepped to block Hawke's path up the stairs. "I suspect there are a few things that you need to hear before you go charging off on the public highway."

"You are delaying me, Brecon," Hawke said. "What use could any small conversation be to me now?"

Brecon smiled, not moving. "You have been married perhaps a month. Yet you have been seen amusing yourself among Madame Mosley's whores, and your wife has fled from town without your knowledge. A conversation does appear in order, Hawke, and somewhere more private than your front hall."

Hawke sighed impatiently. "Very well, then," he said, "but you must be brief, if I'm to make any distance by nightfall."

He went striding toward the ballroom, not so much leading Brecon as permitting him to follow. He wasn't particularly in a humor for picture gazing, but the ballroom was nearby. It wasn't until they'd entered the room that he realized it was also the last place he'd seen Lizzie, the place where he hadn't found the courage to say good-bye when he left.

"What is it you wished to say, Brecon?" Hawke said as he yanked open the curtains to the tall windows himself, scraping the brass rings along their rods. "How exactly do you intend to meddle in my life?"

"Not to meddle so much as to observe," Brecon said, sitting in one of the two armchairs. "From what I know of Lizzie, she is not a lady who would run off like this without provocation."

"Then you do not know her at all." Hawke dropped heavily into the other armchair. Last week's breakfast dishes had been cleared away from the little table, but nothing else had been disturbed since then, as were his orders for this room, with the chairs and leaning pictures exactly as he'd left them. He could almost see Lizzie as she'd sat in that chair beside the window and fussed with her chocolate, her yellow striped dressing gown falling softly over her body. "She has a history of bolting."

"But you do not deny the question of provocation." Brecon rested his elbows on the arms of the chair and made a small tent of his fingers before him. "That is good, because from what I have heard from others, you provoked her most grievously. Given her spirit, you are fortunate she didn't take a pistol to you."

Hawke grunted. "That's not very amusing, Brecon."

"It's not intended to be," he said. "You announced at Lord Merton's house that you intended to return to Italy and abandon your wife, which she in turn was forced to hear from Lady Merton the following day."

"That wasn't my meaning, not at all." He shoved himself free of his chair, unable to sit still any longer, and began pacing back and forth before Brecon. "What I meant was something far more agreeable and civilized. I suggested that when the love and passion between us die away, as they inevitably must, then we part amicably, to seek our own contentment wherever we each should please."

Brecon's expression didn't change. "Which for you would be a return to that winsome villa."

"It would," Hawke said. "I will not deny it. But I was willing to grant Lizzie the same freedom, too, to remain here with her sisters and our children, or wherever else she pleased. My parents followed much the same path with success, and without the distress of those spouses who remained together in misery."

Brecon nodded, lightly bouncing his fingertips together as he listened. "What did you think of your parents' decision when you were a boy? Did you share their happiness when your mother was often in the country with her lover, and your father here in town with his, and with Parliament as well?"

"I was only a child," Hawke said, surprised Brecon would ask such a question. "My opinions were of no consequence to my parents. I had my nurse, my governess, and my tutors, and then I was sent to school, as was expected."

Brecon raised a single brow. "Yet as soon as you came of age, Hawke, you left England and your parents far behind. Only your father's will—and not he himself—could bring you back. Nothing will persuade you to embrace his interests or values. Would you want your own son to have so little regard for you?"

Abruptly Hawke stopped his pacing. He had always thought of his son—the son he must have with Lizzie—as only his heir, a nebulous, formless being who lived in the future. He'd never imagined his son as an actual boy like he himself had been, strong-willed, independent and, if he was truthful, rather selfish. Now, because of Brecon, he could suddenly imagine his son in every detail, down to his feeling the same bitterness and resentment toward his always absent father, the father who was always too busy to bother with him.

As imaginings went, it was not enjoyable. The more Hawke thought of his as-yet-unborn son, the more he wanted to make things different for him. He would teach the boy to ride, himself, and not leave it to the grooms. He would show the boy the secret passage he'd discovered at the Chase one rainy afternoon, something he'd never showed anyone else. He would take the boy to the oldest apple tree in the orchard at Halsbury Abbey, the one with the sweetest apples in the county. He would—oh, he'd do scores of things with his son, all the things his father had never done with him, and he'd do them with his daughters as well, so Lizzie could come along, too.

His sons and his daughters. No, *their* sons and daughters, half Lizzie and half him. His heart and his thoughts were racing headlong toward this future. Why had he never let himself think of these children before? He wouldn't be like his father in the House of Lords. What had made him believe he'd be as wretched a parent, too?

"I know that every marriage is different, Hawke," his cousin was saying. "My dear wife and I followed our own particular path to happiness, just as March and Charlotte have found another, and your father and mother followed theirs. But knowing Lizzie, I do not believe she'd be content with the particular model developed by your parents, living apart from you and going her own way. Nor, truly, do I believe you wish it, either."

Blast Brecon. How could he know?

Because during these last five nights away from Lizzie, Hawke's conscience had plagued him most grievously, as if it had wished to teach him a lesson of its own. Again and again he'd thought of his last glimpse of Lizzie, crumpled on the floor of the ballroom, and each time he'd felt like the most boorish, inconsiderate husband in all creation.

He'd tried to tell himself that it was his wife's youth that had made her so starry-eyed about love and that, once she was older and more experienced, she'd understand the wisdom of what he'd advised about their future. But as justifications went, it wasn't a good one. He'd known the truth, known it from the first night at Madame Mosley's.

He hadn't been able to make his explanation clear to Lizzie because he didn't believe it himself, exactly as Brecon said. He saw that now. He'd bungled badly. Even worse, he'd hurt Lizzie, something he'd never, ever wished to do.

"Damnation, Brecon," he said, raking his fingers through his hair. "I've made as great a mess of things as a man possibly can. How can I ever set this to rights with Lizzie? What can I possibly say to her?"

"Go to your wife and tell her you love her," Brecon advised. "That will go a great way toward mending whatever fences you might have broken down."

But Hawke shook his head, turning away to begin his pacing again. "Perhaps that would be sufficient with an ordinary woman," he said, "but with Lizzie, I do not—"

He stopped, both his pacing and his words, struck completely speechless by the sight before him.

The painting of Naples from Bella Collina sat in the exact place he'd left it five days before. But now the bright blue sky was a muddy gray and the once sparkling bay was dull and gray as well. Splatters of dried coffee grounds clung to the painting's surface, with murky stains in the carpet below where the coffee had dripped. The coffee had been methodically applied, with every inch of the canvas covered, and if Hawke had had any doubts how this might have happened, the silver coffeepot had carefully been left upside down, its four silver feet standing up before the painting.

"Oh, my, my," Brecon said, coming to stand beside Hawke. "Lizzie's handiwork?"

"I have no doubt of it," Hawke said. "That is Lizzie all over."

In humble silence they stared down at the damaged painting. A week ago Hawke would have been furious at what she'd done. But now, in some peculiar way, it seemed only fair, a kind of Lizzie justice. For what he'd said to her, he deserved it.

Besides, he'd already made up his mind. The next time he saw the view from Villa Collina, he wanted it to be the real version, not a painting, and he wanted Lizzie at his side to see it with him.

If only she would forgive him.

CHAPTER

19

Lizzie guided her horse through the long row of cedars, letting her mount set a leisurely pace. She wasn't in any particular hurry, because she'd no particular place to go.

On her first day at Halsbury Abbey, she had raced about like a madwoman, striving to see and learn everything about the house and manor as quickly as possible, and driving the manor's small staff to distraction in the process. But after that, she'd slipped into a much more agreeable routine of rising early and riding the land, reading in the garden, and riding some more. The little mare that had been found for her was far from the elegant mount that Hawke had bought for her in London, but she was sturdy and surefooted, and in her company Lizzie had already spent hours roaming her newest home, letting her thoughts roam as well.

She could still see the house's arched chimney stacks through the trees, sizable landmarks that in the beginning had kept her from becoming lost. This house was the opposite of the rambling Chase, for it had been built when the first duchess was flush with her royal lover's gold. It stood square and elegant, with five bays of windows, three stories beneath a hipped roof, formal pilasters across the front, and a doorway with an elaborate pediment that would have been more at home in London than here in the green hills of Somerset.

Mrs. Short, the housekeeper, had been eager to share old scandals and gossip about the house, all of it at least two decades old and as musty as the furnishings that had been newly freed of their dust-cloth shrouds in her honor. Lizzie had listened politely without really hearing any of it, except the few times when Mrs. Short had offered up tales of Hawke as a boy. There weren't many, and they all seemed to involve Hawke misbehaving wickedly and causing his near-saintly father distress.

In fact, it seemed that in Mrs. Short's eyes, Hawke had done little that was good in his entire life, the most grievous being his disgraceful neglect of the Abbey itself. He had not visited once since he'd come into the title, which was likely why Mrs. Short had been beside herself with joy when Lizzie, as the new duchess, had unceremoniously appeared. The reasons behind her visit didn't matter. To Mrs. Short, having a Duchess of Hawkesworth in residence again made everything right.

If only the same could be said of the rest of her life, thought Lizzie for what must have been the thousandth time. She had told Mrs. Short that she'd come to the Abbey to find peace after the hectic pace of London, but the truth was that she'd run away. She'd run from London, her family, and her marriage; most of all, she'd run from Hawke.

But as she'd soon discovered, running away to Somerset was not the same as running from him through the garden with her skirts flying. She'd expected him to follow her as he always did. He hadn't, nor had he sent so much as a message or letter.

She'd been angry at first, then hurt, but as the days slipped by, she'd become simply sad. Perhaps this was the kind of marriage Hawke had wanted from the beginning, with her here and him somewhere else. Wasn't that what he'd told her that last day? That when he fell out of love with her, he'd leave? In her darkest thoughts, she wondered if he'd already left not only her but England as well and was already on his way back to Naples.

Yet she wasn't alone. At least she didn't think she was. One night, at Margaret's urging, she had finally sat down with a calendar and counted the days since her last courses. To both her shock and delight, she realized that more than seven weeks had passed—seven weeks, when she had always been as regular as the moon itself. There were other small signs, too, such as how weary she was, how long she slept at night, and how already her breasts felt larger and more tender, symptoms she recalled from Charlotte's pregnancies. Hawke might have left her, but at least he'd left her with his child.

Of course she was pleased, and when she imagined holding her own baby, a small, sweet person born from love, she was overjoyed. A baby, an heir, had been the main reason she and Hawke had wed in the first place, and she was sure he'd be proud and excited, as would both their families. But the growing certainty that she carried Hawke's child saddened her, too. He should be here with her so that she might tell him the news to his face and share her happiness with him. If he truly had left for Italy, it might be months, even years, before he returned to see their child—a possibility so melancholy that she tried not to consider it. Mama maintained that beautiful thoughts whilst with child helped produce beautiful babies, and Lizzie resolved to do exactly that.

It was easy enough when surrounded by the beauty of Halsbury's gardens and fields, and before long Lizzie fell into the habit of conversing with her unborn child as she rode out alone each day. This was what she was doing now as she rode beneath the old cedar trees, singing sea chanteys from her own girlhood in Dorset softly to herself and her baby.

She came to the end of the cedar row and followed the narrowing path down into the ruins of the old abbey that had given the newer house its name. Not much remained of the abbey now beyond crumbling stone walls and a few empty windows, their arched frames still pointing toward the heavens. Mrs. Short had told her that the monks had set fire to the abbey rather than have it claimed by Henry VIII's men, and she'd hinted darkly that the ruins were haunted by several of the monks who'd perished in the smoke and flames. Lizzie liked the ruins because they were romantic, with flowering vines climbing through the broken stone tracery.

But she'd ridden only halfway through the ruin when her mare shied, skittishly pulling to one side.

"What is it, Chestnut?" Lizzie said, drawing hard on the reins to control the horse's nervousness. Likely it was only a squirrel or rabbit, though it was uncharacteristic of the mare to be uneasy. "There's nothing here worth being startled over."

Still the horse refused to go forward, her ears swiveling nervously as she backed away. To Lizzie's eyes and ears, there was nothing, yet she couldn't help sharing the horse's fear.

"What is it, Chestnut?" she asked again, more loudly this time, as if bravado alone could conquer her misgivings. "Do you see those ghostly old monks, come to haunt us?"

Suddenly a small white dog with a face like a gargoyle came racing through the doorway and toward the horse. The mare rose, neighing with shrill surprise as she flailed at the dog with her hooves. Lizzie struggled to keep her seat, holding tightly, and if she'd been any less of a rider she would have been thrown for sure. Shaken, she did her best to calm the horse and herself, too. The white dog had vanished as mysteriously as it had appeared—almost, in fact, as if it had been a ghost or demon.

"Best we head for home, Chestnut," she said, her voice quavering. She'd refused the company of a groom, confident enough in her own skill to ride alone, but now she thought only of how close she and her unborn child had come to disaster. "That's sufficient excitement for both of us."

But as she turned the mare's head to return the way they'd come, she heard another noise from the far side of the wall, someone crashing through the brush on horseback. Swiftly she looked back over her shoulder, just in time to see a large man on a larger horse come through the arch. She gasped and very nearly shrieked, tightly reining in poor Chestnut to keep her from bolting.

"Forgive me, ma'am," said the gentleman—for so he seemed from his dress and accent, if not his behavior—"but have you seen a small white bulldog come traipsing through here?"

"Indeed, sir, I have," she said, indignation replacing fear in an instant. "That dog scared my horse, just as you have done again, and both of you should be thrashed for it."

"I am most heartily sorry to have inconvenienced you, ma'am," he said, gallantly sweeping his dark cocked hat from his head. He was not much older than Lizzie herself, and as irritated as she was, she still could not ignore that he was exceptionally handsome.

"To redeem myself I would hand you the cudgel myself, ma'am," he continued, "so that you might thrash me yourself to your satisfaction."

He smiled broadly, determined to charm, but Lizzie wanted none of it. "Do you not realize that you're trespassing on the lands of the Duke of Hawkesworth?"

"Hawke won't mind," he said blithely, "for he'll never know. The duke departed for the Continent over a decade ago, and he is so far entrenched in his foreign ways that he has completely thrown over the care of his properties here. I ride through here whenever I am in this neighborhood. I've always had a liking for the splendid melancholy of this place. Ah, Fantôme, here you are, you ugly little rogue."

The white dog raced across the grass, leaping on its short legs from one broken stone to another until he could make the final jump to his master's saddle, settling comfortably in the open leather saddlebag that appeared designed to hold him. He *was* an ugly little rogue, with a bulldog's crumpled muzzle and large, pointed ears like a bat, and as he sat there snuffling and panting, his pink tongue hanging forward, he seemed to be grinning at Lizzie.

But Lizzie was not about to be distracted by either grinning white dogs or their handsome owners.

"You are still trespassing, sir, whether His Grace is in residence or not," she said sternly. "Let me know your name, sir, so that I might tell him of your presence on his land."

"Sheffield, ma'am," he said, bowing as far as he could over the dog. "That will be name enough for the duke. Now will you honor me with your name, too, so that I might know his lovely champion?"

"I am the Duchess of Hawkesworth, Master Sheffield," Lizzie said, making her voice as frosty as possible. The name was vaguely familiar to her, but she couldn't recall how or why she knew it. "I am His Grace's champion, yes, because I am also his wife."

But instead of being aghast, or even contrite, the gentlemen grinned with rascally content.

"Truly, ma'am?" he asked. "Then I must congratulate my aged cousin for marrying so fair and young a lady."

Now it was Lizzie's turn to be shocked. This young

man was perhaps twenty, while Hawke was only twenty-eight.

"Your *aged* cousin?" she exclaimed. "I will assure you, sir, that while His Grace may be your cousin, he is not aged, not in the least!"

"Hawke was done with school before I'd begun," he explained carelessly, "which made him seem aged to me, and then he left England. In all honesty, I've really never given him much thought, for all that we are cousins."

"Perhaps you should," Lizzie said, striving still to sound solemn. She could see the man's resemblance to Hawke, Brecon, and even March, and a likeness, too, in the same abundant charm that her husband possessed. Now she remembered Hawke mentioning the last of his cousins, another duke likewise descended from the old kin and yet one more mistress. Sheffield had been vaguely described as finishing his education abroad, and it was her own fault that she'd assumed him to be a young boy instead of the entirely full-grown man before her—just as he'd assumed Hawke was a doddering graybeard.

"Yes, cousin," he said, so obediently that she couldn't help but smile. "For we are now cousins, too, Duchess, aren't we?"

"Then you must call me Lizzie," she said, "as cousins should."

He swept his hat grandly from his head, over the white dog. "I am honored, Duchess Lizzie."

Despite how he'd frightened her earlier, she couldn't help but like him: with his dark hair and wide grin, he reminded her too much of Hawke for her not to. By the time they reached the house, they were laughing and chatting as if they'd known each other all their lives, not just a handful of minutes. They had entered the yard as Sheffield had finished telling an uproarious story, and Lizzie was laughing still as the grooms ran up to hold their horses. Lizzie disentangled the skirts of her habit from the saddle's horn while Sheffield dismounted and Fantôme ran looping circles of reconnaissance around the yard. As soon as she prepared to climb down, Sheffield stepped forward to help her, clasping her securely around the waist until her boots had safely reached the ground.

But at the exact moment that Lizzie was sliding down from her mare, they heard another rider arrive in the yard, hooves ringing out on cobblestones. From curiosity, both she and Sheffield turned in unison toward the sound, and that was how they were standing still when Hawke rode slowly into the yard.

"*Hawke!*" cried Lizzie, a week's worth of relief and joy in the single syllable of his name. She slipped free of Sheffield, grabbed her skirts in one hand, and ran across the yard to meet him. She had never been happier to see anyone, and the love she felt for him washed over her so intensely that she almost felt weak from it.

But even before she'd reached him, she saw that he did not feel the same. His face was tight, forcibly without expression as he looked down at her.

"Good day, Duchess," he said, turning her title into a formal rebuke instead of the playful endearment it once had been between them. "I believed you would be here at home alone. I did not expect you to be entertaining company."

His gaze shifted sharply to Sheffield, who'd come to stand beside her,

"Your Grace," Sheffield said, wisely realizing that a formal greeting might be best in the circumstances, even between long-parted cousins. He removed his hat to bow low to Hawke, or rather to Hawke's horse. "Your servant, sir."

"You must bloody well be that and no more, sir," Hawke said, his voice taut with scarcely controlled fury.

"Who are you, sir? Why are you here with my wife? By God, I should send my seconds to call on you, sir!"

"Hawke!" Lizzie called, mortified. She realized what Hawke had seen—Sheffield with his hands at her waist, and both of them laughing together—and she knew what he must have thought, however innocent everything was. "Hawke, please, it's not—"

"I shall speak to you in private, Duchess," he said, his words as harsh as if they'd struck her. "Now I wish to know how this knave dares comes into my home to dally with my wife."

She sensed Sheffield's anger now, too, the air around her crackling with male hostility and foolishness. Even Fantôme growled beside his master.

"I am no knave, Hawkesworth, nor have I dallied with your wife," he began. "Though if I had, I—"

"Hawke, please," she said, her own voice raised to be heard. "Please! This gentleman meant neither of us any ill. Look at him, Hawke, at his face and manner. He is your own *cousin*, the Duke of Sheffield, and he has absolutely *no* designs on me."

Hawke glared, while Sheffield took a deep gulp of a sigh and bowed again.

"Forgive me, Hawkesworth, if I have caused you any offense," he said. "I intended neither harm nor dishonor."

"There now, Hawke," Lizzie coaxing, coming closer to his horse and lowering her voice. "Everything is resolved. Now please, I beg you, climb down so I might welcome you properly."

Still his expression did not soften, though she could sense him wavering, love battling with pride. Oh, she knew him so well, and loved him more!

"Please, my love," she said, looking up to him. "Please."

He looked away, drawing his horse sharply to one side.

"Stand clear, Duchess," he ordered brusquely, and in the next instant he was gone, riding from the yard and away from her.

"I'll go after him," Sheffield said, already halfway to his horse.

"Oh, don't, I beg you," she said, still staring after Hawke as her heart plummeted. "That is, I thank you, Sheffield, but perhaps it would be better if you left now."

"As you wish, ma'am," he said somberly. "You are sure?"

"I am." She sighed forlornly, her mouth twisting as she fought her tears. "His Grace will return to me this night. I am certain of it. He has come all the way from London, and not even he is sufficiently stubborn to turn around and go back tonight."

Sheffield nodded, and after bidding her farewell, he left, too, his dog trotting after him.

Slowly Lizzie forced herself to climb the stairs and enter the house. Both Margaret and Mrs. Short were waiting to offer comfort in their own way, Margaret with a dressing gown and warm water for washing, and Mrs. Short with hot tea and supper on a tray to follow. But as tempting as such comforts were, Lizzie was too distraught to accept them. Instead she stayed in her habit and claimed a tall-backed armchair in the rear parlor, beside the window that overlooked the stable yard, watching and waiting for Hawke's return.

She sat with her hands over her belly, over their child. Again and again she told herself that she'd done nothing wrong, not one thing, and yet all the rightness in the world would mean nothing if her husband did not return to her.

The light faded with the day, and Mrs. Short lit the candles, leaving a pot of tea on the table beside Lizzie in case she relented. She didn't, instead watching as the grooms followed her orders, lighting the lanterns in the yard and leaving the gate open. Yet as vigilant as she intended to be, at some point in the evening she fell asleep, nestled against the chair's tall back. She knew not because she was aware of sleeping, but because she knew exactly when she awakened, at the sound of Hawke's horse entering the yard.

Without pause she ran from the room. She'd known he would come back. She'd known he wouldn't stay away. She hurried from the house and down the stairs, to where the head groom held Hawke's horse, its flanks flecked with sweat and its head hanging low.

The saddle was empty.

"The horse come back in this state, ma'am," the groom said, his wrinkled face reflecting the worry of the others who were gathering. "His Grace weren't with him."

She would not cry or think of how her father had died after being thrown by his horse. She would not panic or wail with fear. She'd be of no use to Hawke that way, and he needed her now.

"Then His Grace must have suffered an accident or other mishap," she said, surprising herself with her calm. "We must search for him. We need lanterns, and dogs. How many of you can come out with me?"

"Not you, Your Grace!" exclaimed Mrs. Short beside her. "You cannot mean to go out into the night. Let the men go, and you stay here."

But Lizzie only shook her head. "No," she said softly. "His Grace needs me, and I will not rest until I find him."

Again Hawke tried to put his weight on his twisted ankle, determined by will alone that it would support him, and again it crumpled beneath his weight, pitching him face-first into the low brush. He swore, long and hard, the only way he had now to fight against the pain.

Two pains, really. He could even diagnose the first one, the pain that felt like a sharp blade attempting to sever his arm from his shoulder. That was where he'd landed when that hell-born beast of a horse had thrown him, square on the same shoulder he'd already dislocated once before. It had taken a surgeon and two helpers to hold him down and push it back to rights the last time it had happened, also when he'd fallen from a horse. He was not looking forward to having the procedure repeated, and intended to make sure he was dead drunk before he so much as let any surgeon within his sight.

The second pain, the one knotted around his ankle, was more inconvenient, if less serious. He'd landed on his shoulder, but he'd also managed to twist his foot beneath him when he'd hit the ground. A bad sprain and nothing was broken, at least not that he could tell. A small mercy, but it still made for a sizable, damnable agony.

He rolled over onto his back, breathing hard from the effort as he stared up at the half-moon. He'd already been heading back to the Abbey, back to Lizzie, back to eat whatever crow she'd accept if she'd only take him back. Who would have guessed that Sheffield had become a man (Hawke had only the vaguest memory of him as a gangly young whelp) or that he'd appear here, of all places, to ogle his wife? Not that it was his cousin's fault. Hawke knew he'd been the one who'd behaved like an idiot. He'd fully intended to apologize. So why, then, had the gods laughed and toyed with him like this? Why had they let him choose to travel the path through the woods instead of keeping to the road? And why, why had they let him trust his neck to a wretched post horse that'd bucked him off for no reason at all?

With an extra oath for hired nags, he reached inside

his jacket, fumbling with the inner pocket until he found the small box tucked deep within. With a sigh of relief he pulled it out and opened the lid, tipping it carefully toward the moonlight.

Brecon had advised that diamonds sweetened every apology, and before Hawke had left town he'd stopped at Boyce's shop for the proper tribute. The little brooch seemed particularly apt tonight: a small besotted (or wounded by a fall from his horse) gold Cupid, haphazardly plunging his arrow into a diamond-covered heart. For a long moment he held it in the moonlight, watching the stones wink back at him as he thought of Lizzie. He was sure she'd love the brooch, but considerably less certain about her feelings for him.

He tucked the box back into his pocket and grunted as he cautiously sat upright. He'd found a thick branch in the bushes beside him, and with that to bear the weight that his ankle couldn't, he finally stood and tried one lumbering, lurching step, cradling his dislocated arm to keep it from swinging.

So this was what he'd come to, he thought with black humor: one good leg, one good arm, and a stick. In the distance he could just make out the arched chimneys of the Abbey, silvered in the moonlight. Another staggering step, a long pause to collect himself, and another step after that. At this rate, he'd be lucky to reach the house in a fortnight.

But Lizzie was there, and he couldn't keep her waiting. He leaned on the stick heavily, and felt it crack beneath him. He pitched forward, unable to catch himself before he once again hit the hard, unyielding ground. But this time the ricocheting pain in his shoulder was matched by a roaring in his head, and he felt himself falling again, slipping away into the pain and the darkness and. . . .

"I found him."

He'd know her voice anywhere, even here in the darkness, and somehow he managed to drag his eyes open to see her. She had a lantern on the ground beside her, and she was kneeling over him and crying as she used her handkerchief to wipe his face.

"Oh, my poor love," she whispered, her tears falling on his cheek. "My poor, dear Hawke!"

This would not do, having her cry over him as if he were dead. "Don't cry, Lizzie," he mumbled. "I'll be well enough."

But that only seemed to make her weep all the more. "You *will* be well, Hawke. You must. We'll take you back to the house and send for the surgeon and you will be *fine*. You must. I could not bear to lose you on account of your own wretched stubbornness."

That sounded more like his Lizzie, and he tried to smile.

"I'm sorry," he said, relieved he'd gotten the words out. "Sorry for being such a stubborn bastard."

"You're not a bastard, Hawke," she corrected, sniffing and snuffling. "You're a duke."

She was blotting her tears and her nose on her sleeve and saying nothing of his apology, which he took to mean she'd accepted it. With his good hand he managed to pull the little box from Boyce's from his pocket.

"Here," he said, exhausted from the effort. "That's for you, Duchess, to show I won't ever leave you. That's my heart."

He frowned, because he was sure he'd planned to say something far more clever than that. Not that it mattered. She opened the box and gasped, and the tears began all over again as she pinned the brooch to the front of her habit.

"You like it?" he asked, shameless.

"Oh, Hawke," she said through her tears. "I'm with child. Your child. Ours."

"Ours." He let the magic of what she'd just said settle around them, magic enough to make him forget his shoulder and his ankle and everything else but her. "Ours, Duchess. No wonder I love you."

Somehow she laughed, even through her tears. "And I love you, Hawke, oh, so much, so much."

He could see other lanterns bobbing toward them, and hear the voices of the men who were coming to help. He wouldn't have much more time alone with her, time to say one last thing that needed saying.

"Lizzie," he said. "Promise me you'll never run away again."

"Yes," she said, bending to kiss him. "Yes to that, Hawke, and to everything else besides."

Bella Collina, Naples
April 1764

Hawke sanded and folded the last of his letters, and pressed his signet into the hot blob of wax to seal it. He'd spent all the morning putting his affairs in order, sending final instructions to the various dealers, agents, and artists in Rome and Florence from whom he'd made purchases for the new gallery in London. He had been buying paintings and shipping them back to England ever since he'd returned to Naples more than a year ago, and now he was eager to see what Sir Lucas had done with what he'd sent. The new gallery was set to open by the end of the summer, and Hawke intended to be there when it did.

With a sigh of accomplishment, he pushed his chair back from the desk and strolled out onto the balcony. In the courtyard below, servants were busily carrying trunks and crates from the house to load into the waiting wagon in preparation for the voyage. In the harbor lay HMS *Theseus*, the stout warship that was the destination of all those trunks and crates. She was an impressive vessel even with her gun ports closed as she sat at anchorage—impressive enough, hoped Hawke, to frighten away any pirates from Tripoli and to make an uneventful and swift voyage back to England. Being able to claim passage on a Royal Navy ship was one of the better privileges of being a duke.

No, decided Hawke, it was likely the very best privilege, especially when he thought of how all he held most dear in his life would be on board that ship tomorrow.

He heard the carriage and horses come up the cobbled drive, and eagerly he leaned over the railing. Sitting like a queen in the open landau was Lizzie, the red ribbons on her hat tossing in the breeze and little Jack in her arms. Hawke didn't have to call down to her; she automatically looked up to the balcony, her smile brighter than the sunshine when she saw him. She turned Jack on her lap so he'd look up, too, and as soon as he'd spotted Hawke, he began to wave his plump baby arm with furious enthusiasm. He'd just passed his first birthday, celebrated with all the pomp due to the young John Charles St. George Halsbury, Earl of Southwell and heir to the dukedom of Hawkesworth. But to Hawke and to Lizzie, he was simply their perfect little Jack, with ruddy cheeks, unruly curls, and sticky baby fingers.

He watched as Lizzie passed Jack to his nurse only long enough for her to climb down from the carriage seat and the small mountain of parcels and provisions she'd bought in town for their journey. Then she took the boy back in her arms and hurried into the house to join Hawke, who met them on the staircase.

"Did you say good-bye to the monkeys at the palace's menagerie?" Hawke asked, kissing Jack on his forehead and Lizzie, a little longer, on her lips. "I'll wager they'll be very sorry to see you leave."

"We did," Lizzie said, handing Jack to Hawke. "All the keepers came out to bid us farewell, and wished us to return to Naples as soon as was possible."

"The Neapolitan monkeys must wait," Hawke said, relishing the feel of Jack in his arms. After an afternoon in the carriage, Jack had a decidedly moist feel to him, but Hawke had long ago put aside his squeamishness where babies were concerned. Shirts could be washed, and it was well worth the pleasure he found in holding his son. "It's high time Jack saw the English lions at the Tower."

"He has a great many English things to see in London," Lizzie said, untying her hat and tossing it on a chair. "Most specifically, he must be introduced to all his relatives."

"I'm sure the harpies cannot wait to make his acquaintance," Hawke said, teasing Lizzie. Much to the consternation of his grandmothers and aunts, Jack had been born not in London but in Naples, an English lordling who'd yet to breathe English air. "In fact, I'm sure he'll set to breaking female hearts as soon as he lands."

Lizzie laughed. "Of course he will. He's your son."

She stood on the balcony, leaning her elbows on the railing as the breeze rippled her gown around her. Once Hawke had believed this view of the bay to be the most beautiful in the world. Now he realized it was even more lovely than he'd dreamed, because his wife was the centerpiece.

"Come into the library, sweeting," he said. "I've something to show you."

"It had better be everything packed and removed to the ship," she said, coming to loop her arm around his waist. "Captain Weathers will have us strung up from the yardarm if we delay him even one moment beyond his tide."

"A pox on Captain Weathers," Hawke said cheerfully. "I'm certain we'll be aboard ahead of his precious tide. My sailor-wife will see to that. Here, Lizzie, now look. Do you approve?"

She stopped in the doorway and gasped, and if he'd any doubt about whether she approved or not, he'd only to see the tears of happiness that had instantly appeared in her eyes—which, if he was honest, had been his reaction as well.

The new portrait showed the three of them sitting on the same balcony, with the bay and Vesuvius in the distance. Hawke stood behind Lizzie's chair, his arm resting protectively on her shoulder, and little Jack nestled in the crook of her arm.

"It's us," Hawke said softly, all he needed to say. "It's us as we are."

"Or as we were," Lizzie said, leaning her head fondly on his shoulder.

Hawke sighed. "The painter did his best, sweeting. But considering how fast Jack grows, it's not possible to show him exactly as—"

"It's not Jack," she said, looking up at him from beneath her lashes. "I mean that by Christmas, we'll likely need another painting to show all our family."

"All?" Hawke's brows rose with surprise. "Another child? You are sure?"

She nodded. "Jack was begun in London but born in Naples. This babe will be just the opposite."

Hawke laughed with happiness, and kissed her so soundly that Jack squawked in protest.

"I don't care where they're born," he declared. "London, Naples, or the moon."

"The place where I'm meant to be," she said. "With you, my love. Always with you."

Read on for an exciting preview
of Isabella Bradford's next novel,

When the Duke Found Love

CHAPTER

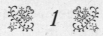 *1*

London
April, 1764

Diana Wylder, the third and final daughter of the late Earl of Hervey, had never particularly believed in fate.

That is, she hadn't, until the afternoon that Mama had explained to her about Lord Crump.

The afternoon began well enough, with a planned drive and perhaps a stroll through St. James's Park with her mother and her older sister Charlotte. They were already waiting in the front hall as Diana hurried down the stairs, for of course Diana was not precisely on time. This time it was her hat's fault, not hers: a splendid new hat with a wide, curling brim and a crown covered with white ostrich plumes and coral satin bows and small sprays of pink silk flowers, too. This hat required a great deal of strategic pinning so that the brim would tip at the exact fashionable angle over her face, yet still permit Diana to see (barely). Her maid had taken a quarter-hour to get it right, and though Diana considered this time well spent, she couldn't help but feel guilty as she saw Mama and Charlotte waiting for her.

"Forgive me," she said breathlessly, pulling on her gloves as she joined them. "I didn't intend to take so long."

"So long as you're ready now," Mama said. "But don't you think you should push your hat back a bit?"

Ever helpful, she reached out to adjust the hat herself, but Diana scuttled backward.

"No, Mama, please," she said, holding the curving brim defensively. "Mistress Hartley assured me that this is the way all hats are being worn this spring in Paris."

"You should care more for how hats are being worn in London, Diana, considering that is where you live," Mama said, but sighed wistfully to show she'd already resigned herself to defeat. "I only wish you wouldn't hide your pretty face behind a hat."

"She looks lovely the way she is, Mama," Charlotte said firmly, looping her arm fondly through Diana's. "Now come. It's far too fine a day to waste standing inside discussing hats."

That should have been a warning of sorts, for Mama generally wished Diana to show less of her person, not more, just as Charlotte, her older, married sister and the famously beautiful Duchess of Marchbourne at that, could seldom resist suggesting improvements to be made in Diana's dress. But Diana was in too good a humor to be wary, and instead she simply grinned and followed her sister and mother from the house and down the steps.

The sun was shining as it rarely did for April in London, and the air was so warm with the first true breath of spring that the side windows were down in the carriage. Charlotte's footmen, gorgeous in their pale-blue Marchbourne livery, hopped to attention as soon as the women appeared, holding the carriage door open and the folding steps steady as they climbed inside. As the youngest, Diana faced backward and slid across the feather-stuffed seat to the farthest side, claiming the window where she could see and—more important—be seen. She'd no wish to have that splendid new hat be wasted where no one could admire it.

"I do like riding in your carriage, Charlotte," she said happily as they began. "Much better than Aunt Sophronia's."

"It's very kind of your sister to invite us to share it," Mama said, settling her skirts around her legs. Mama was still young to be the mother of two duchesses—she wasn't even forty—and with her golden-blond hair and wide blue eyes, still sufficiently beautiful that people often mistook her for one more of the Wylder sisters instead of their mother. "It's also generous of March to have given Charlotte such a comfortable carriage for driving about."

"I like how everyone sees March's crest on the door and makes such a fuss over us because of it," Diana said, watching how even now people on the pavement were bowing and curtseying as they passed by. "It's as good as being a duchess, but without any of the responsibilities."

"You could do with a few responsibilities, Diana," Charlotte suggested gently. "You're eighteen now, no longer a child. It wouldn't hurt you to concern yourself with more important things than new hats."

Diana looked dolefully at her sister. Ever since Charlotte had married four years ago, she'd become more serious, more proper, more, well, dull, and it was all because of *responsibility*. To Diana, Charlotte's entire life now seemed so dutiful and ordered, without even a morsel of excitement. Charlotte's and March's marriage had been arranged long ago by their fathers, and already well sealed with the birth of an heir, plus two other babies besides. As March's wife and duchess, Charlotte oversaw his four households, his servants and his female tenants and their children, his journeys, his charities and subscriptions, his dinners for his friends, and likely many other things that Diana didn't know about. From what Diana observed, Charlotte worked harder at being a duchess than her maidservants did in the scullery, and Diana didn't envy any of it—except perhaps this carriage.

"Don't make a face like that, Diana," Mama said. "Charlotte is only speaking the truth. Unless you wish to return to Ransom Manor—"

"I'm not going back to Ransom," Diana said quickly. Ransom Manor was the only true home that Diana had known: a rambling, ancient house on the southern coast where Mama had retreated from London to raise her three fatherless daughters, or more accurately, where they'd raised themselves. It had been a splendid childhood, filled with pony-riding and boat-rowing and tree-climbing and numerous pets, and very little of the education expected for the daughters of peers. But there were no suitable young gentlemen near Ransom. Not one, especially when compared to the absolute bounty of them to be found in London. "You can't expect me to go back there unless you wish me to marry a—a *fisherman*."

"Really, Di," Charlotte said mildly, opening her fan. "As if anyone would expect that of you! Though an honest fisherman might be considered an improvement over some of the other rogues you've let attend you."

"They weren't rogues," Diana said, folding her arms over the front of her bodice with bristling defense. It was true that she'd been guilty of a few minor, *minor* indiscretions, but nothing worse than most young ladies indulged in to amuse themselves. "They were all gentlemen, every one of them."

"It's of no consequence now," Mama said quickly. "Those, ah, those gentlemen are all better forgotten."

"Exactly," Diana said, pleased that for once Mama had taken her side. "*Much* better to think of all the other ones who will be riding through the park today, ready to admire my hat."

She grinned, tipping her head to one side as if already displaying the hat's magnificence. On the seat across from her, Mama and Charlotte exchanged glances, which only made Diana smile more. They knew there would be young gentlemen striving to capture her attention in the park, just as she would be smiling winningly at them in return from beneath the curving brim of her hat. Such attention followed her everywhere she went in London—in parks, in shops, in theaters and playhouses, at the palace, and even in church—and it had been like that since she'd first come to London to stay two years before. No wonder Diana found her life so amusing, and no wonder, too, that she smiled now at the prospect of the afternoon before her.

But Mama wasn't smiling in return, and neither was Charlotte.

"Diana, my darling girl," Mama said, a disconcerting tremor in her voice. "I know it's been my fault for letting you be so free, but now I hope to make it up to you in the best possible way."

"Nothing's been your fault, Mama," Diana said, confused. "You don't need to make anything up to me, not now or ever."

"But I do," Mama said, pulling a lace-edged handkerchief from her pocket. "If your poor father had lived, he would have seen to this long ago, as he did for Charlotte and Lizzie. You're my baby, you see, my youngest and my last, and I haven't wished to let you go, even though I should."

"But you've always let me go wherever I pleased," Diana said, still not understanding. "You are not making sense, Mama, not at all."

"Yes, she is," Charlotte said. "Mama has accepted an

offer for your hand from the Marquis of Crump. He is going to join us in the Park, so that you may meet him."

"But I do not *wish* to marry!" cried Diana, stunned. "Not now, not yet, and certainly not to a man I have never met!"

"You're more than old enough, Diana," Charlotte said, shifting across the carriage to sit beside Diana, taking her hand. "You're eighteen, the same age as Lizzie and I were. And we hadn't known March or Hawke, either, and look how splendidly everything turned out for us."

"But I thought I would choose my own husband," Diana protested. "I want to marry for—for love, not because I've been *offered* for!"

"Choosing is not always for the best," Charlotte said. "You do recall how narrowly you escaped the disaster of Lieutenant Patrick."

Diana blushed furiously. She had in fact been embroiled in a near-disaster with the very handsome (and as it was discovered, very rapacious) Lieutenant Patrick, but usually, by tacit agreement, his name was never mentioned in the family.

"But that was last year, Charlotte, when I was but seventeen. I'd never make the same misjudgment now."

"Oh, my dear," Mama said, also squeezing onto the seat beside Diana. "I know this must seem something of a shock, but Lord Crump is known to be a most kind and generous gentleman. He has the patience and gentleness to be able to guide you as a wife and lady, something none of those younger rascals could ever do for you, nor does he care about any of your past indiscretions."

"You mean Lieutenant Patrick," Diana said, unable to keep the wounded reproach from her voice. "First Charlotte, and now you, too, Mama. Then you said it wouldn't matter, that everyone would forget, and now—now you're reminding me because of—of this!"

Mama sighed. "We can put the misfortunes of your past behind us, Diana, because we love you. But others have not been as, ah, charitable, and you know how skittish gentlemen can be when it comes to choosing a wife. It's most admirable that Lord Crump has chosen to ignore the tattle, and offer for you in spite of it. A sure sign that he will try his best to make you happy."

Frantically Diana shook her head. It was true that there'd been considerable talk about her last summer, talk that hadn't been very nice. Because of Charlotte being a duchess, Diana hadn't been completely cast out from polite society, but there was a decided chill to her reception in the most noble houses, a chill that would only be cured by an excruciatingly respectable marriage, preferably to an equally respectable peer.

And it was also true that both her sisters had had their marriages arranged for them, and equally true that their bridegrooms had been virtual strangers. But just because Charlotte and Lizzie had fallen in love with their husbands didn't mean that Diana would be so fortunate—especially not wed to a man named Crump who was marrying her because no one else would.

"I'm sure that Lord Crump will come to love you, Di, and you him," Charlotte assured her, as if able to read her thoughts. "True, lasting love, too, and not silly flirtation."

"But why would he ask for me if he's never so much as seen me?" Diana asked plaintively. "He must be attracted only to my fortune, or my connection to you and March, or—or some other mercenary reason. He cannot care for *me*."

"But he will, Diana, just as we do," Charlotte said with a firmness that startled Diana. "Don't pretend you didn't know this would happen one day. You saw it with me, and with Lizzie, too. This is how ladies like us marry. We're not dairymaids or seamstresses, you know."

Diana bowed her head, hiding herself and her misery inside the brim of her hat. Deep down she knew that everything Charlotte was saying was right, because she'd seen it in her own family. If being a lady and the daughter of an earl meant that she rode in a carriage and wore fine gowns and lived in a grand house on St. James's Square, then it also meant that she wasn't permitted to marry wherever her heart might lead.

Her marriage *would* be a mercenary transaction, a legal exchange of property and titles for the sake of securing families and futures. She would simply be another one of the properties to be shifted about by the solicitors in their papers. It didn't really matter that she was surpassing pretty, or that she possessed a kind heart and a generous spirit, or that she could ride faster than any other lady she knew, or that she always defended small animals and children, and it certainly didn't matter that she'd always dreamed of a handsome beau who would declare his love and passion for her alone.

No. She was no different from her sisters or her mother or any other lady of her rank. She must forget all the dashing young gentlemen who'd danced and flirted with her, and sent her flowers with sweet little poems tucked inside. There would be no romance for her, no grand passion, no glorious love like the kind to be found in ballads and novels and plays.

For her there would only be Lord Crump.

And that was the exact moment Diana realized the grim, unforgiving nature of fate.

"There's nothing to weep over, Di, truly," Charlotte said, slipping her arm around Diana's shoulders. "You'll see. March knows Lord Crump from the House of

Lords, and says he's a steady, reliable gentleman, which is exactly what a lady wishes in a husband."

Steadiness was what Diana wished for in a horse. It was not what she dreamed of in a husband, though she knew better than to say that aloud.

"Pray do not misjudge Lord Crump, Diana," Mama said earnestly. "Let him address you, and show you himself how fine a gentleman he is."

Still staring down at her hands, Diana sighed forlornly. "Is he handsome? If he were to ride by this window, would I take notice of him?"

Mama hesitated a moment, exactly long enough for Diana to know that Lord Crump was decidedly not handsome.

"Lord Crump is a good man," Mama said again, carefully avoiding Diana's question as the carriage turned into the park's gates. "A most honorable gentleman."

"There he is, Diana," Charlotte said, leaning forward toward the window. "Come to greet you, just as he promised. There, on the chestnut gelding. That is Lord Crump."

At once Diana looked up, her heart thumping painfully behind her stays. There was only one gentleman mounted on a chestnut gelding within sight, and he was riding purposefully to join them.

And, oh, preserve her, he wasn't handsome. The closer he came, the more apparent that became. He was stern and severe, his face beneath his white wig and black cocked hat without the faintest humor. His eyes were a chilly blue, his thin-lipped mouth pressed tightly shut, and there was a peppering of old smallpox scars over his cheeks. Diana could not guess his age, except that he was older than she; much older, perhaps even thirty or beyond.

"Oh, Charlotte, he—he frightens me," Diana whispered. "He's dressed all in black."

"He's in mourning, silly," Charlotte said, signaling for the driver to stop the carriage. "His older brother died last winter, which was how he came into the title. That's why he has such an urgent desire for a wife and marchioness."

"Smile, Diana, please," Mama whispered even as she turned toward the open window. Mama's own smile was as warm and irresistible as the sunshine as she nodded to the marquis.

But there was no smile in return from Lord Crump.

"Good day, Your Grace," he said solemnly to Charlotte, greeting each of them in turn by rank. "Good day, My Lady. Good day, Lady Diana. I am your servant."

Unable to make herself speak—even if she could find the words to say—Diana ducked her chin in a nervous small nod and smiled as best she could. It wasn't much of a smile, not at all, nor was it enough to thaw Lord Crump's grave expression.

"I trust you are well, Lady Diana?" he asked, his face looming in the window as he continued astride his horse.

"Oh, th—thank you. Yes, My Lord, I am," Diana stammered, her cheeks hot. "Very well. I trust you are also well?"

"I am well, Lady Diana," he said. "Indeed, I am grateful for your solicitude."

She had never felt more devoid of wit or conversation, nor more awkward or tongue-tied in her life—nor, she suspected, had Lord Crump as he stared at her, his pale eyes unblinking.

Not that Mama appeared to notice their discomfiture. "There now, Lord Crump," Mama said, beaming with overbright cheerfulness. "A fair beginning if ever there was one! But wouldn't it be better if you could continue to converse beyond our ears? Diana, why don't you climb down and walk a bit along the path with His

Lordship whilst your sister and I take our turn about the drive. Does such a plan please you, Lord Crump?"

"It does, Lady Hervey." His face disappeared from the window as he dismounted from his horse, and Charlotte called for the footman to open the door.

Not daring to speak aloud from fear the marquis would overhear, Diana shot a look of desperate pleading to her mother. She did not want to walk a bit with Lord Crump; in fact she did not wish to spend so much as a second alone in his company.

But her mother would not relent.

"Pray do not keep His Lordship waiting, Diana," she said, her words full of unspoken warning. "Charlotte and I will come collect you on our way back, no more than a quarter-hour's time. Though the paths are full of people this afternoon, I shall trust you to His Lordship's care."

The footman opened the door and flipped down the steps. Another of their footmen was holding His Lordship's horse for him, while His Lordship himself stood waiting, his arms hanging against his sides, either with patience or resignation.

Oh, preserve her, he had long arms. Dressed in black, he looked for all the world like a crow with folded wings and the black beak of his cocked hat overshadowing his face.

"Diana," Mama said, more warning. "Do not dawdle."

With a gulp, she took the footman's offered hand and climbed from the carriage. As she passed Charlotte, she felt her sister's hand press lightly on her back in silent sympathy. Yet instead of comforting her, the small gesture nearly made Diana burst into tears.

She fussed with her skirts, shaking out and smoothing the ruffled silk to postpone the moment when she must take Lord Crump's arm. At last she couldn't put it off any longer, and she looked up at him before her.

Still he stood without moving, his expression unchanging. He wasn't offering her his arm, either. With any other gentleman, Diana would have been insulted, but now she felt only relief.

"Shall we walk, My Lord?" she said, striving to sound cheerful.

He nodded, and began to walk, clearly expecting her to follow. She hurried forward to join him, her skirts billowing around her ankles. She heard the door to Charlotte's carriage close behind her, and the driver call to the horses to move on, and there she was, alone with the crow she was supposed to wed.

No, she wasn't exactly with him. She was beside him, which, fortunately, didn't appear to be the same thing at all.

The very concept of a walk along the Mall with a lady seemed to elude Lord Crump. Instead of strolling at a leisurely pace, enjoying the sun filtering through the trees overhead and making genteel conversation, he walked purposefully with his head bent and his arms swinging at his sides. While he was the same height as Diana (although the nodding plumes on her hat gave her a distinct advantage), his stride was almost a soldier's clipped march, forcing Diana in her heeled shoes to trot beside him to keep up as they dodged among the park's other visitors.

But Diana was determined to keep pace, and determined, too, to begin some manner of conversation, if for no other reason than to be able to tell her mother she had tried.

"Do you like my hat, Lord Crump?" she asked breathlessly, the exact opening that worked with most tongue-tied gentleman. "It's new. You're the first to see it."

He stopped abruptly to consider the hat. "Do *you* like the hat, Lady Diana?"

"I do," she said. "Else I wouldn't have worn it, would I?"

"Ahh," he said. "Then I resolve to like it as well."

He turned and began walking again, clearly considering his duty both to the hat and Diana complete.

But Diana would not give up, not yet.

"I am sorry for your loss, Lord Crump," she said. "Of your brother, I mean."

Again he stopped, and she stopped, too.

"My brother and I were not close," he said. "He was much older than I, and we were born to different mothers. He fell to smallpox, you know."

"I'm sorry, My Lord," she said again. "It must have been a grievous shock."

"It was," he said. "I hadn't expected to marry at all, but now that I have inherited the title and all with it, I have no choice."

Diana made a small, wordless exclamation of surprised indignation at such an ungallant confession, and more than a little pain, too. How could Mama have praised this gentleman, when he'd speak so callously to her?

"No choice, My Lord?" she asked, her voice squeaking upward. "No *choice*?"

"No," he said bluntly. "You see I am not easy in the company of ladies, Lady Diana. I require a son, an heir, and for that I must have a wife. Your sisters have proven themselves to be fecund, and I trust you shall be, too."

Diana gasped, so shocked she could not bear to meet his gaze any longer, but instead stared down at the path beneath her feet. Of course it was hoped that every marriage was blessed with children, and for noble marriages it was imperative. But for Lord Crump to speak so coldly and with so little feeling of her—her *fecundity*, as if she were a brood mare, appalled her. It wasn't that she was overnice about how those noble babies were to be produced—lady or not, she'd been raised in the country where there were no mysteries about such matters—but the thought of lying with this man as his husband and bearing his children horrified her.

She knotted her hands into fists at her sides, struggling to control her emotions. She couldn't make a scandalous scene here on the Mall. Likely there were already people slowing to observe them, whispering behind their fans, preparing the tattle to share with friends. With a shuddering breath, she forced herself to look up, intending to meet his gaze as evenly as she could.

But Lord Crump wasn't even looking at her. Instead he was staring off down the path, his expression suddenly more animated and eager than it had been since he'd met her.

"By Jove, that *is* Merton," he murmured, marveling. "In the park, of all places.

"Who is Merton?" Diana asked innocently.

He frowned, clearly irritated to have her ask a question that was so obvious to him.

"The Earl of Merton, of course," he said, still looking down the path. "A most important gentleman in the House of Lords. I have been trying to meet with him for days regarding an important trade bill before it comes to a vote, and now here—you will not object if I go speak with him, Lady Diana. I shall be only a moment, and will return directly when I am done."

He did not wait for Diana to reply, but immediately charged off in the direction of the elusive Lord Merton.

Speechless again, Diana watched him go. Although she'd hardly been enjoying his company, it was still preferable to being abandoned here in the middle of the Mall. Already the fashionable crowd on the walk was beginning to gape at her, taking note of the astonishing sight of a young lady standing alone and unattended. Anxiously she smoothed first the sleeves of her gown and then her lace scarf over her shoulders. It was too soon for her sister and mother to return in the carriage, and she'd absolutely no desire to chase after Lord Crump and his precious Lord Merton.

Yet she could not remain where she was, as adrift as if she'd been cast off in a boat in the middle of the ocean. She looked down one way, then the other, and without hesitating any longer, she turned from the main path entirely and ran off among the shady trees, not stopping until she was deep in the shade. Breathing hard, she leaned against the nearest tree and closed her eyes.

A moment alone to think, to calm herself, to swallow back her humiliation and despair. Only a moment, and then she'd go back and wait for the carriage.

But a moment was more than she'd have. She heard the rustling in the dry leaves first, the odd snuffling breathing that was suddenly around the hem of her skirt. She yelped with surprise as her eyes flew open, while the white dog at her feet looked up at her, unperturbed and happy to have her attention. He was smallish, some manner of bulldog, with oversized pink ears like a bat's and a crumpled face that was so ugly that it became endearing. His barrel-like sides quaking as he panted, he seemed to be grinning up at her with his tongue lolling from the corner of his mouth.

She was thoroughly charmed.

"Who do you belong to?" she said softly, crouching down before the dog to ruffle his ears. "Where is your master, to let you run through the woods like this?"

The dog closed his eyes, and made such a grumbling groan of complete contentment that she laughed.

"What a delightful fellow you are," she said. He was obviously someone's much-loved pet; not only was he round and well-fed (perhaps a bit too well-fed), but he wore an elegant red leather collar with silver studs around his neck. There was a silver tag, too, and she tried to turn it around to learn his name. "Come, let me properly make your acquaintance, sir."

"His name's Fantôme," said a gentleman's voice behind her. "It seems he has made a more glorious conquest than his usual squirrels."

With a little gasp of surprise, Diana looked swiftly over her shoulder to the gentleman, and gasped again. He was young, not much older than herself, and he was every bit as handsome as his dog was not. He had broad shoulders and the strong, even features that would make any woman walking along the Mall take notice of him, but it was his smile that captivated Diana, a devil-may-care grin that reached his eyes that made her smile at once in return.

"Fantôme is French for ghost, isn't it?" she asked.

"It is," he said, crouching down to her level with the dog between them. He wore a blue coat and a red waistcoat, both cheerfully bright even here in the shadows, and his light-colored buckskin breeches were tucked into top boots. There were spurs on the boots, which made her suspect he'd been riding, and had somewhere shed both his mount and his hat to chase after his dog.

"Though I fear he's far too corporeal to be a real specter," he continued. "You've only to look at him to see the truth. Isn't that so, *Monsieur le Gros*?"

"Master Fat!" Diana exclaimed, translating for herself. "You'd call this fine gentleman by so dreadful a name?"

"I would," declared the gentleman soundly, patting the dog's broad back with fondness. "He is a French dog, and he is fat. And I do call him Monsieur le Gros, because it's true. All the best endearments are, you know."

"If you call your dog Master Fat," she said, "then I should not wish to hear what you would call your lady."

"Ahh, but I haven't a lady, you see." He sighed deeply

and drew his brows together, trying to look sorrowful, but only succeeding in making Diana laugh again. "I've no use for endearments beyond Fantôme."

"I don't believe you, sir," Diana scoffed. "Gentlemen like you always have ladies."

"That's true, too," he agreed. "More truth: I do not have a lady at present, but I expect to have one again very soon."

Her cheeks warmed. It wasn't the same kind of miserable flush that she'd felt with Lord Crump, but the exciting glow that came from mutual interest and amusement. He was flirting outrageously with her, and if she were honest, she was doing the same with him. She shouldn't be permitting any of this, of course. She should rise and immediately return to the path and to Lord Crump or her sister's carriage, whichever returned first.

But she didn't. "Then we are quite even," she said. "I didn't have a gentleman when I rose this morning, but I do now."

"I congratulate you on your swift acquisition, ma'am," he said, a flicker of regret crossing his face. "Dare I ask the fortunate gentleman's name?"

She shook her head, the flirtation as suddenly done as it had begun. Yesterday, and any other yesterday before it, she would have been gratified to see the regret on this gentleman's handsome face. Any other day, and she would have been pleased to see he was as charmed by her as she was by him.

But today, now, she was promised to Lord Crump. She could vow she wouldn't marry him, that she'd rebel, but her conscience told her that she wouldn't. She'd be as dutiful in obeying her mother's choice as her sisters had been, and pray that her own marriage would be as happy as theirs, too. She would because, truly, a lady had no choice.

And she would never again sit beneath a tree to laugh and flirt with a handsome gentleman like this one.

She scrambled back to her feet. "I must go. I can't stay any longer."

He stood, too, making her realize how much taller and broader and more brilliantly male he was in his blue coat than she thought.

"You could stay if you wished it," he said, as Fantôme, agitated, began to race around them. "Another moment or two. Please. You can."

She shook her head, looking back through the trees to the path. She saw Lord Crump, his black mourning standing out among the others as he waited for her.

"Please don't ask me," she said, beginning to back away. "Because I can't. I *can't.*"

He caught her hand lightly to keep her from leaving.

"Only a moment, sweetheart," he said. He considered her hat, then plucked one of the tiny silk flowers from the crown, as if plucking a real flower from a garden. He tucked the wire stem into the top buttonhole of his coat and gave it an extra pat.

"There," he said softly, smiling. "For remembrance, yes?"

"No," she said, striving to harden her voice and her heart, and failing at both. "Good day, sir."

Then she turned and ran back to the path, to Lord Crump and to her fate as his wife.